The Epic of the Kings

Persian Heritage Series

The Persian Heritage Series aims at making the best of Persian classics available in the major world languages. The translations in the series are intended not only to satisfy the needs of the students of Persian history and culture, but also to respond to the demands of the intelligent reader who seeks to broaden his intellectual and artistic horizons through an acquaintance with major world literatures.

The volumes of the Persian Heritage Series form part of the
UNESCO COLLECTION OF REPRESENTATIVE WORKS

General Editor
Ehsan Yarshater (Columbia University)

Managing Editor
John Walbridge (Indiana University)

Persian Heritage Series
General Editor: Ehsan Yarshater
Number 2

Ferdowsi

The Epic of the Kings

Shāh-nāma
the national epic of Persia

an abridged translation by

Reuben Levy
the late Professor of Persian
University of Cambridge

with a foreword by Ehsan Yarshater,
a preface by Amin Banani,
and a new introduction by
Dick Davis

Mazda Publishers
in association with
Bibliotheca Persica
Costa Mesa, California, and New York

A current list of published titles of the Persian Heritage Series
appears at the end of this volume.

Mazda Publishers
Since 1980
Second edition copyright © 1996 by Bibliotheca Persica.
All rights reserved. First published by University of Chicago Press, Chicago;
Routledge & Kegan Paul, London; and University of Toronto Press, Toronto,
1967. Reprinted by Routledge & Kegan Paul of London in 1973, 1977, and (in
paperback) 1985, and by Penguin's Arkana Books in 1990. For information,
write to Mazda Publishers, P.O. Box 2603, Costa Mesa, CA 92626 U.S.A.

Homepage: http://www.MazdaPub.com

Library of Congress Cataloging-in-Publication Data
Firdawsī, [Shāhnāmah, English]
The Epic of the Kings: Shāh-nāma, the national epic of Persia/ Ferdowsi; an
abridged translation by Reuben Levy ; with a foreword
by Ehsan Yarshater, a preface by Amin Banani, and a new
introduction by Dick Davis.
p. cm.—(Persian Heritage Series, No. 2)
ISBN: 1-56859-035-0 (pbk. : alk. paper)
I. Levy, Reuben. II. Title. III. Series.
PK6456.A1L4 1996
891'.551—dc20   96-22393
CIP

Contents

V   ZĀL   *page* 35

VI   ROSTAM   47

Foreword

Ferdowsi's monumental tenth century epic, the *Shāh-nāma* (Book of Kings), is a compendium of Iranian myths, legends, and events of the ancient past. It is set within a framework of Persian traditional history from the creation to the collapse of the Iranian empire in the seventh century C. E. One of the three major heroic epics produced in Asia (the others being the Indian *Mahabharata* and *Ramayana*), the *Shāh-nāma* has been considered over the centuries the greatest work of Persian literature and the strongest pillar of Persian identity.

A complete English translation in verse of the *Shāh-nāma* was published by A. G. and E. Warner in nine volumes in 1905-25 and a complete translation in prose by Dr. Rahman Surti in 1986-88, but reading these translations requires more time than can be easily afforded nowadays by the busy reader. A large number of scholars have translated excerpts and episodes of the *Shāh-nāma* . Among these the *Shahnama of the Persian Poet Ferdawsi,* an abridgement translated in prose and verse by James A. Atkinson (London: 1832), has been reprinted many times. One episode, the death of the young hero Sohrāb at the hand of his unwitting father, the great warrior hero Rostam, was freely adapted in English by Matthew Arnold as *Sohrab and Rustum.* The same story has also been translated by Atkinson, as well as others, most recently in free verse by Professor Jerome Clinton of Princeton University in 1987.

Another tragic story from the *Shāh-nāma* , that of Siyāvosh, has recently been translated into English verse by the able pen of the poet and scholar Dick Davis of Ohio State University at Columbus and published in the Penguin Classics Series in 1991. Davis has also published *Epic and Sedition* (1992) an eloquent exposition of the *Shāh-nāma* and its significance as a major literary monument.

In 1962 I invited the late Reuben Levy, Professor of Persian at Cambridge University, to prepare a one-volume abridged translation in prose of the *Shāh-nāma,* in order to make the chief episodes of this long epic accessible to the students and the general reader. The result is the present volume, in which the major episodes are

xv

highlighted and the omitted sections summarized. The work thus succeeds in imparting the broad sweep of the epic even though it naturally could not convey the full extent of the poetic quality of Ferdowsi's work nor could it contain some of the fascinating details of the original. The translation did prove a success and went through four reprints. In 1994, as the book was out of print again, I took the opportunity to invite Professor Dick Davis to write an introduction to Levy's translation. The present edition includes this new introduction as well as Professor Amin Banani's essay on "Ferdowsi and the Art of Tragic Epic," and is being published by Mazda Publishers in association with Bibliotheca Persica.

E. Yarshater

Preface

Ferdowsi and the Art of Tragic Epic

to weight more than
it

Ferdowsi's main object is to preserve the 'history' of his father-land, but the sum of the Shāh-nāma's artistic worth outweighs the inherent shortcomings of the poet's conscious scheme. Broadly conceived, it belongs to the epic genre. But it is not a formal epic as the *Aeneid* or the *Lusiad*. Rather, it has the spontaneity of the *Iliad* and its episodic character reveals its kinship with the *chançons de geste*. More than any of its kindred poems, however, the Shāh-nāma is beset with paradoxes and conflicts. Paradoxes that are the protein of its art and the source of tragic nobility. If there is a unifying theme in the Shāh-nāma it is no simple 'wrath of Achilles', but the malevolence of the universe. Yet Ferdowsi is no passive fatalist. He has an abiding faith in a just Creator, he believes in the will of man, the need for his efforts, and the worth of his good deeds.

The pervading paradox of human existence is refracted and made particular in episodes and lives of mortals who, prism-like, reflect the light and shadow of character, the changes of moods and motives, and the many psychic levels of personality. In the strength, variety, and sometimes profundity of its characterization —often achieved with such economy of means—the Shāh-nāma is remarkable in the annals of classical literature. Very few of its many protagonists are archetypes. Alas, all too many of its noblest heroes are prey to the basest of human motives. And even the vilest among them have moments of humanity. Although out-wardly many a character defies all natural bounds, none is exempt from the inner reality of human nature. The goodness of the best is possible and the evil of the most wretched is not incredible.

Nowhere is this depth of characterization more evident than in the person of Rostam, the foremost of Iranian heroes. He is essentially a man of the arena. Chivalrous, intensely loyal, pious, fearless, steel-willed and obdurate, he is nevertheless subject to occasional moods of disenchantment and indifference accom-panied by gargantuan gluttony. He has a mystic reverence for the crown of Iran that inspires him to all his heroic feats. But he is

xvii

quick to take offence and, at the slightest bruise to his ego or threat to his independent domain, wealth or power, he reacts with the full fury and resentment of a local dynast. For all his 'active' temperament he can be very wordy and didactic. When the occasion demands he is wise, temperate and resourceful. Of the more than three hundred years of his life, so lovingly recounted by Ferdowsi, only one night is spent in the amorous company of a woman. It serves the purpose of siring the ill-fated Sohrāb. For the rest, he is infinitely more devoted to his horse. Sometimes he is unable to rein his pride, which results in the two monstrous deeds of his life—and shapes the final tragedy of his life.

It is partly this depth of characterization that enhances and ennobles the tragic episodes of the Shāh-nāma. Jamshid the priest-king, world-orderer, and the giver of knowledge and skills, is the victim of his own hybris. The tragedy of Sohrāb is not merely in the horror of filicide but in the fear and vanity of Rostam and the repulsed tender premonitions of Sohrāb. The tragedies of Iraj and Siyāvush evoke the cosmic anguish and the inconsolable pity of the guileless and the pure, ravaged by the wicked. Forud and Bahrām are the promise of sweet and valorous youth cut down by the senselessness of war. Esfandiyār is rent by the conflict of his formal loyalties and his piety and good sense. But it is his vanity and ambition that send him to his doom. Nor is this moving sense of the tragic reserved for the Iranians alone. Pirān, the hoary Turānian noble, shows compassion to captive Iranians and risks his own life to protect them only, in the end, to lose it for remaining loyal to his sovereign. Even the villainous Afrāsiyāb—a prisoner of his evil nature—is pitiable and tragic in the helpless moments of self-awareness.

Ferdowsi has no set formulae for tragedy, yet in the early and mythical part of the Shāh-nāma an inexorable divine justice seems to balance most of the scales. Iraj and Siyāvush are restored and triumphant in Manuchehr and Key-Khosrow, Rostam is reconciled to his fate as the price for the slaying of Sohrāb and Esfandiyār, and Afrāsiyāb cannot escape his share. The tragic impact of the Shāh-nāma, however, is not simply the sum of its tragic episodes. It pervades the encompassing conception of the work, and the sources of it are to be found in the conscious and unconscious paradoxes that form the personality, the emotional and the intellectual outlook of Ferdowsi.

The overriding tragic fact of the poet's life is that the glory of

which he sings is no more. But this is not to say that the Shāh-
nāma is a defiant nostalgic lament. The intellectual horizon of
Ferdowsi is that of a rational and devout Muslim. Mohammad and
Zoroaster are venerated as if they were of the same root, but
Ferdowsi's pride in Iran is his constant muse. His concept of
history is thoroughly Islamic, but there is no Augustinian
righteous indignation in him. The cumulative emotional tensions
of his 'history' are unresolved. Even in his stark treatment of the
final reigns of the Sāsānian empire, when the succession of evil,
tyranny, rapacity, treachery and chaos is unrelieved by any sign of
grace, he cannot quite bring himself to a condemnation of the
Iranian empire. The only possible catharsis is in the contemplation
of the ideal of justice, essential in Islam—yet already far detached
from the realities of his time. Nor is the holocaust so distant as the
fall of the Sāsānians. Ferdowsi was undoubtedly inspired by the
renascent Iranism of the Sāmānid epoch and may have even conceived of his masterwork as an offering to that illustrious house,
only to witness its demise at the hand of the Turkic Ghaznavids.
The bitterness of the mythical Iranian–Turānian epic struggle that
permeates the Shāh-nāma and gives it its dramatic tension is
largely the pressing phenomenon of the poet's own time. Thus he
has experienced a re-enactment of the final tragedy of his poem.
The necessity of dedicating the Shāh-nāma to the very Turkic
destroyer of the Iranian Sāmānids must have been a bitter and
demeaning fact. Much of the traditional denunciatory epilogue
addressed to Mahmud of Ghazna may be accretions of later times,
but the tone is true.

The tensions and contradictions in the experience of the poet
that are reflected in the tragic paradoxes of the Shāh-nāma and are
a source of validity, profundity, and universality of its art, are not
all conscious or external. The interactions of his innate character,
his inculcated traits, his social position, his changing environ-
ment, and the nature of his creative genius, all fail to achieve a
synthesis. Instead, they fashion a personality marred by unresolved intellectual conflicts and spiritual anguish.

He belongs to the class of *dehqāns*, or landed gentry, and has an
inherited sense of expectation of privilege, which is embittered by
gradual impoverishment. He is not yet free of the impulses of
generosity and noble detachment that sometimes flourish in the
serene and self-assured middle plateaux of wealth and power of
a social class; but he is already afflicted with the material obses-

sions, if not greed and avarice, that characterize the periods of rise and fall of those classes. Thus he seeks, and needs, the patronage and the emoluments of the Ghaznavid court, yet he is too proud, too detached and too dedicated to his 'uncommercial' art to secure that patronage in the accepted mode of the day. He is contemptuous of the servility and the parasitic existence of the court poets, of the artificiality of their panegyric verse, of the ignobleness of their self-seeking and mutual enmity, yet he is not without the artist's vanity, envy and acrimony and, occasionally, he succumbs to the temptation of proving himself in their terms.

Ferdowsi's genuine compassion for the poor and the wronged, his remarkable and persistent sense of social justice, his courageous and vocal condemnation of irresponsibility of rulers, his altruism and idealism—in short, his profound humanity—account for some of the most moving and ennobling passages in the Shāh-nāma and endow it with a consistent integrity. At the same time he had the conservative impulses of the *dehqān*. His yearning for legitimacy, his outrage at disregard of position, his abhorrence of anarchy, his fear of heresy, and his dread of unruly mobs provide the narrative with moments of eerie drama and Jeremiah-like visions and nightmares of the apocalypse.

However much may be said of the formal and philosophical diffuseness of the Shāh-nāma, it is transcendentally successful as a true epic. In that sense only a comparison with the Iliad can be meaningful and instructive. In their origin, nature and functions as well as in form and content, there are arresting similarities between the two poems. This is not to say that the likenesses outnumber the differences. The Shāh-nāma is, of course, the product of a much later and more self-conscious age, and it draws from a vast fund of literary conventions and clichés of 'Near Eastern' cultures. But the Shāh-nāma and the Iliad partake of the fundamental mysteries of epic as art. They both represent the instantly and eternally triumphant attempts of conscious art to immortalize the glory and the identity of a people. It does not matter that neither Homer nor Ferdowsi were the very first to attempt such a task in their cultures. It is the supreme elixir of their art which accomplished the miracle. They ennobled the natural epic without losing its spontaneity. Furthermore, they did so at a time when the cement of past associations was crumbling and the common identity of their peoples was in danger of effacement. Thus by their creations Homer and Ferdowsi succeeded at once in immortalizing the past and bequeathing the future to the language and life of their nation.

The western reader of the Shāh-nāma will learn much—and may gain in enjoyment—by some comparison of its similarities and differences with the Iliad. Although Ferdowsi works with a number of written and even 'literate' sources, at least in the first half of the Shāh-nāma, as in the Iliad the roots of oral tradition are close to the surface. Both poems employ a simple, facile metre and their rhyme schemes are suited to the long narrative and aid in memorizing. The heroes in both epics are affixed with appropriate epithets and are easily recognizable even without mention of their names. Both poems make use of a certain amount of repetition to assist recapitulation. Episodes of battle and heroism are modulated by sequences of chase, ostentatious banquets and idyllic revels, and ceremonious councils and parleys. Semi-independent sub-episodes are interspersed to vary the mood and relieve the tedium of the narrative. Of these, several romances in the Shāh-nāma, particularly those of Zāl and Rudāba and of Bizhan and Manizha in their exquisite lyricism, poignant intimacy and self-contained perfection, have no peers in the Iliad. Both poets lavish masterful attention upon the details of the martial life—the description of armours and weapons, the personal and near magical love of the heroes for their mounts and their armour, etc.—that breed and sustain a sense of epic involvement. Both poems abound in little warm human touches that evoke pathos and enhance the evolving drama.

Transcending these more or less formal similarities are the fundamental parallels of human behaviour under similar relationships and social conditions and the recognizable range of human types in the Iliad and the Shāh-nāma. The affinities of the indispensable hero Rostam with Achilles; of the capricious, covetous, apprehensive and envious monarch Key Kāvus with Agamemnon; of the stolid and martial Giv with Ajax; of the wily and wise Pirān with Odysseus; of the dutiful and sacrificial Gudarz with Hector; of the impetuous and handsome Bizhan with Paris; of the youthful, loyal and pathetic Bahrām with Patroklos; of the impulsive, sensuous and beautiful Sudāba with Helen; of the adoring, meek and resigned Farangis with Hecuba; are only a few of the evocative suggestions of artistic kinship between the two epics. In the fragile social order depicted in the Iliad and in the first half of the Shāh-nāma tension and strife are never far from the surface. But

Ferdowsi has endowed his cosmos with a higher morality and thus the lapses of his heroes are more grave and aweful. In addition to mortal humans both epics are peopled by several supernatural orders of goodly spirits, demons and magical creatures who intervene in the affairs of men and profoundly affect their fate. But the God of Shāh-nāma is the unknowable God of Zoroastrians, Jews, Christians and Muslims. Unlike the deities of the Iliad He is not implicated in the struggle of the mortals though he is constantly evoked and beseeched. Only twice does an angel intervene to alter the course of battle. At other times there is only indirect confirmation of the righteous and chastisement of the wayward. On the other hand prophetic dreams count for more in the Shāh-nāma. Fate is the unconquerable tyrant of both poems, but in the Shāh-nāma it is sometimes unravelled by the stars, robbing the drama of its mystery.

The Shāh-nāma is inordinately longer than the Iliad. Essentially it is made in two segments: the mythical first half and the 'historical' second half. The psychological and artistic seam cannot be concealed. The fundamental affinities with the Iliad are primarily true of the first half. But even there the unity of theme, the limitation of action and time, the rapid devolution of the 'plot', the resolution of the conflict and the uncanny proportions of the Iliad are missing. Ferdowsi's 'historical' mission undoubtedly scatters the artistic impact of the Shāh-nāma and diffuses the focus of its aesthetic concept. But the 'wrath of Achilles', after all, is not the sole catalyst of Homer's art. The validity and viability of the Iliad rests in its general relevance to the human situation. In this sense the artistic 'flaw' of the Shāh-nāma is more than made up by, and perhaps makes for, its greater universality. Thus in the Shāh-nāma we come across characters who have no counterparts in the Iliad, and one must cull the whole of Greek mythology, mystery and drama for parallels. Jamshid, the primal priest-king, the divinely inspired creator of civilization, the bringer of world order, whose hybris causes his fall and plunges mankind into evil and darkness. Ẓahḥāk, the grotesque tyrant, the personification of irrational and demonic forces who grips the world in a thousand-year reign of terror. Kāva, the rebellious *vox populi* triumphant in a just cause. Faridun, the ideal and wise king, compassionate pastor of his people. Siyāvush, the tragic guileless youth, maligned, helpless and martyred. Key-Khosrow, the messiah-king, avenger and restorer. Every one of them is a focal realization of a master figure in the history of man's existence and aspirations.

It is this universality together with its faithful and unresolved reflection of the human paradox that is the essence of Shāhnāma's art and the cause of its timelessness; for it permits every generation to seek its own resolution.

Amin Banani
University of California
at Los Angeles

Introduction to Reuben Levy's
Translation of Ferdowsi's Shāh-nāma.

The Shāh-nāma is the national epic of Iran. Such a bald statement
is both true and misleading; it is literally the case, but the connota-
tions of the word "epic" do not begin to do justice to the work's
extraordinary depth and complexity. As well as being an epic it is
a history, not of a moment in a longer war (like *The Iliad*) or of an
individual (like *The Odyssey*) or of a mythical turning point in a
people's self-creation (like *The Aeneid*), but of many wars, many
individuals, and many such turning points. It is also a work of great
psychological depth, of public tragedy and private pathos, of
national triumph and failure, of earnest ethical exploration; it treats
of politics, of loyalty, familial conflict, duty; of the burdens of
empire and of the resentments and rebellions of the misused, of
service slighted by tyranny, of man's continual attempt to create
justice and civilized order out of the chaos of human greed and
cruelty. Indeed, the more familiar one becomes with it the more it
elicits the kind of admiration usually reserved only for the very
greatest literary masterpieces of a culture—Dante's *Commedia*, the
plays of Shakespeare, the Homeric epics. As with such works, one
feels that all human life is somehow contained within it, potentially
if not always spelt out in the minutest detail; reading it we are led
to believe that everything has been taken into account, that the
author has seen both panoramically and profoundly. We come to
trust him not merely as a writer endowed with immense verbal skill
but as a man whose gaze has given him a wisdom which transforms
literature into a summation of human possibilities, so that it partakes
of that crucial category of ancient literary criticism, the sublime.

Part of *The Shāh-nāma* 's impact lies undoubtedly in its vastness,
both in the sense of the immensity of its subject matter, (which is
nothing less than the history of the Iranian people from the creation
of the world up to the Arab conquest of the country by the victorious
armies of Islam in the seventh century C.E.), and in the sense of its

sheer physical bulk as a work of literature. It is over 50,000 lines
long (and by the standards of English verse they are very long lines;
each line has twenty two syllables, making it slightly longer than a
heroic couplet, so that a more accurate computation for an English
reader would be to say that it is over 100,000 lines long). The
current standard edition of the work runs to nine volumes. But
length alone of course does not guarantee greatness, and the sources
of its particular power as a literary work must be sought elsewhere.

As is the case with major epics from other traditions, the appearance of The Shāh-nāma marks a transitional moment. It is on the
one hand a compilation and summing up of what is believed to have
gone before, and in that sense it self-consciously marks the ending
of an era, so that the poet writes with a sense of belatedness, of living
irretrievably after the golden age he records. But it is also a
beginning, in that a new tradition derives from it; the self-image of
the people whose putative ancestors are celebrated in the work is
cast, by the work itself, into a new mold. The author of The Shāh-
nāma, Ferdowsi, lived at a time when such a recasting of the Persian
tradition was almost uniquely possible—a little earlier or later and
one cannot imagine his poem coming into existence in just such an
emphatic and culturally redefining form. To understand The Shāh-
nāma, therefore, it is necessary to know something of the time in
which it was produced.

The great watershed of Persian history is the Arab/Islamic conquest of the seventh century. From the perspective of the twentieth
century this occurred almost exactly halfway through the historical
record: there are approximately 1300 years of recorded Persian
civilization before this moment (from the sixth century B.C. and the
foundation of the Achaemenid empire), and there are approximately 1300 years from this moment to the present. The longevity
and distinctiveness of Persian civilization during the pre-Islamic
era were a major factor of the ancient world, and though in the West
political power shifted from the Greeks to the Romans, Persia
remained more or less constant as the center of a continuous and
specific tradition of civilization.

The Arab conquest of the seventh century came therefore as an
overwhelming shock, especially since it must have seemed for a
while as though Persian civilization would disappear as an entity
distinguishable from the culture of other countries subsumed into
the Caliphate. An Iranian scholar has dubbed the numbed aftermath

of the conquest in Iran as "the two centuries of silence." One can gather something of the atmosphere of the early post-conquest years in the writing of a Zoroastrian (i.e., an adherent of the religion of pre-Islamic Iran) of the period; "...The Dēn faith was ruined and the King of Kings slain like a dog... They have taken away sovereignty from the Musraus. Not by skill and valor but by mockery and scorn have they taken it. By force they take from men wives and sweet possessions and gardens... Consider how much evil those wicked ones have cast upon this world, than which ill there is none worse. The world passes from us" (*Great Bundahishn*, cited in H. W. Bailey, *Zoroastrian Problems in the Ninth Century Books*, Oxford, 1943, p. 195).

After the conquest there were constant revolts against the new rulers, particularly in the central province of Fārs, which had been the heartland of imperial Iran, and many towns had to be reconquered more than once. The Umayyad dynasty (661–750) had scant regard for Persian civilization and sensibilities and treated even converts to Islam as second-class citizens if they were not of Arab stock (the majority of the indigenous population at this time was still not Moslem and at the beginning of the Islamic period their second-class status went without saying). The Abbasids, who succeeded the Umayyads in 750, came to power partly as a result of a revolt that began in Khorāsān (northeastern Iran) and were generally more sympathetic to Persian civilization and mores than their predecessors had been. The capital was moved to Baghdad, close to the ruins of the Sasanian capital of Ctesiphon—an ambiguous gesture that both reasserted the triumph of the Arabs over the Sasanians, but also signalled the more Persian-oriented direction that came to be taken by the caliphate. The caliph al-Ma'mūn (favorably mentioned by Ferdowsi, see p. 334) in particular was known for his Persian sympathies; his mother was Persian and his chief minister, Faḍl b. Sahl, who was also Persian, ensured that the Abbasid court, extraordinarily enough, adopted much of the ceremonial protocol of the Arabs' defeated enemy, the Sasanians. Iranians became prominent in the Abbasid civil service (the Barmakī [Barmecides] and Naubakhtī families rose to particular prominence) and the Abbasid period saw a general Persianization of the court culture if not that of the caliphate in general. But the Arab yoke still clearly rankled and the early Abbasid period was marked by a series of spectacular revolts throughout Persia against rule from Baghdad.

A gradual weakening of the caliphal power meant that by the tenth century local dynasties controlled much of Iran, though they still nominally held power under the caliph's authority. In the west, including Baghdad itself for a while, the Buyids ruled; this was a dynasty that claimed descent from the Sasanians, revived for itself the Sasanian title of "king of kings," and in its cultural allegiances seemed ready to embrace whatever would distinguish it from the Abbasids. It had strong Shi'i sympathies (the Abbasids of course were Sunnis) and the Buyid court also celebrated the ancient Zoroastrian festivals; this syncretic and quasi-nationalist amalgam is a curious foreshadowing of a much later period of Iranian culture, from the sixteenth century onwards. In the north east the Samanids ruled throughout the tenth century; this highly talented, energetic, and culturally sophisticated dynasty claimed descent from Bahrām Chubina, a Sasanian general whom Ferdowsi treats at great length. It actively promoted an interest in ancient Iranian culture (as its claims to legitimacy of rule came largely from this source), commissioning translations and encouraging an antiquarian interest in the country's past. Most crucially for the later development of Persian literature, the dynasty used New Persian (the language that had developed since the conquest) as its court language rather than Arabic, and a court poetry of great brilliance, in Persian, soon began to flourish in Khorāsān and Transoxania, the area controlled by the Samanids.

It was into this world that Ferdowsi was born, in 940, in a village near Ṭus, a town later to be supplanted in importance by its neighbor, Mashhad, but which was at the time one of the major cities of Khorāsān. He was a *dehqān*, that is a member of the indigenous landed aristocracy, a class which had survived the conquest in a severely attenuated form and which, of course, had had to make its accommodations with the new order. It nevertheless saw itself as the repository of Persian/Iranian tradition and was regarded as "echt-Persian" in its sympathies (so much so that when the two peoples, Arab and Persian, are contrasted in the literature of the period the word "dehqān" is sometimes used as the equivalent of "Persian"). Ṭus was generally controlled by the Samanids, though its local ruler during part of Ferdowsi's lifetime, Manṣūr b. 'Abd al-Razzāq, sometimes tried to play off the Samanids and Buyids against each other, to his own advantage. The revival of interest in indigenous Persian culture, fostered by the Samanids, was clearly of fundamental importance in providing the milieu in which a project such as the writing of The Shāh-nāma , which sought to celebrate the cultural and ethnic inheritance of ancient Iran, could be undertaken. There is also the fact that it was under the Samanids that poetry in Persian came to be extensively written and so developed into a cultural force to be reckoned with; this too indicates Ferdowsi's debt to the general ethos of ethnic and quasi-national self-promotion created by the Samanid court.

Ferdowsi's sources have disappeared. At the opening of his poem he says that he was given access to a composite historical work that had recently been commissioned, and this is normally identified with a prose Shāh-nāma known to have been put together on the orders of the father of the aforementioned Mansūr b. 'Abd al-Razzāq; the preface to this work survives and mentions Ferdowsi, though in a sentence thought to be a later interpolation. The scholarly consensus is that he used oral and written sources, though the exact proportion of the one to the other remains in doubt. One section of the poem, that concerned with the introduction of Zoroastrianism under king Goshtāsp (pp. 191–93), was written by Ferdowsi's predecessor, the poet Daqīqī, and Ferdowsi took over the composition of the work when Daqīqī was murdered by a slave.

Ferdowsi's allegiances are apparent from the opening of the poem, as much from his omissions as from what he includes. He begins with the creation of the world, and the appearance of the first man/king, Keyumars, and then passes on to kings who fight against supernatural evil forces and establish the arts of civilization. Although there can be no doubt whatsoever that Ferdowsi was a sincere Moslem (and there is some evidence that like the Buyids he combined "nationalist" sentiment with Shi'i sympathies) he makes no attempt to include any elements of the Koranic/Moslem cosmology in his poem, nor does he attempt integrate the legendary Persian chronology of the material at the opening of his poem with a Koranic chronology. Unlike other writers who dealt with similar material, and who did attempt to intertwine the two chronologies (e.g. the historians Ṭabarī and Mas'ūdī), he simply ignores Islamic cosmology and chronology altogether and places the Persian creation myths center stage. Further, the first evil person (as against supernatural being) in his poem is the usurping king Ẓahḥāk, who brings disaster on Iran and who is identified as an Arab. The poem ends with the triumph of the Arab armies and the defeat of the

Sasanians, and perhaps the most famous passage of this closing section is the prophecy by the Sasanian commander Rostam, the son of Hormazd, of the disasters that the conquest will bring on the country (pp. 413-14). The poem is thus framed by a fairly forthright hostility towards the Arabs and the political culture, if not the religion, they brought with them.

A Western reader who is unfamiliar with the poem, but who has been told it deals with Iran's history before the coming of Islam, would naturally expect to find the early legendary material followed by stories relating to the Achaemenid monarchs—Cyrus, Darius, Xerxes, and their successors. But the Achaemenids are virtually absent from the poem until just before the advent of Alexander the Great, that is until their decline. Further, the area of Iran which was their homeland, Fārs, (or Pars, from which the word Persia is derived) is hardly mentioned in the first two thirds of the poem at all, and most of the place-names that figure prominently in the pre-Alexander portion of the poem (e.g. Balkh, the river Oxus, the river Hirmand [Helmand], Kabul, Marv) are not within the confines of modern Iran. In fact, the homeland of Iran in *The Shāh-nāma* , at least until the advent of the Sasanians, is Khorāsān, which under the Samanids extended to the Oxus, and the material utilized in the earlier sections of the poem derives from the legends of this area and of Sistan—i.e. eastern Iran and what is now western Afghanistan. It has been surmised that during the dynastic upheavals between the conquest by Alexander and the emergence of the Sasanians in the third century A.D. (and particularly under the Parthians who derived from areas celebrated in these legends) this material gradually replaced the historical record of the Achaemenids who thus to all intents and purposes disappeared from the national record.

The surface of the first half of the poem is concerned largely with tribal warfare, with the river Oxus defining the approximate territorial boundary between the factions; the obvious values celebrated are therefore those of tribal loyalty and military valor. The basic conflict is that between Iran and Turān, i.e. Khorāsān and Transoxania; the conflict is given a mythical origin in the story of the fratricidal conflict of Tur and Iraj (pp. 28-32). The inhabitants of Turān are referred to as "Turks"; this ethnic definition derives from the late Sasanian period when the area was in fact invaded and partially inhabited by Turkish tribes who did constantly threaten Iran. But the legends themselves must be older than this conflict, and, as the story of the common familial origin of the two peoples indicates, the stories, if they have any historical basis at all, must refer to ancient rivalries between different Iranian clans occurring perhaps around the time the Iranian people descended onto the Iranian plateau (a migration which is assumed to have happened some time before the beginning of the first millennium B.C.). The very earliest must refer to an even earlier period as they have parallels in Indian myth and legend (Jamshīd of *The Shāh-nāma*, for example, has been identified with Yama, the Hindu Lord of the Underworld) and presumably derive from the time before the split between the Indian and Iranian divisions of the Indo-European peoples.

Though most of them seem to have come from eastern Iran, not all of the stories in the legendary section of *The Shāh-nāma* derive from the same tradition. Two different dynastic traditions are interwoven, and much of the interest of this part of the poem comes from the relationship between two dynastic families—the Keyānids, who rule Iran as a whole, and the house of Nariman (Sām, his son Zāl, Zāl's son Rostam, Rostam's son Farāmarz) who rule in Sistan but who also function as the Keyānids' chief champions and advisors. This relationship is presented as a gradually deteriorating one: Sām is unquestioning in his loyalty to his Keyānid overlords, acting with the same loyalty towards bad kings as towards good; Zāl is often critical of his kings' actions but always finally supports them; Rostam, who is the preeminent hero of the legendary section of the poem, is openly contemptuous of two of his kings (Kāvus and Goshtāsp) though he too, until goaded beyond endurance, acts with general loyalty; Rostam's son Farāmarz rises in rebellion against his king and is slain.

What is perhaps especially interesting is that in these conflicts between the Iranian kings and their champions/advisors the latter are virtually always shown to be ethically superior to the kings they serve. Given the legendary and tribal nature of the stories, loyalty is obviously a prime virtue of the society described in the poem, but much of the poem's aesthetic interest derives from the fact that those who demand such loyalty are often morally inferior to those whom they govern and that our sympathies are certainly with the governed rather than the governors. A similar situation can be found on the familial level. The three best known stories of the legendary section of the poem—those of Sohrāb, Siyāvosh, and

Esfandiyār—involve the deaths of sons; in each case the death comes about as a result of the father's actions, directly so with Sohrāb, indirectly but equally culpably with Siyāvosh and Esfandiyār. Again, the inferior in the relationship is shown as the innocent (this is particularly clear in the case of Siyāvosh). It is worth remarking also that all three of these slain sons have foreign, non-Iranian, mothers; Sohrāb's mother is from Samangān, a frontier town with ambiguous loyalties, Siyāvosh's is from Turān, the traditional enemy of Iran throughout the poem, Esfandiyār's is from "Rum" (i.e. Byzantium). Here too it seems as if the apparently monolithically authoritarian message of the poem is being somewhat called into question; just as loyalty to kings and fathers is a demand that produces a terrible human cost, so too the very centrality of Iran to the poem's values seems questioned by the sympathy we are invited to give to these sacrificed half-foreign princes. Indeed, Siyāvosh and his son Khosrow, who is presented as the perfect monarch of the legendary portion of the poem, both turn away from Iran for personal, ethical reasons.

Khosrow's abdication (pp. 174–80) directs us to another complexity in the poem, its treatment of the notion of kingship. A surprisingly large number of kings in the poem abdicate, and prominent among these are two of the most ethically admirable of the poem, Faridun and Khosrow. There is a story in *The Golestān*, by the 13th century Persian writer Sa'di, about a king who has a wonderful advisor whom he dismisses. The advisor takes up with a group of religious mendicants and there finds a spiritual peace he had never known at court. The country begins to go to rack and ruin, and the king sends for his former advisor to return, saying he is the one man with enough intelligence to fill the post. The former advisor's answer is that it is precisely his intelligence which prevents him from resuming his position. The same problem, transferred to the ethical plane, haunts much of *The Shāh-nāma* ; those ethically most fitted to rule are precisely those most reluctant to rule. The problem is graphically set out during Khosrow's self-communing before he finally resigns the throne (pp. 174–75).

The relatively frequent abdications, as well as other evidence such as the role Zāl and Rostam play as kingmakers after the murder of the king Nozar (a passage omitted in this translation), are further evidence of the eastern origin of the stories that make up the legendary part of the poem. Two traditions of kingship exist simultaneously in the work. One is that espoused by the Sasanians, through whom Ferdowsi must have received his sources; this is in essence the ancient Middle Eastern notion of kingship, one that ties kingship to religion and to the sanction of God, that elevates the king to a quasi-divine position as God's representative on earth, and that derived from the Babylonian, pre-Iranian dynasties. The other derives from "the practice of the steppe" and involves the acclamation of the king by his peers, the notion that the king can always be replaced if he becomes incompetent (or too old to rule effectively), and that he rules by virtue of his abilities and the consent of the nobility in general. The poem's "abdications" would seem largely to derive from this latter tradition, though in keeping with his practice elsewhere Ferdowsi frequently rewrites the topos as a problem of personal ethical choice. (There is a certain irony in the fact that of the two traditions of kingship it is the eastern, less absolutist one that seems to be authentically Iranian and the western absolutist one that is ultimately Babylonian and non-Iranian; though due to the Achaemenids' espousal of the Babylonian tradition, and its adoption by subsequent Iranian dynasties, especially the Sasanians, it is this tradition which has come to be seen as essentially Iranian).

It should be apparent from even such a brief and necessarily incomplete summary of the themes of the poem's opening section that although it is undoubtedly an epic, and its superficial concerns are those of a dynastic chronicle, the relatively straightforward content we associate with such terms does not begin to do justice to the work's density and artistic complexity.

The poem passes from legendary to quasi-historical material with the appearance of Alexander, though in the earlier sections of this "historical" part the stories are given a more or less legendary treatment (Alexander, for example, is half Iranian, his father being the Iranian king Dārāb, and in common with other Islamic versions of his legend he is presented as much as a seeker after knowledge and enlightenment as a world-conqueror). As with the Achaemenids, the historical record of the Parthians, who ruled Iran from the third century B.C. until the third century A.D., is largely absent from the poem; this is almost certainly due to the success of the Sasanians in deliberately obliterating the memory of the dynasty they replaced.

The closing portion of the poem deals with the Sasanians; here the record is relatively complete and parts of the poem do approach the simplicity of a chronicle. There is also much more circumstantial detail to many of the stories recounted, and they clearly have not undergone the mythological weathering and constant refashioning of the legendary earlier narratives. Much of this section of the poem can be seen as a record of more or less direct propaganda for the glories of Sasanian civilization; the reforms of Ardashir, for example, (pp. 278–82) and a great deal of the narrative concerned with Khosrow (Kasrā) Nushirvān, who is presented as the archetypal king of the poem's "historical" section much as Key Khosrow is of the legendary section. Some themes of the earlier part of the poem continue to be treated; there is as much father-son conflict here as in the legendary section (albeit it is not presented in such starkly mythical terms), and the king-champion conflict receives one of its most extended treatments in the relationship between Bahrām Chubina and his two monarchs Hormazd and Khosrow Parviz. Bahrām Chubina is virtually the only would-be usurper of kingly power whom Ferdowsi treats relatively sympathetically; this may well be because the Samanids, under whose nominal aegis Ferdowsi began his poem, claimed descent from this hero.

But though in the narrative of the Sasanian reigns we may regret the absence of that epic force present in the earlier sections of the poem, there are other compensating virtues to this latter part, which often, incidentally, receives much less attention that the opening half. The circumstantial quality of much of the detail can give the scenes great vividness (e.g. the scene of the minstrel Bārbad playing to Khosrow Parviz, pp. 386–89) as well as pathos (e.g. the events leading up to the murder of Khosrow Parviz, pp. 395–400) and tragic intensity (e.g. the suicide of Shirin, pp. 401–05, a scene which seems in its details to owe something to the story of Cleopatra's suicide over Antony's body in order to escape falling into the hands of Octavian). Few passages of any literature can equal the profound sense of the passing of a civilization that informs the closing pages of *The Shāh-nāma*, in which the cry that "All our long labors will be in vain" (p. 414) seems to call up the whole vast history of a country in its despairing summation. As the Zoroastrian chronicler quoted above wrote, "The world passes from us." These last scenes have a wonderful vividness and pathos; very telling, for example, is the way Ferdowsi emphasizes the pomp and wealth of the Iranian army and its commanders glittering in their jewels and gold, and then contrasts this with the hardiness and poverty of their Arab opponents. Two almost contradictory messages are being given to us at once. The wealth underlines the splendor that is about to pass, it brings home to us the sheer magnitude of what was about to happen, the gorgeousness that had been the indigenous Iranian civilization. The ascetic unconcern of the Arab warrior Sho'ba it also brings home the virtues of spartan simplicity, the laconic uncluttered force that an attitude of *contemptu mundi* can bring with it. In a brief scene (pp. 415–17) of great richness and with consummate skill, Ferdowsi sees and conveys both the glamor of the civilization that is dying and the valor of the new civilization that is emerging.

If Ferdowsi began his poem under the Samanids, and in hopes of contributing to the revival of a politically independent Islamo-Persian civilization such as that promoted by the Samanids and their western neighbors the Buyids, he lived to see such hopes dashed within his own lifetime. In the closing years of the tenth century and the opening years of the eleventh the Samanid dynasty collapsed and eastern Iran was taken over by the Ghaznavid Turks under their energetic king Mahṃūd of Ghazneh. Whether Ferdowsi completely rewrote his poem or simply revised it to suit the new political climate is not known, but as it stands now the work contains frequent episodes of panegyric on Mahṃūd, though the irony of the author of a poem celebrating countless Iranian victories over the Turks writing such passages cannot have been lost on either the poet or the king. Legend has it that Ferdowsi's poem was not appreciated by Mahṃūd and that the poet died a poor and embittered man. The closing lines of the poem (p. 422) certainly attest to resentment at being poorly rewarded for what must have been virtually his life's work.

Just as the politics of Ferdowsi's own time seem to have affected the reception of his work, so too modern politics have played a part in defining the poet's and his poem's reputation. The Pahlavi kings who ruled Iran from 1925 until 1979 were particularly interested in emphasizing Iran's pre-Islamic past as the ultimate source of Persian civilization, and to this end they assiduously promoted the study of Ferdowsi's poem as it takes exactly this past as its subject matter. Since the Islamic revolution of 1979 in Iran, the Islamic component of Persian culture has received emphatic state support, and the pre-Islamic period has been downplayed as a factor within the culture. In each case scholarship, both Western and Iranian, has tended to follow the current political fashion. Scholars writing on Iran before the revolution tended to emphasize a continuity of culture across the Islamic watershed; some recent writing tends to suggest that little of significance survived the conquest, that Iran became a wholly new cultural entity after its incorporation into the Islamic world. (Similar arguments as to the sources of national tradition can of course be found in other countries' histories; in Greece, for example, there are both partisans of continuity between ancient and modern Greek civilization, and those who assert that the coming of Christianity and the fashioning of a distinctive Byzantine civilization virtually negated all that had gone before in the culture.) But Ferdowsi's poem has survived other political vicissitudes and its immense value both as a literary work and as an unrivalled source of Iranian legendary material will certainly ensure its continued vitality as a component of the culture. Whatever else it is, *The Shāhnāma* is the one indisputably great surviving cultural artifact that attempts to assert a continuity of collective memory across the moment of the conquest; at the least it salvaged the pre-conquest legendary history of Iran and made it available to the Iranian people as a memorial of a great and distinctive civilization.

The translation of such a long and complex work is by no means an easy task. Reuben Levy's prose translation reprinted here takes the reader from the opening of the poem to its end, and this gives it a considerable advantage over all translations of single narratives from the poem. He manages this by summarizing considerable portions of the poem. Probably any reader would have his own notions of which passages should be translated in full and which summarized, but it is fair to say that Levy's version does give a general panoramic view of the work which does not traduce its essential sweep and force. The reader should be aware, however, that something is inevitably sacrificed, not least the sense of the huge architectural structure of the poem, which adds immeasurably to the power of many episodes; the tragic consequences of Rostam's duel with Esfandiyār, for example, owe much of their strength to the reader's mind being steeped in Rostam's innumerable battles on behalf of the Persian throne; the closing pages of the poem have a greatness and finality that draws substantially on the reader's sense of the multifariousness of what has gone before, and this is unavoidably diminished by summary and compression. A summary prose

translation of *The Shāh-nāma* must inevitably be a little like tran-
scribing Wagner's *Ring* for piano and then cutting it to an hour's
length. Much of the transcription may be brilliant, and the choice
of cuts felicitous, but one cannot pretend that nothing will be lost.
Given this, it is impressive how well Levy brings off his massive
task, and he is particularly persuasive in the relatively neglected
Sasanian section of the work, especially in his versions of the reign
of Khosrow Parviz, the death of Shirin, and the last confrontation
with the armies of Islam.

Since Levy worked on his translation views of the text have
changed somewhat. From 1966 to 1971 a new edition of the text
was published in Moscow, under the general editorship of Y.
Bertel's. This edition rejected as spurious many lines and even
whole episodes that previous editors had allowed to stand and
which Levy had translated (for example, the testing of Salm, Tur
and Iraj by their father Faridun, pp. 26–27). In 1977 a manuscript
of *The Shāh-nāma* was discovered in Florence which predates all
previously known manuscripts by some sixty years; this text has
served as the basis of an edition of the poem by Djalal Khaleghi-
Motlagh which is still in the process of being published. In the
portions that have appeared so far, this edition suggests that even
more of the text than had been questioned by the Moscow edition
is perhaps spurious. In general one can say that recent textual
revisions have tended to excise incredible, magical, or overly
supernatural episodes, and to reveal the poem as a more sober and
less fantastic creation than it has sometimes been considered. Such
minutiae are perhaps mainly of interest to scholars, even if cumu-
latively they do alter our general perception of the work. In overall
terms, though, the poem continues to exist as it has done over the
centuries, telling the same legendary and quasi-historical tale of
Iran's pre-Islamic past, as does Levy's translation for the English-
speaking world.

Dick Davis
Ohio State University

Prologue

Before the land of Iran was converted to its present religion of Islam, or Mohammadanism, it had for many centuries followed the doctrines of Zoroaster. His religion, known in the West as Zoroastrianism or Mazdaism, had a literature of its own, which concerned itself largely, as might be expected, with doctrinal and ritual matters. But in its later stages there had also grown up a small body of secular works, of which some at least dealt with the history of the land, its monarchs and heroes.

The conquest of Persia by the Mohammadan Arabs, an event which took place in the years after 636 of the Christian era, wrought a profound change not only in the religion of the people but in its language and literature. The older Pahlavi script was displaced by the Arabic alphabet, and the older language, while remaining basically Indo-European, was blended with a great number of Arabic words relating not only to the new religion and the new worship, of which the sacred language was Arabic, but also to everyday life. In a measure it was a precursor of what happened to the Saxon vocabulary after the conquest of England by the Normans.

The Shāh-nāma* and its author

Of the writers in the new Persian, the Iranians themselves look upon seven as outstanding, and of these the earliest and most linked with national sentiment is the poet known as Ferdowsi, author of the Shāh-nāma (literally 'King-book', i.e. 'The Book of Kings'). This work provides a more or less connected story, told in metrical and rhymed verse, of the Iranian Empire, from the creation of the world down to the Mohammadan conquest, and it purports to deal with the reigns of fifty kings and queens, the section devoted by the poet to each bearing little relationship to the length of his or her reign.

The author himself is normally spoken of by his poetical name of 'Ferdowsi (or Ferdausi)', i.e. the 'Paradisal', whose honorific

* Vowels are pronounced as in Italian: ā, i and u are long, representing the long vowels which occur in the English words 'father', 'chief', and 'rule', while a, e, and o are short, as in 'cat', 'egg', and 'lot'.

title was Abo'l-Qāsem. His personal name is unknown and the
dates of his birth and death are both conjectural, though the latter
probably took place at some time between the years 1020 and 1025
of the Christian era. He came from the neighbourhood of Tus in
the province of Khorāsān and appears to have been a member of
a family not wealthy but which owned a certain amount of land
that they cultivated themselves. They belonged in fact to the
'Dehqān' class, which seems to have been the depository of national
and local tradition and which educated some, at any rate, of its
sons.

The origins of the Shāh-nāma

Ferdowsi had in his possession a prose book on the history of the
Persian kings, and possibly also one in verse, but it was not until
middle life that he began his own poem which, from beginning
to end, took him about thirty-five years. He was not continuously
employed at it and this is known from the fact that here and
there he tells us what his age was at the time when he was composing some particular episode. This énables us to deduce that the
various portions of the work were not done in the order in which
they appear in the final form of the Shāh-nāma. His method was to
select episodes as the fancy took him and he, or a redactor, later
put them together in the chronological order of the reigns.

The contents of the Shāh-nāma

As a whole the work is a collection of episodes, providing a fairly
continuous story of the Iranian Empire from before the creation of
the world down to Iran's submergence under the Muslim Arabs.
The material was of ancient origin and much of it had been stored
up in the minds of Dehqāns, who were able to refresh their memories from records written in Pahlavi [Middle Persian] or in Arabic
prose translations. Ferdowsi indeed did not invent the legends he
put into verse form; in other words, he was not a fiction-writer
drawing on his imagination for the central characters or the actual
plots of his stories. They were established parts of the national
tradition. But he elaborated what he found already in existence
and he himself composed the innumerable speeches he put into the
mouths of his heroes, as well as the many long letters written at
the dictation of the kings and other principal characters.

The narrative begins with the creation of the world 'out of nothing' and continues by narrating how the primordial kings invented the crudely conceived basic requirements of civilization. During the reign of Jamshid, who was king for seven hundred years, there appeared, born of a family with Arab blood in its veins, the monster Zaḥḥāk, who was finally overcome by Kāva the Blacksmith, whose famous banner was for long the palladium of the Iranians. Another great character who appears in the primeval era is Faridun, whose division of the earth between his three sons, Iraj, Tur, and Salm, leads to the murder of Iraj by the other two, and, hence, to the long feud between Tur (Turān) and Iran.

Manuchehr it was who avenged the blood of his father Iraj; then later in his reign appears the warrior Sām. His son Zāl fell in love with Rudāba, by whom he became the father of the prince Rostam, mightiest of all the heroic figures who enter upon the scene in the Shāh-nāma. He makes his appearance intermittently during a number of reigns which between them cover a space of over three centuries. Born in the reign of Manuchehr he does not die until Goshtāsp is on the throne of Iran, when he is killed, treacherously, in vengeance for having caused the death, howbeit involuntarily, of the Shāh Esfandiyār. Even in his last moments the hero had strength enough to slay the miserable wretch who had betrayed him.

It was during the reign of the inept Shāh Kāvus that most of Rostam's heroic feats occurred, and also his combat with his son Sohrāb, who died tragically by his hand. During that reign also the war between Iran and Turān flared up with renewed strength. This was in part due to a quarrel between Kāvus and his son Siyāvush, who fled to the court of the Turanian king Afrāsiyāb. For a time all had gone well with the fugitive prince, to whom Afrāsiyāb had given his daughter in marriage, but then the Turanian king became offended with him and had him murdered. The need to avenge his death therefore became imperative. Key Khosrow, the son of Siyāvush, had grown to manhood in Turān and been with difficulty rescued from it. It was he who brought the war to a successful conclusion, Afrāsiyāb being killed after a long pursuit.

It is here that the romance of Bizhan and Manizha is inserted into the narrative.

After Key Khosrow there ascended the throne the Shāh

Lohrāsp, member of a parallel branch of the Kaiānid dynasty. In his reign occur most of the adventures of his son Goshtāsp, who became the lover and husband of the daughter of the Caesar of Rum, i.e. Eastern Rome. It was in Goshtāsp's reign that Zoroaster introduced his new religion, being supported by the Shāh's son, Esfandiyār. He was kept from the throne long after his succession was due and was slain in the end by Rostam, who had to employ magic to achieve his aim.

The reigns of Dārā and Dārāb, both of which names represent Darius, are followed by that of Sekandar [Alexander] with the accounts of his more or less mythical adventures. Then comes Ardashir, with whom the narrative enters the historical period of the Sasanian Shahs, though it is interspersed with much that is romantic and legendary. Interest is chiefly concentrated on Bahrām Gur, one of the favourite heroes of Persian romantic poetry, and on Kasrā (Khosrow) regarded as the paragon of kingly wisdom. To another Bahrām, known as Chubin, who revolts against Kasrā, is devoted a lengthy portion of the Shāh-nāma and much attention is given also to the fall of the second Khosrow and the rise of his son Shiruy (Qobād).

With sympathetic detail the poet describes the fall of the Iranian Empire under its last Shah, Yazdegerd, after his army, led by a second Rostam, had been defeated by the Arab invaders at the battle of Qādesiya. Then the long story is brought to its close in a brief section containing some dates which purport to give the author's age at the time of his putting the finishing touches to the work.

The character of the Shāh-nāma

The various episodes which compose the narrative are strung together very loosely, for, as we have seen, they were not composed in the chronological sequence proper to a work of history. The whole can be likened to a vast canvas on which the great heroes of Iran's past are depicted against the background of the poet's beloved country. From the nature of the work it cannot be an exact portrayal, for it begins from before the creation of the world and describes the careers of the Shahs who reigned during the era of myth and legend. Nevertheless it took the place of history with the audiences who listened to the stories recited to them; they were not concerned with the fact that no one could have been an eyewitness to the scenes described to them or could have been close to them in time.

There is in the Shāh-nāma an amalgamation of the Persian equivalents of chapters in the book of Genesis, the Odyssey, Paradise Lost, Chaucer's Canterbury Tales and Shakespeare. It is indeed astonishing how often the vocabulary of Shakespeare suits the incidents described in the Persian epic. Drama, comedy, tragedy—all are here. Nature has a conspicuous and felicitous place in the Shāh-nāma. Tree lore has a prominent part. The vast scene of operations is bathed in a wondrous light.

In two types of passages Ferdowsi's art is often at its highest: the laments for the fallen kings and heroes, and the descriptions of sunrise. Perhaps Ferdowsi has intended an organic artistic link between these two themes that like a great antiphony run through the whole of the Shāh-nāma. The endless procession of death is punctuated by the recurrent birth of the source and symbol of all life itself. For the technical solution to the difficult task of treating repetitive material Ferdowsi borrows a prevalent and highly-regarded art form, namely theme and variations, and proves himself a consummate master. The full range of poetic arts are brought into play so that no two sunrises are described in the same terms and the same manner and no two laments are identical. There is an unsentimental pathos and a measured humanity in these laments. They often contain some of the profoundest lines in the whole poem.

But the poet's main object is to tell the story of his fatherland. We are stirred by the constant clash of arms, more particularly caused by the attacks and counter-attacks that throughout the passage of time recurred between Iran and its enemies, the most formidable of whom was Turān, the great national antagonist. The air is nearly always filled with the dust of battle, the roll of drums of war or the clash of heavy mace on steel helmet when a warrior meets his adversary in single combat.

Yet there are intervals for peaceful pursuits, when the monarchs, their coronets firmly attached to their heads, play polo or go hunting the onager—their favourite game—or the gentle gazelle. Following on triumphs in the field of battle or the hunting ground they seat themselves before huge trays laden with viands of every kind, being waited on by moon-cheeked maids who are constantly at hand with flagons of red wine. From time to time they engage in amorous dalliance.

The events and characters described suffer no terrestrial limitations as they range over land and sky, though it is only rarely that anything is said of adventure by sea. In this connection it may be said that Ferdowsi was as little trammelled by the facts of geography as was Shakespeare. Territories separated by vast stretches of road are traversed in an instant or else brought for convenience into close proximity. Monarchs dictate their behests to the whole world from the height of their thrones and proclaim themselves the direct instruments of God's will. The prehistoric kings, and heroes such as Rostam, live and wage war for hundreds of years. Throughout the whole poem the struggle with the national foes is associated with the struggle between good and evil, where the good must in the long run gain the upper hand.

Cambridge, 1966   R. L.

Translator's Note

In accordance with the scheme laid down by the editors of the Persian Heritage Series, which is meant for 'the general reader', I have stressed before all else the narrative and literary value of the Shāh-nāma. The general reader in view here is presumably one who is not necessarily a specialist in the field of Persian language or literature, though such a one would not be excluded. He or she would appreciate a good story and would be willing to concede that such a thing can exist in surroundings other than Western and that its setting need neither be modern nor confined to what we know of the classical world. Such a reader would further be willing to accept the rendering of the stories into conventional English prose, tinged by archaisms introduced in the endeavour to create the right atmosphere. The original Persian text is in metrical verse, rhyming in hemistichs, in which as a rule a sentence is contained within the compass of a single line and does not often overrun into a second. Given the scanty stock of rhyming words existing in English it would have been impossible to imitate the form and style of the original.

The Persian text used was that of Vullers and Landauer for the early part and that published by Beroukhim (Tehran, 1934-) for the remainder. Notes on points of difficulty have been confined to the minimum necessary for the understanding of the narrative.

Some repetitive sections of the original have been omitted and some of the poet's moralizings also. Where it has been necessary to summarize or abbreviate passages I have put them in my own words enclosed within square brackets [ ]. The numbers of the chapters and sub-sections are arbitrary. They have been allotted to the anecdotes concerned with the chief characters in the work, not necessarily at their first appearance on the scene but when they ascend the throne or are otherwise shown as getting into their stride.

On the question of the transliteration of proper names and Persian words certain rules have been laid down by the editor of the Series and have normally been obeyed by me in accordance with the footnote on page xv. Very occasionally I have been in a dilemma when both a Persian and an English form of name exists, but I have as a rule come down on the side of the Persian.

xlv

For example, instead of speaking of Darius I have called him Dārā or Dārāb, as Ferdowsi did, and I have written Sekander instead of Alexander, for whereas the Macedonian was an actual historical figure, the Persian counterpart was in some degree a legendary character about whom many myths have gathered.

I have not sought to improve on the poet, but I have not been a slave, as he sometimes was, to metre and rhyme. I have used the English equivalent best suited to the Persian without seeking to subordinate sense to sound. Apart from that, I have tried to represent the poem 'warts and all'. The choice of what parts of the poem to omit has been my own. It would have added little to the interest or value of the work to have translated everything in it.

The Epic of the Kings

The Poet's Introduction

The opening of the book

In the name of the Lord of the soul and of wisdom, than Whom thought can conceive nothing higher; the Lord of all things nameable and of all space; the Lord who grants sustenance and is our Guide; the Lord of the universe and the revolving sky, who kindles the Moon, Venus and the Sun. He is beyond all naming, indication or fancy and He is the essence of anything a limner may design.

[The poet repeats his asseveration that the mind of man has no means of attaining to a knowledge of God by any power of reason.]

In praise of wisdom

Wisdom is better than aught else which God has granted to you. Wisdom is the guide and is the heart's enlivener; wisdom is your helper in both worlds. From it comes happiness and all human welfare; from it you gain increase and without it you experience loss. Thou, Wisdom, art the creation of the Creator of the world and knowest all things patent or hidden. Do thou, O man, ever keep wisdom as your counsellor, whereby you may preserve your soul from all unworthiness. When you have acquired an insight into any branch of a matter, you will understand that science does not reach down to the root.

On the creation of the world

As a beginning you must know precisely what the material of the elements was in origin. God created matter out of nothingness in order that his power might be manifested; out of it was produced the substance of the four elements, without effort and without expenditure of time. Of these elements one was fire, which arose shining; then the wind and the water came, above the dark earth. First the fire was stirred into motion and so dryness appeared because of the heat of fire. When it was still again, cold manifested itself, and then, out of cold grew moisture.

I

When these four elements were once in existence they came together to form this fleeting abode of the world. Thus they were compounded each with the other to make up every genus of the proudest order of phenomena, such as this swift-moving dome [the sky], displaying ever-new marvels. It is master of the twelve [Signs] and the seven [Planets], each of which takes up its due position. Through God generosity and justice came into being and He has granted fitting reward to all who recognize Him.

The heavenly spheres were constructed one within the other and set in motion once the structure had been completed. With sea, mountain, desert and meadow the earth became bright as a shining lamp. With the mountain towering high, waters coalesced and the heads of growing plants reared upwards. But to the earth itself no place on high was allotted; it was a central point, dark and black. Overhead the stars displayed their wonders, casting their brightness on to the earth. Fire ascended, water poured down and the sun revolved about the earth.

Grass sprouted, together with trees of several kinds, whose tops happily grew upwards. These things grow and have no other power; they cannot move in any direction in the way that animals can. These moving creatures brought the growing things into subjection. They ever seek food, sleep and repose and find all their satisfaction in being alive; with neither tongue for utterance nor wisdom to make investigation they nurture their bodies on thorn and stubble. They do not know if the outcome of what they do is good or ill; the Lord demands no service of them.

The creation of man

Going beyond these creatures Man appeared, to become the key to all these close-linked things. His head was raised up like the cypress, he was endowed with good speech and applied wisdom to use. He received sense, reason and wisdom, and all animals whether wild or tame are obedient to his command. By the path of wisdom you may perceive in some small measure what the significance of man may be. Perhaps you know mankind as a distracted thing and can find no indication of its being ought else. You were produced out of two worlds and nurtured in some respects to be a go-between; although first in nature you must regard yourself as the latest in time. Thus you are; therefore do not devote yourself to triviality.

The creation of the sun

The blue vault of heaven is made of red coral, being composed neither of wind and water, nor of dust and smoke. With its brilliance and light it is bright as a garden in the Spring. There is in it a heart-warming element which moves and from which day receives its illumination. Each dawn like a golden shield it raises its glowing head out of the East, clothing the earth in a garment of light in such fashion that the universe stands revealed. When it travels onwards from the East towards the West, dark night raises its head out of the East; neither seeks to overtake the other and nothing can be more orderly than this succession.

The creation of the moon

The moon is a lamp provided for the dark night (never turn to evil if it is within your power). For two days and two nights it does not show its face, the circle of it fades away; then it reappears thin and yellow, its back bent like the back of a person who has suffered the torment of love. Even as the beholder gazes on it from afar it vanishes from sight. The next night it reappears larger and provides you with more light. In two weeks it becomes full and whole again and then returns to what it was at first, becoming more slender each night and moving nearer to the sun. Thus did God establish a just path for it and as long as it exists it will pursue this same course.

In praise of the prophet and his companions

[Here follows a section belauding the Prophet Mohammad and his four Companions, the 'Upright' Caliphs, of whom the poet regards the prophet's cousin Ali as the most to be revered.]

How the SHĀH-NĀMA came to be composed

From early times there existed a work in which were contained an abundance of legends, and it was shared out between a number of [Magian] priests, each of whom held a portion. It happened once that a personage of high rank, belonging to Dehqān [landed gentry] stock, a man of noble character, liberal disposition and high intelligence, came to be interested in primeval days and sought for histories of times gone by. Accordingly, he assembled from their various provinces the aged priests who had learnt that work by heart and he put questions to them concerning the kings who had once possessed the world and about other famous and illustrious men.

'How did they,' he inquired, 'hold the world in the beginning, and why is it that it has been left to us in such a sorry state? And how was it that they were able to live free of care during the days of their heroic labours?'

Little by little these revered men unfolded to him the histories of the kings and told how the world's vicissitudes had come about; and when this great knight had heard all that they had to tell him, he laid the foundations of a noble book that achieved fame throughout the world and received universal adulation from all people, high and low.

'Who was it first,' that gifted Dehqān had inquired, 'who invented the crown of royalty and placed a diadem on his head?'

They answered, 'The time of that goes far back in the memory of human beings. A son learnt of it from his father, and told about it, in every detail, as he had received it from his begetter.'

And now that inquirer into ancient legend, who recounts the story of the Heroes, has this to say:

I

The Reign of Keyumars

The ceremonial of throne and crown was introduced by Keyumars, who was king and ruler over the whole world. He placed
his residence at first in the mountains, where his fortunes and
throne were raised on high. Like his people he clothed himself in
leopard-skin; nevertheless it was through him that civilization
came, because clothing was something new, as also was food. He
ruled the world for thirty years, benevolent as the sun everywhere
and as resplendent on his throne as the two weeks old moon
shining above a slender cypress. All living creatures, wild or tame,
on seeing him, assembled from every part of the world and took
refuge with him, bowing low before his throne. And so it was
that he grew in majesty and power. All came to him in the attitude
of reverence, and hence religion took its rise.

II

The Reign of Hūshang

[Keyumars had a son, Siyāmak, who was killed while giving battle
to the Black Demon, son of Ahrimān, the Maker of Evil. The
demon was in his turn attacked by Siyāmak's son Hūshang and by
Keyumars himself.][1]

Once Keyumars had made his resolve to exact vengeance and give
battle [to the demon] he summoned Hushang, whom he loved
dearly, and informed him of the stratagems he must employ, and
imparted all his secrets to him, saying,

'I will mobilize an army and set alarming rumours on foot. You
will have charge of all, for I must die and you shall be the new
commander of the army.'

He then mustered the peris [fairies], the leopards and the lions,
together with all the other ravening beasts, such as the wolves and
the fierce tigers, so that it became an army composed of animals
wild and tame, birds and peris, commanded by a chieftain endowed
with pride and courage. Keyumars himself was in charge of the
army's rearguard, while his grandson led the van.

In fear and trembling the Black Demon advanced, making the
dust rise to heaven; and, when the two forces engaged, the
demons were thrown into rout by the ferocious beasts. Hushang,
stretching out a hand like a lion's foreleg, shut the world down
tightly upon the raging demon, whose hide he split from top to
toe. The monstrous head he severed, cast it down and trampled
it under foot in contempt. Thus having achieved the vengeance
he desired, Keyumars reached the end of his life.

Hushang the all-powerful, endowed with the spirit of wisdom
and justice, now set the crown on his head in his grandfather's
place, and being seated on the throne of splendour he made this
proclamation,

'I am lord of the seven climes, supreme over all and obeyed
universally. By command of Almighty God I am ready to dispense
justice and deal generously with all men.'

[1] Passages within square brackets provide links bridging gaps, sometimes
lengthy, left by omissions in the translation. These are required in places
where the poet has introduced material that interrupts the course of the main
narrative or which is repetitious. [Translator's note.]

6

With that he set about the task of bringing prosperity into the world and providing equitable conditions in every part. As a beginning he procured a wondrous touchstone and by science separated the rock from the iron. That wonderful metal, the substance which he had extracted from the hard ore, he made his prime material, and, once he had become familiar with its qualities, he invented the craft of the smith, whereby he was enabled to fashion axes, saws and mattocks.

With that achievement completed he began to devise schemes for water, which he drew from the river in order to cultivate the plain, making a way for it along channels and ducts. By his royal *Farr*[1] he reduced drudgery. To the pasture-lands of people he added sowing of seeds, cultivation of soil, and reaping of harvests. And so each one was able to better his own livelihood, and to recognize and develop his own homestead. Before these tasks had been carried out no foods had existed but fruits, and no part of man's labours had gone to the storage of provisions, and his clothing was nothing but leaves.

The discovery of fire

Man's ancestors had possessed a number of ceremonial rites and a religion and the worship of God was practised. In those early days fire with its gorgeous colouring was the cynosure towards which men faced, as the Arabs do towards the niche that shows the direction of Mecca. And fire first appeared out of stone and became the source from which light was diffused about the world. It happened one day, while the king of the world was making a journey towards the mountains with some of his retinue, that there came into view, moving at speed, an elongated creature black in colour. In its head were two eyes like pools of blood and from its mouth there poured black smoke covering the world with gloom. Hushang observed it keenly and steadily, then took up a stone, which he gripped firmly and, with the strength granted to heroes, let fly against this world-devouring monster, which leapt aside from the world-conquering Shah.

---

[1] A certain refulgence or 'nimbus', symbolizing Divine favour, and reserved for kings and other royal personages. It had almost a physical character, being as it were a palladium, talisman or mascot, which was recognizable by beholders and implied infallible greatness and good fortune as long as its possessor held the favour of the Divine Powers.

The small stone dashed against a greater one, both were shattered by the impact, and from between the two there flashed out a spark whose brightness set the heart of the stone aglow. The monster was not slain, but, out of the realm of the hidden, fire was discovered from that stone. So that whenever iron is struck against stone a spark appears. On that first occurrence the world-possessor went to the Creator of the world and worshipped him, calling down blessings on him for having granted him the gift of the spark. And he appointed the fire to be the objective to which men turn in worship.

'This spark,' he proclaimed, 'is God-given; if you are wise you will worship it.'

Night came, and with it the fire blazed mountain-high, the king and his retinue being gathered about it. That night he feasted and drank wine and gave the name *Sada* to this happy occasion.

By virtue of his divine *Farr* and his royal powers he was enabled to set apart the beasts which are hunted, such as the onager and the wild antelope, from domestic animals like donkeys, cows and sheep. And he fostered all things that would serve man. He bred the swift animals whose fur is good and he skinned off their pelts. They were such animals as fox, marten and smooth ermine, as well as the sable, whose fur is warm. With the skins of such fast-running beasts he clothed the bodies of human beings.

III

The Reign of Jamshid

[After Hushang came his son Tahmuras, who subjugated the demons and earned the title of 'Demon-binder' and reigned for thirty years. He was followed by his son Jamshid.]

For a time Jamshid had respite from war, since all the demons, birds and peris were subject to his command. 'I am,' he declared, 'endowed with the divine *Farr* and at the same time both king and priest. I shall stay the hand of the evil-doers from evil, and I shall guide the soul towards light.' He first devoted himself to the making of weapons of war, which he gave to valiant heroes eager for renown. By virtue of his kingly *Farr* he was able to mould iron into such equipment as helmets, chain-mail, and laminated armour as well as missile-proof vests, to swords and horse-armour, all of which he invented by his perspicuous intellect. He spent fifty years at this task, part of the time being devoted to the accumulation of stores.

For the next fifty years he gave his mind to the subject of apparel and such matters as the dress appropriate to feasting or to battle. Hence he contrived materials of linen, silk, wool and floss as well as rich brocades and satins. He taught men how to spin and weave and how to interlace the warp with the weft; then, when the weaving was completed, they learnt from him how to wash the materials and how to sew.

When that task was completed he turned to another employ, which was the bringing together of all the men engaged in each craft. Over that he spent fifty years. The class of men known as 'Kātuzi', regarded as being specially charged with the rites of worship, was set apart from the common herd of mankind. As for the priests, the mountains were allotted to them as temples, where they were to devote themselves to worship and to supplication of their divine Master.

In contrast to them he established the caste whom men call 'Neysāri'. They are lion-hearted warriors who shed lustre over the army and the whole land and because of whom the king sits securely on the throne. Through them the term 'manliness' was established.

The third group claiming recognition was that of the 'Nasudi'

caste. They give homage to no man; tilling, sowing and themselves reaping. They heed no person's censure when the time
comes for eating. Their heads refuse to bow to command; they are
men of independence although clad in rags, and their ears are deaf
to abuse. By them the earth is kept under cultivation and clear of
strife and discord.

The fourth class is named 'Ahnukhwashi', who industriously
spend themselves in all crafts. Their work is consummately skilled
and their minds teem with ideas.

Over that task Jamshid consumed another fifty years, distributing benefits generously in every region. Thus he assigned to every
living creature the right rank or station [proper to it] and directed
[it on] its path, so that each might be aware of its place and understand the measure of it. Upon the demons he laid the duty of
mingling earth with water, and when they understood what could
be produced with clay they quickly fashioned moulds for bricks.
With stone and mortar they built walls, upon which they were the
first to erect works of masonry such as baths and lofty arches and
castles which could provide refuge against attack.

For a length of time the king sought for gems amongst the
rocks and by experiment discovered their lustre. Precious minerals
of various kinds came into his hands. They included jacinth,
yellow amber, silver and gold, which he extracted from the rock
by magic art, the key to unloosening any bond of conglomeration.
He also distilled sweet perfumes in whose fragrance men delight;
essences like balsam, camphor, pure musk, aloes, ambergris and
limpid rose-water. These are drugs and restoratives for those who
suffer disease, and they are of use in health as well as during
illness. All these hidden things he brought to light, there being no
equal to him as a discoverer in the whole universe.

After that he went over the water in a ship, voyaging swiftly from
one clime to another. In that way he spent another fifty years. And
then he set foot even beyond greatness. With the aid of the royal
Farr, he fashioned a marvellous throne, which at his bidding was
lifted by demons into the air. He sat upon that throne like the sun
in the firmament. To celebrate, that day was called a new day—the
festival of Now-Ruz—the first day of the new year.

Thus another three hundred years went by and men never saw
death, remaining unacquainted even with toil and hardship, for the
demons waited ever ready to serve. All men were obedient to the
king's command and the world was pervaded by the pleasant

sounds of music. And so years went by until the royal *Farr* was wrested from him. The reason for it was that the king, who had always paid homage to God, now became filled with vanity and turned away from Him in forgetfulness of the gratitude he owed Him. He summoned those of his followers who were held in highest esteem and in these words addressed his nobles of long experience,

'I recognize no lord but myself. It was through me that skills appeared on earth, and no throne however famed has ever beheld a monarch like me. It was I who adorned the world with beauty and it is by my will that the earth has become what it now is. Sunshine, sleep and repose all come through me, and even your clothing and what enters your mouths originate from me. Power, crown and kingship are my prerogative. Who can claim that anyone but I am king? By means of drugs and other medicaments the world has been brought to such a level of health that sickness and death befall no one. Who but I have banished death from amongst mankind, although many kings have been upon the earth? It is because of me that you have minds and souls in your bodies. And now that you are aware that all this was accomplished by me, it is your duty to entitle me Creator of the World.'

The priests to a man remained with heads bowed low, none daring to ask 'Why?' or 'How?'. But as soon as he had made his speech the *Farr* departed from him and the world became full of discord. Men deserted his court and no one desiring repute would remain in his service, for when pride combines with power of action it brings ruin in its train and converts good fortune into bad. Jamshid's destiny was overcast with gloom and his world-illumining splendour disappeared.

(i) *The story of Zaḥḥāk*

In those days there lived a man who came from the deserts where men rode horses and brandished spears. He was a person much honoured for his generosity and one who in his fear of the Lord trembled as though shaken by a gale. The name of this noble man was Merdās. This true believer and prince had a son, whom he loved with a love beyond measure and who was called Zaḥḥāk, a youth of high courage, swift in action and bold. Of each day and night he spent two parts out of three in the saddle on noble enterprises, never for any unlawful purpose.

Now one day Eblis [the Devil] arrived on pretence of being a visitor who wished to pay him homage. The visitor's speeches fell agreeably on his ear, for he had no inkling of his character, and he surrendered to him with his whole mind, heart and pure soul, and humbled himself before him. Eblis, feeling that the prince had been completely won over by him, rejoiced beyond measure at his own cunning and said,

'I have many things to impart to you which no one knows but me.'

'Tell me then,' replied the youth, 'and hold nothing back. You are the man to give good advice. Instruct me.'

'First,' said he, 'I require an oath of you, and then I shall reveal such matters as I have to impart.'

The youth was innocent of heart. He gave his word, swearing an oath in which Eblis demanded that he would never disclose any part of his secret to anyone and would obey his every word. Eblis then said,

'Within this palace, my noble lord, what need for a being other than yourself? Why is a father necessary when a son like you exists? Listen to counsel. Over this aged nobleman long years have passed; he lingers on while you endure in wretchedness. Seize upon these riches and this palace; the high rank which he enjoys in the world is well suited to you. If you will have trust in what I say, you will be the only ruler in the world.'

As he heard this Zaḥḥāk became pensive, but his heart filled with pain at the thought of taking his father's life. 'It would conflict with all justice,' said he to Eblis. 'Suggest some other plan, for that is something which I cannot do.'

'If you fail in carrying out my advice,' replied Eblis, 'you will dishonour your pledge and the oath which you swore to me; that oath and your bond will lie heavily upon you. Moreover you will linger on as a person disregarded by all, while your father continues to command reverence.'

The head of the Arab [Zaḥḥāk] fell into the net and he was cowed into submission to the other's will. He asked what scheme he advised and declared he would not reject the slightest detail.

Now within the palace bounds the king had a garden which rejoiced his heart, and into it every night he went to prepare himself in privacy for the rites of worship by washing his head and body. The servants who accompanied him carried no lanterns, and on the path leading into the garden the vile demon, in pursuance of his evil plan, dug a deep pit, and covered it with straw. Night fell and the Arab chief [the king], that noble lord ever zealous for his good repute, arose to enter the garden. As he approached the abysmal pit, the royal fortunes sank heavily; down into it he fell and lay there broken. So departed that benevolent and God-fearing man.

Ẓaḥḥāk, despicable malefactor, seizing his opportunity, usurped his father's place and set on his head the crown of the Arabs, amongst whom he became the giver of good and evil.

Once Eblis understood that he had brought this matter to an end with success, he began to elaborate a further scheme. He said to Ẓaḥḥāk,

'When you turned to me for aid, you won all that you desired. If you will make another such compact with me, leaving nothing undone that I suggest and obeying my commands, the sovereignty of the whole world will be yours. Every living animal wild or tame, together with the birds and the fishes, shall be in submission to you.'

So saying he departed to further this scheme and to devise another strange artifice.

(ii) *Eblis turns cook*

Having tricked himself out as a young man, glib-tongued, active and clean-limbed, Eblis found his way into the presence of Ẓaḥḥāk, whom he addressed in the language of flattery and said,

'If I am agreeable to your Majesty, I am myself a renowned and perfectly-trained cook.'

Ẓaḥḥāk accepted this with approval. He had a place got ready for him where he could prepare his viands, entrusted him with the key of the royal kitchens and gave him full oversight of all. In those days flocks were not plentiful, and living creatures were rarely killed for eating. Except for herbs men had nought to eat and it was the ground that produced all, until Ahriman, the Evil-doer, conceived and lodged in the minds of men the thought of killing animals. Out of every genus both of birds and quadrupeds he contrived eatables, making use of all. With their blood he fed Ẓaḥḥāk, as though it were milk, in order to make him stout of heart. And Ẓaḥḥāk obeyed every word that Eblis uttered, giving his mind in pledge to his command.

First Eblis gave Ẓaḥḥāk the yolk of an egg to eat and for a time kept his body in good health with it. Zahhāk ate and, finding it agreeable to his palate, gave praise to Eblis. One day Eblis said to him,

'Proud monarch, may you live for ever! Tomorrow I will prepare a dish that will give you the perfection of sustenance.' Then he went to rest and all night long his mind was occupied with the thought of the wondrous dishes his cook would concoct on the morrow. Next day, when the azure vault [of heaven] raised aloft and displayed the yellow jacinth [of the sun], Eblis cooked a dish of partridge and white pheasant and brought it in with his mind full of expectation, and as the Arab king stretched out his hand to the tray of food, his foolish head betrayed him into a partiality for Eblis.

On the following day the tray was decked by Eblis with chicken and lamb as well as with other viands. On the next day again when he set his tray before the king, he had prepared a saddle of veal enriched with saffron and rose-water as well as with old wine and clarified musk. When Zahhāk partook of this delicacy and savoured it, he was filled with admiration at the man's skill and said to him,

'Consider what you would most desire and then ask me for it.'

The cook replied,

'May your Majesty live happily for ever, endowed with all-powerful command! My heart is wholly devoted to love for you and from your countenance comes all that sustains my spirit. I have one petition to make of your Majesty, although I am not of the degree to aspire to it. It is, if your Majesty command, that I may be permitted to kiss your shoulders and rub them with my eyes and face.'

Zahhāk heard the words and, little suspecting what lay behind all the doings of Eblis, replied,

'I grant your desire. Mayhap your fame will get advancement from it.'

And so he let him have his wish, as though he were his dearest friend, to kiss him on his shoulders. This Eblis did, and immediately vanished into the ground—a marvel such as no man in the world has ever seen.

From Zahhāk's shoulders now two black serpents thrust their heads out, filling him with terror. On every hand he sought for a remedy and at last had recourse to cutting them off. But, just as branches sprout anew from trees, so those two black serpents grew again from the royal shoulders. Learned physicians crowded about him, each in turn advising what should be done; and every kind of wizardry was tried. Yet no remedy was found for the affliction. And then Eblis appeared again, this time in the guise of a physician. Presenting himself gravely before Ẓaḥḥāk, he said, 'This is an occurrence predestined by fate. Leave all alone. Since they are there, you must not cut them off; rather let food be prepared and given them to eat so that they can be propitiated. That is the only proper expedient. For food let them have nothing but human brains, and it may be that given that kind of nurture they will die.' [And in this his secret intent was to empty the world of people.]

(iii) *Jamshid's fortunes decline*

Days passed, and then, [God having withdrawn His favour from Jamshid] a mighty discontent arose throughout Iran. On every hand strife and turmoil erupted and glorious bright day was turned to darkness. Jamshid's allies broke away from him, his divine *Farr* became tarnished and he took to crooked paths and folly. On every hand new kings sprang up, on every frontier men sought a way to power. They gathered armies and made war, their hearts having been emptied of all affection for Jamshid. By ones and twos a host of men forsook Iran and went along the roads towards the Arabs, in whose land, they had heard, was an awe-inspiring king with a dragon's body.

Iranian knights, in search of a new king, turned their glances in unison towards Ẓaḥḥāk and, saluting him as sovereign, they proclaimed him king of Iran.

Swift as the wind the dragon-king journeyed to Iran, where he assumed the crown. In Iran and from amongst the Arabs he chose an army composed of the champions of every region. Then when fortune had withdrawn its face from Jamshid, the new king hemmed him in closely until he came and surrendered throne and crown, his high rank vanishing with his diadem, treasure and retinue. The world grew black in his sight, so that he hid himself away and no one saw him again for a hundred years. At last he, prince of besmirched faith, appeared in the sea of China. There Ẓaḥḥāk had him seized and, without granting him a moment's respite, had his body sawn in two, thus cleansing the world and ridding it of all fear of him.

After Ẕaḥḥāk had enthroned himself as emperor, a thousand years accumulated over him, an era during which the ways of rational men disappeared and the wishes of the devil-possessed everywhere prevailed. Virtue was humiliated and wizardry esteemed; truth hid itself and evil flourished openly. Now it became the practice that each night two young men, either humbly born or sons of noble families, were carried away to the royal palace by a cook, who out of them provided something for the solace of the king. He killed them and then drew out their brains, from which he made a dish with which to feed the dragon.

IV

Farīdūn

(i) The birth of Farīdūn

[Ẓaḥḥāk dreamt one night that a hero named Farīdūn would appear to dethrone and slay him.]

A long time went by, spent in anxiety by Ẓaḥḥāk, and then Faridun, blessed by fortune, came into the world. He grew up as beautiful as a slender cypress, and the royal *Farr* radiated from him. It had been inherited from Jamshid and he was refulgent as the sun that shines in the heavens, and as needful to the world as rain to the earth and as appropriate as knowledge to the mind. Over his head in affection for him the skies revolved in benignity.

[To discover Faridun's dwelling-place] Ẓaḥḥāk filled the world with hue and cry, hunting for him and searching in every direction. Faridun's father, Abtin, when the world narrowed about him, fled away in despair of his life but unsuspectingly fell into the lion's toils, for vile guards found him and carried him, bound like a tiger, into the presence of Ẓaḥḥāk, who put an end to his life.

[Farānak, the hero's prudent mother, at that took flight with her child and after a number of adventures settled in a hiding place in the Alborz mountains.]

(ii) Ẓaḥḥāk and Kāva the blacksmith

Day and night the thoughts of Ẓaḥḥāk were occupied with Faridun, of whom he was constantly speaking. Fear of him caused his upright stature to become bowed and because of him his heart was ever pervaded with dread. One day, seated on his ivory throne and with his turquoise crown placed on his head, he summoned the princes charged with ruling over his provinces in order to secure from them their affirmation of his sovereignty. He then addressed his ministers, to whom he said,

'My revered and talented counsellors, I have a hidden enemy; a fact which is patent to men of understanding like yourselves. And,

17

however despicable an enemy may be, I do not hold him in contempt, for I am ever doubtful of the malice of fate. I therefore stand in need of a large army, in which demons and peris shall be enrolled along with men, and such an army I am about to raise. Since I am unable to support the burden of it alone, you must ally yourselves with me in the project. And now I desire you to subscribe to a proclamation on my behalf that as commander in chief I have sown no seed but that of uprightness, that I have never spoken anything but the truth and that I would never fail to maintain justice.'

Being in awe of the monarch, those upright men allied themselves with him in his scheme and, old and young, willingly or unwillingly, wrote on the dragon's proclamation the assurance he desired. Just then an unexpected petitioner for justice entered the king's palace. He was a man who had been grievously wronged and, being summoned into the royal presence, was given a seat before those famous men. With an anxious countenance the monarch said to him,

'Tell me at whose hands it is that you have suffered wrong.'

Striking his head with his hand at seeing the king himself, the man cried out,

'Your Majesty, I am Kāva, seeking for justice. Grant me justice! I have come here running and I implore you with grief in my soul. If you are active in doing justice, then the esteem in which you are held will be heightened to the extreme. Most of the wrong done to me comes from yourself. It is you who constantly thrust the lancet into my heart. If as you say you would not suffer an outrage upon me, why then do you inflict harm on my children? I had eighteen alive in the world, and now only one remains. Spare me this one child, or my spirit will everlastingly be tortured. My king, what crime have I committed? Tell me. If I am innocent, do not seek pretexts against me. Misfortune has bowed me down, as you see; it has left my heart devoid of hope and my mind full of misery. My youth is gone, and without children I will have no ties left in the world. There is a middle and a limit to injustice; even then it must have a pretext. If you have an accusation against me, present it, for you plan my destruction.

'I am a simple blacksmith, doing no wrong; yet fire descends on my head from your Majesty. Although you have a dragon's form, you are the king and it's your duty to let me have justice in this thing. You have sovereignty over the seven [planet-ruled] climes;

why should the fate allotted to me be all grief and misery? You and
I must come to a reckoning, and then the world will stand in
amazement. Perhaps the reckoning with you will make clear how
my last son's turn has come, how it was that from amongst all the
people it was my son's brains which had to be sacrificed to your
Majesty.'

The monarch at this speech opened his eyes wide and he was
overcome with astonishment at the words. The man's son was
restored to him and an effort was made with kindly treatment to
win his support for the king. However, when the king commanded Kāva to add his testimony to what was contained in the
proclamation, Kāva perused the document from end to end and
then, turning swiftly to the elders of the land, he cried out,

'Henchmen of the Devil, you have cut off your hearts from fear
of the Lord. All of you have turned your faces towards Hell and
surrendered your hearts to obedience of the Devil. I will not lend
my testimony to this proclamation, nor will I ever stand in awe of
the king.'

With a cry he sprang up trembling, tore the proclamation into
pieces, which he trampled underfoot. Out of the palace he went
thundering into the street, his son ahead of him.

[In the audience-hall] the nobles made sychophantic speeches to
the king.

'Most famous king of the world,' they said, 'even the cool winds
of heaven do not venture to pass over your head on the day of
battle. How then dare this crude-spoken Kāva address you in
anger as though he were your equal? He has destroyed our proclamation containing the covenant made with you and rejects
your authority. His heart and head are swollen with wrath and he
has gone as though to make common cause with Faridun. Never
have we beheld viler conduct; we stand outraged by his actions.'

'Listen to a strange thing that has happened,' said the king in
speedy reply. 'When Kāva appeared in the audience-hall, as soon as
my ears heard the sound of his voice there immediately arose
between him and me in the chamber what seemed a mountain of
iron, and then, when he struck his head with his hand, the thing
fell, shattered in pieces. I do not know what will emerge from this
portent; nobody knows Heaven's secrets.'

Meantime, when Kāva came out after leaving the king's presence, the people crowded about him in the market-place. He
called out, summoning men to come to his aid and urging the

world to demand justice. On to the end of a spear he fastened a piece of leather, of the kind which blacksmiths wear in front of their legs when using their hammers, and as out of the market-place the dust rose high, with the spear held aloft he began to march, crying out as he went,

'Noble worshippers of God, let all who side with Faridun liberate their heads from the yoke of Zaḥḥāk! Let us go to Faridun and find refuge in the shelter of his *Farr*. Let us proclaim that this present king is Ahriman [the Maker of Evil], who is at heart the enemy of the Creator. By means of that leather, worth nothing and costing nothing, the voice of the enemy was distinguished from that of the friend.'

As the stout-hearted man marched onwards, an army of no small size rallied about him. He knew where Faridun lay and went directly towards the place, and as they at last approached the castle of the young prince they greeted him with a shout when they espied him in the distance. His eye caught the piece of leather attached to the spearhead and he beheld in it the foundation of prosperity to come. The leather he decorated with Greek brocade and as background to it had a golden figure outlined with jewels sewn on it. Ribands of red, yellow, and violet cloth were hung from it and it was given the title of 'The Kāviāni Banner'. Since those days anyone who has assumed kingly rank and placed the crown of royalty on his head has added fresh jewels to that trifling thing of blacksmith's leather.

With him as his constant companions Faridun had two brothers, both older than himself, and to them he opened his heart, declaring that the skies revolved only to a benevolent purpose and the diadem of greatness would inevitably come to him.

'Get me cunning smiths to fashion me a heavy mace,' he bade them, and outlined in the dust a figure portraying the likeness of a buffalo's head.

(iii) *Faridun makes war on Zaḥḥāk*

Proudly Faridun raised his head sun-high and girt himself tightly to exact vengeance for his father's death. On an appointed day he eagerly began his undertaking beneath a happy star and with omens that brightened his day. At his palace, whose pinnacles reached the skies, troops massed about him with massive elephants, and buffaloes laden with the army's provender. In the forefront of the troops rode Kāva, head on high, moving spiritedly from the halting-place and bearing aloft the the Kāviāni Banner, regal emblem of majesty.

Faridun set his face towards the Arvand river as a man determined to find a crown. (If you are ignorant of the Pahlavi tongue, you call the Arvand by its Arabic name of Dijla [i.e. the Tigris].) When he reached the stream he sent salutations to its wardens and commanded them quickly to launch ships and other vessels.

'Ferry me and my soldiers across to the other bank,' he said, 'and leave no man behind on this side.'

The chief river-guard however, ignoring Faridun's command, brought no ships, but said in answer to him,

'The King of the World [Ẓaḥḥāk] secretly ordered me to launch no ship unless I had first obtained a permit from him, attested by his seal.'

Faridun was stirred to wrath by these words. Without fear of the deep flood, he fastened his royal girth tightly, sprang upon his lion-hearted steed and, with his mind sharply intent on vengeance and battle, spurred his rose-coloured horse into the torrent. His comrades, similarly girt for action, charged into the river with him, sinking on their swift-footed mounts as deep as the saddle. Coming to dry land on the opposite side they continued on their way to Jerusalem, which is now in Arabic called 'The Immaculate Abode', where Ẓaḥḥāk, you must know, had erected his palace.

From across the desert the warriors approached the city in high hopes of storming it. At the distance of a league Faridun observed it, and what caught his eye in the royal city was a palace whose pillared hall appeared to rise higher than the planet Saturn, so that you could have imagined it sweeping the stars out of the sky. There it shone against the heavens like Jupiter, as though it might be the abode of joy, peace and love. But he knew that it was the lair of the dragon and the seat of his power, a place filled with treasure. He said to his comrades,

'I am afraid that one who on the dark earth can build up so mighty an edifice, raising it out of the bowels of the ground, is in a conspiracy with the earth. Our best course in this campaign is to attack at once and permit no delay.'

With the words Faridun stretched out his hand to grasp his [bull-headed] mace and gave the rein to his swift-galloping courser. You would have said that fire burst forth of its own free will as he charged the men on guard. He raised his heavy club above the

E K—D

saddle, and, as the earth seemed to crash together in folds, he rode
into the great palace—a youth inexperienced in the world, but
stout of heart. Not a man of the sentinels had remained at the
gates, and Faridun gave blessings to the Creator of the world.

(iv) *Faridun and the deputy of Ẓaḥḥāk*

At such times as the land was unoccupied by Ẓaḥḥāk's presence,
there remained in his stead a certain worthy dignitary who occupied the throne, the treasury and the palace, since his master had
great admiration of his trustiness. He was named 'Kondrow'
['Slow-mover'], because he walked with deliberate pace when in
the presence of his tyrannical master. This Kondrow now came at
a run into the palace and in the pillared hall saw a young man of
princely stature at his ease in the place of honour, looking as
beautiful as a tall cypress topped by the sphere of the moon. The
citadel swarmed with his troops, every man ready for action, while
others were arrayed in the portals. Kondrow showed no trepidation nor did he inquire the reason for this enigmatical occurrence,
but approached uttering salutations and with blessings on his lips.

Faridun invited him to come forward and disclose to him the
inner purpose of his arrival, then commanded them to set out the
appurtenances of a royal banquet.

'Bring wine,' he bade, 'and call the musicians. Fill cups and let
platters be decked. Let all who are able to provide me with music
come to the feast and enliven my spirits. And invite to my dais such
company as shall be in harmony with my good fortune.'

As he drank his wine and made his choice of music Faridun
celebrated a night of feasting that accorded with his circumstances. At dawn, however, Kondrow swiftly withdrew from his
new master and, mounted on a willing beast, rode off in search of
Ẓaḥḥāk. When he had entered the royal presence he told of what
he had seen and heard.

'King of the mighty,' he said, 'signs have appeared that your
fortunes are in decline. Three great men with troops have arrived
from a foreign land. The one that stands between the other two is
the youngest, but he has the stature of a cypress and the visage of a
king. Although he is youngest he is superior in dignity and it is he
who stands forth amongst them. He wields a mace like a fragment
of mountain and in any assembly he shines out. He rode on horseback into your Majesty's palace with those two mighty warriors,

one on either side, and when he arrived at your Majesty's throne he sat on it, making nothing of your interceptors and your magic talisman. As for those stationed in your pillared hall, whether human beings or your own demons, he cut off all their heads as he sat on his horse, and mingled their brains with their blood.'

'Let him stay,' replied Ẓaḥḥāk. 'Perhaps he is a guest, and must be entertained.'

'A guest?' queried his steward. 'A person who boldly seats himself in the place where you yourself rest, who expunges your name from your crown and girdle and converts unfaithful creatures to his malpractices? If you wish to acknowledge such a one as your guest, do so!'

'Do not protest so loudly,' bade him Ẓaḥḥāk. 'An arrogant guest is an omen of the happiest kind.'

'I hear you,' retorted Kondrow. 'Now listen to what I have to say. If this renowned warrior is your guest, what business has he in your women's quarters? There he sits with Jamshid's sisters, discussing every kind of topic with them, with one hand fondling the cheeks of Shahrnāz, with the other the red lips of Arnavāz. When the night grows dark his conduct is even worse. Under his head he lays a pillow of musk, which is nothing other than tresses of your two beauteous ones, who were ever your favourites.'

Ẓaḥḥāk was roused to fury like a wolf. At hearing this speech he cried aloud for death. With foul obloquy he raged in savage tones against the unfortunate steward.

'Never again,' said he, 'will you be my warden.' To that the steward replied,

'I believe now, my king, that you no longer enjoy fortune's favour. How then will you be able ever again to give me charge of the city? Since you are to be deprived of your office as ruler, how will you entrust to me the task of acting in your stead? You have been torn from the place of majesty as a hair is plucked out of dough. Now, my lord, make your plans and look to what needs to be done, for this is an occasion that has had no precedent.'

(v) *Faridun takes Ẓaḥḥāk prisoner*

Ẓaḥḥāk boiled with rage at this exchange of talk and determined on speedy action. He commanded that his horse, swift of foot and of the keenest sight, should be saddled and at a breath-taking gallop he set off with a great army entirely composed of male demons inured to war. Moving by a devious way he reached the palace, whose gates and roof he occupied, with no thought in his head but that of exacting vengeance. Faridun's army received news of this and made by untrodden paths for the same goal, where, leaping in a spate from their war-horses, they attacked the closely guarded palace. On every roof and in every doorway stood the men of the city who had any strength to fight. But all sided with Faridun, for their hearts were sore at Zaḥḥāk's oppression, and although missiles rained down—bricks from the walls, stones from the roofs and, in the streets, javelins and poplar-wood arrows—in the city the youths, like their battle-hardened elders, deserted to Faridun's army in order to escape the wizardry of Zaḥḥāk.

He, meanwhile, cast about for a means of sating his venom. Leaving his troops he entered the palace clad in iron armour from head to foot in order to avoid recognition. In his hand he carried a lasso sixty cubits long, by the aid of which he quickly climbed to the top of the lofty building. From there he beheld that dark-eyed Shahrnaz, full of enchantment, in dalliance with Faridun, her cheeks bright as day and her tresses like night. He opened his mouth with curses, understanding that this was God's will and that he could not evade the clutch of evil. With the fires of jealousy searing his brain he flung the end of his lasso down into the portico and, reckless of throne and precious life, he climbed down from the palace roof. From its sheath he plucked his sharp dagger and, without a word that would reveal his secret, without calling on any name, and holding the tempered steel weapon in his clutch, he came forward athirst for the blood of the peri-cheeked woman. No sooner, however, had he set foot on the ground than Faridun advanced upon him with the speed of a storm-wind and dealt him a blow from his bull-headed mace that shattered his helmet. But at that instant an angel approached at speed and said,

'Do not strike him down; his time has not yet come. He is wounded; bind him firmly as a rock and carry him up to where two mountains close together will come in sight. Tie him securely inside one of them, where neither his kinsfolk nor his associates can have access to him.'

Faridun heard the words and with little hesitation carried out the behest. He got ready a noose of lion-skin and with it tied Zaḥḥāk's hands and waist so tightly together that a raging elephant could not have loosened the bond. Afterwards he seated himself on Ẓaḥḥāk's golden throne and cast down the symbols of his wicked rule, while at the palace gates a proclamation was by his command uttered in these words,

'You noble men of worth and good sense, it is not fitting that you should remain burdened with the weapons of war and be forced to seek fame and repute in this fashion. That soldiers and workmen should both win merit in one and the same way is not right; some are craftsmen, others wield the mace, and each man's occupation displays its worth in its own fashion. When, therefore, one group seeks to perform the other's task, the whole world becomes confused. That fellow who was so vile is now in fetters— that creature who kept the world in terror. As for you, may you live long and remain ever happy. Now depart to your tasks with song.'

In accordance with the advice which he had been given, Faridun, blessed by fortune, drove the tightly-bound Ẓaḥḥāk towards Shīrkhān and into the mountains. There he would have stricken off the demon's head, but the benevolent angel appeared once again and gently spoke a quiet word in his ear, telling him to take the captive at the same good pace as before to Mount Damāvand. No escort was to accompany them but one composed of men whose services were indispensable and who could be of assistance at a difficult moment. Accordingly, swift as a rumour, he brought Ẓaḥḥāk to Mount Damāvand, where he left him in fetters. There he remained hanging, his heart's blood pouring down on to the earth.

(vi) *Faridun sends Jandal to seek wives for his sons*

By the time that Faridun's age had grown to fifty years, three fine sons had come into the world for him, two of them born of Shahrnāz and the third and youngest of Arnavāz. From delicacy he did not give them names even when they had the strength to outrun elephants in a race. He watched them grow until they were ready for thrones and then, one day, he summoned the most valued of his illustrious counsellors, a man named Jandal, who was ever zealous in his master's service. To him he said,

'Journey about the world and select three maidens of royal birth who in beauty shall be a match for my three sons and worthy of being linked with me. Their father must likewise out of delicacy have refrained from giving them names, so that no one shall have been able to discuss them. They must be sisters by the same father and mother, peri-faced, lovable and of regal character. In figure and appearance they must be so alike that no person shall be able to recognize the least difference between them.'

Leaving his royal master's presence and accompanied by a number of willing attendants, Jandal began his search. All over Iran he travelled making inquiries and hearing reports; wherever there was a prince who in his inner chambers had a daughter, Jandal probed into the secret with caution and heard all names and tittle-tattle. At last the honest sage and counsellor came to Sarv, King of the Yemen, and found that in truth this prince had three daughters of the quality demanded by Faridun.

[Sarv was reluctant to let his daughters go and tried on various pretexts to prevent their departure from him. In the end Faridun's sons came in person to win his favour and consent, and were allowed to take their wives home with them.]

(vii) *Faridun puts his sons to the test*

When Faridun received tidings that the three princes were on their way back, he journeyed out on the road by which they were coming with the object of ascertaining their spirit and ending any uncertainties he had about them. He therefore advanced on them in the guise of a dragon from which not even a lion might escape unharmed. He raged and fumed as though boiling with fury and out of his mouth he belched flames. As he saw his three sons approaching, spying them through the gloom as three dark hills, he stirred up clouds of dust, spat out foam and caused the world to re-echo with the thunder of his roaring.

First he went towards his eldest son, greatest in dignity and worthy to bear the crown, who said, 'A man who has acquired wisdom and power of judgment does not face dragons in battle.' With that he swiftly turned his back and fled.

The father moved on to confront his middle son, who, seeing him at close quarters, fastened a bow-string to his bow and drew it taut, saying, 'When battle is afoot, what matter if the enemy is a raging lion or a mounted warrior?'

When the youngest son came near, he uttered a great shout at seeing the dragon and called out,

'Begone! You are nothing but a lynx, so do not venture on the pathway of lions. If King Faridun's name has reached your ears, engage in no battle of this kind. We are his children, all three of us his sons, ready to wield the mace and thirsting for battle. Your best course is to vanish from this road into the wilderness, otherwise I will crown you in a way you may dislike.'

With satisfaction Faridun heard and beheld all this, and, having ascertained the qualities of his sons, disappeared from the scene. But then he came again, this time in his own person as their father, in dignity and with due ceremony, being accompanied by drums and fierce elephants. In his hand was his bull-headed mace while behind him followed the men of highest rank in his army. The world was now patently in his grasp.

(viii) *Faridun names his sons:—Salm, Tur and Iraj*

Beholding the face of the Shah, the noble youths dismounted and came running towards him, then kissed the ground, while in the cheering of the crowd the thunder of the elephants and the drums was overwhelmed. He caught his sons by the hand and blessed them, raising their honours to the highest degree. He then said to them,

'That fearsome dragon, which would have consumed the world with its fiery breath, was your father seeking to test your courage. He found enlightenment and so returned in happiness. Now I have bestowed names on you, as is proper for a man of sense.

'You, the eldest, your name shall be "Salm". May the whole world resound with your prosperity [*kām*], because you chose safety [*salāmat*] from the dragon's mouth [*kām*] and did not delay when the moment came for evading him. The man who is rash enough not to fear elephant or lion should be called a fool and not a courageous hero.

'You, my middle son, who from the first showed your stoutness and whose ardour was only increased by the fire, I name "Tur", a brave lion which no elephant can overcome. Courage is a virtue on the throne; no poor-spirited man should ever hold lofty rank.

'Next come you, my youngest, a man of resolute and warlike spirit, capable both of speed and deliberation. You chose the middle way between earth and fire, the only proper course for a man of sense. Though headstrong and young, you have an alert mind. It is only such men as you that deserve praise in the world. "Iraj", therefore, is the fitting name for you. Greatness in every respect should be your destiny, because from the outset you showed leonine courage and at the moment of peril displayed your manliness.'

(ix) *Faridun divides the world between his sons*

When he had realized the intention which he had kept concealed, Faridun divided the world between his sons. To one he granted Rum [Greece] and the West, to the next Tur [Turania] and China, and to the third the plain of the heroes and the land of Iran. First consider Salm. To him he allotted the region of Rum and the West, commanding him to lead an army against the West, whose throne of sovereignty he ascended with the title of 'Lord of the West'. Then he allotted to Tur the Turanian land, making him master of the Turks and of China. When it came to the turn of Iraj, his father selected him to be king of Iran, and moreover master of the plain of the lance-wielders [Arabs] too. Also, beholding that he was worthy, he yielded to him the dais of royalty, the princely diadem, the sword, the seal, the ring and the crown. Those princes who had insight, good sense and judgment entitled him 'Sovereign of Iran'.

All three sons reigned in peace and happiness as Lords of the Marches.

(x) *Salm's jealousy of Iraj*

A long space of time elapsed, with destiny holding a secret concealed in its heart. Faridun the sage grew old in years and dust covered the garden of Spring. Salm's feelings moved out of their accustomed channel and he changed in his behaviour and opinions. His heart was pervaded with envy as he sat communing with his advisers, for his father's allotment had ceased to be in accordance with his liking. Faridun had assigned the Golden Throne to his youngest son [Iraj], so covetousness filled the heart of Salm, and frowns spread over his face. At last he sent a messenger to [Tur] the king of China to reveal to him the thoughts he had in his mind. He said in his dispatch to his brother,

'Think, you who are king of the Turks and of China, whose illuminated heart has lost hope of a just division, how we have been compelled to reconcile ourselves to injustice, and how our esteem has been lowered although we stand as tall as cypresses.

With your alert mind scrutinize this history, the like of which was never heard from the time of the most ancient annals. We were three sons, adornments to the throne, and it was the least of us who was promoted to the greatest fortune. Since I am fullest of years and wisdom, fortune should have put its seal on me. If crown, throne and diadem were passing me by, they should not fittingly have come to anyone but you. Is it right, then, that we two should remain humiliated by this wrongful act committed against us by our father? He gives Iran and the plain of the warriors and Yemen to Iraj, Rum and the West to me, and allots to you the land of the Turks and China. Thus it is the youngest of us who reigns over the land of Iran. I will not abide by a division of this kind; there is no reason in your father's brain.'

The dromedary which he dispatched made such good use of its legs that it was not long before the messenger was standing in the presence of the lord of Turan. He had learnt his instructions well, and having remembered them perfectly he filled the brainless head of Tur with vapour. When the valiant Tur had heard the dark tale he was immediately roused, like a quick-tempered lion. His answer was,

'Tell the king—bear this well in mind—that while we were young our father deluded us. This tree which he has planted bears bloody fruits and its leaves are vainglory. You and I must meet face to face to discuss this matter; we must make cunning plans and together build up an army.'

Accordingly, the one brother coming from Rum and the other from China mingled poison with honey, and meeting together, discussed all things open or concealed.

(xi) *Salm and Tur send a message to Faridun*

The two selected a quick-witted priest eloquent in speech, perspicuous in mind and of retentive memory. Clearing their apartment of all not in their confidence they began to consider all manner of schemes. Salm first entered the parley, with eyes washed clear of any reverence for his father. He said to the envoy,

'Take to the road, and let not even the wind or the dust overtake you. Swift as the storm-wind go to Faridun, letting your every movement be concerned with nothing but your journey. When you dismount at his palace, first convey greetings to him from his two sons, then say,

' "The fear of God is needful both for this world and the next. Holy God granted you the universe, from the shining sun above down to the dark earth beneath. You, however, have demanded that all laws and expedients should conform to your will and have paid no heed to God's command. Crookedness and treachery were the only motives of your action, and you had no justice in view when you made your allotment. You had three wise sons, all brave men, the eldest clearly to be distinguished from the youngest; it was impossible for you to have discerned in any one of them a virtue that would have justified his being made superior to the others. Yet against one you contrived the dragon's breath, while you raised another aloft to the clouds, placing a crown on his head for him to be alongside your couch. Only at his coming did your eyes light up with pleasure. Yet by birth we are not his inferiors either on our mother's or our father's side, or in any way that would disable us from occupying the royal throne.

' "Dispenser of justice, Lord of the world, never let this kind of justice be called blessed. If the crown falls from the undeserving head, let the wearer suffer banishment and the earth be rid of him. Assign to him some remote corner of the world, where he may exist as we do powerless and obscure. If you refuse, we will launch against you the cavaliers of the Turks and Chinese as well as those of Rum, all of them warriors eager for vengeance who are combined into a single mighty army that will destroy both Iraj and Iran." '

[To this message Faridun returned a reproachful answer and gave his son Iraj warning of his brothers' intentions. He proposed to meet them with overtures of peace.]

(xii) *Iraj visits his brothers*

Iraj approached the spot where his brothers lay, without being aware of their dark intention. They received him with the ceremonial customary amongst them, marching all their forces out to welcome him, but although they saw their brother's face bright with affection they showed the darker side of their countenance to him. Yet their army held him in good esteem, for he had the stature fitted for throne and crown, and the two brothers were disturbed at the army's favour to him. Salm looked askance at it, his heart burdened at the troops' behaviour. He entered his pavilion his heart overflowing with hatred and his face lined with frowns, cleared the place of all assembled there and then with Tur seated himself to take counsel. They explored their difficulty by every door, discussing the kingship, the crown and the several provinces in turn. As Tur was speaking, Salm broke into his words to say,

'Why did the separate troops form into pairs as they made their way back [into camp]? Did you not observe them? The whole time that they were marching they did not turn their eyes from Iraj. Our two armies were one thing as they marched to meet Iraj, but a different one on the return. My mind is despondent over Iraj and my apprehensions mount. When I looked at the troops of our two lands I saw that they desired no king but him. If you do not tear his roots out of the ground, you will tumble down from your exalted throne to a place beneath his feet.'

In this mood they arose from where they sat and all night long pondered on their schemes.

(xiii) *Iraj is killed by his brothers*

When the veil lifted from the face of Sol, dawn broke and sleep had been cleansed away, the two contemptible men resolved to clear their eyes of anything that might display their conduct in a shameful light. With swaggering gait they strode towards the pavilion of Iraj, who, seeing them approach, came running towards them with affection in his heart. All three entered the pavilion, speaking of this and that.

'Why is it,' Tur demanded of him, 'that although you are younger than we are, you wear on your head the diadem of supremacy? For you it is that Iran and the throne of the mighty are reserved, whereas I must stand girt as a servant at the gate of the Turk. Your elder brother lives in misery in the West, while on your head reposes the crown and under you lies the treasure. That division executed by the emperor was all in favour of his youngest son.'

Iraj listened to the speech of Tur and replied in a conciliatory mood,

'My renown-worthy brother, if you wish to achieve your aim, you may do so peaceably. I have not at this present moment any desire for kingly crown or high position. I do not demand a title of authority, or the army of Iran, or Iran itself, or the Western land, or China, or kingship, or the wide-spread expanse of the earth. Magnificence that declines into obscurity is a form of grandeur deserving of tears, for in it, even if at first high heaven lies under your saddle, in the end your pillow will be of clay. Though the throne of Iran exists beneath me, I am now weary both of crown and throne. I surrender to you both diadem and ring; do not bear me ill-will any further, for I have no quarrel or dispute with you and you have no cause to feel aggrieved against me. I have no desire that fate shall harm you, even if I am exiled out of your sight.'

Tur listened to the words from beginning to end without raising his head. The speech of Iraj held nothing pleasing to him nor had a reconciliation with his brother any value in his eyes. Angrily he stepped down from his dais and uttered many words, meanwhile stamping the ground with impatience. Then, lifting the heavy golden throne in both hands he brought it down on the head of [Iraj] the emperor, wearer of the crown. Iraj pleaded with him for his life.

'Does not the fear of God fall on you?' he demanded. 'Will you not find dishonour in your father's sight? Do not kill me; in the end fate will seize upon you for my blood. Do not let yourself be a murderer. You will not find any further trace of me, for I will content myself with some far corner of the earth and win my bread by my own toil. You have desired the world for yourself; now you have it. Do not by killing me arouse Almighty God to anger.'

Tur heard, but made no answer. His heart was filled with rage and his mind with vain ambition. Out of his boot he drew a dagger and with it covered Iraj from head to foot with a curtain of blood.

(xiv) *A child is born to the daughter of Iraj*

Time passed. One day Faridun, on a visit to the women's quarters of Iraj, reviewed its fair occupants and came upon a handsome-faced handmaiden whose name was Māh-Āfarid. Iraj had loved her deeply and she was now pregnant with his child. Upon her Faridun now centred his ambition, solacing his heart with the hope that she would bear a son to avenge his father's death. But, when the time came, Māh-Āfarid bore a daughter and the Shah's imminent hopes were cut short.

[Yet he brought up the child with kindness and in due course gave her in marriage to a descendant of Jamshid's to whom she bore a son, Manuchehr. He was reared by his grandfather to be a warrior whose sole aim in life was to be the exacting of vengeance for Iraj. At last the occasion presented itself.]

(xv) *Faridun sends Manuchehr to war against Tur*

From Turān two armies were led against Iran, the men composing them being invisible beneath their coats of mail and helmets. With them went ferocious elephants and munitions in abundance—and two men thirsty for blood, their hearts steeled with hatred. As soon as the message came to Faridun that troops had crossed the Oxus river to the Iranian side, he issued a command that Manuchehr was to march his army from the frontiers and on to the plain of battle. In the forefront went the Kāviāni Banner, and in each man's grasp was a sword of blue steel. Manuchehr, accompanied by the elephant-bodied Qāren, emerged from the forest of elms and passed in front of his army to set his forces in due array on the vast plain. In command of the left wing he placed Garshāsp and over the right he set the heroic Sām together with Qobād. The combatants on either side drew up in battle array while Manuchehr with Sarv remained in the centre of his own force.

To Tur and Salm news had been brought at a gallop that the Iranians were ready for onslaught, that they had emerged from the forest and been put into order of battle, the blood from their stricken hearts bringing foam to their lips. At the same moment the two murderous princes, with rancorous hearts, led their immense forces out and took up their positions on the battlefield. Qobād advanced into a forward position and Tur, being informed of this, swiftly came and called out to him,

'Go to Manuchehr and say to him, "You unfathered boy-king, Iraj may have had a daughter born to him, but how can you have a right to throne, crown and ring?" '

Qobād, approaching the Shah, repeated to him what he had heard from his vengeful opponent. But he laughed and said in reply,

'None but a fool could speak in that vein. Praise be to the Ruler of both worlds, who is aware of all things patent and concealed, he knows that Iraj was my grandfather, and Faridun the blessed vouches for me. When we join battle, my birth and lineage will become evident. I will be avenged on him for my blessed father and I will throw his empire into confusion.'

(xvi) *Manuchehr joins battle with Tur*

As darkness fell on the sun-illumined earth and sentinels were being posted about the battlefield, Qāren the champion stepped out before the army [of Manuchehr] with his counsellor Sarv, king of the Yemen, and delivered this oration,

'Men of fame! Lions of the Shah! Understand that this onslaught is made by Ahriman [Maker of Evil], who at heart is the foe of the Creator. Be ready and alert, though you are all under the protection of the Emperor. The man who is slain on this battlefield enters Paradise absolved of all transgression, and any man who sheds the blood of the armies of China and Rum, or seizes territory from them, shall win everlasting fame and dwell in the glory foretold by the priests.'

When dawn arrived a great shout went up from the troops and spears were brandished to the skies; by the time that bright day had passed the meridian the hearts of both armies were ablaze with fervour. Yet each side acted with caution, planning stratagems by which they thought how when darkness fell they would by night-attacks cover the fields and the plain with their foemen's blood.

The two tyrants got their troops ready and launched their troops as they planned. But spies quickly caught wind of it and bore the news to Manuchehr, who, after hearing their reports, transferred command of his army to the warrior Qāren. He promptly determined on a place of ambush in which he stationed thirty thousand picked men. With the onset of night, Tur with a hundred thousand men emerged ready for battle, but Qāren fell on them from his ambush, leaving Tur no way of escape in any direction. At the same moment Shah Manuchehr came up from the rear and overwhelmed the ill-famed tyrant. Into his back he thrust a spear, so that the other's dagger fell point downwards to the earth. Then snatching him from the saddle he dashed him headlong to the ground and cut the head from the body, providing a feast for all animals, wild and tame.

[Subsequently, after a number of adventures, the second brother, Salm, was slain by Manuchehr, who succeeded to the throne after the death of Faridun. Amongst Manuchehr's courtiers was the mighty hero Sām son of Narimān.]

V

Zāl

(i) *The birth of Zāl*

In the women's quarters of his house Sām possessed a lovely maiden, her cheeks as ruddy as rose-petals, her hair black as musk. From her he had hopes of a son, for she was sunny-cheeked and seemly; but in her pregnancy she suffered great distress from the weight of the burden she bore. When the child was severed from his mother his face was beautiful as the sun, but his hair was entirely white, and for a whole week because of his strange appearance news of his birth was not brought to his father Sām. Those who lived in the inner quarters of that noble warrior's mansion stood weeping before the child, none having the spirit to tell Sām the Hero that the son borne to him by his beautiful wife was hoary-headed.

Yet Sām had a nurse whose courage was that of a lion, and it was she who boldly approached the warrior with the happy news of the birth of a son to him. She said, calling down benedictions,

'Fortune prosper Sām the Hero! May the hearts of his ill-wishers be torn out! God has granted what you have desired. Embellish your soul with the fulfilment of your wishes. Behind the veil in your palace, illustrious prince, a handsome son has been born to your wife; a young paladin with the heart of a lion. Even now, in his baby state, he shows himself to be of sturdy nature; his body is of pure silver, his face like Paradise. You will see no ugly feature in him, his one blemish being that his hair is white. That is something which destiny has decreed for you, illustrious prince, and you needs must be reconciled to it, not permitting your spirit to be ungrateful or your heart downcast.'

Sām the Hero at once descended from his throne and entered behind the veil to where his son lay like fresh Spring. His eyes fell on a handsome boy whose head was hoary in a fashion that he had never beheld or been told about. Every hair on the child's body was like snow, but his cheeks were ruddy and beautiful. On seeing his son thus, with his white hair, Sām felt his worldly ambitions frustrated and, in great fear that he might become the butt of

35

ridicule, he strayed from the path of wisdom and chose a strange course. With his face turned towards Heaven he prayed for indulgence for any act he might be about to commit.

'O Thou who art above all crookedness and imperfection,' he prayed, 'blessings are multiplied when Thou desirest. If I have committed a grave sin or if I have allowed myself something that belongs to the religion of Ahriman, then let the Lord of the World in consideration for my repentance grant me forgiveness even if it be hidden from me.

'My blackened soul writhes with shame, the blood surges hotly within my body because of this child, which, with his dark eyes and hair white as the syringa, resembles a child of Ahriman. When proud noblemen come to make enquiries of me they will see this ill-omened boy, and then what shall I say of this demon-child: that he is a parti-coloured leopard, or an entire peri? The great ones of the world will mock me because of this infant, both openly and in secret. Because of this disgrace I must depart from the land of Iran and refuse my homage to this country and clime.'

All this he spoke in his anger, with contorted face, and so disputed with his fate. The child, he commanded, was to be removed from the land and abandoned in some remote place. Now there was a mountain called Alborz, nearing the sun in height and far from association with men, where the Simorgh [that fabulous bird] had its nest, an abode inaccessible to all. Upon that mountain the child was placed and there left.

A long time passed by. The hero's innocent babe could distinguish neither black nor white. His father had severed all affection for him and cast him away with loathing. (A story is told of a lioness who, as she sated her cub with her milk, said to it, 'When I gave you my heart's blood, I demanded no gratitude, for you are as living a part of me as my own heart, which would be rent from me if you departed.' How much kinder to their offspring are the wild and tame beasts of this earth than men!) In that spot where the little child had fallen he lay without shelter day and night, and for a time he sucked his own finger-tips and cried. Now when the Simorgh's brood grew hungry she flew aloft from her nest and so caught sight of a babe weeping. The earth around him appeared as an ocean in storm. His cradle was of thorns and his nurse was the ground. His body was bare of covering and his lips clean of any milk. Round about him were gloomy deep chasms, while above him blazed the sun, high in the heavens. Had even leopards been his parents they would have sheltered him from that sun.

The Simorgh swooped down from the clouds, thrust out her claws and lifted the babe from the torrid rock, then carried him to that point of the Alborz mountains where lay her eyrie and her brood. She offered him to them for a victim, urging them to pay no heed to his bitter weeping. But God the beneficent delivered him and granted him hope of the prolongation of his life, while the Simorgh stood gazing in astonishment at the little babe with the tears of blood trickling from his eyes. Picking out the tenderest portions of her own prey she fed her milk-starved guest on their blood.

A long time went by, during which the child remained there undiscovered, while he was ever growing in strength. Then, one day, a caravan crossed the mountain. The child had grown to manhood; his stature was that of a free-growing cypress, his chest a silvern mountain and his waist slender as a reed. Report of him spread abroad throughout the world—for neither good nor evil endures in concealment—the news about this happy youth and his splendour at last reaching Sām son of Narīmān.

(ii) *Dastān takes leave of the Simorgh*

Sām now came in haste to that region of mountains to make a search for his child thus cast away. He scanned the steep crags and saw the fearsome bird and the hazardous situation of the nest, built so high that its topmost level touched the skies, for no toiling hands had built it, nor was it made of stones and earth. As he sought for some way of climbing up to it he wondered how even beasts, wild or tame, could find a path to so inaccessible an object. With prayer on his lips he roamed about the mountain, but although he ventured far from the trodden road he could find no means of approach. He prayed,

'O Thou who art loftier than all earthly places, than the bright arch of the sky or than sun and moon, I bow down my head in supplication before Thee and in reverence for Thee do expend my spirit. If this child indeed derives from my loins undefiled and not from the seed of evil-souled Ahriman, then help Thy slave to ascend here and permit my sinful being to become acceptable to Thee.'

No sooner had he uttered these prayers to the Lord than they were answered. The Simorgh, glancing down from the mountainous height and descrying Sām and his retinue, knew that his coming was for the sake of the child, and that it was not for love of the Simorgh that he had undertaken the laborious journey. She addressed the son of Sām and said,

'You have suffered the hardships of this nest and this eyrie while I have been your guardian and nurse. I have reared you and been the source of your welfare. I bestow on you the name of 'Dastān-e Zand', because your father practised *dastān* ('Trickery') and enchantment on you. When you return to your own place, command the warrior who will be your counsellor to call you by that name.

'Your father is the warrior Sām, paladin of the world, whose head is exalted above all the nobles. He has come to this mountain in search of his son, for you have acquired worth in his esteem. And now I must raise you up and bear you to him unharmed. When the time comes for you to take possession of the crown and of the highest rank, of the sovereign honours and the diadem, this eyrie will no longer be worthy of you. Yet make a trial of fortune. I part from you for no reason of enmity; I do but entrust you to an empire. For me it would be well if you remained here, but the other course is better. Yet take with you a single feather from my wing and with it you will continue to be under the protection of my influence. If ever a difficulty overtakes you or any dispute arises over your actions, good or ill, then cast this feather of mine into the flames and you will at once experience the blessing of my authority. I will come as a black cloud, with speed, and transport you unharmed to this place.'

When she had thus given him assurance, the Simorgh lifted him and majestically flew aloft with him into the skies, then in one swift stoop brought him down to his father. Dastān's hair at this time reached below his chest, his body was strong as an elephant's and his face was radiant as the Spring. At sight of him his father burst into bitter weeping and quickly bowed his head down before the Simorgh, uttering many words of benediction and greeting.

'Queen of birds,' he said, 'the Giver of justice granted you power, ability and honour because you come to the aid of the helpless. May you remain thus ever strong!'

Followed by the gaze of Sām and all his retinue the Simorgh then flew away to the mountain.

When Sām turned to look at his son he beheld him worthy of a crown and a royal throne. Except for his hair he could see no flaw in him and all his scrutiny disclosed no other blemish. As he perceived this, the heart of Sām became as blissful as the highest heaven and he rained blessings on his handsome offspring, to whom he said,

'Let your heart relent towards me. Do not remember what is past, and let your heart be warm. I will exert myself to fulfil your desires whether good or bad. Henceforward your will shall be done, whatever it be.'

[Sām then gave his son the name 'Zāl-zar' (or 'Zāl'), which he bore in addition to that of 'Dastān' bestowed on him by the Simorgh, and proclaimed him his heir.]

(iii) Zāl visits Mehrāb, king of Kābol

[After his accession] Zāl proposed to himself to make a round of his kingdom and set out upon the road with his bodyguard of warriors, all at one with him in thought and faith. He planned to make his first destination the land of the Hindus, going by way of Kābol and Danbar, Margh and Māy. In whatsoever place he came to an encampment was set up, and there he called for wine, song and minstrels; the treasury doors were opened wide and cares were banished, as is the custom in this fleeting world.

It was from Zābol that the king began his journey to Kābol, with due state but joyously and in light-heartedness. The king of Kābol was Mehrāb, a man possessed of power, wealth and abundance. By origin he was of the stock of Arabian Zaḥḥāk and he held all the land of Kābol, for which he paid yearly tribute to Sām since he was unequal to opposing him in battle. Now the following story was brought by a nobleman to the ears of Zāl the world-paladin,

'Mehrāb has a daughter in the women's quarters of his palace who is more radiant than the sun. From head to foot she is white as ivory; her face is a very paradise and for stature she is as a plane-tree. About her silvern shoulders two musky black tresses curl, encircling them with their ends as though they were links in a chain. Her mouth resembles a pomegranate blossom, her lips are cherries and her silver bosom curves out into breasts like pomegranates. Her eyes are like the narcissus in the garden and her lashes draw their blackness from the raven's wing. Her eyebrows are modelled on the bows of Terāz powdered with fine bark and elegantly musk-tinted [dark]. If you seek a brilliant moon, it is her face; if you long for the perfume of musk, it lingers in her tresses. From top to toe she is Paradise gilded; all radiance, harmony and delectability.'

The description set the heart of Zāl fluttering with such eagerness that self-control and ease of mind forsook him. His mind was ablaze with desire, prudence was banished and passion became the only wisdom.

Mehrāb, one morning as he passed through the inner apartments of his palace, met in the pillared hall two young women beautiful as the sun, one being his daughter, the lovely-featured Rudāba, and the other his prudent and affectionate wife, Sindokht. Rudāba questioned him about his comings and goings. 'What kind of man,' she asked him, 'is that hoary-headed son of Sām? Are his thoughts of the throne or of the nest? Does he possess the qualities of civilized beings and display the manners of a man of birth?'

Mehrāb answered,

'There does not exist in the whole world a warrior-hero who can follow where Zāl leads. On the frescoes of the pillared hall you never saw anyone depicted with such arms as his, and for manipulation of the reins and for his seat in the saddle there never existed a horseman to equal him. He has the heart of a lion and an elephant's strength. For generosity he is as bounteous as the Nile. That his hair is white is something which only cavillers could select as a blemish. His hoariness is indeed a mark of beauty, by which he may win people's affection.'

Rudāba heard the words and blushed until her cheeks flamed as red as a pomegranate. About her were the five Turkish slaves who were always in attendance on her and were her willing servants. To these prudent girls she said,

'I wish to tell you a secret. I foster a love as violent as the sea in storm flinging its waves to Heaven. My heart is filled with passion for Zāl and in my sleep at night my thinking of him never ceases.'

Their answer was,

'Do you desire to take to your bosom one who rejected your father's offer of friendship? He is a creature that was reared by a bird in the mountains. In every company people point a finger at him and say that no human being was ever born old of his mother and that he cannot be truly of the stock of his begetter. For you, with your face and figure and hair, there will be a husband like the sun in the fourth sphere of heaven.'

When Rudāba heard their words, her heart flared up like fire in a gale. 'Your arguments are crude,' she retorted, 'and your words deserve no heed. My heart is torn for a star; how then should I be happy with the moon? I aim at no Caesar or any emperor of China, nor at anyone who wears the Iranian crown. Zāl son of Sām is suited to my measure; he has the forearm of a lion and the shoulders and chest of one. Let people call him old man or young boy, he is the happiness of my heart and soul.'

The slave-girls being now more fully aware of her secret and hearing her agitated words declared themselves her bondswomen, who loved her dearly and were her devoted servants. One of them said,

'Cypress-stature, let no one know of this. Yet, if it be necessary for us to learn magic and deceive men's eyes with spells and incantations [we shall do so]. Or we will take flight with birds or turn ourselves into witches, learn to gallop and, if need be, become gazelles, if we can thereby induce the king to come to the embrace of yourself, the moon.'

Rudāba's lips of ruby curved into smiles at this and she turned her saffroned cheeks towards the girl.

'If you can bring about this wizardry,' she said, 'you will plant a lofty fertile tree that will daily bear jacinth fruits and wisdom shall gather its fruits.'

(iv) Rudāba's slaves contrive to see Zāl

The slave-girls departed and Rudāba waited in expectation of what their scheming might contrive. They donned clothes of Greek brocade and decked their hair with flowers, then all five went down to the river bank as perfumed and adorned with colour as the joyous Spring, for it was the month of April and the new beginning of the year. On the other bank lay the camp of Zāl; on this side the girls chattered of Zāl as they went along the brink of the river picking flowers, their own cheeks like gardens and their bosoms adorned with blossoms. Moving here and there as they went along plucking the flowers they came to a spot opposite to the pavilion of Dastān [Zāl], who, seated on a lofty throne, caught sight of them and asked,

'Who are these flower-worshippers?'

Someone replied,

'The Moon of Kabolestān ever sends her servitors down from the castle of the illustrious Mehrāb to where the flowers grow.'

Dastān's heart fluttered when he heard this and the warmth of his ardour kept it from tranquillity. At the moment of seeing the slave-girls it chanced that he had called for a bow and had his arms extended to aim at a duck which he had seen on the river. A cry sent the bird up from the surface and, loosing his arrow, he brought it down in flight so that it dropped with its blood staining the water.

'Cross over,' he called out to a slave, 'and retrieve the bird. It is wounded in the wing.'

The massive Turk so addressed went over in a boat and was met by one of the slave-girls, who said,

'Warrior, be so agreeable as to tell me who that man is with the arms of a lion, that elephant-bodied hero. Of what people is he the king? I mean that man who shot the arrow from the bow with such skill. What terrors the enemy must suffer who faces him! Never have we beheld a cavalier more handsome or anyone so sure with bow and arrow.'

Sharply the slave put his teeth on his lip.

'Do not speak in so loud a voice about the king,' he warned her. 'He is ruler of Nimruz [Sīstān] and the son of Sām, who is called Dastān by other princes. The sky revolves over no other knight like him and destiny will never see another man of such renown.'

So the slave and the comely girl jested together. She said to him,

'Don't talk such folly. In his palace Mehrāb has a handsome beauty who out-tops your king by a head. In figure she resembles the teak-tree, though she is like ivory for whiteness, and her face is crowned with a diadem of musk. We have come tripping here from Kabolestān to Zabolestān's king to see if we can make those crimson lips acquainted with the lips of the offspring of Sām. It would be proper, and very suitable, for Rudāba to become the wife of Zāl.'

When the slave returned laughing, the illustrious son of Sām inquired with whom it was that he had been jesting and what the girl had said.

[Being told all that had passed, he then called for rich presents, which the slave-girls were to deliver to Rudāba.]

(v) *Rudāba and her slave-girls*

The pretty slave-girls went their way and Zāl returned to his palace, where the night endured as tediously for him as though it were a year long. When the maids, each with two bunches of flowers in their arms, reached the gates of their [mistress's] palace the porter with a glance at them prepared himself for strife. He sharpened his tongue and made his heart flinty, saying,

'You went out of the gates at an unlawful hour; it is a wonder to me how you got out.'

The girls had their answer ready and, stirred to indignation, they answered,

'Today has been no different from other days, and there is no demon of contrariness in the flower-garden. Spring has come to the rose-beds and we were picking blooms and taking hyacinths from the ground.'

The porter answered,

'Today was not the time to act as usual. Never before has the great commander Zāl appeared in Kābol and the ground has never been so covered with pavilions and troops. Have you not seen how our lord of Kābol rides out from his palace each night? All day long people are coming and going before him, for all these are close friends. If he saw you like this, with flowers in your arms, he would trample you into the dust.'

Into the palace went the girls and, when they were seated in the presence of their mistress, they told her what they had observed.

'Never,' said they, 'have we seen a man so splendid, with cheeks like roses, though his countenance and hair are white.'

Rudāba's heart burned with passion and the hope that she would see his face, and, when the girls had set down his gifts of gold and jewels before her, she questioned them on every item that occurred to her mind. She asked,

'How were your dealings with the son of Sām? Is he better in his actual presence than are reported by rumour and gossip?'

When they found the opportunity to answer their mistress the five girls hastened to assure her that Zāl was the noblest knight in the whole world and that he had no peer for distinction and splendour.

Their royal mistress observed,

'You have altered your views, then, and your speech? This Zāl, reared by a bird and looking like a hoary-headed withered old man, now has the beauty of the Judas blossom, has acquired a graceful figure and a handsome face and has turned into a great warrior? You spoke in flattering terms of me to him, and for your speeches may expect a reward.'

She told them that when darkness fell that night they were to go swiftly to the prince with a happy message and were to listen with care to what he might reply.

'Tell him,' said she, 'that his wishes are granted and that he must set to work, for he is to see the Moon in all her glory.'

Rudāba herself began swiftly to make preparation and arrange to achieve her purposes with those who were in her confidence. She had a chamber pretty as the Spring, bedecked with pictures of the heroes. It was adorned with Greek brocades and equipped with golden bowls, into which she had caused wine, musk and amber to be mingled, the coral and the emerald being poured together. Violets, roses, narcissi and judas-blossom decorated one side and on two other sides were sprigs of syringa. The goblets were all of gold and turquoise and the viands were contained in rose-water bowls, so that the fragrance from the apartment of that sunny-cheeked maiden arose to the sun itself.

(vi) Zāl visits Rudāba

When the shining sun had gone down, although the door of their apartment was locked and the key hidden away, the slave-girls went out in search of Dastān son of Sām. They told him all that had been contrived and urged him to set forth. The hero accordingly turned his face towards the palace, as a man seeking his mate must do. She, dark-eyed and with blushing cheeks, had gone up on to the roof and, when Dastān came into sight, the royal maiden loosed her twin tresses and called out,

'Welcome, son of a noble sire! The Creator's blessing be on you! May Heaven's revolving dome be the ground you tread! You have come a far distance on foot from your palace; your royal limbs are fatigued.'

As the gallant prince heard the voice from the tower, he gazed upwards and saw the sunny-cheeked maiden. At once the roof-top became a shining jewel to him; the very earth turned to ruby and jacinth from the lustre of her visage. He answered her,

'You who are as beautiful as the moon, accept my salutation and Heaven's blessing. How many nights, my gaze turned upwards, have I implored holy God and prayed that he, Lord of the world, might vouchsafe to me the sight of your ever-hidden face. Now at last I am gladdened by the sound of your voice, by these gentle words and this loveliness. Devise some means for me to behold you. How can you remain thus on your tower while I languish here on the road?'

As soon as she heard the gallant hero's words, the peri-faced maiden unloosed her tresses and from the height of the tower let drop her locks till the ends reached the turret's base. From aloft she called out,

'Warrior's son, hero-fathered, leap strongly and put forth your middle. Let your lion's chest expand, then reach out with your warrior's arms and take hold of this black hair of mine. My tresses will be sufficient for you as a rope.'

Zāl gazed up at the lovely maid, astounded at her words, and he pressed a kiss on the musky noose, so that the sound came to her ears.

'That cannot be,' he called out, and, seizing a lasso from his attendant, he looped it up and in an instant threw it aloft. The rope encircled the pinnacle and he immediately climbed from base to summit. As he seated himself on the roof, the maiden came applauding him, and then, with her hand held in his, they went together intoxicated with love, down from the roof. There were kisses, embraces and wine, and to his beloved the warrior spoke as follows,

'When Manuchehr hears the history of this he will be no party to it, and Sām will shout and cast his arms about in rage against me. Yet I swear before the Lord who is my judge that I will never depart from my oath to you.'

'I too swear before the Lord of my religion and faith,' she answered, 'that no one shall be king over me but the world's hero Zāl-zar.'

So their love grew; wisdom fled and passion came nigh. When dawn approached Zāl took leave of his loved one, whose breast with his body had been as warp and weft.

(vii) *Zāl consults his advisers over Rūdāba*

When the sun in glory came up over the mountain, Zāl sent a herald to summon his wise nobles. [To them he said,]

'I have this story to tell, namely that the rose and narcissus which grow in the garden have become mine. My heart has fled away from me and my good sense has departed; tell me what remedy I can apply for this condition. All of Mehrāb's palace holds my affection; to me its very earth is as precious as the revolving sky. My heart has been enslaved by Sindokht's daughter. Tell me, will Sām submit willingly to this? If Shah Manuchehr hears of it he will regard it as a misdemeanour for which youth alone is answerable.'

The clerics and warriors closed their mouths and the shrewd man's lips held back all utterance, for the ancestor of Mehrāb was Zaḥḥāk, and the king himself had constantly intrigued against them. None therefore ventured to speak openly, for none had ascertained how much bitter poison might be compounded with the honey.

[Reassured by promises of immunity if they gave their honest opinion, they at last advised him to write a full account of the circumstances to Sām. The letter provoked a reply, which led to further correspondence and argumentation over a period of time, in the course of which it became evident that Rudāba was pregnant and that the parturition would be attended with grave danger.]

VI

Rostam

(i) The birth of Rostam

To Rudāba's pillow Zāl hastened, his cheeks wet with tears and his heart sorely grieved. The women living behind the veil in the palace tore their hair, left their heads uncovered and flooded their cheeks with tears. Then into Zāl's memory a thought came which brought alleviation to the pain in his heart, for he had remembered the Simorgh's feather. Joyfully he bore the news to Sindokht. They called for a brazier, in which a fire was kindled, and in it they burned one of the barbs of the feather. In an instant the air darkened and out of the gloom the great bird appeared, eager to serve. Her coming was as though she had been a cloud raining down seed pearls; but what she brought was far better than pearls, for it meant balm for sore hearts. Zāl invoked abundant blessings on her, gave her praise to the utmost and uttered prayers for her. The Simorgh inquired,

'What means this grief? Why these tears in the lion's eyes? From this silver-bosomed cypress, whose face is as the moon for loveliness, a child will issue for you who will be eager for fame. Lions will kiss the dust of his footsteps and above his head even the clouds will find no passage. Merely at the sound of his voice the hide of the fighting leopard will burst and it will seize its claws in its teeth for panic. For judgment and sagacity he will be another Sām in all his gravity, but when stirred to anger he will be an aggressive lion. He will have the slender grace of a cypress but the strength of an elephant; with one of his fingers he will be able to cast a brick two leagues.

'Yet, by command of the Lawgiver, Provider of all good, the child will not come into existence by the ordinary way of birth. Bring me a poniard of tempered steel and a man of percipient heart versed in incantation. Let the girl be given a drug to stupefy her and to dull any fear or anxiety in her mind; then keep guard while the clairvoyant recites his incantations and so watch until the lion-boy leaves the vessel which contains him. The wizard will pierce the frame of the young woman without her awareness of any pain and will draw the lion-child out of her, covering her flank with blood, and will sew together the part he has cut. Therefore banish all fear, care and anxiety from your heart. There is a herb which I will describe to you. Pound it together with milk and musk and place it in a dry shady place. Afterwards spread it over the wound and you will perceive at once how she has been delivered from peril. Over it all then pass one of my feathers and the shadow of my royal potency will have achieved a happy result.'

Speaking thus she plucked a feather from her wing, cast it down and flew aloft.

[Zāl took the feather and obeyed his instructions. When his son was born he named him Rostam.]

Ten foster-mothers gave Rostam the milk which provides men with strength and then, when after being weaned from milk he came to eating substantial food, they gave him an abundance of bread and flesh. Five men's portions were his provision and it was a wearisome task to prepare it for him. He grew to the height of eight men so that his stature was that of a noble cypress; so high did he grow that it was as though he might become a shining star at which all the world would gaze. As he stood you might have believed him to be the hero Sām for handsomeness and wisdom, for grace and judgment.

(ii) *Rostam slays the white elephant*

Seated with Rostam one day in his garden drinking wine while music played in key high and low, were his noble companions, happily quaffing the ruby liquor from goblets of crystal until their heads were in a maze. After the company dispersed, each man having received gifts of lavish value, the king [Zāl] retired to the women's apartments, as was the practice and custom, and Taham-tan ['Giant-bodied' Rostam], his head full of wine, went roaring to his own bedchamber, where he lay down. Scarcely had his head sunk into sleep when in at the door came someone who shouted,

'The king's white elephant has escaped from its chain and wounded several men.'

As the cry fell on Rostam's ear his valour and energy woke swiftly to life. He broke into a run with his grandfather's mace in his grasp and made his way at once to the gateway. But there the guardians in charge of his quarters attempted to bar his path, demanding of him how they could face the king's wrath if they opened the gates in the darkness of the night with the elephant loosed from its fetters. Maddened by the words of the porter who spoke, Rostam launched a blow at his head which made his head roll off sideways like a ball. Then he turned towards the others, who shrank away from him, and strode to the gate, the chain and bar of which he shattered with another blow of his mace. Like a blast of wind he swept through the gateway, shouldering his mace and with his head filled with turbulence, and at a gallop made towards the maddened beast. It raged like the Nile in flood and he could see his warriors bounding away like sheep when the wolf appears. He himself, roaring like a lion, rushed fearlessly upon the elephant, which wildly raised its trunk for battle, but with his mace he dealt it a blow on the head that doubled up the mountainous carcase as the beast fell dead.

(iii) *Rostam and Afrāsiyāb*

[Here follow accounts of a number of kings who lived and died as rulers of Iran, the most important being Manuchehr. During their reigns the hostility between Iran and Turān grew in strength. When Pesheng, king of Turān, heard of the death of Manuchehr he became ambitious to occupy the throne of Iran in addition to his own and to avenge the murder of Tūr. With that object he summoned his son Afrāsiyāb, who commanded the Turanian army, and ordered him to begin a campaign against Iran. A long series of campaigns ensued, with fluctuating fortune, victory falling now to one side now to another. After Shah Garshāsp the Iranian throne was vacant for a time, and it was then that the hero Rostam appeared more persistently on the scene in an active role. He begged his father Zāl for leave to attack the Turanian hordes under Afrāsiyāb. But Zāl hesitated.]

'My gallant youth,' said Zāl, 'chief of the illustrious and mainstay of warriors, you have recounted to me your prowess at Mount Sepand [whose fortress he had stormed] and against the white elephant and given me joy by it. They, surely, were easy tests and undertakings, about which my heart could have felt no apprehension? But while this activity of Afrāsiyāb's continues I dare not go to sleep when the darkness of night fails. How can I send you against so intrepid a monarch, one so eager for battle? For you this is the age for feasting to the strains of music, for wine-bibbing and listening to lays of heroes. It is not yet the time for you to make war, to seek reputation, to give battle and stir up earth's dust as high as the moon.'

Rostam answered Zāl son of Sām with these words, 'I am not the man for luxury and wine-cups. These shoulders and these long fingers did not win their strength for a career of ease. If the battle-field is cruel and the fighting harsh, God will be my associate, and my fortunes will triumph. You will see how I acquit myself in the fray, how on my rose-coloured charger I plunge into bloodshed. I have in my hand a cloud which has the lustre of water [tempered steel] but which rains blood; with its matter it kindles fire and its head crushes the skulls of elephants. When I cover my breast with armour the world will have reason to fear my quiverful. No fortress that once has suffered the on-slaught of my mace, of my breast, arms or shoulders, will again fear ballista or mangonel or call for engines of war to guard it. When my lance goes into battle, even a stone will have its heart drenched in blood.

'But I need a horse of mountain height, one that no man but myself can take in a noose, one that will have the power to bear my fury in battle yet will not be impatient when the occasion demands steadiness. Further I require a mace like a mountain-fragment, for there is a horde advancing upon me from Turān. When they come, then even bereft of an army I should do battle against them, fiercely enough to make you believe that blood was raining down from the clouds over the battlefield.'

(iv) *Rostam chooses his horse Rakhsh*

[To enable Rostam to make his choice] every drove of horses that was in Zābolestān, together with those that were in Kābo-lestān, was brought in and driven in parade before him, the brand-mark of each princely owner being called out. Whenever Rostam drew a horse towards him he pressed his hand down on its back; each time with the potency of his strength its spine yielded until its belly touched the ground. At last there arrived a troop from Kābol, and a spate of horses of every colour rushed before him. One which galloped swiftly by was a bay mare whose breast was like a lion's, her haunches short, her ears two shining daggers, her chest and shoulders stout, though she was lean in the flank.

At her foot sported a colt as large as herself, his buttock and breast of a size with her own. His eyes were black, but his body was not of a single colour; his tail curved high, his testicles were black and firm, his hoofs of steel. His skin was bright and dappled as though flecked with petals of red roses on saffron. At night he was able to see an ant's footprint on a black cloak two leagues away. His strength was that of an elephant, for speed he equalled any racing-camel and for courage any lion on Mount Bisetun. No sooner had Rostam caught sight of the mare than he also saw this splendid colt and at once began making a loop in his royal lasso to pluck him out of the troop. But the old herdsman in charge called out,

'Master, do not take another man's horse.' 'Whose horse is he then?' inquired Rostam. 'His haunches are clear of any brand-mark.'

'Look for no brand-mark,' came the answer, 'because there is a deal of talk about this horse. We call him "Rakhsh", this red bay with a skin that shines like water and has the colour of fire. None of us knows who the owner is and we simply call him "Rostam's Rakhsh". He was put under saddle three years ago and he has often been picked out by the eyes of the great ones. When his dam sees a rope, or when someone tries to mount him, she comes forward and fights like a lion. Noblest of warriors, we do not know what the mystery is that surrounds him. You are a man of experience, but be cautious. Do not approach even the dust of this dragon too closely, for if the mare begins to fight she will tear the heart out of a lion or split a leopard's hide.'

Rostam on hearing the words fathomed the meaning of what the old man had said and, casting his royal lasso, swiftly caught the bay's head in the noose. Like a raging elephant the mare bore down upon Rostam and was on the point of wrenching off his head in her teeth when he uttered a roar like that of an infuriated lion, at sound of which she withdrew daunted. Bracing his mighty legs he drew in the slack of the rope and then extended his powerful arm to press down on the back of the bay colt. Not in the least degree did it yield to the pressure; you would have said that he had not even been aware of it.

'This,' said Rostam to himself, 'is my horse. And now it is my duty to set to work.'

To the herdsman he said,

'For how much will you sell this dragon? Who knows the value placed on him?'

The man replied,

'If you are Rostam, use him to bring redress into the face of the land of Iran. His value is the whole of our Iranian fatherland, and, mounted on him you will set the whole world to rights.'

Rostam laughed, his lips looking like corals, and called down blessings on the man. He saddled his rose-coloured steed, whose head filled with zest for strife and battle. So [precious] did he become that rue was burnt [as a charm] to protect him from onslaught at night. You would have thought that however regarded, whether from right or left, he radiated enchantment and in battle would become a very gazelle [for swiftness].

(v) *Kāvus summons the king of Māzandarān*

[The war against Turān continued its slow progress, Rostam taking a prominent part. At one period there occurs the episode in which King Kāvus summons a Div-like vassal to submit. Upon the vassal's refusal Kāvus makes an ill-prepared foray into Māzandarān and is taken captive. He manages to send a message for aid to Zāl and Rostam. Rostam sets out for Māzandarān alone via a perilous short-cut. On this journey he is challenged every day and performs seven heroic labours to overcome a ferocious lion, traverse desolate poison-aired, waterless desert, combat a dragon, slay a sorceress, and kill the Great White Div who had taken Kāvus prisoner. Kāvus is freed and once again calls upon the vassal king of Māzandarān to submit.]

Upon white silk a clever scribe wrote in a good hand a letter containing words to inspire fear and hope and referring to matters mortifying and agreeable. First he praised the Lord, through whom virtue was made manifest in the world, who provided wisdom, created the revolving skies, ordained harshness and savagery as well as charity and granted us the discretion of doing good or ill. [He then continued,]

'If you are just and your faith is pure, you will receive nought but praise from mankind; if you are malevolent and an evil-doer, retribution will come to you from high Heaven. Since the universal Ruler has acted with justice, how is it that you have come to transgress his command? In the acts of God you may perceive how he requites sin, as in his destruction of the demons and of the wizards of Māzandarān. If the experience of that has enlightened you, and your own spirit and wisdom have been your instructors, forsake your throne in Māzandarān and present yourself at this court according to the rule for vassals. Furthermore, since you have not the strength to oppose Rostam in battle, I require you immediately to pay tribute and impost to my satisfaction. So only, if your place in Māzandarān is essential to your existence, will the way be kept open to you. Otherwise, like Arzhang and the White Demon [both slain by Rostam] you must surrender all hope of life.'

When the scribe had felicitously brought his missive to a close, he affixed to it a seal of musk and amber. The Shah then summoned Farhād, wielder of a mace of steel and elect among the great ones of the land, a man unacquainted with the need to labour or with any discomfort, to whom the king said,

'Bear this letter, which is rich in counsel, to that Div escaped from his bonds.'

Farhād the warrior listened to the king's words, kissed the ground and bore the missive to a city where there dwelt men who were soft of foot, riders of horses and strong-jawed. There the king of Māzandarān resided and there also lived his valiant troops, all doughty warriors. Ahead of himself Farhād sent a herald to announce his business, and the king, hearing that an envoy from King Kāvus was approaching after a long journey, sent out a numerous party of stout warriors, Māzandarāni lions, to receive him. Each had been chosen by the king himself anxious to win repute, and he addressed them as follows,

'Today the human aspect of you must be set apart from the demonic and you must put into practice the ways and habits of leopards. So seize the heads of these rational creatures in your claws.'

They advanced therefore to receive Farhād with scowling faces. But matters did not go to their liking. As they came up to the heroic Farhād, one of their noted champions trained to feats of strength seized him by the hand and gripped it as though meaning to crush both sinews and bones. Farhād's face, however, did not blanch and he neither blushed nor frowned with the pain. He was then escorted into the presence of the king, who inquired about King Kāvus and the travails of the journey. Farhād placed the letter down before the scribe, and, when the material of it had been sprinkled with wine and musk, he recited it to the king.

That great warrior writhed at its contents. Once, when he heard the story of Rostam and his conflict with the Div, his eyes had filled with tears of blood and his heart with fear. He had said to himself, 'The sun will set and the night, time for ease and sleep, will come. But with Rostam the world will never be at ease, and his name will never disappear.' Now, when the king's letter was read to the end, his eyes shed the blood with which his wounded heart was filled. For three days he kept the envoy as his guest, amongst his nobles and his own companions, and on the fourth day he said to him,

'Go back to your witless newly-fledged king and give this answer to Kāvus, "Lacking the essence of the wine, the jar is dark within. Am I one who can be commanded to leave my land, home and throne and present myself at that place of audience? My palace is loftier than yours and my troops number a thousand or more times a thousand. Once they set their faces to battle they leave no stone undisturbed nor any ordered comeliness. Prepare yourself for toil and give yourself no respite, for I am preparing war. I shall bring against you an army to be composed of men like lions, and shall rouse your heads out of their sweet slumbers. Twelve hundred elephants will be in that army, whereas your empire contains not one. I will so plough up the gloomy earth of Iran that a hill will not be distinguished from a pit." '

Farhād perceived how rancorous the king was and observed his pride, ferocity and arrogance. But he continued to dispute with him until he received the [written] reply to the missive of Kāvus. He then turned his rein homewards to the sovereign of Iran, to whom he related what he had seen and heard, and for whom he rent the veil of all secrets.

'He is above the heavens,' he said, 'and his lofty view does not descend beneath them. He turned his head away from anything I had to tell. In his sight the world is a thing of nought.'

Upon that the emperor summoned the hero [Rostam], to whom he recounted all that Farhād had said. To that the elephant-bodied warrior replied,

'I will rescue our people from this shame. It is my duty to take him an answer, which will be the drawing of my sword from its scabbard. A missive trenchant as a sharp sword is needed, a despatch having the quality of a thunder-cloud; and I will myself go to him as envoy and make blood flow in the runnels with what I have to say.'

In answer King Kāvus said,

'Ring and crown are both made illustrious by you. You are not the simple carrier of a message; you have the courage of a tiger and are foremost where strife is afoot.'

When the king had sealed the letter that was written, the world-ambitious Rostam set out on his journey, with his heavy club laid ready on his saddle, and, as he neared Māzandarān, the king received warning that Key Kāvus had sent an envoy with a message, the ambassador's appearance being that of a wild lion. On his saddle-strap he carried a lasso of sixty bights, under him was a proud-stepping horse and in body he was like an elephant in fury. This ambassador the king welcomed and said,

'You are Rostam, for you have the chest and arms of a Pahlavān [Champion warrior].'

Rostam replied,

'I am only a humble servitor, even if I were worthy of such servitude, for compared with the position of my master I am little to the purpose. He is the Pahlavān, the noble Champion and gallant knight.'

[The answer given to the message he brought was one of defiance. Thereupon, scornfully rejecting the gift offered him by the king, Rostam returned to Iran, where he urged Kāvus to make war on the Māzandarāni forces, composed of Divs and Pahlavāns.]

(vi) Kāvus makes war on Māzandarān

As soon as Rostam departed homewards from Māzandarān, the king of the magicians [i.e. of Māzandarān] made ready for war. His pavilion was transported from the capital and he led all his troops out into the open, their dust rising out of their midst so thickly that the very colour of the sun was obscured. Plain, valley and mountain were lost to sight, and the earth wearied with the tread of elephants. Like the wind he drove his men, without seeking a moment's respite.

When tidings came to Shah Kāvus that the army of the Divs was close at hand, he ordered Rostam (the son of Zāl) to be the first to tighten up his girdle for the fray, and he gave further command to the noble warriors Tus, Gudarz (sons of Keshvād), Giv and Gordin to get their forces ready and to furbish their spears and shields. The royal pavilion and the tents of the captains were then despatched to the battlefield of Māzandarān.

In front of the array went the elephant-bodied Rostam, who had never known defeat in combat, while on the Māzandarāni side was a noted warrior, bearer of a massive battle-axe upon his shoulder, whose name was 'Juyā' ['Seeker']. He was, in truth, a seeker after fame and a man of much talk. By leave of his king Juyā went forward and flaunted himself before Kāvus, Chief of the army. Armour shone on his body and the flashes from his sword were earth-consuming. In front of the Iranians he passed and repassed, mountain and plain re-echoing to his voice.

'Who seeks to do battle with me?' he said. 'He must be such a one as can raise dust from off the water.'

No man ventured out against him and you would have thought that [in those challenged] neither blood nor pulse moved, until at last the monarch exclaimed,

'What has happened to you stout warriors and men of action that your hearts are so dismayed at this demon and your faces so gloomy at sound of his voice?'

No reply came to the king from the warriors. It seemed as though the army had withered before Juyā. But now Rostam turned his rein and, laying his gleaming spear along the neck of his steed, he said,

'Let your Majesty grant me leave to encounter this contemptible demon.'

'This is a fitting task for you,' replied the king. 'Nobody in Iran but you would seek a combat such as this. Go, and may the Creator be your ally. Let every Div and wizard fall before you.'

The hero spurred his gallant steed Rakhsh forward, in his grasp a head-crushing spear. On to the field of combat he charged like an elephant in fury, with a tiger under him and a dragon in his fist. He called out to Juyā,

'You evil creature, your name should be expunged from the calendar of nobles. For you the moment to repine has arrived. There is no longer time for ease and peace. Let her who gave birth to you shed tears; it would have been better for her if she had crucified you.'

To this Juyā retorted,

'Permit yourself no freedom from care concerning Juyā and his head-reaping sword. For now it is your mother's heart that will be broken; it is she that will weep over your armour and helmet.'

Rostam heard these words to the end, in a loud voice mentioned his name and began to stir from his place like a mountain in motion. His adversary's spirit sank in gloom. He pulled on his reins and turned away, for it was not Rostam that he wished to meet in combat. Yet behind him Rostam came close as his own dust, and, directing his spear-head at Juyā's girdle, he thrust his shaft at the fastenings of his armour and coat of mail, so that no link or knot remained unloosed. Then, parting Juyā from the saddle, he lifted him up and twirled him about like a chicken on a spit, at last throwing him down on the ground, where he lay with his mouth full of earth and his armour in fragments. The warriors and champions of Māzandarān were thrown into dismay at the sight; the army felt its courage broken and every man's face grew pale, while from the field of battle arose a babel of talk.

The commander of the Māzandarāni army immediately issued the order that his troops as one man should lift up their heads and go into battle displaying the courage of tigers. Each man drew the sword of vengeance and the armies flung themselves upon each other. On either side resounded the trumpets and drums, the air became blue [with dust] and the ground black as ebony. Like the lightning that flashes from the midst of the dark cloud, so rays flickered from battle-axe and sword. The air gleamed red, black and violet from the multitude of the lances and the colours of the banners. At the shouts of the Divs and the noise made by the black dust rising, the thunder of drums and the neighing of war-horses, the mountains were rent and the earth cleft asunder. So fierce a combat had been seen by no man before. Loud was the clash of the battle-axes and the clatter of swords and of arrows; the warriors' blood turned the plain into marsh, the earth resembled a sea of pitch whose waves were formed of swords, axes and arrows. Panting horses floated, like ships at sea, speeding onwards till they sank. Axes rained blows on helmets and skulls as fast as autumn gales blow down the leaves in showers from the willow-trees.

[For seven days the battle raged with unabated fury and at last Rostam broke through the Māzandarāni lines and confronted the enemy king himself. He was on the point of thrusting him through with his spear when the king, being possessed of magic powers, in full view of the Iranian troops transformed himself into a mountainous boulder.]

King Kāvus ordered that the boulder should be brought from where it lay to his throne. But though every sinewy athlete in his army thrust against the rock with all his force and strenuous effort, the heavy stone in which the Māzandarāni king lay embedded would not stir from its place. It was then that the giant hero stretched out his arms and, without any aid in that ordeal,

lifted the stone with such ease that the troops were left in amazement. He walked with it over the shoulder of a mountain, with
the crowd roaring at his heels, brought it to the Shah's pavilion
and there cast it down as victim to the Iranians. Addressing it he
said,

'Now show yourself. Leave this cowardice and wizardry, else I
will shatter this rock into fragments with my sharp steel and axe.'

The Māzandarāni heard the words and transformed himself into
the semblance of a wisp of cloud, topped by steel and with a coat
of mail covering his body. Rostam seized him by the hand,
laughed and turned towards the king.

'Here is the mountain boulder,' he said. 'Fearing the axe he has
come meekly into my hand.'

King Kāvus with a glance at him judged him a person unfitted
for the throne and crown. His visage was ugly, his body too
elongated and his head, neck and teeth resembled those of a wild
boar. Kāvus remembered his ancient grievances, the days when
his heart had been sore and his lips full of cold sighs, and he
ordered the executioner to hack the Māzandarāni into pieces with
a sharp sword.

(vii) *Kāvus builds a palace*

[Occasionally Ferdowsi interrupts his tales of bloody battles and
feasts of triumph to portray a peaceful idyllic scene. This is how
he describes a royal dwelling built by Key Kāvus in the Alborz
mountains.]

It was such a dwelling as a man's heart would covet at sight, in a
place where day lasted long and never shortened. It suffered
neither torrid July nor chill December; its air was perfumed with
amber and its rain was wine. The whole year round it enjoyed
the climate of Spring and its flowers had the tints of rosy-cheeked
girls. In that spot the minds of men were remote from distress,
grief and vexation, and if there was pain it was suffered by the
bodies of Divs. Each day laid its head down in slumber in contentment and spread the lesson of justice done.

[Prosperity afterwards led Kāvus into the paths of wickedness.]

(viii) *Eblis leads Key Kāvus astray*

At early dawn one morning Eblis [the Devil] held a secret conclave with the Shah [Kāvus]. But he had beforehand informed the Divs that the royal fortunes had declined into a state of trouble and difficulty.

'What is needed,' he said to them, 'is an alert-minded Div, acquainted with the forms and ceremonies of intercourse with kings whereby he may be able to lead the soul of Kāvus astray and induce him to end his persecutions of Divs. That Div must turn the king aside from favouring the pure gods, thereby contriving to besmirch his Majesty's repute.'

They all listened, but fear of Kāvus prevented any of them from consenting to take action, until at last one evilly-disposed Div rose to his feet, saying,

'This delicate task is one for me to accomplish; I undertake to pervert him from the religion of God. Nobody but me could carry this out efficiently.'

Eblis then instructed the Div, who was one of his personal attendants, a fluent speaker and accustomed to the regimen of courts, how to act; and the youth awaited his opportunity, which came when the illustrious monarch left his palace to go hunting. Kissing the ground before him and presenting a nosegay of flowers to him he said,

'The splendour of your kingly majesty makes the revolving sky your throne. The whole surface of the earth has submitted itself to your might; you are the shepherd and the mighty are your flock. There is but one achievement lacking to ensure that your fame will never be obscured. It concerns a secret which the sun holds concealed from you; and that is, by what means it revolves, first sinking and then rising. Further, how does the moon change, and what are day and night? Who directs the setting in motion of this cycle? You have acquired control of the earth, as was your ambition; now the sky should be submissive to your command.'

The king's heart was led astray by the Div and his spirit lost the power to reason. He fancifully thought to himself, 'The revolving sky shows its face to me as I stand here on earth. The Creator of the world cares nothing for it all, whereas both sky and earth are my essential interest.'

He brooded long, considering how without wings it might be possible for him to ascend into the aether. Of the learned he made inquiry about the distance which lay between the earth and the sphere of the moon and listened with care to the astronomer's reply. Upon that he hit on a distorted scheme devoid of sense. It was, that when all were asleep, a group of men should make their way to the nests of the eagles and carry off a large number of the young birds, only leaving behind one or two in each nest. These birds he fed unceasingly for a year and a month on fowls, roast meat and whole lambs, until they acquired the strength of a lion, capable of bearing aloft a horned fighting-ram.

Then out of aloes-wood he constructed a throne, holding all fast with gold, and to each side he attached long poles on which he tied legs of mutton, a plan to which he had devoted careful thought. He then brought four strong eagles and bound them securely to the throne, on which he seated himself, with a goblet of wine set before him. When the eagles felt the pangs of hunger they sprang towards the mutton, thus lifting the throne from the ground until it rose from the earth's surface into the clouds.

The time arrived when the strength of these winging birds failed and they fell into distress, their pinions dissolving in sweat. Down they came from the dark clouds, dragging with them the spears and the Shah's throne, and came to earth in a forest belonging to the land of China. There, humiliated and grief-stricken, he rested for a time devoting himself to adoration of the Creator.

(ix) *Rostam rescues Key Kāvus*

While Kāvus lingered on where he was, begging forgiveness for the sin he had committed, his army sought for him in every direction. At last, Rostam and the heroes Giv and Ṭus got news of him and with a great force of troops and drums marched off to find him. [On their return with the king,] Goudarz the Elder remarked to Rostam,

'Since the day when my mother suckled me I have seen many crowns and thrones, and kings and chieftains whom Fortune keenly favoured. But never, amongst either great or small, have I beheld a man so self-willed as Kāvus. Of wisdom he has none, nor has he any faith or judgment, for neither his sense nor his heart is in the right place. You would say he had not a brain in his head, seeing that not a single thought of his has any worth. No man of note before has ever proposed to go up into the skies. Like all lunatics he is bereft of sense and judgment and is moved from his place by every breeze that stirs.'

Other paladins approached, roused to disapproval of Kāvus and eager to wrangle with him. [Addressing him] Goudarz continued, 'A hospital is a place more suited to you than the capital city. You are for ever surrendering your position to the enemy. You have wandered about the earth carrying on warfare and now you have made an attempt on the sky. In time to come they will relate the legend of how a king ascended to the spheres above in order to view the moon and the sun and to count the stars in their order.'

Kāvus was abashed and thrown into confusion by these men of renown and warlike prowess. He replied,

'True it is that nothing can be lost by justice. You have spoken justly and there is nothing false in what you say. My spirit can find no release from your strictures.'

Shamed by these noble men he humbled himself, gave up his prideful gait and closed the gates of his audience-chamber. He did penance, accustoming himself to pain and toil and giving away much of the treasure he had stored up. In adoration of God the Pure he ground his face into the dark earth and, when he had spent an age in tearful prayer, the Creator granted him forgiveness.

(x) *The combat of the seven champions*

I have heard that one day the giant-bodied hero [Rostam] gave a banquet to the circle of his comrades in a place called Navand, where there were many lofty palaces. The nobles of Iran at that festal resort assembled in their glory as a great company, each of the chieftains being escorted by a retinue which in itself formed a notable and mighty force. This multitude never ceased from its activity, being always engaged in polo, archery, wine-bibbing or the chase. Several days passed in this way, every man's heart being light with pleasure and music.

One day in his intoxication the hero Giv said to Rostam,

'Illustrious warrior, if you have a taste for the chase, if the speedy panther brings joy to you, let us cover the shining face of the sun in the hunting-grounds of the mighty Afrāsiyāb with the dust of horsemen, of panthers and falcons. We will point our long lances, bring down the swift onager with our lassos and with our swords drive the lion into fetters. With our javelins we will take the boar and with our hawks the pheasant throughout the livelong day. Let us go hunting on that plain of Turān to such effect that it will be talked of throughout the world.'

Rostam answered,

'Let all the world go according to your desire, and may good fortune be your lot. At dawn tomorrow we will go into the plain of Turān and not rest from hunting and raiding.'

With one voice they agreed to this proposal, not a man uttering a different opinion. At dawn then, as soon as they were awake, they began carrying their purposes into effect, setting off with panthers, hawks and gear. Curvetting and galloping the horses made for the river Shahd and the hunting-grounds of the mighty Afrāsiyāb, keeping the mountain on one hand and the river on the other. Beyond lay the city of Sarakhs, before which spread the plain covered with herds of gazelle and wild sheep. Everywhere on the plain tents large and small were now pitched by the hunters, who were struck with amazement at the multitude of the game.

Predatory lions were absent from the plain, but the birds of prey became aware of what was afoot. Soon wildfowl and other game lay in heaps on every side, either dead or pierced by arrows; while the hunters, cheerful and blithe of heart, ceased not for a moment from laughter. Thus passed a week, which they spent cup in hand and with joy in their hearts as worshippers of wine. On the eighth day at dawn Rostam proposed an admirable plan to the assembled company. He said to those noble princes, chieftains, proud warriors and headmen,

'Afrāsiyāb has by now become aware, as cannot be doubted, of our being here. That ill-omened miscreant must not be permitted to consult with his well-known chieftains so as to make plans for issuing against us to do battle. That would make the plain too straitened for the panthers to pursue their victims. We must station a sentry on the road, who, on the least warning, shall come in and raise the alarm about the enemy's coming. This evil-minded fellow must find no way of approach to us.'

Gorāza [a noted warrior] strung his bow and issued forth ready to carry out his duty [as sentinel]. With a watchman like him the army cared little for enemy devices and gave themselves up to hunting, with no thought at all for the foe. But one dark night the alarm came to Afrāsiyāb while he lay asleep. He summoned the veterans of his army and with them discussed at length concerning Rostam and the seven brave warriors and cavaliers [in the retinue

of Kāvus], each of them a veritable lion. He said to his own
renowned warriors,

"This is no time for us to delay. We must have a plan to attack
them while they are unprepared. If we can seize the seven champions, we can make the world a narrow place for Kāvus. We must
go out as though in pursuit of game and throw our strength
suddenly upon them.'

Of his swordsmen Afrāsiyāb chose out thirty thousand, all
noted for prowess in battle, and he gave them orders to avoid the
[trodden] road. Accordingly they galloped out by way of the
desert, all with heads raised high for war, and in every direction he
sent large bodies of troops which should close the roads to the
proud [Iranian] army. As they approached the hunting-ground,
coming in eager haste for vengeance, Gorāza caught sight of the
[Turānian] army's dust and came up to inspect it, then turned
swift as the storm-wind, with a hail and a cry and a loud shout.
When he came on to the hunting-ground, he said to Rostam, who
was engaged with his retinue drinking wine,

'You lion-man, Rostam, you must leave this merrymaking, for
their army is measureless, their troops cover mountain and plain
alike, and the banner of the malevolent Afrāsiyāb shines out above
the dust like the sun.'

Rostam laughed aloud as he heard this, and said,

'Triumphant fortune is with us. Why do you so fear the king of
the Turks and the dust of the Turānian land's cavalry? His army
numbers not more than a hundred thousand horsemen tugging at
the reins and mounted on armoured steeds. Were there only myself on this plain, with my mace and Rakhsh and my armour, there
would be no cause for qualms about Afrāsiyāb and his numerous
army, nor any need for perturbation. Even if there were only one
of us on this field of strife, the whole might of Turān would be of
no avail against him in battle. We need this field of campaign, and
I require no army from Iran. We are here a company of seven
knightly warriors, famous swordsmen, each backed by two thousand five hundred valiant cavaliers skilled with the lance. Cup-
bearer, fill a Bāboli cup to the brim with Zāboli wine!'

The steward poured the wine and deftly handed it, and soon
Tahamtan was enlivened by what the man proffered. Holding the
gleaming goblet in his hand he first drank to King Kāvus.

'Let us call on the name of the king of the age,' said he. 'May he
ever remain whole in body and spirit!'

Again he took the goblet. And now he kissed the ground and said,

'This wine is drunk to the name of Ṭus.' But the gallant knights came forward and begged the hero not to give them more.

'We cannot contain all these beakersful,' they said. 'At wine the devil himself cannot keep pace with you. None but you has such capacity for wine, or for making the battle-axe kill with one blow, or for a fight.'

He answered,

'A brother drains a brother's cupful. He is a lion who takes this cup.'

[After a series of battles, in which Rostam plays a conspicuous part, Afrāsiyāb's army is routed, although he himself escapes, and Rostam returns to Iran in triumph.]

(xi) *Rostam loses Rakhsh*

I will here interpolate a story from ancient legend told me by the Dehqān, who had it from a priest. One morning, Rostam was gloomy of spirit when he arose, and proposed to go hunting. He made himself ready, filled his quiver with arrows and flung his leg over Rakhsh [his horse], which he roused to a gallop, turning his face towards the Turānian plain. Like a bloodthirsty lion he sought about for game and as he approached the hunting-ground he saw that it swarmed with onagers. The cheeks of the bestower of crowns [Rostam] glowed like a rose. He laughed aloud as he put spurs to Rakhsh, and with bow and arrow, club and rope he brought down birds and beasts in number. Then, with thorn bushes, litter and branches of trees he made a fire. Once it was well alight he looked about for a tree which he could use as a spit, and on it, weighing no more than a feather in his hand, he impaled a male onager. This he roasted through, rent into pieces and ate, squeezing the marrow out of the bones. He then lay down and rested after the exertions of the day, while Rakhsh roamed about the plain grazing.

It chanced that across the hunting-ground there passed a group of seven or eight Turānian horsemen. They caught sight of the hoof-prints left by Rakhsh and followed them along a water-course. As the horse came into view on the plain, they hurried in the attempt to snare him, and men from the mountains also galloped up on all sides. One of them threw a 'royal' noose, but as Rakhsh perceived the rope and the horseman he flew into a wild rage. Two of the pursuers he brought down with a kick from his hindlegs and he tore off the head of a third with his teeth, so that of the small cavalcade he had slain three, while his own head was still unfettered by a noose. But now they cast lassos from every side and at last they held his neck in tight bonds. They made him fast and bore him off with them at a gallop into the city, where they hoped to breed and gain from him.

When Rostam awoke from his sweet slumber he looked for his high-stepping mount, but scanning the meadows he could nowhere catch a glimpse of the horse. Anxiety filled him when he failed to discover his steed and he hastened distractedly towards [the town of] Samangān, thinking to himself,

'On foot, running, whither shall I go in my disgrace and with my gloomy spirit, all girt as I am and laden with quiver and battle-axe, a helmet such as this, my sword and leopard-skin cloak? How shall I traverse the wilderness, and what can I do against any that may attack me? What will the Turks say? Only this—"Who carried off his Rakhsh? Tahamtan [Rostam] fell asleep, and so died." Now I needs must continue and reconcile my heart to sorrow, tightening my armour and girding up my loins. It may be that I shall find him somewhere.'

Thus he went forward, his heart full of pain and grief, his body racked with torment and his spirit in agony.

(xii) *Rostam comes to Samangān*

> [Grieved and angry Rostam arrived at Samangān, where he was greeted by the king, who offered him soothing words and the assurance that Rakhsh was too well known for his hiding-place not to be soon discovered.]

Tahamtan was placated by the king's words and his spirit was liberated from anxiety. He felt pleasure at going to the house of the king and he in turn rejoiced at the tidings that he was to be Rostam's host. He provided a lodging for him in his own palace and remained standing to wait upon him. To the cooks he gave orders to prepare a festive table which was to be set before the warriors, who took their places, as did the musicians, in a manner to ensure that Tahamtan would extinguish any ill-will that he harboured. The servers of wine, the singers and minstrels all were black-eyed and rosy-cheeked charmers of Terāz [renowned for the beauty of its inhabitants].

With intoxication, sleep began to possess Rostam, who grew impatient at prolongation of the feast, until at last the host allotted him a fitting place for his repose and sleep, where he set musk and rose-water before him.

(xiii) *The king's daughter, Tahmina, visits Rostam*

When part of the dark night had gone by, although the morning star had yet to appear on its revolving path, there took place some mysterious and secret conversation and then the door of the sleeping-quarters was softly opened. Towards the unconscious warrior's pillow stepped a slave with a perfumed candle in her hand, while behind her came a creature lovely as the moon, radiant as the sun and fragrant in her beauty. The colour of her cheeks was that of the corals of Yemen, her mouth small as the heart of a lover contracted with grief. Her soul was ripe wisdom, her body pure spirit uncontaminated by earthly element. At sight of her Rostam the lion-heart was cast into amazement. Calling down the Creator's blessing on her, said,

'What is your name? What seek you in the darkness of the night and what do you desire?'

She answered,

'I am Tahmina. You would say that I am rent in twain with longing. I am daughter of the king of Samangān and I come of the stock of lions and leopards. On earth I have no peer among persons of royal birth; indeed beneath the dome of heaven there rarely exists anyone like me. Outside the veil no one has ever beheld me, nor has anyone ever heard my voice. But of you I have heard from all men as a legend and have been told histories of you in plenty; that you fear no Div, lion, leopard or serpent, and how bold you are in action. I have craved for your shoulders and arms and breast. Now God has vouchsafed your presence in this city. If you desire me, I yield myself to you, and neither bird nor fish will set eyes on me [hereafter]. One thing is sure, that I have so devoted myself to you as to have killed wisdom in favour of love. It may be that the Creator may place a child of yours in my bosom, one who will resemble you in manly qualities and strength and to whom Heaven will grant fortune through Saturn and the Sun. Another thing to say is that I will restore

Rakhsh to you, even though I trample all Samangān under foot.'

Rostam's heart was touched by the gracious woman's speech. He listened eagerly to all she said and, gazing upon this resplendent creature, he saw her endowed with every good quality. Moreover, when she thus gave him tidings of Rakhsh, he could foresee nought but felicity as the outcome of this adventure. He commanded that a virtuous priest should come and crave her for him from her father, who, being told of the matter, rejoiced and arose like a free-growing cypress to give his daughter to the champion, according to custom and the law.

The dark night, shared in seclusion with him, passed without tedium. When the bright sun in his lofty sphere was about to cast off his musky noose, Rostam gave his bride the jewelled amulet which he wore on his arm and which had acquired fame throughout the world. He said,

'Guard this. If a daughter is granted to you by fate, take and bind it on her tresses to secure good fortune and as a talisman to brighten the world. But if the stars send a son, bind it upon his arm in token of his father. He will attain the stature of Sām son of Narimān, and he will have the valour and spirit of noble men. He will bring down the eagle in swift flight out of the clouds, and the sun will not shine on him with overpowering heat.'

[At dawn] Tahmina turned away in tears from Rostam, who shared her grief and pain. The much-venerated king then came to him to inquire about his sleep and repose and, further, gave him good tidings of the discovery of Rakhsh that rejoiced him greatly. He went to where the horse stood and caressed him, put on the saddle and, with the speed of wind, departed for Sistān and thence to Zābolestān, telling no one what he had heard and seen.

(xiv) *Tahmina bears a son, Sohrāb*

Nine moons passed over the princess, and then a child was born, glorious as the moon. You might have said he was the elephant-bodied hero Rostam, or Sām the Lion, or Niram. When he smiled and his face showed pleasure, Tahmina gave him the name of Sohrāb. After but a single month had passed, it was as though he was a full year old, and his breast matched that of Rostam son of Zāl. At three years old he began the exercises of the battlefield; by his fifth year he had acquired the courage of lion-like men, and when he reached his tenth year there was no man in the land who would venture to stand in combat with him.

One day he came to his mother and said boldly to her,

'Tell me—since I am taller than all who were my foster-brothers and my head almost penetrates the sky—of whose seed I am and of what stock. What shall I say when someone demands to know who my father is? If [the answer to] this question is kept hidden from me, I will not continue to exist for you in this world.'

To this his mother replied,

'Listen to what I have to say; rejoice at it and cease your dis-pleasure. You are the son of the hero Rostam, the elephant-bodied, sprung from Dastān son of Sām and from Niram. The reason for your head's out-topping the sky is that your stock derives from those noble origins. Not since the World-Creator brought the universe into existence has there ever appeared such a knightly warrior as Rostam, nor has there been anyone like Sām son of Narimān, whose head the skies themselves did not venture to touch in their revolution.'

She then brought a letter from the warlike Rostam which she showed him secretly, together with three glowing rubies and three purses of gold sent for him by his father from Iran at the time when he was born. She continued to say,

'Afrāsiyāb must be kept in ignorance of this, from beginning to end, for he is the enemy of glorious Rostam and, further, mis-fortune lies heavy on the land of Turān because of him. Let him not become your enemy and destroy the son for hatred of the father. Yet if your father became aware of the handsome condition into which you have grown, he would become boastful and over-bearing and would immediately summon you to him, so that your mother's heart would suffer the torments of grief.'

Sohrāb replied,

'It would not be possible for anyone in the world to keep this thing concealed. For long past all the great warriors have been narrating the story of Rostam. Never has there been such ancestry as mine; what excuse was there for keeping it concealed from me? Now I shall raise an army from among the Turks that shall have no bounds. I will stir up Kāvus from his lair and blot out all trace of Ṭus from Iran. Then I will bestow on Rostam the treasury, the throne and the crown, and set him in place of the Shah Kāvus.

And I will march from Iran against Turān and set one king face to face with the other. I shall seize Afrāsiyāb's throne and raise my lance above the sun. And you I will make queen of the land of Iran, myself displaying the courage of lions in the struggle. Since Rostam is my father and I am his son, there can be none else in the whole world fitted to wear the crown. When the faces of sun and moon are both illuminated, how can a star display its diadem?'

(xv) *Sohrāb chooses a horse*

To his mother Sohrāb said,

'Now you will see some triumphant deeds from me. But I need a high-stepping horse, which for hooves shall have rock-shattering steel, for power shall be an elephant, for fleetness a bird, in the sea a fish and on land a gazelle. It must have strength to carry my battle-axe and mace and my warrior's chest and shoulders.'

[The steed he required was obtained for him by his mother, who sent word of his demands to all the herd-watchers in the land.]

Then exclaimed Sohrāb with self-gratulation,

'Since my horse has come into my hands in this wise, I must mount and turn Kāvus's day into darkness.'

From every side troops gathered about him, men of substance and those who could wield the sword. Then going to his grandfather in supplication, he begged for permission to depart and for aid.

'I wish to go to Iran,' he said, 'to see my much-praised father.'

The king of Samangān, admiring his powerful arm, granted him stores of every kind. He opened his hand with liberal gifts and laid before him both munitions of war and the furniture of kings.

(xvi) *Afrāsiyāb sends aid to Sohrāb*

News was brought to Afrāsiyāb that Sohrāb was launching ships upon the water, that an army had rallied about him and that he was lifting his head high as a cypress in a meadow. Though the smell of [his mother's] milk still issued from his mouth, yet thought of sword and archery came to him. But what need is there to speak at length of all this? Qualities too noble for his origins are becoming visible in him.

When Afrāsiyāb heard these words he was so gratified that he laughed and openly displayed his pleasure. From his own army he chose out the most gallant chieftains, skilled in wielding the heavy mace. To them he said,

'Devise your stratagems anywhere in the world, but keep all under cover. The son must not know who his father is, nor anything of his kinship in spirit, nor of affection, nor of his ancestry. When the two are brought face to face, Tahamtan [Rostam] will with little doubt seek to gain the upper hand, and then perhaps the aged hero will find his death at the hands of this lion-man. Once we have got Iran without the presence of Rostam into our clutches, we can make the world a narrow abode for Kāvus. Later we can deal with Sohrāb, overwhelming him with eternal sleep some night. And if he is slain by the hand of his own father, that noble man's heart will be consumed with grief.'

[There are now interposed descriptions of several incidents in the career of Sohrāb, one of them being his encounter in battle with the Amazon Gordāfarīd. Another was his advance with a Turānian force on Iran, whose king, Kāvus, wrote to Rostam at his home in Zābolestān warning him of the danger that threatened the country from the northern invaders and about the remarkable warrior who was their leader. Rostam replied that a warrior of such prowess could not have sprung from the Turānians. He himself had had a son by the king of Samangān's daughter, but that son was still too young to be identified with the Turānian warrior. He took lightly the plea of Kāvus that he should treat the matter as one of urgency. Instead, he set himself to a drinking bout, news of which reached the ears of Kāvus, who manifested his wrath when Rostam finally came into his presence.]

The furrows on the brow of Kāvus deepened, and he held himself taut as a lion in a thicket.

'Who is Rostam?' he demanded, 'that he should hold my behest in contempt and remove himself from his sworn allegiance to me? If there were a sword by me, I should slice his head from his body like an orange. Seize him and hang him alive from the gallows; and let no person open his mouth to me on his behalf.'

At this speech the heart of the warrior Giv was perturbed.

'Would you thus stretch out your hand against Rostam?' he asked. The king's anger at that flared out as much against him as against Rostam, while the whole assembly remained aghast.

'Go, and hang them both from the gallows,' he ordered Ṭus,

and he himself, raging as though he were a fire set alight, leapt from his place. In the meanwhile Ṭus had come over to Rostam and grasped him by the hand, his warrior comrades standing and wondering who would deliver him from Kāvus and who in that perilous circumstance might commit some act of treachery. Tahamtan was stirred to wrath against the king and said,

'Nourish no such fire in your breast. Each act of yours is worse than what went before it; the kingship is unsuited to you. Hang the Turks alive on the gallows; storm against them and overthrow those who are your enemies, such as the Greeks, the Sagsar [Dogheads], Māzāndarān, Egypt, China and Hāmāvarān. They count no more than grooms to my horse Rakhsh; their hearts are run through by my sword and arrows. You yourself only exist in the world through me, why then scarify your heart with wrath against me?'

[Resentful of the way in which he had been treated, Rostam vowed to leave Iran to its fate, but the nobles, after pointing out to the Shah where he had erred, went in pursuit of the great national hero and persuaded him to return, on the plea that it was the land and not its king that would suffer if he (Rostam) forsook it. On his arrival back, Rostam is welcomed by Kāvus and the two agree on leading an expedition to repel the foreign invaders led by Sohrāb. After the usual bouts of boastful outpourings, Sohrāb attacks before Rostam has had time to prepare. When the messenger from Kāvus arrives, Rostam says to him,]

'When a prince has called to me without warning, it has been either for purposes of war or to go feasting. From Kāvus I have received nothing but the tribulations of strife.'

(xvii) Sohrāb attacks Rostam

[Before the battle Sohrāb captured one of the Iranian knights and asked him to point out Rostam to him. The Iranian, overawed by the might of Sohrāb, was afraid that if Rostam should be killed by Sohrāb the news would heighten the Turānians' courage. He therefore lied and told Sohrāb that Rostam was not present in the Iranian camp.]

He [Rostam] ordered that Rakhsh should be saddled and that his cavalry should furrow their brows with wrinkles [of determination]. As he gazed out of his tent on to the plain, there came into his vision first Giv, who was on his way to place the shining saddle on Rakhsh, then Gorgin, who was calling out to the men to make haste, Rahhām who was tightening the horse's girths, and Ṭus holding the horse-armour ready. Each man was urging his neighbour to speed. Tahamtan said to himself as he heard the voices,

'This war is fought against Ahriman; such turmoil is for no human's sake.'

He stretched out his arm to don his leopard-skin cloak, then fastened the kingly girdle about his middle and, mounting Rakhsh, he set out on his way, having first set Havāra to keep guard over the encampment and the troops. Along with him his banner was borne and he stepped out grimly determined for combat. Soon he caught sight of Sohrāb, endowed with great shoulders and thighs and a chest rivalling in size that of the warrior Sām, and called out,

'Let us go aside from here and choose out a site for battle without the defects of this place.'

Sohrāb rubbed his palms together and went over to the ground where they could give battle to each other. He said to Rostam,

'Let us come here and stand man to man as one warrior to another. We require no one else either from Iran or Turān; let there be only me and you in this encounter. Yet you are not fitted to be my opponent in battle; you cannot stand against one of my fists. You may be tall enough and possessed of shoulders and arms, but they have been worn down by a multitude of years.'

Rostam gazed at this man of proud bearing, at his shoulders and hands and long thighs, then said gently to him,

'My delicate young man, the earth is hard and cold and the air soft and warm. In my long life I have seen many a battlefield and many an army have I brought low. At my hands many a Div has met his fate and in no contingency have I ever suffered defeat. Observe me well during the continuance of this battle, for if you remain alive you will never again fear a dragon. Seas and mountains have beheld me in conflict and the stars are witness to my prowess against the most renowned warriors of Turān. When it comes to valour the whole earth is below my feet. My heart urges me to be compassionate towards you and I am loath to detach your soul from your body. Possessed of such arms and shoulders you are unlike any Turk, and even in Iran I know no parallel to you.'

While this speech was being uttered by Rostam, the heart of Sohrāb leapt towards him so that he said,

'Let me ask you a question and let all be established on a foundation of truth. Recount your origins to me with every detail, and let me be rejoiced by your kindly story. It is my belief that you are Rostam and that you derive from the noble seed of Niram.'

Rostam answered,

'I am not Rostam nor am I of the stock of Sām son of Niram. He is a hero and I a humbler being, possessed neither of throne nor rank nor crown.'

After his lively expectations Sohrāb now fell into despondency and the face of bright day became dark before him.

(xviii) *Rostam battles with Sohrāb*

Seizing a lance Sohrāb went on to the field, turning over, with perplexity in his mind, what his mother had once told him. A narrow arena had been prepared and the men wielded short lances. Soon neither fastenings nor heads remained on the lances and both antagonists twisted their reins leftwards, laying on with Indian swords and striking continuous fire out of the iron. At last in the exchange of blows, which provided a foretaste of the Resurrection, the swords broke in pieces. Heavy spars were thereupon seized with which they pounded each other. These bent under the weight of their blows, while their horses stamped about and the men themselves were overcome with faintness. From off the horses the armour came clattering down, the chain mail dropping in fragments between the two warriors. Now the horses became exhausted and the valiant heroes grew too weary for their tasks, so that hand and arm availed to neither man. Their bodies ran with sweat, their mouths filled with dust and their tongues cracked with thirst. For a while the two champions disengaged, the father being racked with torment and the son loaded with grief. To himself Rostam said,

'Never have I beheld a dragon who fought so fierce a battle, beside which my battle with the White Demon was only trivial. This man's courage leaves my heart without hope, though he has never been about the world, is not reckoned a champion nor famed as belonging to the great. He has reduced me to the state of being satiated with the world, even while our two armies look on at our contest.'

The two men's horses now were rested from the stress of the

combat, from the struggle and the contention, and the warriors strung their bows; the youth and the older man too. But since each wore armour and a shirt of mail and was protected by a leopard-skin shield, no injury was caused by shaft or point. Rage against his opponent filled each man and each seized the other by the girdle at his waist. If Tahamtan were to grasp at a rock he could snatch away pieces from black basalt on a day of battle, and he now endeavoured by seizing Sohrāb's belt to wrest him from the saddle. But the youth's middle evaded any touch and he contrived by his suppleness to leave the hand of Rostam empty.

Once more Sohrāb raised his heavy club from the saddle, contracted his thighs and dealt a crippling blow at his opponent's shoulder. He writhed with the pain but endured it with fortitude, but Sohrāb laughed and shouted out,

'You are a knight, but you cannot withstand the wounds dealt by a warrior, and Rakhsh under you is no better than a donkey. Worst fault in a knight is to have both hands occupied, and, let a hero be of cypress stature, a young man may succeed where an old one proves futile.'

To such straits were the two reduced, so narrowed now was their field of strife, that both yielded heart and soul to terror and turned away from each other. Tahamtan, swift as a leopard sighting its prey, rode off to make onslaught upon the army of Turān, while the warrior Sohrāb for his part gave rein to his horse and rode at speed towards the Iranian army, where he destroyed many a noted champion.

Meanwhile fear had seized upon Rostam that harm might befall Kāvus at the hands of this valorous Turk so newly appeared. He therefore galloped in haste back to his own camp, and there beheld Sohrāb, under whom the ground was stained ruby with the blood he had spilt. Maddened with fury at seeing his antagonist there, he cried out,

'Why did you not end your combat with me instead of descending on the flock like a wolf?'

Sohrāb answered,

'As for that, the army of Turān are remote from any concern with this conflict and are innocent of offence, yet it was you who began by turning to attack them, when no one sought hostility or harm.'

To this Rostam said,

'It is now dark. When the sword-ray of the world-illuminating sun shows itself [tomorrow] there will be present both a gallows and a [royal] dais, for this glorious world is subject to the sword. But since the sword is a weapon with which you are familiar, even though you still smell of your mother's milk, you cannot be a mortal. Yet at dawn let us return with our swords of combat. Now depart, to await what the Creator shall decree.'

(xix) *Rostam and Sohrāb renew their battle*

As the effulgent sun spread out his wings and the fleeting black raven [of night] buried its head, Rostam donned his leopard-skin and mounted his spirited dragon [Rakshh]. The armies here were two leagues apart, but no one dared permit his loins to remain ungirt, and Rostam, having fitted on his head his helmet of iron, entered the field of combat. (All rancour stems from ambition; therefore let us have no contact with envy.)

In the other camp, Sohrāb had spent the night with wine and minstrels. To Humān [a Turkish warrior] he said,

'That lion of a man who is returning to do battle with me has a stature not less than mine and in combat his heart never quails. His chest, shoulders and arms are equal to mine, as though an expert had applied a measuring-cord. At sight of his legs and thighs my feelings are stirred until shame is brought into my face. I perceive the tokens of which my mother told me and in my heart there is torment. Fancy tells me that he is Rostam, since there are few warriors in the world like him. I must not venture to give battle to my father and shamelessly confront him.'

Humān's answer to that was,

'Rostam has often encountered me in battle and you must have heard how he acquitted himself with his heavy mace in the war against Māzandarān. This steed bears a resemblance to his Rakhsh, but these are not his legs nor does this horse leave the same traces with his hooves.'

At dawn, with the first glowing of the sun, the warriors' heads emerged from sleep. Sohrāb donned his battle armour, his head full of thoughts of strife and his heart of feasting. With a shout he entered on to the battlefield, on his lips a cry and in his grasp a bull-headed mace, and smiling at his opponent as though he had spent the evening with him he asked,

'How did you pass the night and in what mood have you

awakened today? With what weapons have you equipped yourself
for war? Throw away those arrows and your vengeful sword,
thrust your brutal claws into the earth and let us two make an
end of standing. Let us rather seat ourselves and brighten our
scowling visages with wine. Let us make a pact before the Lord
and may our hearts repent our pursuit of war. Others can go to
war; do you come to an agreement with me and let us prepare a
feast. My heart has conceived an affection for you and the tears of
shame rain down on my face. You must of a certainty spring
from a line of heroes and you will tell me what your origins are.
You cannot hide your name from me, since you and I are engaged
in this one bout together. Are you not the son of Dastān son of
Sām the warrior? Are you not the most elect and famous Rostam
of Zābolestān?'

To him Rostam thus replied,

'Noble youth, I have never before held such a conversation as
this. Yesterday our talk was all of our wrestling, and I will not be
beguiled by you. Do not attempt to enter that door. You may
yourself be a youth, but I am not a babe. My middle is girt fast for
combat. Let us fight, and let the outcome be whatever is ordained
by the command and decision of the Ruler of the world. I have
roamed afar over hill and dale and am not the man to indulge in
lying and deceitful speeches.'

Sohrāb answered,

'You are aged, so that my counsel will have no effect upon you.
Yet I had hoped that you would live to die on your couch in the
fullness of time, and one that you left behind would raise a monument to you. But if your life is to come into my power, let us
stretch out our hands towards God's decree.'

At that they dismounted from their steeds and began to move
warily about in corselet and headpiece, until like a pair of lions
they sprang on each other so that sweat and blood poured from
their bodies. Now Sohrāb thrust at Rostam like a maddened
elephant, dislodged him from his place and brought him low.
Then, as when a lion buries his claws in a male onager at the end of
its powers, he drew a dagger of tempered steel and aimed to cut
off his head. Rostam caught his intention and called aloud,

'The secret must now be disclosed. Our custom is not this, and
our law demands a different practice. When a man engages in a
wrestling contest and thrusts his older opponent's head into the
dust, he does not on first pressing his back down on to the ground

cut off his head, even to exact vengeance. If he brings him down a second time, he receives the title of 'Lion' for his prowess, and it is then lawful for him to sever the head from the body. Such is our custom.'

By this cunning talk Rostam hoped to escape from the clutches of the dragon and find a way out of destruction. The gallant youth bowed his head to the older man's argument even though it was not to his liking. This he did first out of gallantry, next because it was destined and again, without doubt, out of generosity. Releasing his opponent from his grasp he emerged on to the open plain. There the gazelles leapt before him and he at once went in pursuit with no further thought of the man who had striven in conflict with him. On he rode until, out of the dust, Humān came into view and questioned him about the struggle. In his reply he told all that had passed and repeated the words which Rostam had spoken to him.

'Alas, my youthful friend,' remarked Humān. 'Have you wearied of life? Alas for that chest, those arms and that stature of yours, those long thighs and heroic legs. You have let loose the lion you had trapped in your net and now all your matured achievement is unripe again.'

In reply to Humān he said,

'Drive all care from your breast. Tomorrow, when he enters the contest with me you will see the halter placed about his neck.'

It happened that Rostam, when he escaped from his opponent's clutches, made his way to a stream of running water, having recaptured his life as though he had retrieved the water which had flowed away. He drank from the stream and, having washed his hands and body, turned aside to pay his devotions to the Creator, to whom he prayed for victory and strength, unaware of the fate allotted to him by sun and moon.

I have heard that from the outset of his existence Rostam had been endowed by God with such vigour that stepping on to a rock his feet sank into it. Because of this vigour he was ever led into difficulty, which he was far from desiring, and he therefore implored the Creator to remove part so that he might be able to walk upon the roads. In accordance with his petition God diminished the vigour in his mountainous body. Now, however, with this new task confronting him, his heart was ill at ease for fear of Sohrāb, so that he implored God to watch over him in his trial and restore his vigour to what it had been in the beginning. As he desired it was given back to him, being increased by the amount which it had lost.

From the stream Rostam went across to the place of combat, his heart laden with care and his face pallid, but Sohrāb came on like an elephant in rage, a lasso over his shoulder and a bow in his hand. As he beheld him thus equipped he began to estimate the gravity of the struggle facing him, whereas Sohrāb, on turning to see his opponent, felt his heart beating with the new wind of youth. Yet, on approaching nearer, he realized the other's *Farr* and the mightiness of his frame, and said,

'You escaped from the claws of the lion; why have you with such recklessness returned to me? Have you no regard for your own well-being?'

(xx) *Sohrāb is slain by Rostam*

When evil Fortune is stirred to wrath, then granite rock is softened like wax. The two warriors began by seizing each the other's girdle at his waist. Then Rostam angrily stretched out his arm to encircle his opponent's head and shoulders, but he fought like a leopard and bent him low until he was all but at the end of his strength. Swiftly then he drew a dagger from his girdle and with it cleft the chest of his bold-spirited son. Writhing, and uttering a deep sigh, his power to think of anything good or ill came to an end, and he said,

'This has come upon me through myself; Fate has set the key of me into your hand. In this you are innocent; the vault of heaven reared me and now, too soon, puts me to death. Men will speak in jest of the fewness of my years and of how this mighty frame of mine was brought low into the dust. My mother gave me tokens whereby I might know my father. Now, because of my love, my soul departs from me. I sought for him that I might see his face, and, in gaining my desire I yield up my life. Alas that my travails have profited nothing and that in spite of them I have not beheld my father's face.

'Yet, though you were now to become as a fish in the ocean, to be plunged like night into blackness, to find a place in the sky as a star, or to exclude the sun from shining on the earth's surface, my father would still exact retaliation from you for me when he perceives that the clay is my pillow. Someone among the mighty and proud will carry to Rostam the tidings that Sohrāb is slain and overthrown in ignominy, his one desire being only to find him.'

On hearing these words Rostam was thrown into dismay and the world grew dark in his eyes. When his senses returned he set about plying his adversary with questions. Sobbing and with his tears running he said,

'What tokens have you of Rostam (whose name be expunged from the scroll of the mighty!)? I am Rostam. Let my name perish and the son of Sām prostrate himself in mourning for me.'

Sohrāb answered,

'If you are indeed Rostam, you have slain me without cause in your ill nature. Now unloose the knots of my armour and behold my unclad body shining. Once, the sound of war-drums coming loudly through my door, my mother entered to me, her cheeks in-flamed with grief. Her spirit quailed at my departure and on my arm she tied a seal-ring, telling me it was a memento of my father which I must preserve and hold in sight, so that it might bring me succour in case of need. And now the time has come to bring it to effect. The battle has been fought and the son has been vanquished by his father.'

The shining sun declined from out the sky but Rostam did not return to the camp from the battlefield, so that from amongst his troops twenty alert men came forward to discover what had befallen in the arena of battle. There were the two horses standing covered with dust on the plain, but Rostam was absent. Since they failed to espy the champion in the saddle in that place of wrath, they imagined him slain and galloped back to King Kāvus with the news that the seat of greatness had been vacated by Rostam.

[When the Iranians discovered the grief-stricken Rostam, he tried to kill himself but they restrained him. To Goudarz he said,]

'Famed champion, bright spirit, bear a message from me to the king and tell him what has befallen us; how with my dagger I have pierced my son's heart. If he has any memory of my past deeds then let his heart be moved for a little on my behalf. It were fitting were he now without delay to send to me, mingled in a cup of wine, a portion of that panacea which he holds in his store for healing stricken bodies. It may be that by the virtue of his Majesty's destiny Sohrāb may recover and, like me, become a supporter of his throne.'

With the speed of wind the warrior departed and forthwith brought the message to Kāvus. His reply was,

'Whose honour is more precious to me than that of the elephant-body? Never would I desire evil to befall him; with me his esteem is of the highest. Yet, were I to grant him this remedy, the champion [Sohrāb] would remain alive and Rostam would overcome you all with his power and so doubtless would then bring me to ruin. If ill befalls me from him how could I exact condign vengeance from him? You heard how he once said, "Who is Kāvus? And if he is king, then who is Ṭus?" How can he, with that *Farr* and stature, those arms and thighs, be contained within this wide world? How could he continue to stand as vassal before my throne, and how would he conduct himself under my royal *Farr*? If his son remains alive, I have nought in my hand but dust. He that nurtures his own enemy spreads ill report about himself throughout the world.'

Goudarz, as soon as he had heard these words, returned at speed to Rostam, to whom he said,

'The king's evil nature is a bitter colocynth-tree ever in fruit. There is not his like in the world for hard-heartedness and he is no healer of others' ills. If you wish to inject light into his gloomy soul you must go to him yourself.'

[But no sooner had Rostam mounted his horse than the news reached him that Sohrāb was dead.]

VII

Siyāvosh

(i) *The story of Siyāvosh*

And now my narrator, alert of wit, compose me a tender tale, in words that shall make good sense and which the minstrel's genius may set to music.

I will continue then with a story that the Dehqān told me, one stemming from ancient legend. An aeon has passed and such tales as these have become old, but fate now restores what is old to new freshness. When a man has reckoned fifty years and eight, many a strange event has passed over his head; yet his desire for years does not diminish. And I for one seek eagerly to ascertain my destiny from almanacs and omens.

Now let us turn to the saga told me by the Dehqān and see what the sweet singer has to tell.

(ii) *The mother of Siyāvosh*

Thus speaks the man of ancient lore. It chanced one day that Ṭus, at the time when the cock begins to crow, was riding merrily with Giv and Goudarz and a company of knights out of the city gate. Their purpose was to hunt in the forest of Daghui; so, curvetting and cantering they pursued the game, catching or shooting an abundance of victims, enough to provide their victuals for forty days. In the vicinity there lived a Turk, whose land was over-spread with pavilions, and ahead of the hunters, in the distance, there appeared a forest that extended as far as the land of the Turānian knights. Into it and ahead of the rest rode Giv and Ṭus, with some brave attendants following them.

The two knights, once having penetrated into the forest, cast about for a time in search of game, and as they pressed forward they came upon a ravishing maid, towards whom, with smiling lips, they hastened. For beauty she had not her peer in the whole world; there was no detail of her loveliness in which a flaw was to be discovered. Said Ṭus, addressing her,

'Enchanting maiden, who was it guided you into this forest?'

She said,

'My father beat me yesterday night, so I forsook my land and home. In the darkness of the night he had returned in a drunken state from a wedding feast. When he saw me in the distance, in the confusion of his mind he drew a gleaming sword and would have hewn my head from my body.'

The hero [Ṭus] questioned her about her kinship and she replied recounting every detail, saying that she came of the family of Garsivaz and that her lineage ascended to [King] Faridun.

He then asked,

'How came you here, being on foot, horseless and lacking a guide?'

She said,

'My horse lingered behind, having in its exhaustion left me seated on the ground. I had money and jewels beyond counting and, on my head, a golden crown. Over there they took my led horse from me and someone beat me with the scabbard of a sword. I ran away in fear and came into this forest weeping tears of blood. When my father is restored to sobriety again he will undoubtedly send knights in search of me with speed. My mother too will come in haste. I have no desire to forsake my country or my home.'

The hearts of the two heroes warmed towards her and the head of Ṭus son of Nowzar was unsteadied. This prince said,

'I found her. That is why I galloped so fast ahead.' But Giv said,

'Commander-in-chief, surely you were together with me, and there was no escort with you.'

At that, Ṭus son of Nowzar became inflamed and said,

'How? My horse reached here first', to which the other retorted,

'I galloped ahead seeking for game. Do not utter falsehoods for the sake of a slave-girl. No man of honour seeks a quarrel.'

To so high a pitch of violence did their wrangling come that they were on the point of cutting off the girl's head. At last a nobleman intervened to say,

'Carry her to the king of Iran and obey such command as he imposes.'

When Kāvus caught sight of the maiden's face he smiled, but kept his lip within his teeth, saying to the two warriors,

'The hardships of your journey are now at an end. This is a

mountain-doe, truly a heart-ravishing gazelle; but game appro-
priate only to the highest. We will spend the day telling the story
of how certain warriors caught the sun with hunting cheetahs.'
To the girl he said,
'What is your kinship, for your face is lovely as a peri's?'
She answered,
'On my mother's side I am a princess and on my father's I am
of the stock of Faridun. My grandfather is the puissant commander
Garsivaz, whose encampment lies on the frontier there.'
He then said,
'Can one throw such a face and hair and lineage as yours to the
winds? It would be my task to set you in a palace of gold and
make you queen over my loveliest ones.'
In reply to that she said,
'I have gazed upon you and chosen you out from amongst all
the mightiest.'

(iii) *The rearing of Siyāvosh*

[In due course the girl bore a son, Siyāvosh, who was entrusted to
Rostam for training in the arts of war and peace.]

He taught him horsemanship, archery and how to wield lasso,
rein and stirrup, and what and when and how; the rites of con-
vivial society, of formal ceremony and the symposium; hawking,
falconry and how to hunt with the cheetah; what was justice or the
lack of it; what the throne and crown meant; how to deliver
orations and how to go to war and lead an army. All these arts did
Rostam teach Siyāvosh, who spent over them much labour that
afterwards bore fruit.

(iv) *Sudāba falls in love with Siyāvosh*

King Kāvus was one day seated with his son Siyāvosh, when in at
the door there entered Sudāba [the first wife of Kāvus]. She became lost in thought at beholding the young man's face, and her
heart beat fast. It was as though the fine brocade of her being had
been turned into crude fibres, or as though ice had been set close
to the fire. [Some time later] she sent an attendant secretly to him
with a message saying that if he appeared without previous warning in the women's quarters of the royal apartments it would cause

no surprise. When the messenger arrived bringing the missive it greatly disturbed the honest youth. He said,

'I am no frequenter of women's quarters. Do not ask me. I practise no deceits and impostures.'

Next morning Sudāba went with dignity into the king's presence and said,

'Your Majesty, sun and moon have never beheld a monarch like unto you nor anyone on earth equal to your son. Send him into your women's apartments to his sisters and your beloved ones. All those veiled ladies are sore at heart with love of him and the tears rain down their cheeks. We will cover him with adulation and scatter largesse before him, bringing the tree of praise into full bearing.'

'These are fitting words,' replied the king. 'You would show him the affection of a hundred mothers.'

Thereupon he summoned Siyāvosh, to whom he said,

'The blood in your veins and natural love cannot be concealed. God the Immaculate has so designed you that all who behold you conceive a love for you. God granted you noble lineage and never has anyone born of a mother had as proud birth as you. How can it fare with them who are knit to you by ties of blood that they see you only from afar? Beyond the curtain veiling off my quarters you have a sister, and Sudāba is as fond as a mother. Go then behind the curtain to look upon them who are veiled and remain there for a while, that they may give you their blessings.'

Siyāvosh cast a glance of astonishment at the king on hearing this speech. He remained for a while communing with himself and endeavouring to wash the dust [of suspicion] from his heart. He imagined that his father sought to elucidate what he had in mind, for he was a man who had been acquainted with many things, of easy speech, sagacious, shrewd and of a nature given to doubting. He said to himself,

'This thing is wicked, and it is through Sudāba that this suggestion has been made. If I go into his women's apartments, I shall suffer scandal in abundance because of Sudāba.' His answer therefore was,

'Your Majesty has granted me power of command as well as a throne and a diadem, so that it is as when the exalted sun on rising endows the earth with a thing of value. No king who has ever worn a crown is your equal for virtue or knowledge, for justice or beneficence. Direct me to them that are possessed of

wisdom, to noble and experienced counsellors, or else to men who
wield the mace, the battle-axe, arrows or lasso; or else let me go
feasting, playing music or wine-bibbing. What shall I learn in the
inner apartments of your Majesty? How can women guide me to
knowledge? Yet, if it be your Majety's command, I can be granted
leave to proceed there hereafter.'

'Well spoken, my son,' exclaimed the king. 'May you ever be
the foundation of wisdom. I have rarely heard words of such
excellence; let your spirit swell at such praise. Harbour no ill
suspicion in your mind; prepare for happiness and cleanse away
all anxiety. Go then and see the children for a little while; they
will derive pleasure from it.'

[Siyāvosh answered that he would go on the morrow.]

(v) *Siyāvosh visits Sudāba*

Now there was a certain man named Hirbad, whose heart and
breast and mind were filled with evil. It was his duty to ensure
that none entered the women's apartments, for it was he who held
the key to the inner quarters. To this person the king said,

'When the sun brings its sword out of hiding, go you discreetly
to Siyāvosh and see you carry out what he commands. Tell Sudāba
also that she must strew the path before him with largesse of
precious stones and sweet perfumes, the slaves at the same moment
scattering emeralds and saffron.'

[Siyāvosh then set out with Hirbad.]

As Hirbad lifted the curtain from the door, Siyāvosh had fears
of some mischief. The harem occupants all approached in a body,
gaily arrayed, the house from end to end being covered with
musk and gold coins and filled with saffron. Silver coins were
poured in his path and mingled together with rubies and emeralds.
Chinese brocade covered the floor and the surface of the ground
was strewn with pearls of purest lustre. Everywhere to be found
were wine, music and minstrels' songs, and each lady of the harem
wore a diadem on her head. The whole apartment was a Paradise
richly dight, with lovely women and precious objects in abundance.

As Siyāvosh entered, he beheld a throne of shining gold inlaid
with emeralds, over it being laid a cover of brocade. Upon the
throne sat the resplendent Sudāba, angel-like, all endowed with
the fragrance of beauty, and as Siyāvosh approached from behind

the curtain she descended gracefully, with all dignity stepped towards him and greeted him. Then she took him in her arms in a long embrace and said,

'Glory be to God a hundredfold. I will give praise to Him every day and night in all three watches. Surely no person has a son to equal you, and the king himself has no other such kinsman.'

Siyāvosh perceived the nature of her love and understood that the affection she displayed had no element of purity in it. Quickly he strode towards his sisters, since in the place where he stood the behaviour was unseemly.

[While he went apart, Sudāba contrived with the Shah that Siyāvosh should visit the harem again, her pretext being that she wished him to marry her daughter. At his next visit she says to him,]

'I wish to give you my daughter. But [first] look upon my face and head and crown. What reasons have you for turning away from love of me, from my person and charms. Since I gazed upon you I have been as one dead, have wept and raged and been in torment. Make me happy secretly; grant me but one day of your youth and I will adorn you with crown, throne and diadem far more precious than the world-possessing Shah has given you. But if you turn away from my desire and your heart will not consent to solace me, then I will bring your princedom down in ruin, so that sun and moon will grow dark before your eyes.'

'Never will I throw my head to the winds for the sake of my heart,' replied Siyāvosh. 'How could I behave so disloyally towards my father and break with all honour and sense? You are the king's wife and the sun of his palace; it ill becomes you to be guilty of sin such as this.'

In anger and spitefulness she arose from her throne and seized him in her embrace, saying,

'I told you the secret of my heart, while you concealed your evil thoughts. In vain you think to disgrace me and pretend before the wise that I am a trivial person.'

Stretching out her hands she tore her garments and with her fingernails slashed her cheeks. Turmoil broke out in the apartment and the rumour of it issued from the palace into the open street. From hall and portico a clamour arose and it was as though the Night of Resurrection had arrived. Its echo, reaching the monarch's ears, caused him to descend from his royal throne and in bewilderment to stride towards his sleeping-quarters. As he entered he beheld Sudāba with her face scarred and heard how the place resounded with clamorous voices. This one and that he questioned and was troubled at their replies, for he suspected nothing of the wiles of stony-hearted Sudāba. She came towards him wailing aloud, weeping abundant tears and tearing her hair. Then she said,

'Siyāvosh came up on to the dais, stretched out his hand against me and embraced me savagely, although body and soul I am filled with love for you.'

The king was weighed down with thought at the words and probed deeply into every side. To himself he said,

'If this woman speaks the truth, pursuing no evil ambition in this conduct, then must the head of Siyāvosh be lopped off; that alone is the key to the undoing of this wickedness.'

He dismissed all who were in the harem and, remaining there alone, he summoned Siyāvosh and Sudāba before him. Sagely and with prudence he said to Siyāvosh,

'It is your duty not to conceal the inward truth of this from me. It was not you who brought about this evil; it was I. By my foolish talk I have harmed myself. Why did I invite you into the women's quarters? Now there comes sorrow to me, and to you come deceit and imposture. Look only to the truth. Show me your face and tell me how the matter went.'

Siyāvosh repeated the course of events and told the cause of Sudāba's being stirred to anger.

'That is not the truth,' exclaimed Sudāba. 'Of all the women here he chose out none but me. I told him what the King of the World desired to give him; I explained the inwardness and outwardness of it all, telling him what I would add to it and the goodly things I would give to my daughter. He replied that he had no concern with wealth and no desire to see my daughter. He said that I alone was needful to him there and that without me no treasure and no person was of value to him. He wished to make me yield by force to his passion, and seized me with hands as hard as rock. I did not obey his behest and he therefore tore my hair and my face was cut. Lord of the World, I have within my body a child of your seed and, because of my suffering, it was near to being killed. The whole world became straitened and dark to me.'

To himself the monarch said,

'This is no time for haste. Anxiety but wrests wisdom astray.

I must consider which of these two is to blame and deserving of punishment for wickedness.'

With that end in view he began to seek about. He smelt the hand of Siyāvosh, his breast and arms, his head and body. In Sudāba the king perceived the odour of wine and musk and the scent of rose-water. That smell he did not find on Siyāvosh and discovered no sign that he had touched her. The king was troubled and the worth of Sudāba was lowered in his eyes. But Siyāvosh was innocent of the evil act, and the king acknowledged his virtue.

(vi) *Sudāba hatches a plot*

Sudāba swiftly perceived that she had fallen low and that the king's heart was no longer attached to her. She therefore cast about for means whereby she might extricate herself from her difficulty and plant anew the tree of vengeance. Behind the veil with her there lived a woman who was abundant in devices and stratagems, in spells and incantations. This woman was heavy with child and because of her burden her life passed unhappily. Sudāba took the woman into her confidence, first requiring of her an oath of secrecy, and asked for a scheme.

'Concoct some potion,' said she, 'that will cause you to miscarry and leave you empty. I will tell Kāvus that the child was mine, thus slain by the devil's hand, and it may be that it will suffice against Siyāvosh. Now see how you may bring this about.'

The woman replied,

'I am your slave; I bow my head to your command and counsel.'

When the night became dark the woman drank a medicament, and her devil-begotten progeny fell from her. It was composed of two identical demon-conceived twins, for what else could hap when a witch brings forth? Sudāba brought out a golden tray, and, not telling her attendant what was afoot, she placed upon it the devil-begotten pair. The mother she concealed and then laid herself down. Soon from under her bed-coverings cries were to be heard in the palace and the servants present in the hall swiftly made their way to Sudāba. There they saw the two babes dead on the tray, while the women's wailings rose above the palace as high as Saturn.

Kāvus was aroused from his sleep by the clamour that issued from the hall, and tremblingly he opened his ears and inquired what was amiss. They told him what mischance had befallen his beautiful wife and he was smitten with grief, so that for him the night passed without a moment's slumber. At dawn he arose and came gloomily to where he saw Sudāba lying, the harem being all in turmoil and the two babes laid piteously on the golden tray. Sudāba poured forth tears from her eyes.

'Behold all in clear sunshine,' she exclaimed. 'I told you what wickedness he had performed, yet it was his word that you so rashly believed.'

The heart of Kāvus felt deep suspicion and he remained long in thought after his departure, wondering what expedient he could employ, for this was a matter not to be considered lightly.

(vii) *Kāvus inquires into the affair of the children*

King Kāvus then looked for men who observed the stars, and in friendly manner he summoned them into his presence. He inquired how they did and seated them on golden chairs, the talk being concerned with Sudāba and the struggle with Hāmāvarān [her father]. The purpose was that they might be informed of the question affecting her and with full knowledge understand her behaviour. Much he said of the two babes, bringing the secret into light. Thereupon they took out their almanacs and astrolabes and for a whole week pondered the matter. At last they said,

'How could wine ever be poured into a cup that has once been filled with poison? These two children are the offspring of a person not the Shah, nor are they the offspring of this mother. Had they been of royal origin, that would easily have been revealed by these almanacs. But the secret that lies behind all this is not patent either in the heavens now nor in the earth. It is a strange thing which you must realize.'

They described the features of the ill-designing and sinful woman to the king and the assembled company, Sudāba meanwhile with tears demanding justice and appealing to the king himself for aid. She had, she declared, been his helpmate when he lay wounded and when he had been cast from the throne.

'My heart has been tormented because of my murdered children,' she said, 'so that there are times when my mind parts company with my body.'

He exclaimed,

'Woman, be still. Why utter words which cannot be accepted?'

All the palace guards were commanded to issue forth and traverse every town and every desert until they brought the evil-working woman into the light. They found a clue not far away, and men of experience hastened to the spot, whence they dragged the ill-starred woman on to the road and brought her ignominiously before the Shah. He questioned her in gentle mode and nurtured her with hopes and for many days fed her with promises. But she confessed nothing that was pertinent; the illustrious king remained outside her confidence. Then they bore her out of the Shah's presence and spoke to her of the sword, the gallows and the pit. But the witch replied,

'I am innocent. What shall I say in this glorious presence?'

This they reported to the Shah, adding that God alone knew what lay behind it all.

[Sudāba herself on being summoned protested that the real truth was being concealed through fear of Siyāvosh and his influence. After she was dismissed, wise ministers were summoned and they advised a trial by ordeal for the discovery of the truth. They said,]

'Since the cause between these two has reached the present pass, then one of them must needs go through the fire; it being the command of high Heaven that no harm shall befall the innocent party.'

The world-possessor thereupon summoned Sudāba into his presence and gave her a place beside Siyāvosh in order that he could engage them both in conversation. Finally he declared that there would be no certainty in his mind concerning them nor clarity in his spirit until fierce fire had revealed the one guilty of the offence, who would then swiftly be disgraced. Sudāba's reply to this was,

'I miscarried the king's two children. What greater offence could there be than that? Siyāvosh must set matters right, for he it was that committed the foul deed and brought about the calamity.'

Turning to his young son the king of the world asked,

'To what conclusion does your thinking over this matter lead?'

He said in reply,

'In an affair like this, Hell itself would be a trivial thing to me. Even were it a mountain of fire I would pass through it. It would be contemptible could I not clear myself of this disgrace.'

(viii) *Siyāvosh passes through the fire*

Oppressed was the spirit of King Kāvus by reason of his son and the ill-starred Sudāba. If either of these two was guilty, who hereafter would acknowledge him to be a ruler? His son and his wife were as blood and marrow to him; to whom could this matter be of profit? He now gave command to his minister that the chief cameleer should bring in from the open country a hundred caravans of racing camels, of the red-haired kind, all laden with wood. They piled this into two lofty mounds, in size beyond compute, so that it was visible at a distance of two leagues, and men said, 'This is the means by which the key to this crime is to be found,' for they were eager to discover the essence of the truth and where in this matter the crookedness and deception lay. 'When this story is heard from first to last,' they said, 'one sees it is best not to put one's trust in women. Never seek any woman in the world but one who is truly pious. A sinful woman brings you dishonour.'

In the open the wood lay piled in two mounds and the whole world clustered about them to see the spectacle. The illustrious king commanded that black naphtha should be poured over the fuel and then two hundred men came to kindle the blaze and fan it. You would have said that night had turned to day.

Now to his father came Siyāvosh, a golden casque set upon his head, alert, clad in white, with a smile upon his lips and his heart filled with confidence. He was mounted on a black charger, the dust from whose hooves reached high as the moon, and, as was the practice in the rites of burial, he had sprinkled himself with camphor. When he was close to the king, he dismounted from his steed and did homage to his father, to whom he said,

'Do not grieve. Fortune's wheel has turned in this fashion. If any head is filled with shame and thoughts of destruction, it is mine; if I am guiltless, deliverance will be mine; but if I have any guilt in this thing the Creator will have no regard for me. By grace of God, giver of all good, I will receive no scorch from this mountain of wood.'

As he approached the fire, Siyāvosh prayed to God the Almighty saying,

'Suffer me to pass through this fire and relieve my person from my father's reproach.'

Having uttered this petition he put spurs to his black horse and

swiftly rode in. A shout arose from plain and city, and anxiety fell
on the whole world as he did so. But he thrust his black steed
onward as though he were in league with the fire, despite the
flames that leapt upwards as though to make Siyāvosh and his
horse vanish from sight. The whole plain became a sea of blood-
washed eyes staring to see if he would emerge from the flames.
As they caught sight of him, the roar went up, 'The young prince
has come out of the fire!'

[King Kāvus, now convinced of his son's innocence, called
Sudāba before him to hear a denunciation of her wickedness. He
spared her life, however, at the instance of Siyāvosh, and after an
interval restored her to favour despite her persistent malevolence.]

(ix) *Kāvus receives tidings of the arrival of the Turk Afrāsiyāb*

The king of the world was engrossed in love-making when he
heard a report from his men of affairs that Afrāsiyāb was close at
hand with a hundred thousand horsemen of the Turks. His heart
was clutched tight as his thoughts turned from festivity to warfare. He called for an assembly of the Iranians well disposed towards their rulers and to them he said,

'Afrāsiyāb could surely not have been compounded by God out
of the elements of air, fire, earth and water; rather must the sky
have moulded him out of different clay. After he has sworn so
many oaths of loyalty and given so many smooth-tongued
pledges, he gathers war-thirsty men about him and turns aside from
his covenants and oaths. I must go and endeavour to be avenged
upon him, transforming his bright day into blackness and causing
his name to perish from off the earth. Else, swift as an arrow from
the bow, he will without warning muster his troops and attack
Iran, so as to bring desolation on this land and countryside.'

To him a counsellor said,

'Your army is vast. Why go out to the battlefield yourself? Why
throw money to the winds or open the doors of your treasury
wide? Twice have you renounced your illustrious throne to your
enemy over-hastily. Now choose out a number of doughty
warriors who are strong in battle and able to avenge us.'

He answered,

'I see none in this array with the ability and power to confront
Afrāsiyāb. I must launch myself swiftly as a boat on water. You

yourself return home until I have concerted my plans with my advisers.'

Siyāvosh at these occurrences had become pensive and his spirits were as entangled with thought as a forest. He said to himself,

'I will prepare for this war. I will speak smooth words and request the king to let me go. It may be that God will grant me release from Sudāba and my father's discussions [concerning her]. Moreover, I may win fame for myself by inveigling an army of that size into a trap.'

[Siyāvosh is in fact given leave to do as he wishes. With Rostam as his guardian and lieutenant, and under the protection of the Kāviāni Banner, he marches out against the forces of Turān. Meanwhile, the Turānian king, Afrāsiyāb, has a dream of evil omen which causes him to delay his advance against Iran, whom he attempts to placate with gifts of precious metals and jewels. 'If I stitch up the eye of destiny with treasure, the sky should not keep me in travail,' he says.]

(x) *The dream of Afrāsiyāb*

When a part of a dark night had passed, as occurs when a man is shuddering with fever, a cry came from Afrāsiyāb, who lay trembling on his bed of ease and sleep. Swiftly his attendants were aroused and everywhere agitation was seen. News was brought to Garsivaz that the royal spirits were stirred to gloom, and at speed he hastened to the palace of the king, whom he saw lying on the ground in his path. He took him to his breast and questioned him, saying, 'Tell me, your brother, what has occurred.' The king replied, 'Do not question me. Speak no word to me now or until I find my wits again, but take me in your arms and hold me close for a while.'

A short time passed. As he returned to sober sense he saw the world filled with weeping and turmoil. Candles were set up and he ascended his throne still continuing to shake like a twig on a tree. Garsivaz, that seeker after fame, begged him to open his lips and reveal what this strange event had been. The puissant Afrāsiyāb replied,

'May no man else ever behold in a dream the vision I saw in the blackness of the night. Never have I heard the like either from old or young. In my dream I saw a desert covered with serpents, the

earth being shrouded with dust and the heavens obscured by
eagles. The earth was desiccated, an arid waste to which you
would have said that the sky had never shown its countenance
since the world came into existence. On its margin my pavilion
was pitched, and about it was stationed a guard of doughty
warriors.

'A storm-wind laden with dust arose and cast my banner headlong, while on every hand a torrent of blood began to flow.
Pavilion and camp were flattened down and, of my guard, a
countless number lay with heads severed and bodies prostrate.
An army from Iran it was, coming up like a heavy storm, part
bearing spears and others bows and arrows. Every spear bore
a skull aloft and every horseman had a skull in his embrace. They
rode full charge at my throne, a hundred thousand men, clad in
black and brandishing spears. They thrust me from the place in
which I sat and galloped over me, my hands fettered.

'I gazed about me hard on every side. Of those who were constantly in my presence there remained not one. A notable champion of proud bearing took me swiftly into the presence of
Kāvus. A throne stood there whose top reached almost to the
moon, and on it was seated the warrior king Kāvus. At his side
sat a youth whose two cheeks were lovely as the moon, his years
no more than twice seven. When he saw me held captive before
him he roared like a thunder-cloud, then slashed at my middle
with his sword. At the pain I shrieked aloud and my cries
awakened me.'

To the king Garsivaz said,

'This dream of your Majesty's can have nothing but a favourable import. All shall be according to the desires of your heart and
in support of your crown and throne, while the fortunes of your
enemy are entirely in reverse. For the interpretation of the dream
there is required someone who is deeply versed in this science.
Let us summon alert-witted priests who know the stars, as well as
sages familiar with the knowledge of such philosophy, whether
they be far afield or at your Majesty's gate.'

All such men were assembled at the king's gate, where they
wondered about the reason for his requiring them. He invited
them to enter and, having seated them before him, unfolded the
matter to them in its fullness. Thus he spoke to these noted
priests, astrologers and savants,

'This dream and these words of mine are something that must

not be heard by any person, whether openly or in secret. Should any one of you breathe a word of it, I will not leave his head and body together.'

Yet he gave them gifts beyond measure of gold and silver that they might not linger in fear of him, and proceeded to tell them what he had seen in his dream. The chief priest, when he had heard what the Shah had to tell, was seized with dread and begged assurance for his life. He said,

'We dare not tell the truth concerning this dream unless the king grants his slave a promise and gives his tongue in pledge for our reply, which is to the effect that we shall disclose to his Majesty all that we have in mind concerning this matter and that we shall be treated with justice.'

The king gave his word that he would grant them security and would not take amiss anything unpleasing to him which they might say. Their spokesman was a person of keen understanding who opened his discourse in delicate words, saying,

'O king of the world, I will reveal to you, now that you are awake, what has been concealed. A heavy force is on the way from Iran with bold commanders. In the forefront is a prince, with whom are many astute counsellors, and the equal of whose ascendant star no king possesses. He will bring desolation on our soil and land. If your Majesty makes war on Siyāvosh, the face of the earth will become as a piece of red satin [with gore] and no single Turk will survive. The king will fall into distress because of the war; and yet if Siyāvosh is slain by the king's hand there will be left in Turān neither head nor throne. The whole land will be invested with turmoil because of Siyāvosh, because of strife and vengefulness. You will then call to mind the truth which I have uttered, namely that the land will become a waste through lack of people. Even if the lord of the world should become a winged fowl, he can find no way of escape through this revolving wheel.'

When the sky had turned half its course and the glowing sun revealed its face, the nobles came to the palace of Afrāsiyāb as servitors, wearing helmets. From amongst them he formed a council of wise men of alert mind, well tried in affairs, and to them he said,

'From destiny I experience nought but strife. Many a famed hero belonging to the Iranians has been destroyed by me in war, many a castle has become a residence for the sick, many a garden a wilderness of thorns and many an orchard has been my battle-ground, everywhere bearing the marks of my army. Because of the tyranny of the Iranian king all good disappears into hiding; the wild ass does not bring forth at its due season, the eye of the young falcon is blinded, wild creatures stem the flow of milk to their breasts, water in the springs turns to pitch or dries up in the wells everywhere, the musk lacks perfume in its pod. Because of crookedness honesty flees away and in every directions deceit flaunts itself. My heart is sated with war and evil; I wish to seek the path of God, to restore wisdom and justice and bring comfort in place of grief and suffering. Let the world have peace from us for a season; it is not meet that death should befall us before its time. Two parts of the world are under my foot, for my dwelling is in Iran and Turān. If you agree with me, I will send a message to Rostam and knock on the door which leads to peace with Siyāvosh. In addition I will send them a gift of aught you desire.'

[The nobles and counsellors agreed with Afrāsiyāb's proposals, but suspicion of the peace overtures caused Rostam to hesitate. Siyāvosh, however, accepted them and sent Rostam to King Kāvus with a report of the successful end to the negotiations. But the king would not consent to peace. Addressing Rostam, he said,]

'I look upon him [Siyāvosh] as a youth whom no evil has ever befallen. But are you not a man with experience of the world who has seen good and ill of every kind? Have you not beheld the wrongs committed by Afrāsiyāb which have brought annihilation to our sustenance, tranquillity and sleep? He has flattered your soul with despicable gifts, goods wrung by himself from innocent people. That is how he turned your head aside from the right path, giving you as hostages a hundred miserable low-born Turks who did not know their fathers' names. For those hostages he cares as little as for the water that has flowed by in the river.

'I myself am not wearied of the hardships of war, even if you refuse to set your wits to work. I am about to send to Siyāvosh, who is possessed of some wisdom and astuteness, a message commanding him to light a vast fire and to place heavy fetters on the legs of those Turks. On to the fire he is to throw all those gifts, not retaining a single object. The captives he is to send to me; I will sever their heads from their bodies. He is then to go to Afrāsiyāb's court considering nothing but war.'

[Rostam tries to dissuade Kāvus from this course, declaring it would mean that Siyāvosh would act dishonourably in breaking faith with Afrāsiyāb. A quarrel breaks out, Rostam is exiled to the distant province of Sistān and Siyāvosh goes over to the camp of Afrāsiyāb. Relationships between the Turānian king and the Iranian prince remain friendly for a while. Siyāvosh marries the king's daughter Farangis and on one occasion is able to display his prowess to him in a game of polo.]

(xi) *Siyāvosh displays his skill before Afrāsiyāb*

One night the king said to Siyāvosh,

'Let us be ready at dawn tomorrow to go out into the open country with ball and mallet, so that we can canter about for a while and entertain ourselves. I have heard from all quarters that on the meydān [open square] no warrior can see your mallet [for speed].'

When the night had passed, the warriors went out on to the square with cavorting and laughter. Said the king of Turān to the prince,

'Let us choose our team-mates for a game of polo. You remain on this side while I take the other, the company being thus divided into two teams.'

'Noble lord,' asked Siyāvosh, 'which of these will venture out for the ball? These are your Majesty's escort, whereas I am alone, the only one possessed of an [effective] mallet. If your Majesty will grant leave I will bring horsemen from Iran on to the field, and they will be my mates in playing the game in an appropriate manner on both sides.'

The great general listened to his proposal and concurred with it, whereupon Siyāvosh chose out seven Iranians fitted to take part in the contest. The sound of kettle-drums spread about the ground, from which the dust arose as high as the sky. You would have said that with the clash of the cymbals and the blare of the trumpets the whole area moved from its place. The commander made the first stroke on the meydān, hitting the ball magnificently high so that it rose into the clouds, but then Siyāvosh put spurs to his horse and, when the ball fell within reach, did not let it reach the dust. Instead, he took aim at it as it neared the ground and smote it so high that it disappeared from sight. At that the great king commanded that another ball should be brought to Siyāvosh, who placed it to his lips to the accompaniment of a salvo from the bugles and the drums.

He then mounted a fresh horse, threw the ball up out of his

hand and struck it with the mallet until it appeared to come alongside the moon. You would have said the sky had sucked it up.
Afrāsiyāb laughed aloud at the play, and, when the nobles had
recovered from their amazement, with one voice they declared that
they had never seen so notable a horseman in the saddle. The king
then told his own team that the ground and the ball were theirs
[to show what they could do]. There ensued between the two
teams a tussle so fierce that the dust rose up to the sun. This way
and that, with much talk, the ball passed from one side to the
other. Each time the Turks attacked for a goal the Iranians beat
them to the ball and frustrated the Turks. Siyāvosh was angered
and said to the Iranians in the Pahlavi tongue,

'Is this a ground where games are played, or is it a battle-field?
Give way and let the Turks take the ball for once.'

[The time comes when Garsivaz, brother of Afrāsiyāb, is driven by
jealousy of the favours accorded to Siyāvosh to incite the monarch
against the Iranian prince. He is accordingly seized and made to
suffer a cruel death. In the lengthy passage which Ferdowsi devotes
to these incidents he expresses the venom that he as a patriotic
Iranian felt for the traditional enemy of his country. The bitterness
is somewhat relieved by an account of the rescue of Farangis,
daughter of Afrāsiyāb and widow of Siyāvosh, by Pirān, chief of
the Turānian army.]

VIII

Key Khosrow

(i) The birth of Key Khosrow

One dark night, when the moon was obscured and all creatures—birds and beasts, wild and tame—were deep in slumber, the commander Pirān saw in a dream that a candle was lit by the sun and Siyāvosh, seated sword in hand on his throne, kept calling out, 'It is not fitting to be idle. Free your head from this sweet sleep and give a thought to the fate of the world. For this is a day of new dispensation and new festivity, and tonight is the night when the Shah Khosrow [Chosroes] is to be born.'

In the midst of his sweet slumber Pirān trembled and Golshahr [his daughter], her face bright as the sun, was awakened. He told her to go quietly to Farangis and tell her that he had that moment in a dream beheld Siyāvosh, more resplendent than moon and sun, saying, 'Why do you sleep so long? Do not delay, but come to the feast of the Emperor Khosrow.' Golshahr went running to the young woman and saw that she had just been delivered of a prince. At that she swiftly returned and soon the whole palace resounded with the story. Coming blithely to Pirān she said, 'Here is a new kind of sun, lying beside the moon.' The general, when he came and beheld the prince, gave thanks to God. His eyes filled with tears for [the murdered] Siyāvosh and he cursed Afrāsiyāb, saying to the assembled company of nobles,

'If my life is destroyed for these words, I will not permit the king to stretch out his hand against him, though he should throw me into the maw of the sharks.'

When the sun next displayed his sword and black night retired to rest, Pirān came in haste, being filled with mingled fear and hope, to the king [Afrāsiyāb]. He waited till the hall was cleared and then, approaching the illustrious throne, he said,

'My Lord, Peer of the Sun, Emperor, alert-minded Worker of miracles, to your felicity a new slave yesternight accrued, whose substance might be supposed to consist of honey. For beauty he has no equal in the world, for as he lies in his cradle he is the very Moon, and Tur himself restored to life would be compelled to

admire [the babe's] countenance. This boy could be declared to be
of the stamp of the hero Faridun, possessing his *Farr* and visage,
his arms and legs. Cleanse your spirit of anger, add lustre to your
crown, and let your heart be lifted up.'

The Creator gave Afrāsiyāb such enlightenment that all
thought of strife, injustice and rancour departed from him. His
soul grieved for his past conduct and a cold sigh issued from his
heart. He said to Pirān,

'The times are full of war's alarms. I learnt from my tutor that
of the seed of Tur and Key Qobād a king would appear of their
combined stocks, that the world would come to need his love
and that both in Iran and Turān men would bless him. And now
there has come about all that was predestined, so that grief,
rancour and apprehension are no longer valid. Do not retain him
in places where men congregate; rather send him to the shepherds
in the mountains, so that he may never know who I am and why
I have entrusted him to them. Let him never be given knowledge
of his birth, nor learn about what has occurred in the past.'

(ii) *The youth of Key Khosrow*

[The boy prince grew up to manhood in his wild surroundings.]

One dark night, in the period when men rest and sleep, a
messenger from Afrāsiyāb came to the famed warrior [Pirān] to
summon him, and their talk was of events that were past.
Afrāsiyāb said,

'My heart is constantly in torment through forebodings of evil
and I cannot rid myself of unhappiness. Because of the child
which has sprung from Siyāvosh you would say that daylight had
departed from my life. How could it have been in accord with my
good judgment to have this grandchild of Faridun reared by a
shepherd? If it is written [in destiny's book] that evil is to befall
me from him, it will not be averted by any precaution, since it is
divinely ordained. And even if no ill is to be foreseen, his head
should be lopped off, as was his father's.'

'Your Majesty,' replied Pirān to him, 'you stand in need of no
advisers. A young boy is like a witless person. What memory has
he of the events of the past? One reared by shepherds in the
mountains is no better than the beasts, whether tame or wild.
What knowledge has he? Only yesterday I heard from the man
who nurtures him that the boy, although having the face of a peri,

is possessed neither of reason nor sense. Concern yourself no more with him and make no effort on his behalf. What did that very sage philosopher say? "He that rears a child is more important than his begetter." And only the mother knows the truth. If your Majesty commands, I will immediately bring the dear youth to you. First rejoice me with a promise and swear a royal oath. Faridun gave assurance to the truth by [an oath on] his crown, throne and diadem; and Tur also swore by the Lord of the Universe when *Farr* and fortune were his.'

Hearing these words from Pirān, Afrāsiyāb's head was lulled into slumber. He swore a solemn and kingly oath by bright clear day and azure night, by earth and time and space, that no harm would befall the youth from him and that he would never even speak a harsh word to him. Pirān kissed the ground and said,

'Lord of equity, peerless and without equal, may wisdom ever be your guide to godliness, and may the world and time be the dust at your feet.' He then hastened away to Key Khosrow, his cheeks empurpled but with joy in his heart, and said to him,

'Put all sanity away from your mind. When he speaks of battle, answer him about wedding-feasts. Never go to him save as a man whose wits have gone astray and do not move your tongue except to talk folly. Make no least approach to sanity, so that perhaps the day will leave you unharmed.'

On Key Khosrow's head he placed a royal diadem and fastened a kingly girdle about him. Softly he called for a high-stepping horse, which the clear-visioned hero mounted and so came to the palace of Afrāsiyāb, where the whole world shed tears at sight of him. He came pressing on while men called out, 'Clear the way. Here is a new kind of hero demanding a throne.'

Then the commander Pirān brought him into the presence of the warrior king. Close to Afrāsiyāb he came, his grandfather's cheeks running with tears of shame at how he had dealt with the youth, while the commander's body trembled like an aspen-leaf, being without hope that Key Khosrow's life would be spared. But the king gazed long at the youth and, summoning his love and abandoning his cruelty, was overcome with admiration of his majestic shoulders and powerful grasp, at his gait and dignity and wisdom. He said to him,

'Young shepherd, how do you reckon the days and nights? What have you done with your flocks and how do you count your goats and your ewes?' He answered,

"There are no animals to hunt, and I have neither bow nor bowstring nor arrow.'

The king then questioned him about his tutor and about the good and ill which fortune's wheel had brought him. He replied,

'Where the leopard is, there the heart of sharp-clawed men is rent.'

Again, Afrāsiyāb put questions to him about Iran and his city and his mother and father. He answered,

'A caravan dog cannot bring down a ravening lion.'

He then answered him,

'Will you go hence to Iran? Will you go to thé king of the valiant?'

He answered,

'On mountain and plain a horseman passed me by the night before last.' The king laughed and expanded like a flower. He said gently to Key Khosrow,

'Would you not like to learn to read and write? Would you not like to get vengeance from your enemy?' He replied,

'There was no cream left on the milk. I would like to drive the shepherd off the plain.' Again the monarch laughed at what the boy said, and turning to the warrior Pirān he remarked,

'This boy's mind is deranged. When I ask him about the head he gives me an answer about the foot. Neither ill nor good will come from him. Men who pursue vengeance are not of this kind. Go and deposit him gently in his mother's care by the hand of some trustworthy man. Send him to the city of Siyāvoshgard; let no counsellor of evil touch him. Give him all that is needful of goods and money, horses, slaves and all things else.'

[Ferdowsi returns, after reciting this incident, to the main narrative concerning the long struggle between Iran and Turān. He takes up the story at the point where report comes to Iran of the death of Siyāvosh. Rostam vows vengeance. He begins by dragging Sudāba out of the women's quarters by the hair and killing her for being the first to put Siyāvosh on the path of destruction. He then musters an army of experienced warriors which was to march against Turān and bring Afrāsiyāb to his death. Panic-stricken at Rostam's approach, Afrāsiyāb retreats to his own country, and there proposes to Pirān, commander of his forces, that Key Khosrow should be killed, otherwise Rostam would carry him back to Iran. Pirān, however, counselled avoidance of bloodshed. Instead, the young prince was carried off to Khotan on the fron-

tiers of China, while Afrāsiyāb deserted his own country, his place
on the throne being taken by Rostam.

For seven years Rostam spread havoc in Turān, and then, hearing that Key Kāvus was becoming too old to direct the affairs of
Iran, he returned home. Almost immediately thereafter the hero
Gīv went secretly to Turān to find Key Khosrow and after a long
search recognized him by his *Farr* and by a certain birthmark
inherited by him from Key Qobād. With his mother Farangis the
young prince fled the country. News of this was brought by the
humiliated Pirān to the ears of Afrāsiyāb, who in a fury ordered
him to be exiled to the remote province of Khotan while he himself
went in pursuit of the fugitives.]

(iii) *Giv disputes with the toll-gatherer*

Pirān in gloom set out for Khotan while the mighty sovereign
hasted in the opposite direction. He and his noble retinue held on
towards the Oxus, in their anger dragging their skirts through
blood. To [his courtier] Humān he gave the command to race
ahead to the river-bank, for once Giv and Khosrow had crossed
the Oxus all his exertions would have been in vain.

'An augury has come,' he said, 'in what has been related to me
by truthful men, that a sage of ancient times prophesied that a
king would appear of the two-fold lineage and that he would convert the land of Turān into a thorny waste, leaving no city in all
the country undevastated. His heart would turn in love towards
Iran, whereas towards Turān he would display a countenance full
of hatred.'

Now Giv and Khosrow arrived at the stream, which they were
in great haste to cross. But they entered into a wrangle with the
collector of the tolls about which ship was available at the toll-
place, about whether there was a swift one, if its sails were new,
and whether the seating was worthy of Key Khosrow. The toll-
collector remarked to Giv,

'To flowing water it makes no matter whether a man be a slave
or a king. If you need to cross this river you must make an offer
for a ship.'

To him Giv answered,

'Ask what you wish. Give us passage, for the [Turānian] army
is close behind.'

When the toll-gatherer heard these words, he turned a sharp
visage to Giv and said,

'It is no trifling fare that I demand of you. I require from you one of these four things: I want your armour, or that black horse, or a slave-girl, or a handsome serving-youth.

'You have lost your wits,' said Giv to him. 'How can this be proper talk? If every time you took a fare it was from a king, you would have an outstanding share of this world's goods. Who are you that you make such demands of a king? Are you such a courser of the winds, you base-born wretch? Do you desire the king's mother or require the king's crown as your fare? Or else do you demand a horse like Behzād here, who can leave the wind behind in its paces? As for the fourth thing, the armour which you so impudently request, you would not even know how to unloose its fastenings. Metal of that kind is not tarnished by water, nor does fire touch it, nor lance nor Indian blade nor arrow. Yet you demand it as fare over this pond. The water is ours, though the ship is yours; the possession is ours, and yours is the toil.'

[Being unable to come to terms with the man, Key Khosrow and his mother, with Giv, thereupon braved the swollen stream on horseback. The pursuing Turānians, however, were daunted by the flood and turned back frustrated. On his arrival in Iran, Key Khosrow was acknowledged as a future king of kings by all the provincial rulers except Ţus son of Nowzar, who claimed that he was, after Rostam, the most illustrious Pahlavān (or warrior champion) in the Iranian army and that he came of the stock of Faridun, whereas Key Khosrow was descended from Afrāsiyāb the Turānian. The rival candidate put up by Ţus as claimant to the throne was Fariborz son of Key Kāvus, who declared that he would name as his heir that one of the other two princes who should succeed in storming the enemy castle of Bahman. Both made attempts, but in vain. Key Khosrow himself achieved the victory by attaching to the castle wall an imperious command, which caused it by divine intervention to collapse. Thereupon he returned in triumph, to be crowned as successor to Key Kāvus.]

(iv) *The rule of Key Khosrow*

When Key Khosrow the Shah attained to his high dignity, the whole world became aware of his history. He seated himself upon the throne of the king of kings and on his head placed the crown of sovereignty. He spread justice abroad in the world and tore out of the ground the roots of tyranny. Wherever there was a man of independent power, one possessed of a crown or born of kingly stock, whether he was the king of a province or a victorious warrior, and anyone who had achieved fame, he came to him. There was no person in the world who failed to place his head in the king's net. Where there was waste land he put it into cultivation, and he delivered the hearts of the sorrowing from their grief. He caused showers to rain down from Spring clouds and from the surface of the earth he cleansed away corrosion and sorrow. The world became a painted Paradise, full of the treasures of justice and liberality; the earth was covered with kindliness and security and the hand of Ahriman was tied so that it could work no ill.

(v) *Key Khosrow vows to Key Kāvus to take vengeance on Afrāsiyāb*

When the shining sun sharply uprose to spread its ruby light over the dark earth, the world-emperor took his place with Key Kāvus —both proud monarchs of blessed augury. With them were the valorous Rostam and also Dastān. Key Kāvus spoke of matters great and small, of which the first was the subject of Afrāsiyāb; and as he spoke his cheeks were moist with the blood-stained tears shed by his eyes. He told how Afrāsiyāb had behaved against Siyāvosh and what great stretches of Iran he had laid waste. Many had been the champion warriors who had been slain and numberless the women and little children made to suffer.

'Many are the cities of Iran which you see to be in ruins, laid waste by the rancour of Afrāsiyāb. You [Khosrow] have all the divine qualities required, such as stature, knowledge and strength of arm. You have the royal *Farr* and, as well, a fortunate star. In every essential you are above all other kings. And now I require an oath from you, one from which you will not diverge in any particular. Swear that you will endue your heart with hatred of Afrāsiyāb, never quenching the breath of your fire in water; that you will disregard your mother's kinship with him; that you will not be led astray because of it nor hearken to any word spoken in his favour; that you will not be beguiled by treasures or money, whether height or depth presents itself before you. Swear by your battle-axe and sword, by your throne and crown and promised word that you will not go aside from the road in his company.

'I speak to you of the foundations for your oath and of what will convince your understanding and your spirit. O King, swear

by the Lord of the sun and moon, by crown and throne, by seal
and diadem, by the memory of Faridun, by our law and custom,
by the blood of Siyāvosh and by your life, by your *Farr* and
felicitious star, that you will not turn aside to evil courses, that
you will seek no arbiter but sword and battle-axe and that out of
your mighty stature you will maintain a greatness of spirit.'

On hearing these words, the young prince turned his countenance and spirit towards the Fire. He swore an oath by the all-
possessing Lord, by white day and azure night, by sun and moon,
by throne and crown, by seal and sword and royal diadem, that
he would never turn with favour to Afrāsiyāb and would not,
even in a dream, look upon his face. They wrote a script [of it]
in Pahlavi in black ink on royal parchment, and it was witnessed
by Dastān and Rostam and also by the men of the highest rank in
the army. For security this sworn document and sealed demand
for justice was placed in the hands of Rostam.

Then trays of food were called for and the nobles formed themselves into an assembly of a different nature. For a week they
lingered over music and wine in the palace of King Kāvus. On the
eighth day the monarch laved his head and body, took repose and
then repaired to the temple, where he stood before the Lord of the
revolving heavens and poured out his adoration in worship.
Throughout the darkness of the night and until the sun arose he
remained imploring God with tears in his eyes.

[Key Khosrow then set before his warriors his scheme for attack-
ing Afrāsiyāb and obtained their consent to it.]

(vi) *Key Khosrow distributes treasure to the warriors*

To that open space on the encampment where the horses were
allowed to wander freely, the herdsmen brought their troops of
horses. Each man who wielded a lasso or was brazen-bodied in
war was commanded by the king to cast his rope over the Arab
steeds and seize their heads in a noose. Afterwards the conquering
world-possessor placed himself mace in hand on a golden throne,
threw open the door of his treasure-house stored with gold and
said,

'The riches of the proud should not be left hidden. When strife
appears and the ardours of war, then stores and money sink to
nought in men's sight. Every man shall by us be endowed with
goods and a throne and the fruits of our trees shall be piled high

as the sun. Why waste one's life over gold at a time when treasure may be put to good use by men?'

He caused a hundred robes of Greek brocade to be fetched, entirely jewelled and with gold for background. Others to the like number were of silk and of the finest weave. A beaker filled with precious stones was then placed before the great Shah, who addressed his troops as follows,

'This valuable prize is for the valueless head of Palāshān, the vile male dragon whom Afrāsiyāb calls Champion Warrior, through whose watchfulness he himself is enabled to lay his head down in sleep. On the day of battle who will bring that head, with his sword and horse, fast as blown dust to our camp?'

Swiftly Bizhan son of Giv leapt to his feet and declared himself ready to slay the dragon. He claimed the robes and the golden beaker with its varied precious stones, heaped blessings on the Emperor and prayed that his crowned head might exist for ever, and then returned to where he had been seated, holding in his hand the beaker full of jewels.

The sovereign now commanded the treasurer to bring two hundred pieces of cloth of gold, gauzes also, and brocades and silks, and two rosy-cheeked slaves with waists begirdled for service. He said,

'All these I will present as a gift—declaring myself ever indebted—to the man who will lay before me, or before this venerable assembly, the crown of Tazhāv. It is one which Afrāsiyāb put on his head when he named him as his daughter's husband, declaring him a man born under a lucky star.'

There again the same Bizhan son of Giv sprang up, his arm being mighty in battle, and claimed the slaves and other gifts, while the assembly were left in amaze. He called down blessings on the king and resumed his place with happy countenance. Then Key Khosrow bade the treasurer bring out ten slaves begirdled for service, ten proud-stepping horses with golden bridles, and ten veiled maidens richly bedight.

'All these horses and pretty girls,' said the alert-minded Shah, 'are for [him who shall act] when Tazhāv swerves, since that lion-heart probably has no great courage. On the day of battle he is squired by a page-girl whose voice tames the leopard. In face she is pretty as the Spring and in figure she is like the cypress; her waist is a reed and her gait graceful as a pheasant's. He that finds her must not touch her with the sword, for such a one as she must be spared from that, but let him take her with a loop of the lasso and lift her [from her horse] in such fashion that she falls on his bosom.'

For that prize too Bizhan touched his breast with his hand and came forwards towards the all-conquering Shah.

[Once more the king called for rich articles from his treasury and said,]

'This gift is for him who will grudge no effort to secure fame and wealth, will go from here to the Kāsa river and bless the spirit of Siyāvosh. At the river he will see a mountain of wood, in height exceeding ten lassos' length, which Afrāsiyāb piled up at the time of crossing the river. His desire was that no other person should tread that road and that none should pass from Iran into Turān. Some man of valour must go from here and set fire to that pile by the Kāsa river, so that if ever there is a battlefield there the army may not be barred by that timber.'

And Giv said,

'That is my prey. Burning the mountain shall be my task. If an enemy shows himself I will not shirk a battle, and in the fray I will invite the vultures to a feast.'

The king said,

'This [further] gift is designated for the man whose pure spirit is ruled by sagacity. He must be bold, far-sighted and eloquent, and in battle will not flinch from a lion. He shall carry a message to Afrāsiyāb, in fear of whom no tear shall come to his eyes, and he shall convey to me what he says in reply.'

It was Gorgin son of Milād then who stretched out his hand, declaring himself ready to set out on the journey.

(vii) *Key Khosrow sends Rostam to Hindustan*

When the mountains turned to red orpiment in the daylight and the crow of the cock rose high to the clouds, Rostam presented himself before the Shah and discoursed of Iran, the crown and lofty rank, and they took counsel together on matters great and small. Said Rostam to the Shah of the world,

'In Zābolestān [Sistān] there was once a province, part of whose territory was held by Tur. Manuchehr cleared it of Turks, and it was a beautiful and pleasant country. When Kāvus lost his mind and became senescent so that fame and *Farr* and power departed from him, the Turānians seized the land and no Iranian remained there. Now the people pay tribute and impost to Turān, without any regard for Iran's king. An abundance of elephants and treasures is to be found in the land, yet the innocent inhabitants suffer tyranny. Because of the constant raids and killings and harassment they are ready to raise their heads in opposition to the winds of Turān. At this moment in Iran the sovereignty is yours, all of it from ant's foot to lion's claw, and there is need for a great army to be dispatched [to Turān] under a doughty warrior. If the inhabitants will offer tribute to the Shah, all is well; otherwise let their heads be brought to this court. When we have got possession of that province we can conquer the whole land of Turān.'

The Shah's answer to Rostam was,

'May you live for ever! That is our plan. Consider how large an army we require for the task; choose out the most notable of our warriors. A territory which shall be adjoined to your land is one that accords well with your deserts. To Farāmarz [son of Rostam] give a strong force consisting of valiant men of war and let the battle be opened by his hand; let the hook that catches in the shark's jaw be his.'

The face of the warrior brightened and he abundantly blessed the Shah, who then bade his court chamberlain to bring in platters with food. Wine too he brought and summoned minstrels, at whose voices all remained lost in admiration. When the gleaming sun appeared above the mountains and the minstrels had become wearied with their recitals, the roll of drums was to be heard at the king's gate and the troops were drawn up about the palace. A brazen drum was then bound on to an elephant and the sound of trumpets blared out. On the back of another elephant a throne was affixed and the royal scion now began to bear fruit; that is, the Shah advanced and seated himself having first placed on his head a jewelled diadem. A regal collar studded with jewels was about his neck and in his hand he held a bull-headed mace, while from his ears hung two rings enriched with pearls and jacinths. On each arm was a bracelet of jacinth and gold, and his girdle was made up of fine pearls, gold and emeralds.

The [king's] elephant advanced in the midst of the army, with golden bells and cymbals upon it. A pebble was flung into the bowl in the Shah's hand and at once the huzzaing of the troops rose high as Saturn. [It was a signal for] a pavilion to be brought out from the palace on to the open plain, and, at the loud acclaim, the very heavens were stunned.

[All the great warriors then passed before the king in review, each accompanied by a standard representing some creature from the animal world.]

(viii) *Ṭus marches on Turkestān*

The sun displayed his full greatness, sate on the throne in his rightful place, overwhelming the Sign of the Ram, so that the world from end to end assumed the colour of yellow wine. Then it was that from the portals of Ṭus there arose the sound of trumpets and the roll of drums. A tumult was let loose throughout the province, the air became saturated with clamour and the earth was moved to trembling. Because of the tramp of horses and the shouting of the soldiery the moon was made to stray from its heavenly course, and from the clash of weapons and the trumpeting of elephants you would have said the earth was being overrun by the Nile flood. The flash of the Kāviāni Banner and the wheeling of the Goudarzi knights with the Kāviāni Star amongst them caused the air to appear red, yellow, blue and violet.

When the troops were assembled about the king, having proudly marched in with their banners and helmets, he commanded the general-in-chief to lead the most notable of the warriors into his presence. To them he said,

'Ṭus is commander and leader of the army. He holds the Kāviāni Star and you must therefore be ready to obey his orders.'

Before the whole army he accorded him a seal, declaring him Chief and Pathfinder. Addressing him then he said,

'Do not forsake your loyalty to me, but observe my law and my behest. On the march let harm come to none—that is the law of throne and diadem—be he cultivator of the land or craftsman or anyone else who strives not against you in this war. Let no cold wind blow upon him, and attack none but your opponents. Inflict no suffering on any that are innocent, for this fleeting world abides for no one. Also do not go by way of Kalāt. If you do, you would have broken your promise. May the soul of Siyāvosh be radiant as the sun; let him enjoy a place of hope in that other world. He had a son born of a daughter of Pirān who could hardly be distinguished from his father. My brother also resembled me, being young, of like age with myself and of happy disposition. He lives in Kalāt now with his mother and his army. He knows the name of no man in Iran. You must keep away from his direction [at Kalāt], for he has an army and men renowned in war, and there

lies a mountain difficult and steep in his way. Instead proceed
by way of the desert. It is not easy to pluck out the lion's claws.'
Ṭus then addressed the monarch and said,
'Fate cannot disregard your counsel. I will go by the path which
you advise, for nothing but good can come of your behest.'
Quickly then the commander set out, while the Shah returned
to his palace accompanied by his well-wisher Rostam. With him
he held a council at which there were also present warriors and
priests and Khosrow of the pure body. Much he discoursed of
Afrāsiyāb, of his own sufferings and the torment undergone by his
father.

As for Ṭus and the army with him, they marched on until they
were confronted by two roads, one of them leading to the desert,
arid and lacking all moisture, and the other towards Kalāt and the
direction of Jaram. The elephants with the drums halted until Ṭus
the commander should arrive and decide which of the two roads
he preferred and whither he would order the army to go. When
Ṭus with easy pace came up with the leaders he spoke of the road,
which was waterless and hot. He said to Goudarz,
'If we press on swiftly and for the length of the whole day
across this arid waste, even though its sand produced ambergris
and its soil were musk, we shall require water and rest. Better
therefore that we should aim at Kalāt and Jaram, making a halt at
Mayam. There there is cultivated land to right and left; why
should we make choice of the desert and of travail for ourselves?
Occasion arising, I once journeyed that road, Gazhdaham being
the guide for our army, and I saw none of the hardships of a long
journey, save that there was an abundance of descent and ascent.
It were best for us to take the army by this route and disregard
both desert and leagues.'
To him [Ṭus] Goudarz made answer,
'Our illustrious king made you leader of this army. Take the
troops by the road which he indicated and do not let the journey
be one of hardship. Do not turn aside from the king's behest; or
the troops may be exhausted by this march.
'Noble hero,' Ṭus thereupon replied, 'have no anxiety over
that. The Shah will not be troubled by it and you need suffer no
distress on that account.'
Ṭus gave orders accordingly for the men to proceed and take
the road to Kalāt and Jaram, thereby disregarding the behest of
Khosrow. See how in the end a storm blew up [about this]!

(ix) *The adventures of Forud*

[News came to Forud, the son of Siyāvosh, of the Iranian army's
approach under its commander Ṭus, and, on the advice of his
mother, he climbed a mountain with his chief counsellor Tokhār
to spy out the invaders and identify their leaders. The two were
observed by Ṭus, who sent his general Bahrām to discover their
purpose and dislodge them from their position.]

Then said the prince [Forud],
'Who is this that advances so boldly? He surely can have no
apprehension of us that he climbs so briskly towards us.'
   The counsellor replied,
'We must not thrust him back too harshly. I do not know him
by name or by his emblems, but I think he is of the Goudarz
family. When Khosrow came to Iran, a royal helmet disappeared
from sight and I fancy that I see it on his head, and on his breast
also the royal corselet; surely therefore he is of the stock of
Goudarz. We must question him.'
   As Bahrām came near to the summit, he roared out in a voice of
thunder,
'What man are you on the mountain there? Do you not see this
immense army? Do you not hear the noise and the roll of the
drums? Have you no fear of Ṭus, that alert commander?'
   Forud in answer said,
'You have seen no threat, therefore make none. Moderate your
words if you are a man understanding affairs. Do not sully your
lips with harsh language. You are no warrior lion, nor am I a wild
ass of the plains. You cannot pass this way in any manner that you
may regard as possible. In no respect have you the advantage over
me, whether in experience of war, in courage or in strength.
Observe me and see whether I have head, foot and hand, heart,
brain and wit, as well as an eloquent tongue and eyes and ears. If
I possess them, do you make no futile display of force. I ask you
a question. If you give me an answer I shall rejoice, provided
that your decision is a felicitous one.'
   Bahrām retorted,
'Say on, then. You are the heavens and I am here on earth.'

[At that, Forud inquired who commanded the army, who its
officers were and what the reason was for the hostile incursion.
After further questions and answers Bahrām and Forud disclosed

their identity, and Bahrām, by means of certain birthmarks, recognized Forud as the son of Siyāvosh. The young prince then said,]

'Had my eyes seen my father alive, they would not have been more gladdened than by beholding you thus, happy and cheerful of spirit, full of virtue, perspicacious and a champion warrior. I ascended to this summit to learn who the noteworthy men of the Iranian forces were, to ascertain who the commander was and who was famed for prowess in battle. I will now hold a feast that shall have all possible splendour and in joy look upon the faces of these warriors. Afterwards I shall proudly march at the head of the army against Turān, my heart being aflame and eager for vengeance. And I have the right to seek this vengeance; in war I am a raging fire in the saddle.

'It were well if you told the Pahlavān [Commander] to come to this mountain, in happy spirit; and it will be needful for us to remain together here for a week in consultation over matters great and small. On the eighth day, when the roll of the drums swells forth, let the commander of the army of Ṭus mount into the saddle. I will prepare myself for the duty of going out to avenge my father and giving battle; with that torment in my heart it will be in a fashion which will instruct the lion in the art of war and to which the flight of vultures overhead will give testimony. None of the haughtiest in the world will ever have made such preparation for exacting vengeance.'

To him Bahrām said in reply,

'Prince, you have youth and skill, you are a warrior and a knight. I will inform Ṭus of all that you have said and will kiss his hand in supplication. Yet the commander of the army is not a man of sagacity, and his mind and brain are not endowed with wisdom. He has courage, wealth and lineage, but of sagacity he has no inkling in his heart. He has contended against Giv, Goudarz and the king himself on behalf of Fariborz and the throne and crown; he speaks ever of his being of the seed of Nouzar and of being worthy to occupy the throne of the world. Doubtless he will resent what I say and will have recourse to onslaught and battle with me.

'Of them who approach you let none but myself behold your head and helmet. He told me to ascertain who it was on the mountain-top, but not to ask the purpose of it. It was for me to inquire with mace and dagger only why anyone was upon the mountain. If Ṭus relents I will bring you tidings of it and bring you happily to our camp, but if anyone but myself comes from the camp, do not trust him overmuch. It would be only a solitary horseman who would come; that is the rule of this noble warrior. And now consider deeply your plan of action. Fasten the gates of your fortress and make your position strong.'

(x) *Bahrām returns to Ṭus*

When Bahrām returned to Ṭus he said,
'Let wisdom be mated to your spirit. You must know that that man is Forud son of king Siyāvosh who was slain for no sin of his own. He showed me the sign which at birth they received from Key Kāvus and Key Qobād.'
The presumptuous Ṭus thus replied,
'It is I who possess this army, with its trumpets and drums. I bade you bring him to me; make no plea to me on his behalf. If he is a prince, what am I? In that fortress of his what does he declare my purpose to be? A Turk's son, black as a crow, has he closed the passage of my army to the mountain? Am I to endure nothing but loss to my army from these arrogant descendants of Goudarz? You were thrown into panic by a single, worthless horseman; no fierce lion was that on the mountain there. He viewed the army and then had recourse to a trick, so that you made the journey up and down the mountain to no purpose.'
Turning then to his chief warriors, he said,
'Noble men of war, slayers of your foes, I call for a man of note who is eager for fame, one that will breast the mountain and con-front this Turk, will sever his head from his body with a knife and bring it to me here in this assembly.'

[Two noted warriors, despite their being discouraged by Bahrām, volunteered for the task. They were slain by arrows discharged by Forud, against whom Ṭus himself then advanced.]

(xi) *Ṭus gives battle to Forud*

A shout went up from the army of Iran and the warriors all seized their helmets. In haste Ṭus donned his armour, his heart bleeding and his eyes shedding tears, and climbed into the saddle like some great mass being loaded on to the back of a stout elephant. Now he turned the reins in the direction of Forud, his mind seething with rage and his head full of wild thoughts. Tokhār, the eloquent, gave tongue and said,

'Approaching us up the mountainside is a very mountain in a fury. It is the commander Ṭus, coming to give battle. You cannot stand against this wily dragon. Let us go and barricade the fortress gate and bide our time until we see what fortune shall determine. Since you have destroyed his son and his daughter's husband in warlike fashion [with your arrows], you can pay no further thought to feasting.'

In rage the young Forud turned on Tokhār and said,

'When war is afoot and strife, what matter if it be with Ṭus, or elephant, or raging lion, or fighting leopard or ravening tiger? In war man should be heartened; when fire is meant to blaze fiercely, none feeds it with earth.'

The veteran Tokhār replied,

'Princes do not reject counsel. You are but a simple knight, though a man of iron and capable of dislodging a granite mountain from its base. On this mountain thirty thousand Iranians of note will come into battle against you; no castle will be left here, not even a stone or a particle of its soil. They will sweep all clean away. And if any harm should come to Ṭus from this encounter, unhappiness will descend on Khosrow for the hurt that befalls him. While he undertakes to avenge your father, there will come upon you a defeat from which you will not recover. What need have you for war and for conflict with a lion? Return to your castle and do not wage war uselessly.'

He left unsaid the words which he should rather have spoken and which he kept hidden. By the fault of that worthless and crude adviser, Forud came to consider the strife to his advantage, thereby bringing his life to ruin. This young man Forud's castle was multitudinously inhabited. Within it he had eighty attendants and on the roof his beauteous women stood gazing. Greatly were they distressed at seeing him turn in flight, twisting his reins and pressing [his horse] with his thighs while he fitted another arrow to his bowstring. Addressing the war-thirsty prince, Tokhār said,

'If you are determined on battle, it is not likely that you will overcome Ṭus. Your best course is to shoot down his horse, for princes do not fight dismounted, however difficult and perilous their situation. But it may also be that his career will not be brought to an end by one single shaft from your bow, and, if he reaches the mountain summit, doubtless his escort will support him from the rear. You are not on an equal footing with him in combat and you have never yet faced his arrows in their flight.'

As soon as Forud heard these words of Tokhār's he strung his bow and let fly an arrow. The shaft, launched in the way proper to a knightly bow, struck the commander's horse, so that the beast went down headlong and lay dead. The heart of Ṭus filled with rage and his head with wild thoughts. He returned to his camp with his shield about his neck, on foot, covered with dust and his head bewildered. And after him Forud hurled stinging gibes.

'What has happened to this renowned warrior?' he called out. 'He would not face one mounted man. How would he appear before an army in battle array?'

The slave-girls laughed aloud and sent up a shout higher than the spheres, crying, 'An old man frightened of an arrow fled tumbling from aloft before a boy.'

The Commander reached the base of the mountain, where warriors anxiously came to meet him.

[After a number of other champions had been killed by Forud, the Pahlavān Bizhan son of Giv undertook to accomplish what the others had failed to do and, in addition, to avenge their death. Forud's mother, disturbed by an ominous dream, roused him from his sleep.]

'Wake up, my son,' she bade him. 'Evil comes upon us from our star. The mountain is covered with the enemy; the gateway of the castle is full of spears and armour.'

The young man replied,

'How long will you continue trembling in despair? If my life is to end, you cannot reckon that anyone's time can be extended to more than has been allotted. My father was killed while he was still young; and my fortunes like his have been reversed. His fate came upon him from Garui; mine is approaching relentlessly upon me from Bizhan. I will fight; I shall die, regretfully but like a man. I desire no mercy from the Iranians.'

To his men Forud served out battle-axes and armour, while on his own head he placed a costly helmet, fastened on his body a corselet of Greek mail and came forth grasping a royal bow. Down from the castle wall he came, accompanied by the most gallant of the Turks who were there. The mountain-top then began to resemble a sea of pitch because of the dust thrown up by the horsemen and the density of the flights of arrows. There was

no level ground or any area for battle, and the steepness of the
rocks threw the horses into confusion.

[Forud resisted the oncoming Iranians with great valour.]

Of the Turks no knight had survived at his side and he was left
single-handed to continue the battle. At last he turned his rein
and at speed climbed towards the castle. But Rahhām and Bizhan
had laid an ambush for him and so drove him upwards and then
down again. When the young Forud espied Bizhan's helmet his
hand swiftly plucked a battle-axe from his girdle and like a lion
in fury he leapt on his foe, unconscious of the fate held in store
for him by the vaulted skies. At his opponent's head he aimed a
blow which was like to have crushed both helmet and head, and
Bizhan groaned aloud at it, all sense departing from his mind and
his body left powerless. Rahhām perceiving this came up from the
rear with a shout, holding an Indian scimitar in his hand. He
thrust at the gallant youth's shoulder and left his arm without
power to move.

Though wounded thus in arm and back, Forud urged on his
horse with a shout. But up came Bizhan towards the castle and
pierced the horse's hind-leg through so that Forud dismounted,
and he with some of his squires, exhausted with combat against
doughty warriors, were compelled to take refuge in the castle on
foot. Its gate they swiftly closed. (Alas for the warlike heart and
pride of Forud!) To him came his mother and her attendants
and the veiled women took him to their hearts. Weeping they
laid him on an ivory throne although the day and moment for
a crown were past. Their perfumed tresses and curls the slaves,
and his mother too, rent in sorrow. Opening his eyes and sighing
grievously he turned to his mother and slaves and said, when
he could part his lips,

'This rending of your tresses does not cause me wonder. Now
the Iranians will enter with all their efforts directed to plundering
the castle. They will take my slaves captive and destroy castle,
horses and the whole mountain. You whose hearts are in torment
for me and whose cheeks are on fire for my departing life, ascend
in your purity to the castle wall and cast yourselves down so that
none of you shall remain for Bizhan to enjoy. I myself remain here
but a little while, and it is he who has cut short my dear life; he is
the fatality that has overtaken my youth.'

Thus he spoke and his cheeks blanched; his soul then departed
in sorrow and pain.

E K—K

[Jarira, Forud's mother, mutilated and killed all the valuable Arab horses in the castle stables, then laid herself on her son's body and stabbed herself to death. Ṭus and the Iranian army entered the castle, where those of them who were of royal birth mourned their kinsman Forud.]

When Ṭus the Commander had ended the war against Forud, he descended from the castle. Three days he remained at Jaram; on the fourth, at a blast of the horn, he mustered his army and caused trumpets and drums to sound until the ground from mountain to mountain was ebony-black with troops. Wherever they saw men of the Turānian army they slew them and threw their bodies into pits, while the countryside was ravished all the way to the Kāsa-rud [Kāsa river]. There the army encamped, the ground disappearing from sight because of the number of the tents.

Tidings now came to Turān of how an army from Iran had come to the Kāsa-rud and halted there on its march. So from amongst the Turks there came forth a gallant youth named Palāshān, an alert-minded hero, to spy on the invading army and to count the banners and pavilions. In the midst of the encampment lay a high hill, the main body being to one side, and on it Giv and Bizhan were seated in discussion of matters great and small when on to the road there came into sight from out the army of Turān the banner of Palāshān. Seeing him in the distance, the doughty Giv stretched out his hand and drew his sword from his girdle.

'I will go,' he said, 'and sever his head from his body, or else bring him in fetters into the presence of these troops.'

To him Bizhan replied,

'If the king gave me a robe of honour for this combat and commanded me to undertake it, I would assume the task of giving battle to this war-thirsty Palāshān.'

The valiant Giv retorted,

'Be not over-temerarious in attack upon that male lion. It is possible that you will not be his equal in combat, and then you will put me in difficulty for the battle. Palāshān is like a lion on the battlefield; all he demands for prey is a warrior.'

Then said Bizhan,

'Do not put me to shame before the emperor with such words as these. Give me the armour of Siyāvosh for the combat and you will see how a leopard takes his prey.'

Giv handed over the armour to the valiant warrior and Bizhan covered his body with it, then mounted a swift horse and galloped boldly on to the plain, spear in hand. Now Palāshān had just shot down a gazelle, gobbets of whose flesh were laid over the fire; and while his horse moved about and cropped the grass he ate, lasso over his arm. When his horse became aware of Bizhan's in the distance, it neighed and snorted violently, making him realize that a horseman was approaching, so that he advanced, ready for conflict. In a loud voice he called out to Bizhan,

'I am the lion-breaker, he that holds demons in thrall. Tell me plainly what your name is, for your star is about to shed tears over you.'

The gallant warrior replied,

'I am Bizhan. In battle I am an elephant with a body of bronze. My grandfather was a battling lion; my father is Giv the warrior. Even now I can perceive victory before me; on the day of havoc, when it comes to the battle, you on the mountain there will be no more than a wolf devouring carrion. You will be consuming smoke, ashes and blood at a time when you should be leading your army on to the field.'

Palāshān made no comment in answer; instead, he spurred that battling elephant [his horse] into movement. Fiercely the two knights grappled with each other, stirring up a cloud of black dust. The spear-heads were shattered as one met the other, and the warriors stretched out their hands to their swords. In the cut and thrust the scimitars fell into fragments and the two men were left trembling like leaves. Their steeds were drowned in sweat and their own heads ached beyond enduring. Now they seized heavy poles, both men like lions with head erect and both still active enough for battle.

They paused, until Bizhan with a cry lifted the pole from his shoulder, thrust at the middle of Palāshān's body and broke his spine. His body crashed headlong from the horse's back to the ground and lay there covered with helmet and armour. Light as a mote Bizhan was down from his own horse and had severed the slain warrior's head from the body. He then bore off the famous man's weapons, head and horse to his father, Giv, whose head had been racked with travail wondering how the wind would turn when the battle was fought.

(xii) *The Iranians suffer hardship from the snow*

[Afrāsiyāb the Turk learnt of the Iranian victory and bade his chief
commander Pirān to gather an army together without argument.]

A strong wind arose such as no man in Iran could remember.
Close behind it followed a great cloud and men's lips froze together with the cold. Pavilions and tents turned to ice and a
carpet of snow was spread over the mountains until the whole
region was lost to view because of it. And for a whole week none
saw the surface of the plain. Food, sleep and repose became scarce
and you would have said that the surface of the earth was stone.
Without a thought for the day of battle men killed and ate their
war-horses. Many were both the men and the steeds that perished
and no man had a war-horse remaining to him.

On the eighth day the sun shone forth strongly and the whole
world turned into a sea of water. Then the commander gathered
his troops together and discoursed to them at length concerning
the day of battle.

'Here,' he said, 'our army perished through hardship. We must
ride away from this field of strife. Let there be no blessing on
these lands, nor on Kalāt, nor the White Mountain nor Kāsa-
rud.'

From amidst the proud warriors Bahrām spoke. 'This,' he
said, 'must not be hidden from the Commander. You silence us
with your speech, but it was you who waged war against the son
of Siyāvosh. I advised you not to do so, seeing that it was not
right. Now behold how much has been lost by your deed and the
further evil which may accrue to you. The buffalo is still in its
hide!'

Ṭus responded,

'Let us not continue to discuss the past and whether one or
other was unjustly slain. Giv received a robe of honour for undertaking to burn the mountain of wood and remove it from our
path. Now the time has come to burn it and to light up the skies
with the blaze. Thus perhaps the army's path will be cleared and a
passage forced through along the road.'

'This matter offers no difficulty,' said Giv in response. 'And
even if there be any it does not lack reward.'

This speech brought unhappiness to Bizhan, who replied, 'I
do not consent to these words. In toil and hardship you reared
me and never hurt me with your words. It is not possible for me

with my youth to lag behind while you in your old age are prepared for deeds.'

Giv replied,

'By what I have done I have achieved honour. The time is still
left for me to make myself ready; it is not the moment for old age
and repose. Be not troubled at my going, for I could set alight a
mountain of granite with my ardour.'

It was with difficulty that he passed to Kāsa-rud, for ice and
snow formed the warp and weft of the world. When he came to the
mountain of wood he could not estimate its height or thickness.
On an arrow-head he lit a flame, shot it into the mound and set
the wood ablaze, and for the space of three weeks, because of
the flames, the wind and the smoke, none was able to pass by the
fire. In the fourth week they were able to make their way across,
for both river and fire had begun to subside.

(xiii) *Afrāsiyāb learns of the invasion by Ṭus*

[After some skirmishing, a massive invasion of Turān was
launched by the Iranian army under Ṭus. Information was brought
to Afrāsiyāb by a subordinate officer, who reported,]

'The heads of Palāshān and those other notable warriors have
fallen miserably in the dust; the enemy have burnt up the whole
country and destroyed all the cattle.'

He was downcast at hearing this report, but at once began to
lay his plans, having first addressed Pirān son of Visah [his chief
general] in these words,

'I bade you gather an army together from every region, but
you delayed because of your folly, senility, unwisdom and sloth.
Of my kith and kin many have been slain, and misfortune
has come on many a man once happy. Now no further time
for delay remains; the world has tightened about the men of alert
mind.'

Pirān the commander hastened away from the presence of
Afrāsiyāb. He now in every district called up men fitted for war,
gave out arms and money and set his forces in movement. Troop
on troop the army marched on, [so numerous] that neither plain
nor river nor mountain was to be seen. Pirān commanded,

'You are to go by untrodden ways. From here you will ascend
swiftly into the mountains by the shortest path. The enemy must

get no warning of you notable captains or of your fine troops. I will bring this mighty force down on that army suddenly, like a mountain.'

The most experienced men he dispatched at once to search out keenly what was stirring in the world, and they swiftly turned to the task eager for war. First they turned in the direction of the city of Gerowgerd, and their reports went back to men understanding affairs. Those notable men conveyed the matter to Pirān, whom they told that the [Iranian] commander Tus had settled in a certain place but that no sound of a drum issued from the encampment. The men were all either tippling or intoxicated; day and night they had wine in their hands. They stationed no sentinels on the roads, careless of the movements of the Turānian force. When Pirān heard this he summoned his warrior chieftains and addressed them at length concerning his troops, telling them that never in the course of the war had they held so great a chance of victory over the Iranian army.

(xiv) *Pirān's night attack on the Iranians*

From amongst his famous troops Pirān chose thirty thousand sword-wielding knights, and these, when the darkness was half gone, set forth without beat of drum or sound of trumpet. Their commander Pirān led his force on until between the two armies there remained a space of seven leagues. First he came upon herds of horses which had been allowed to roam freely in search of pasture on the plains of Turān, and of these he seized a goodly number which his troops drove along with them. By the malice of fortune they left no harm undone; for they slew the guardians of the herds and the herdsmen too, the Iranian fortunes being in adversity.

Like a black cloud the Turānians then descended on the Iranian army, whom they found all drunk, seated about in groups with their belts unfastened. In his tent, however, Giv was awake and the general, Gudarz, was sober and alert. Sudden clamour broke out and there was the noise of the beating of drums until the warlike Giv was bewildered. But, ready saddled at the door of his pavilion stood an armoured horse, and he himself, having donned the corselet of Siyāvosh, became bold as a male lion. Like a leopard he flung off his sleep, and shame overtook him at his slothfulness. He said to himself,

'Bestir yourself! What has happened this night that my brain is filled with fumes and not with thoughts of war?'

He flung his leg across his steed and swift as the wind he galloped away, though he saw the world darkly through the dust and the night. At last he arrived at the commander's pavilion and to him he called out,

'Arise! The enemy is here, but these gallant men of the Shah's are sunk in sleep.'

Clutching his bull-headed mace he went on from thence to his father, then moved swift as smoke about the camp to rouse any men that were sober. He wrangled with Bizhan, inquiring, 'Is it the time for war or for wine?'

Each army plunged into the dust of the other, and a clamour arose from the field of strife. The intoxicated men fell into a stupor. Beneath their drunken heads the pillows were soft; over them the lances, swords and arrows were sharp. At dawn, when the Lion struck up his head above his castle, the valiant Giv surveyed his encampment. He saw the whole plain strewn with the Iranian dead and the ground cut up into segments like clay. Gudarz looked about him in each direction and saw how with every moment the troops increased until they were a multitude as of ants or locusts sweeping over their scanty opponents. The commander peered out but could descry no [Iranian] warrior or any of the valorous or men of daring. The banners were torn, the drums reversed and the cheeks of those still remaining alive were ebony-hued.

In that plight the men marched to Kāsa-rud lacking equipment and bereft of all material, whereas behind Ṭus the Turānian knights advanced with rancorous spirit and blasphemous tongues. From behind also you might have said that axes rained down blows as though from the clouds upon breastplate, helmet and corselet. In the combat no man stood fast, every Iranian warrior taking refuge in the mountains; men and horses wearied of conflict, none retained hold of their wits or considered delay. No surgeon came to the pillow of the wounded. All was occasion for sorrow and blood-stained tears.

Through his defeat in the battle the Commander [Ṭus] took leave of his senses, so that his mind became a stranger to reason. The much-travelled Gudarz was left with hoary head and without son, grandson, land or estate. In depair the veterans came to him seeking a way of deliverance, and he commanded a noted warrior

from amongst the Iranians to gird up his loins tightly and carry
tidings to the Shah of what had occurred and what plans the
chief had made, of the ill-fortune which had beset the Iranians
and of the calamity which had resulted from this attempt at
vengeance.

(xv) *Key Khosrow recalls Ṭus*

[Angry at the defeat and death of his half-brother Forud, Khosrow
recalls Ṭus, who on presenting himself before the Shah is addressed as follows,]

'You miserable wight, may your name vanish from amongst the
proud. Have you no fear of God the Pure; are you not ashamed or
abashed before these warriors? I granted you a royal diadem and
girdle and sent you out to do battle with the enemy, bidding you
not to divert your road to Jaram. Yet you did so, thereby plung-
ing my heart into misery. First you satisfied your hatred of me and
then deprived the offspring of Siyāvosh of his life. You slew my
noble brother Forud, whose peer has never existed in the world,
one whose equal would be desired by fortune as a commander.
Then, when you went to the battlefield, all your activity was
devoted to music and feasting. You have no place in the capital
city. It were best for you to be fettered in a hospital for the insane.
You can have no further employ among free men, for your judgment is no longer balanced. Your descent from Manuchehr and
your white beard alone give you some hope of life; were it not
for them I should have commanded some person evilly disposed
towards you to sever your head from your breast. Go! Your house
is from henceforth your prison, your jailer being your own evil
character.'

(xvi) *Fariborz begs a truce from Pirān*

[Ṭus was replaced as commander of the Iranian army by Fariborz
son of Key Kāvus.]

On his head Fariborz set a diadem, for he was both a Pahlavān
and the son of a king, and he invoked Rahhām to bring lustre to
his birth and name by going to the mountain on which Pirān
lay encamped, addressing him eloquently and hearing his reply.
He said to him,

'Go in your dignity to Pirān and carry a friendly message to him. Say that the working of the revolving sky has ever been alike, whether for hate or love; it raises one man aloft to the summit of the wheel and casts another low into grief and misery. Now as for the man who seeks destruction for gallant warriors— onslaughts in the dead of night are not the habit of gallant folk; they are not required by the courageous, by the men who wield the heavy battle-axes. If you are for a truce, we shall have a truce; if your thoughts are on war, we shall make war. But we need a truce of a month's duration for the wounded to recover their powers.'

Rahhām departed from the presence of Fariborz bearing the message and the letter. A sentinel, seeing him on the path, required his name and the place whence he had come. He answered, 'I am a man of war; noted, alert and possessed of authority. I carry hither a message from Fariborz, son of King Kāvus, to Pirān.'

From the sentinel a horseman went swiftly to report all that had passed, saying that Rahhām son of Gudarz had come from the battlefield to the commander of the army. The order being given that he should be admitted, cheerfully and with pleasant mien they brought him in, but when the pleasant-voiced Rahhām stood in the presence of Pirān he was in fear of what his enemy contemplated in secret. Pirān on beholding him paid him compliments, asked how he fared and seated him on a throne. And Rahhām disclosed his confidential message and delivered the message of Fariborz.

Pirān answered to Rahhām the warrior, 'This can be regarded as no light matter. You were beforehand in this struggle; we found no interval for delay with Ṭus, for he came on to the field like a rabid wolf and recklessly slew both small and great. A vast multitude he slew and a vast multitude took captive. In this land he reckoned good and evil all alike. Now you have received requital for this wickedness, although you hasted away without warning. But, since you are the Pahlavān of your army, demand of me what it is that you need. If you desire a truce for a month, not a knight from my army shall issue forth in combat. Then, when you seek the battle, I am willing to wage it: prepare yourselves and draw up your array. When you have reckoned up the month and are ready to traverse the spaces of this land of Turān, lead your army back to your own country, with alert mind judging your own powers. If you fail, we will press you hard in battle; there will be no time of respite for you then.'

He ordered that there should be got ready a robe of honour suited to his fame for Rahhām, who returned to Fariborz with a letter as he had before. Being given his month's truce, Fariborz like a lion stretched out his claws in every direction; the strings on purses were loosened and from all sides spears and bows were brought in. Men went about to recruit forces, and stores of material of every kind were got ready.

(xvii) *The Iranians suffer defeat from the Turānians*

When the month was at an end and the time come for battle—for the Iranians had never disregarded their word, their repute and their honour—there arose the clamour of troops advancing with one accord to the battlefield. Haranguing his men Fariborz said,

'Our energies have retired into hiding. But let us today give battle like lions and close the world in upon our enemies, or else, because of our past disgrace, battle-axes and Greek helmets will for evermore scoff at our troops.'

The hail of arrows they loosed was sharp as the autumn wind leaping on the trees and thick enough to leave no room for the birds. The tussle between Gudarz [the Iranian] and Pirān [the Turānian] became fiercer, reaching a climax where none could perceive the ground, the earth's surface having vanished under the many dead.

[Defeat now overtook the Iranian side.] One by one they yielded ground to the enemy; of the Iranian warriors not one stood fast. No longer were drum and banner to be seen at their stations, and men's eyes were purpled by the stress of battle. Even the most valiant turned their backs and all their striving profited them no more than wind in their clutches. Down went drums, banners and spears, and no longer could stirrups be distinguished from reins.

As the enemy massed on every side, Fariborz departed for the slopes of the mountains and every Iranian still alive went with him. (Shed tears for such survival!) There still remained in their places Gudarz, Giv and, from among the troops, a goodly number of brave men. Then, when Gudarz, Keshwād's son, lost to sight the banner of Fariborz son of Kāvus and the champions of the

army, his heart flared up like fire and he turned his rein purposing
to flee. But a tumult arose amongst his men. Giv said to him,
    'Mine ancient captain, you have seen much of axes, maces and
arrows. If you wish to flee before Pirān, pour dust on my head.
Of warriors none is left alive in the world, nor any veteran. You
and I have no escape from death, yet no misfortune lingers so
long in its coming. Now that this harsh fate has come upon us, it
were better for your face rather than your back to be seen. As
for me, I will not turn my mind from the battle here; let us not
bring shame on Keshwād's dust. Have you not heard the sage's
proverb, received by him from ancient lore, that if two brothers
stand back to back, the earth in a mountain's bulk amounts to no
more than a handful? You are still here and with you are seventy
warrior sons, among your own stock being many men who are
stout as elephants and male lions. With the sword we shall burst
the hearts of our enemy, and were he a mountain we would sever
him from his base.'
    When Gudarz heard the speech of Giv and beheld the heads
and casques of his valorous kinsmen, he repented of his timidity
and reasoning and set his foot firmly in its place. Gorāza then
advanced and Gostaham and Barta and the martial Zanga too.
They swore profound oaths that there would be no breaking of
promises here; that from this field of strife they never would turn
their face away, let the blood from the battle-axes flow in a river.
They would everyone stand back to back in hope of regaining
their departed glory. So they established themselves firmly in
their positions and manfully wielded their axes in the fight until
many a man was slain. Fortune had now turned towards evil. Then
said the ancient Gudarz to Bizhan,
    'Go swiftly from here with axe and arrows, make your way to
Fariborz, and to me here bring the Kāviāni Star. If Fariborz
himself comes with the standard he will cause the enemy's face to
blanch.'
    Bizhan heard, put spurs to his horse and sped like lightning to
Fariborz, to whom he said,
    'Why do you linger in hiding here? Turn your rein like a man
and dally no longer on this mountain summit. If you will not
come, give me the standard, together with mounted men and
violet-hued scimitars.'
    But though Bizhan argued thus with him, Fariborz would not
let his mind be paired with wisdom. He shouted to Bizhan,

'Go! You are quick to act and new in war. The king happily entrusted this standard and these troops to me, and he gave me the rank of Pahlavān and a crown and diadem. The standard is not meant for such a one as Bizhan son of Giv, nor for any other warrior in the entire world.'

Bizhan at that seized a sword of tempered metal and struck a sudden blow at the middle of the standard, cutting the Kāviāni Star in two. One half of it he seized and so left the place to regain his own encampment. When the Turks perceived the Star on the path, a lion-hearted group of them eager for battle charged down on Bizhan wielding maces and swords of tempered steel and ready to do battle [in order to capture] the Kāviāni standard.

'That is the Star in which lies the strength of Iran,' said Humān. 'If we can bring that purple ensign into our grasp, we shall make the world a straitened place for the Shah.'

[Bizhan, however, warded off the attacks of his pursuers and regained his own camp. His men rallied about the standard, but in vain. The day ended in an Iranian defeat.]

(xviii) *The Iranians return to Khosrow*

The dispersed forces assembled once again, each man having a story to relate of how many of the Iranian army had been slain and how the fortunes of the commander had suffered decline. So great had been the victory of the Turks that now no profit was to be gained from continuing the war. Without fail the army must return to the Shah and discover what fate held in store. If he had no mind for war, then it was not for this man or that to propose it. Fathers had been deprived of their sons, sons of their fathers. Many had been slain and those still living were stricken at heart. If the Shah were to order the war to be renewed, he would muster a notable army and all would come again with their hearts full of martial ardour, and they would ring the world tightly about the foe.

[The message was brought to Afrāsiyāb the Turk that his land had been liberated from the enemy.]

The commander [Pirān] rejoiced at the tidings, for he was now free of care and anxiety. His troops in gladness of heart tied up banners along the path of the great warrior, covered roofs and walls with woven stuffs and rained money down on him. When he approached the king, he was welcomed with the scattering of coin. Greatly was he felicitated and often assured that he was without peer. For two weeks the music of harp and rebeck resounded from Afrāsiyāb's palace, then, in the third week, Pirān resolved to return to his own home. To him the king then said,

'You must continue to be amongst my counsellors and remain of alert mind, keeping your troops ever watchful of the enemy. In every direction despatch secretly men who are clever and understand their duty, for Key Khosrow is today well supplied with treasure and his country prospers because of his justice and generosity. Do not be sure against the enemy's return, and from time to time seek to be freshly informed. In a place where Rostam is the Pahlavān, if you lie down without care, your soul may suffer torment; my apprehensions are about him alone, for his sole purpose is to seek vengeance and I fear he may be roused out of his place to lead an army from Iran against Turān.'

Pirān, being commander of his troops and also his kinsman, fell in with his counsel. He and his escort then turned their thoughts in the direction of Khotan.

(xix) *The Iranians renew the war*

From Turān, Fariborz with his company, among whom were such men as Gudarz and Giv the army-breakers, sorrowfully and with tears directed their faces towards the road leading to Iran. As the troops set foot on the road for Jaram, with Kalāt above them and the river Mayam below, they remembered Forud's battle; and all was regret, pain and woe. Shamed in spirit they approached the Shah, their hearts broken and their souls conscious of sin, for his brother had been slain for no cause and his ring and diadem surrendered to the enemy. With burning hearts and with hands on breasts like slaves they went into his presence. Khosrow looked with anger upon them, grief in his heart and his eyes wet with tears. He thus addressed God,

'Giver of justice, thou didst grant me throne, fortune and power. Now I stand in shame before Thee, for Thou art more aware of What and How than I am. Else should I command that a thousand gallows be at once set up on the meydān, whereon should be hanged the bodies of Ṭus and of all the others who acted with him. Upon the kin of Gudarz evil came from Ṭus—curses be on him, on his elephants and his drums! I gave him robes of honour and other gifts. Did I send him to war against my brother? May there never more be a captain like Ṭus son of Nowzar! May no Pahlavān like him lead the army! Alas for Forud son of Siyāvosh! He was stout of heart, and stoutly he wielded axe and sword. Like his father he was slain being innocent of harm, and by the hand of my Commander and my troops. I know of no man in the world more despicable than Ṭus, who is fit only for fetters and the dungeon. He has neither brains in his head nor sinews in his body. In my sight Ṭus is no more than a dog.'

In rage for his brother and grief for his father's innocent blood he remained tormented and broken-hearted. He degraded his generals and drove them out, and ever kept shedding from his eye-lashes the tears of blood that arose from his heart. Against his army captains he closed the doors of his audience-chamber, for his heart was sore in his grief for his brother.

[At Rostam's intercession, Khosrow pardoned Ṭus and the other warrior chieftains, these being then despatched to renew the war against Turān. On their arrival Pirān sent smooth messages to them and in return was invited by Tus to forsake Turān for Iran, where he would be received with honour. He reported this information to Afrāsiyāb, whom he advised to build up a strong force to overwhelm the Iranian invader. Various battles and bouts of single combat then took place, fortune favouring neither side. In the end the Turānians had to have recourse to magic for aid.]

(xx) *The Turānians employ magic against the Iranian army*

Amongst the Turks there was a man named Bāzur, who had travelled everywhere in the practice of enchantment, having learned the arts of chicanery and magic and acquired a knowledge of Chinese and Pahlavi. To this wizard Pirān said,

'Go from here to the highest mountain summit and suddenly on to the Iranians cause a storm of snow, frost and raging wind to descend.'

As soon as the wizard had reached his destination, there came a storm of snow and furious wind, which so disabled the hands of the Iranian spearsmen that they could not engage in combat. In that moment of terror and intense cold the cry of the Turānian warriors was heard, accompanied by a rain of arrows. At the same time Pirān was commanding his troops on the field of battle to launch an immediate assault, and, since the Iranians' hands were

frozen on to their spears, none was able to show fight. Humān
then uttered a shout and rushed like a demon into attack, and so
many Iranians were thus slain that a river of blood flowed in
the midst of them. Both valley and plain were covered with snow
and blood and the Iranian horsemen were thrown into headlong
confusion. Commander and captains raised woeful petitions to
Heaven, saying,

'Thou who art too lofty for men's knowledge, mind or comprehension, who art above no place or within any place and yet
dost exist in every place, we all are Thy sinful slaves and in our
helplessness call to Thee for justice. Thou art an aid in man's sore
straits and hast power over fire and frost; deliver us from this
intensity of cold, for apart from Thee we recognize no lord.'

There arrived at that moment a man who was a student of the
sciences and pointed out to Rahhām the place on the mountain
where the vile Bāzur stood exercising his enchantments and
wizardry. Thereupon Rahhām turned away from the scene of
battle and rode his horse out of the midst of the troops. Midway
up the slope he left the road and climbed on foot to the summit.
There the wizard caught sight of him and advanced to attack him,
holding in his hand a pole of Chinese steel. But as he approached,
Rahhām swiftly plucked a sword from his belt and with its sharp
blade cut off the other's hand. Suddenly a wind arose as though it
were the Day of Resurrection and in front of the storm the black
cloud was carried away. Down from the mountain now descended
the warrior Rahhām, first having imprisoned the wizard's remaining arm, and coming on to the plain, he remounted his horse.
The weather now had returned to what it had been before, the
sun shone and the skies were blue.

[The Iranian army retreated to the mountain of Hamāvan, where
it was beleaguered by Pirān and the Turānians. Hearing of its
plight, Key Khosrow called on Rostam to go to its assistance,
while on the other side the Khāqān of China and Kāmus, a warrior
chieftain of Transoxiana, came to aid Afrāsiyāb.]

(xxi) *The Khāqān of China spies out the army of Iran*

When the sun had led his troops into the arch [of the sky] to rout
the dark night and cause it to disappear, the Khāqān of China
assembled a small force of the nobles and warriors of the Turānian
land. He said to Pirān,

'We shall not engage in battle today, for we need a whole day's respite in order that our proud warriors and these knights inured to carnage shall have repose from the hardships of their long journey and their difficult riding across depths and heights. Let us see the aims which the Iranian pursue on this field of battle and who their allies are.'

Pirān replied,

'The Khāqān of China is a wise and fortunate king. Today he does as his heart desires, for he is lord over the whole army.'

From the [royal] pavilion a shout went up, then came the roll of drums and the blowing of trumpets. Thrones were set on the backs of five elephants, their gear being all of Chinese embroidery. The thrones were studded with emeralds and covered with cloth of gold thread and of turquoise colour. The bridles were of gold, the housings of leopard-skin; while the bells large and small and the gongs also were of silver. Garlands in brilliant colours covered the heads of the elephant-drivers, all of whom were brightly garbed and wore necklaces and earrings. From the multitude of red, yellow and violet banners, the scene was like a Chinese market.

On to the field of combat rode a detachment whose appearance roused the desire and expectation of a feast. The ground, for vividness of colour, took on the likeness of a cock's eye, and there was an abundance of sound and ornament, of fifes and drums. The kings and their escorts moved off, the air filled with the notes of the trumpet; spears glittered, the horsemen curvetted and the whole surface of the earth was black with soldiery. From a distance, Tus the Commander espied all this and drew up in battle array the troops that remained to him, the captains made themselves ready for action and Giv brought up the Kāviāni Banner. From the plain of combat to the very summit of the mountain the Iranian forces stood in their detachments, but as spectators on the Hamāvan mountain rather than as men boldly confronting the foe.

When the Khāqān of China, however, observed them from afar and heard the clangour made by the Iranian horsemen he admired them, saying,

'Behold here an army of knights fit to overthrow their enemies and eager for battle! The Commander Pirān has differently represented them, but people's true qualities should not go unrevealed. For the commander of troops to cover over a pit with thorn-bushes and with his horse ride into it on the day of the hunt is better than to underestimate the enemy on the day of battle. Never have I beheld horsemen and proud knights as good as these for martial spirit and valour.'

Pirān remarked,

'On this battlefield we regard so small an army as of no account.'

Thereupon the Khāqān of China inquired,

'What action can we now take on this field of combat?'

Pirān answered him,

'You have trodden a long road and endured its descents and heights. Let us remain for three days on this field of battle so that the troops can rest. Then I will divide them into two halves, the day of strife and terror having come at last. From dawn to noon intrepid cavalry who can set the world on fire will attack; with javelin, sword, axe and spear they will seek to engage the enemy. At noon the second contingent will take up the conflict until night comes up over the mountain. In the dark of the night I will lead into battle the men who have rested and will continue until the Iranians are forced into straits. Our cavalry, eager and well equipped, will allow them no respite.'

Kāmus replied,

'That is not an acceptable plan. I see no ground for this delay. With this force of men and this kind of battle, why seek to wait so long? Let us act and launch an immediate assault so as to make valley and mountain too narrow for them. From here we shall lead an army into Iran, where we shall leave neither throne, crown nor king, shall bring desolation on every region and province and give full satisfaction to our courageous lion-like men. No woman or child, no elder or youth, no king or satrap, no champion warrior shall we leave in Iran, nor any vaulted palace, pillared hall or pavilion. Why permit so many days to go to waste and needlessly suffer anxiety, pain and care? Tonight, when they retreat from this battle, do not leave the way open. When the wind of dawn begins to blow, all our army must be on the march. On the summit of the mountain tomorrow you will see a mound of dead Iranian warriors. It will be a place which Iranians will never more behold without weeping.'

To him the Khāqān said,

'That is the only plan. Nothing is better than a short battle.'

With one voice the notables agreed with the scheme which Kāmus the lion-killer had prepared.

E K–L

[This was followed by boastful exchanges between the subordinate commanders on either side and there were bouts of single
combat. At last Rostam came to reinforce the Iranians. With
elaborate ceremonial Iranians and Turānians prepared their forces,
after which Rostam engaged in a series of preliminary bouts with
champions, in ascending order of repute, put forward by the
Turānians.]

First a vainglorious Koshāni named Ashkabus, who roared in a
voice like a drum-beat, came forward to challenge any amongst the
Iranians willing to do battle and desirous of laying his opponent's
head in the dust. He yelled,

'You famous warriors, which of you will emerge for combat?
Who will enter into a struggle with me, so that I can strike a
river of blood out of him?'

As this speech came to the ears of Rahhām he roared out and
began to boil like the sea. He seized his bow and let fly a hail of
arrows against that illustrious challenger. But he was protected
by steel, so that on his coat of mail an arrow was of no more
effect than a puff of wind. Rahhām then drew an axe so heavy that
chieftains' arms were exhausted with carrying it in combat, but
on his opponent's helmet it made no indentation and his head
all the more eagerly thirsted for battle. Ashkabus in his turn took
up a heavy axe—the air turning the colour of iron, the earth to
ebony—with which he dealt such a blow at the head of stout
Rahhām that it shattered his helmet. At that he took fright at the
Koshāni, turned about and made for the mountain.

Out of the centre of the army thereupon Ṭus sprang, putting
spurs to his horse to charge upon Ashkabus; but Rostam too
leapt up, saying to Ṭus,

'Rahhām's only comrade is the wine-cup. It is at feasts that he
makes play with his sword and bears himself proudly amongst
warriors. Where is he now, with his face like red lead? While you
keep the centre of the army in good array, I shall undertake this
combat on foot.'

He flung his bow over his arm by the string and placing arrows
in his girdle he called out,

'My well-tried warrior, someone has now come whom you
may fight. Do not depart.'

The Koshāni laughed and showed surprise. With a pull at his
reins he smilingly said to Rostam,

'What is your name? Who is it that must weep over your headless body?'

Tahamtan retorted,

'You flimsy-bodied weakling, why ask my name in such company as this? My mother named me death to you and destiny made me the hammer for your skull.'

Said the Koshāni,

'You have no horse. You expose yourself to death at once.'

Tahamtan rejoined,

'You who so rashly look for combat, have you never seen a man on foot who can give battle to a rival and put his head under the stone? In your country, do the lions, leopards and sharks ride into battle? Now, my gallant horseman, I on foot will teach you the art of combat. Ṭus sent me unmounted for the express purpose of depriving Ashkabus of his horse and setting him on his own feet like me, so that everyone present may laugh at him. On this ground, on this day, on this field of combat one man on foot is better than three hundred mounted men like you.'

The Koshāni returned,

'Where are your weapons? Other than lies and sneers I see nothing.' To this Rostam said, 'You will see the arrow and the bow which are about to put an end to your life.' Regarding him seated at his ease on his splendid courser, he fixed an arrow to his bow and let fly. It struck the horse, which fell its full length to the ground. And Rostam laughed aloud and said, 'Place yourself on the ground by your splendid companion. It would be fitting for you to embrace his head and rest yourself from combat for a while.

For reply Ashkabus strung his bow, his body trembling and his face as red as orpiment, and began to rain arrows on to Rostam's leopard-skin shield. But Rostam said,

'It is in vain for you to fatigue your body, your arms and malevolent spirit.' With that he thrust his hand into his girdle and chose out a poplar-wood arrow, which had a shining head and was feathered by four eagle's plumes. He caressed his Chāchi bow with his hand, put his thumb into a sheath made of the hide of a wild stag and, making a firm column of his left arm, he bent the right. The Chāchi bow uttered a creak as it bent and as the notch of the arrow came close to his ear the cowhide whistled. With the arrowhead kissing his finger, his arm stretched backwards beyond his spine, he aimed his shaft at the breast of Ashkabus and on the instant Heaven touched his hand with a kiss. Fate said, "Take" and destiny said "Give"; the sky said, "Good" and the Angel said, "Well done!" And then the Koshāni gave up the ghost; it was as though his mother had never brought him into the world. The armies facing each other gazed on the two men engaged in combat, Kāmus and the Khāqān of China expressing admiration of their arms and build, their strength and spirit. As Rostam turned away the Khāqān urgently sent a mounted man to pluck out the noteworthy [fatal] arrow, which down to its feathers was drenched in blood. Men passed it amongst the troops from hand to hand and they thought it to be a javelin; and as the Khāqān looked at the feathers and arrow-head, his youthful heart aged. He inquired of Pirān.

'Who is this man? How is he called amongst the warriors of Iran? You told me they were a contemptible group, of the lowest grade of the patricians. But now I find this arrow of theirs equal to a javelin. A lion's heart is of small value in combat with them. You have represented this affair as trivial, but from top to bottom all has been other than what you have said.'

Pirān replied,

'In the army of Iran I am acquainted with no one who has such power, no one whose arrow can pierce a tree. I do not know what object this ill-conditioned fellow has in mind. The true men amongst the Iranians are Giv and Ṭus; they have brilliance and strength on the day of battle. In the fray Humān [my brother] has often caused the world to appear of darker hue to Ṭus, but I do not know of anyone in Iran who might be this person, and there is no man in this army of ours who could be his match. I will go and inquire in the royal pavilion and ascertain his name without fail.'

[Pirān discovered that the mighty Iranian champion was no other than Rostam. Once again the two armies confronted each other and again there were rounds of single combat. In one of them Rostam challenged Kāmus, who had slain the Iranian warrior Alvā.]

(xxii) Kāmus is slain by Rostam

Tahamtan [Rostam] grieved over Alvā and in torment untied his lasso from the saddle-strap, for since he had purposed to fight alongside the other warriors he had lasso and battle-axe with him. Lasso over his arm and axe in hand he advanced, roaring like an elephant enraged. To him Kāmus called out,

'Do not be so confident in the strength of that thread sixty coils long.' To that Rostam replied, 'A lion roars bravely on first catching sight of his victim. It was you who first girt your loins up to take vengeance in this fashion, yet you also killed a nobleman of Iran. You called my lasso a thread; now you will see the noose tighten. Fate impels you, my Koshāni. When you have reached this point, there will be no more earth left for you [to tread].'

Kāmus the warrior put spurs to his charger, and, seeing his adversary standing firm and strong, swung his flashing sword at him with the intention of severing his head from his body. The point of the blade struck Rakhsh in the neck and cut his war-armour, yet without causing any injury to the horse's body. The elephant-bodied hero made a loop in his lasso and, while stirring his horse to move forward, launched it, encircled the waist of Kāmus, brought him up to his thigh and made fast, while Rakhsh thrust ahead like an eagle mightily winged. Strongly the rider pressed his thighs on him; the reins were let go and the weight was all in the stirrups.

The stupid victim sought to break the bight of the rope by his bodily strength and so release himself from his captivity, but though he strove insanely he could not break the bond. The elephant-bodied hero brought Rakhsh under control, turned his rein and flung his victim down from the saddle on to the ground. Dismounting he fastened him with a turn of the rope and said,

'Now you can do no further harm. Trickery and witchcraft are outside your power and your spirit is the hireling of any demon.'

He bound the hands of Kāmus behind his back as firm as a rock, seized the loops of the rope, put the vindictive fellow under his arm and so walked with him into the Iranian camp, where he said to the warriors,

'This war-thirsty fellow in his great might and boastfulness came out to confront me. This bold headstrong warrior, who has constantly been engaged in combat with lions, came to Iran with the purpose of making it desolate, and to our land, which he designed to convert into hiding-places for lions. He declared he would never loosen his grasp on his mace until he had destroyed Rostam son of Zāl. Now, his helmet and corselet have become his shroud, his diadem is clay and his shirt the dust. What think you of killing him, since the career of Kāmus must now come to a halt?'

He threw the man into the dust before the chieftains, whereupon the captains issued from amongst the troops and hacked his
body to pieces with the sword, until the stones and earth beneath
him were drenched with his blood. That is the habit of the skies
and fate; sometimes they are laden with pain and grief and sometimes they are full of gladness.

(xxiii) *Rostam and the Khāqān of China*

The tidings came to the Khāqān of China that Kāmus had been
slain on the field of vengeance and that because of his death the
spirits of the Koshāni and Shakni warriors and of the heroes of
Balkh had been darkened and embittered. Men turned to each other
and asked who this skilful and battle-trained vanquisher could be,
what kind of man he was and what his name was. Was there
anyone in the world who could confront him in battle? If the
heroic Kāmus could be caught up in the coil of a rope on the
battlefield, then this man could seize an elephant's head on the
day of conflict and bring it crashing to the ground.

As one man the troops made their way to the Khāqān, grieved
to tears because of Kāmus. Having greeted him, Pirān said in his
distress,

'You who are loftier than the azure dome, you have heard the
history of this battle from end to end and from your place beside
the troops have been a spectator of it all. Discover some scheme
for us of your own designing, conferring with no other person.
Consider well which of the veterans amongst the troops is
capable of investigating matters secretly. Let him find out who
this lion-hearted man is and whether there is not someone in this
army who has the power to confront him in battle. Then we can
set our whole force to slaughtering and, on the field of combat,
direct our attentions towards him.'

[In one of the passages at arms between champions from either
side, the Khāqān of China himself challenges Rostam, who hoists
him out of his saddle and takes him captive. Thereupon the whole
of the Turānian army turns its back and flees. Rostam angrily up-
braids the Iranians for missing a chance of destroying their enemy
completely.]

He loosened his tongue in scorn and said,

'Has not one of you a brain that is mated with sense? When
your enemy is thus hemmed in by two hills, fortune favours you

when he runs away. Did I not tell you to set outposts and turn
the slopes and dales into so much level plain and desert [because
of the multitude of the enemy dead]? You delivered over your
heads to comfort and slumber, leaving the toil and the marching
to your foes. Sloth of the body bears grief and pain as its fruit,
whereas exertion produces treasure. How can I promise that we
shall some day enjoy ease for our bodies? For the present we must
tremble in our anxiety for Iran.'

Turning furiously as a leopard on Ṭus, he continued,

'Is this a bed of repose or a battlefield? From now onwards
watch this plain with your troops for Humān and Kolbād as well
as for Pirān, Ru'īn and Pulād. You belong to one province and I,
Rostam, to another. Make war by yourselves, if you have the
resources. No longer will you have me as your ally. When I turned
victoriously from the field they had all been destroyed and the
task was completed. Now look to your sentinel and ascertain to
what force he belongs; discover the name of him who commands
that detachment. When you find the man who has acted as out-
post, pound his hands and feet immediately with the bastinado;
seize his possessions and shackle his feet. Then set him on a high
elephant and send him thus to the Shah, at whose court he will
surely be tamed. Observe moreover which amongst the Iranians
have money, jewels, ivory thrones, brocades, diadems or other
treasured articles or a throne. Demand that all such valuables be at
once produced. Many kings have there been on this plain, all of
them men of note in the world, who came from China, Saqlāb
[Sclavia], Hind and Vahr. All were possessed of great treasure
and were lords of great empires. Foremost out of it all there needs
to be a gift for the Shah, and then a portion must be sought out
for me and you.'

[In the course of his campaign against Turān, Rostam undertook
an expedition to destroy the ogreish Kāfur.]

He beheld a city, the name of which was Bidād and which was
fortified, inhabited by people whose food was human flesh and
from amongst whom the beauteous damsels were constantly
disappearing. At the table of its debased king nothing was served
but little children and the only food on his tray consisted of
beautiful slaves of faultless appearance and figure. Such was this
king's provender. At Rostam's command three thousand armoured men and others mounted on mail-clad horses set out

under Gostaham against the fortress, with him being two outstanding warriors, one of whom was Bizhan son of Giv and the
other Hazhir, vigorous in battle.

The name of the city's ruler, who held authority [from the king
of Turān], was Kāfur. On his hearing that an army from Iran had
arrived and that its general was a noted warrior, he donned his
martial gear, the whole city accompanying him with the ferocity of
leopards. There were lasso-throwers and wrestlers and others also
who in combat were as stone on anvil. First Kāfur grappled with
Gostaham, then both armies engaged. Of the Iranian warriors
many were slain and the minds of the remaining soldiers were
confused with grief.

When Gostaham understood how events were proceeding and
saw the world falling headlong into the grasp of the Div, he gave
orders for a shower of arrows on them and an ambuscade of
mounted men to lie in wait for them. Kāfur meantime was saying
to his captains,

'Iran shows no sign of being affected by arrows. Let every man
use sword, axe and lasso and get the hands of these arrogant
fellows into bonds.'

For long the warriors struggled together, fiercely enough to set
the river on fire. At last Gostaham said sharply to Bizhan,

'Touch your rein for an instant and move. Tell Rostam not to
delay over long but to put spurs to his horse and come with two
hundred knights.'

Bizhan son of Giv departed like the wind and recounted to
Rostam what was afoot. He at once set his foot into the stirrup
and came, his troop recking nought of mountain or dale. On to
the field of battle he dropped like a torrent falling from a black
mountain. Recklessly Kāfur attacked that royal and fruitful tree,
letting fly a sword as though it were an arrow that might by
chance land on the lion-overwhelming hero. But Rostam held
out his shield, on which the sword fell harmlessly. Kāfur then cast
his lasso over the son of Zāl, but his shoulders nimbly evaded it
and he in return aimed a blow at Kāfur's head which crushed it
and his helmet and shoulders together, so that his brains gushed
out of his nostrils. With the same vigour Rostam carried his
attack against the fortress, which great and small alike defended.
They barred the gates and rained down arrows from the walls,
shouting out,

'You have strength and sense; you are an elephant dressed in leopardskin. What name did your father give you at your birth? Are you a rope-thrower or the very sky of combat? You waste your effort against this stronghold, which the knowing call the city of war. When Tur, Faridun's son, rode forth from Iran, he called men skilled in every craft. One of them laid the foundations of this wall with stone and timber, brick and reed. He raised its top to its present height with wizardry and toil, drenching himself with sweat and emptying his treasury. Many a valiant fighter has exerted his strength to destroy this fortress wall, but none has ever mastered it, and no effort against it has any worth. We have weapons and there is food in abundance here, while beneath us is a passage by which more can be brought in. Though you strive and attack for years, you will gain nothing but more toil. No mangonel has ever come up against this wall, because of the wizardry of Tur and the whisperings of the priest.'

Rostam heard the words and his mind was troubled. His bellicose heart was confused as a jungle, for this was a contest that did not progress as he wished. He arrayed his forces in all four directions, setting Gudarz on one side, Tus on another and beyond him Giv with trumpets and drums. On the last face was a Zāboli force armed with Kāboli daggers. The wily Rostam seized a bow and then, when the whole fortress looked down in curiosity, he promptly shot through each head which appeared over the wall, with an arrow that confided its secret to the brain within that skull, although the two were associated only for ill.

Soon Rostam began to sap the wall and bring the defenders down from the rampart. At its foot were placed beams over which black naphtha had been poured and to which fire was applied when the wall had been pierced half-way through. Down came the ramparts built by Tur and from every side troops came pouring through the dust into the city.

'Attack!' commanded Rostam. 'Put bows and arrows to work.' The warriors in the fortress, concerned for their goods and children, their homes and kinsfolk, recklessly exposed their heads to destruction. It would have profited them more had they never been born of their mothers. The most valiant [Iranians], on foot, seized bucklers, arrows and bows and went with the spearsmen, in the van being Bizhan and Gostaham. From then onwards the attack was continued with spurting fire and with a hail of arrows which none could evade. Those of the occupants who emerged from the citadel walls fled panic-stricken and in tears out on to the open plain.

Now it was the warlike Iranians who barricaded the gates in order to devote their efforts to looting and slaughter. Great were the numbers they slew and many the captives young and old whom they carried off from the city. Gold, too, silver and precious goods in plenty, slaves male and female the Iranian soldiery carried away to their baggage-camp. Thereafter Rostam went, having washed his body and head, into the presence of the World-Creator, bidding the Iranians to confess what was concealed rather than what was patent and to render thanks for their victory and the benefits which had been granted them.

[Afrāsiyāb the Turānian king now called on his army commander Pulādvand to make a stand against the Iranians.]

(xxiv) *Pulādvand encounters Giv and Ṭus in battle*

When the sun flourished his shining banner and the violet satin of night turned saffron, there issued from the royal palace the roll of drums and the shout of the army reached to the clouds. Out in front of the troops stepped Pulādvand, immense in body, a lasso over his arm. As the two opposing forces drew up in their ranks, the air became violet with the dust and the ground was black [with their multitude]. Meanwhile Rostam donned his leopard-skin cloak and mounted his fierce elephant [his charger Rakhsh], roused himself to movement and charged the right wing of the Turānians, many of whose heroes he overthrew.

Pulādvand, seeing this, unloosed his writhing lasso from his saddle-strap and grappled with Ṭus like an elephant enraged; the lasso over his arm and a club in his hand. He seized his foeman by the girdle, lifted him with ease from the saddle and dashed him to the ground. Giv, looking on at the contest, beheld the son of Nowzar flung headlong and at once put spurs to his courser Shabdiz. With body and mind prepared for the struggle like a male lion he engaged the Div; he himself being dight in his harness, in his hand a bull-headed mace. But Pulādvand cast his lasso and in a moment the head of the valiant Giv was ensnared.

Now making their way to the field of battle were Rahhām and Bizhan, who saw what was afoot and observed that mighty arm and that power. They came up to Pulādvand with the object of pinioning his arms in a noose of their lasso, but he was keenly

watching. He put out his arm, stirred his horse into movement
and exerted all his strength, flinging down into the dust these two
bold and stout-hearted warriors, these proud lions capable of far-
reaching defence, and bringing them low in humiliation before
many knights who stood looking on. Then he approached the
Kāviāni Standard and, with his dagger, cut it into two. A cry
arose from the Iranian troops, no man on the field remaining unmoved. Fariborz and Gudarz with other proud knights who saw
this act of the demon warrior called out to Rostam, exactor of
vengeance,

'On this battlefield Pulādvand has left not a single man of note
in the saddle; not one knight amongst the army's champions
remains whom he has not brought low into the dust with axe and
dagger, arrow and bow. The whole field is a scene of mourning,
and in this crisis Rostam is our only succour.'

(xxv) *Rostam encounters Pulādvand*

Rostam heard the words and was saddened; he trembled like a
leaf on a tree. Approaching closer to Pulādvand he saw him as
though he were a lofty hill, and grieved for those four brave
warriors destroyed like wild asses by their enemy the lion. He saw
that the greater part of his own troops were wounded, while on
the other side the men continued to give battle. To himself he
said,

'Surely now the cycle [of fate] has turned against us; fortune,
once alert on our behalf, has been lulled to sleep.'

He pressed his thighs against Rakhsh and stirred him into a
gallop, having roused himself to excitement and the resolution to
attack.

[After charging each other on horseback, with the usual vituperative exchanges, the two combatants agreed to dismount and decide
the issue in a wrestling contest.]

Those two proud warriors eager for vengeance now got ready
for a wrestling match. On both sides the armies had sworn an oath
that no enraged partisan would leave his own side to give aid to
either combatant; the two forces being half a league apart. The
stars were spectators of the struggle as the two fierce lions grappled with each other. First each touched the other's hand and then
seized the belt about his middle. As Shida [Afrāsiyāb's son] closely

observed Rostam's chest and shoulders he heaved a cold sigh that
came from the depth of his being. He said to his father,

'This man of strength whom you call Rostam, with his force and
overwhelming power, will bring the demon warrior's head down
into the dust. One cannot foresee anything but defeat for our
warriors, therefore do not let us defy the inexorably-turning
spheres.'

Afrāsiyāb gave this answer to Shida,

'My brain teems with swift-moving thoughts over what is
occurring. Go out and see how Pulādvand fixes his holds in the
wrestling. Direct him in Turkish and demonstrate the proper way
in which he may from behind throw Rostam from his footing.
Tell him that when he has got his man underneath he must continue the fight with his sword.'

Shida answered,

'Your Majesty's oath to him in the presence of the army was
not in those terms. If you break your word and yield to ill-con-
sidered ideas, the result of your act will be lacking in honour. Do
not let the esteem which you enjoy be converted into black infamy,
so that any caviller may condemn you.'

At that the king unloosed his tongue abusively, stirred himself
to fury and began to harbour suspicions against his son, to whom
he said,

'If the Div Pulādvand suffers any harm from this malevolent
fellow, not a man shall remain alive on this ground. The only skill
which you possess is with your tongue.'

With that he turned his rein and came raging like a lion to the
spot where the two doughty rivals struggled. For a time he
regarded their exertions as they roared lion-like, then said to
Pulādvand,

'Mighty lion, if in a bout you get him underneath, slit his
midriff with your dagger. The task you have in hand is to use
your skill and to settle this business, not merely to boast of a
triumph.'

Giv, watching Afrāsiyāb and noting the despicable advice and
vicious scheme, put spurs to his horse and came up in haste as the
treacherous king thus broke his word. He said to Rostam,

'What order have you for us who are under your command?
Pay regard to how Afrāsiyāb acts, to his treacherous words and
to his underhand trickery. He has come to give heart to your
opponent, telling him to use his dagger while he is wrestling.'

Rostam answered,

'I am a fighter and in wrestling I am slow. Yet why be afraid and why let your heart be riven like this? I am on the point of bringing Pulādvand head and shoulders down from the sky into the dust. Even if I have not the strength of arm for this encounter, why break my heart over it vainly? Now that this foolish wonder-worker is transgressing the oath given by him before God, why should you fear his breach of the oath, since by it he has brought death pouring down on to his head?'

So saying he stretched out a lion-like claw and gripped the master-fighter's arms and chest. Though Pulādvand put out all his strength, Rostam uprooted him from his position like a plane-tree, seized him by the neck and dashed him to the ground, with praises to God. A mighty shout arose from the Iranian army and the drummers marched out along the road, the blowing of horns ascended the sky, cymbals clanged and Indian bells were set pealing. To Rostam's mind not a sound limb had been left in Pulādvand's body and his face had taken on the appearance of the wild saffron. Rostam, mounting his courser Rakhsh, left that dragon-body where it lay.

As soon as the lion-taking hero had departed to his own army, Pulādvand looked about him keen as an arrow and ran with sore heart and tearful countenance to Afrāsiyāb. Then for a time the warrior's senses departed and he lay prostrate on the dark earth. Tahamtan, seeing the warrior still alive and the whole ground covered with his troops, cried out to the veteran Gudarz the command that his forces should send a rain of arrows and make the aether look like a shower in Spring. To his own army Pulādvand said,

'Our throne, treasure and high repute are departed. Why cast our heads to the wind or think of resisting further?'

With that he set his troops on the march and so departed, the links of his spirit having been broken by Rostam.

[After the rout of his army Afrāsiyāb fled into hiding, while Rostam came in triumph back to Iran, where there were great festivities. He then entered on a new series of adventures.]

IX

Rostam and Akvān the Div

(i) *The Div appears*

It happened once, when an hour of the day had gone, that out of the wilderness a herdsman arrived at the palace. He presented himself before the king, kissed the ground and said to that prince of blessed birth,

'Amongst my horses a wild ass has appeared like a demon escaped from its bonds. You would think it a male lion for savagery, for it can break the neck of any horse. In colour it exactly parallels the sun, as though the heavens had dipped it in liquid gold, and from its neck to its tail a stripe black as musk is drawn. From its rounded haunches, its fore-legs and hind-legs you would judge it to be a powerful bay charger.'

Khosrow perceived that this was no wild ass, for no onager could surpass a horse in strength. Moreover he had seen much of the world and heard much from men of experience. He knew therefore that there existed a spring where Akvān the Demon dwelt, because of whom the world was overwhelmed by sorrow and lamentation. It was there that the herdsman kept his troop of horses, though letting them roam freely and safely for pasture. He said to the herdsman,

'That is no onager, as I now understand. Linger here no further.'

To his escort he said,

'Noble men, all endowed with splendour and lofty rank, from amongst you warriors I need a champion of leonine daring who will devote himself to this endeavour.'

As he spoke he looked keenly about him, but no warrior there met with his approval. For this high endeavour only Rostam son of Zāl was fitted to be of service. To him then he wrote a letter full of kindliness and due gratitude and handed it to the warrior Gorgin son of Milād, to whom the king of blessed fortune said,

'Bear this missive of mine to Zāl's son. Travel night and day as swift as smoke; there must be no resting in Zābolestān. Salute him warmly on my behalf, with the prayer that Heaven itself may not

146

exist without him. When he has read the letter, tell him that my
Farr owes everything to him. Show your face there but for a
moment, then rise and return here. Once you have perused his
reply do not linger in Zābol.'

Gorgin set off like a storm-wind, or like an onager in peril of its
life. When he arrived in Zābol, in the presence of the famous hero,
he surrendered the king's letter to him, and he, on receipt of the
royal command, departed at a gallop for the king's court. There
he kissed the earth at the foot of the throne and prayed for the
king's good fortune. Then he said,

'O king, you summoned me. Here I stand to learn what you
have thought out and wait with loins girt to hear what your behest
shall be. May greatness and goodness be ever associated with your
name.'

The king answered,

'Elephant-body, a task has arisen for which I have chosen you
out of all my forces. If you do not deem it irksome, you must be
ready at my bidding to strive for a throne and treasure. A herdsman has informed me that an onager has appeared amongst his
troop of horses. And now, you must assume this further undertaking and once again burden yourself with a combat. Go, but be
strongly on your guard, for this may be Ahriman the vengeful.'

Rostam commented,

'With fortune favourable to you, nobody who serves your
throne can harbour fear. Whether this be Div, lion or male
dragon, it will not escape my sharp sword.'

(ii) *Rostam seeks out the Div*

Out in pursuit of his prey went the male lion, lasso at hand and
with his dragon [i.e. Rakhsh] under him; out into the wilderness
travelled this fierce lion to where the herdsman kept his troop of
horses. For three days he sought for it over the grazing-grounds;
on the fourth he saw it galloping over the plain and overtook it
like a wind from the north. It was a beast of shining gold, yet
underneath its hide was a hideous canker. Rostam put spurs to his
swift courser, but on coming close up with the beast he changed
his purpose, saying,

'This creature must not be put to death. I must ensnare it in a
loop of my lasso and not destroy it with my dagger. So I can bring
it to the king alive.'

He thereupon cast his royal lasso with the purpose of entangling its head in the noose. But the powerful onager, espying the rope, suddenly vanished from his sight, making him understand that this was no onager and that to deal with it demanded guile rather than strength. He thought, 'This can be nothing but Akvān the Div and must be dealt a sword-thrust swifter than wind. I have heard from a sage that this is its abode and that by some marvel it has assumed the hide of an onager, so I must employ the sword with cunning if I am to let blood pour over that yellow gold.'

At that moment the onager reappeared from out of the wilderness, and the champion put spurs to his swift-moving steed. He fitted a string to his bow and made Rakhsh gallop faster than the wind, while he loosed an arrow that was quick as lightning. But no sooner had he drawn his royal bow than the onager vanished from his sight once again. He galloped his courser over the wide plain in pursuit until, when a day and a night had thus passed, the need for water, and for bread too, overcame him, and his head struck the saddle-bow in sleep. Then, as his thirst for limpid water pressed urgently on him, there appeared in front of him a spring sweet as rose-water. He dismounted and watered Rakhsh, then out of weariness closed his eyes in sleep. From his royal saddle he unloosed his girth and laid down the saddle-cover of leopard-skin for a pillow, while Rakhsh moved off to graze. Then he spread out the felt underlay of the saddle alongside the water.

(iii) *Akvān the Div casts Rostam into the ocean*

When from afar Akvān beheld Rostam asleep, he transformed himself into a storm-wind to gain approach. He dug round the earth all about him and [on this bed of earth] raised him aloft from the plain to the skies, so that on waking Rostam was smitten with fear. He writhed about in panic and his head filled with apprehension as he said to himself,

'This foul demon has spread a bloody snare for me. Alas now for my courage and strength and these shoulders of mine! Alas also for my swordsmanship and mace-wielding! This happening will bring my world to ruin and everything will foster the ambitions of Afrāsiyāb. Gudarz will not survive, nor Khosrow nor Ṭus, nor will throne or crown, elephant or drum. Through my own act evil will descend on the earth, so slack has my market become. Who will wreak vengeance on this accursed Div? There is none to confront him on equal footing.'

As Rostam contorted himself in his distress, Akvān thus addressed him,

'Elephant-body, speak your wish and declare where you would desire the air to cast you down. Shall I thrust you down into the waters or on to the mountains? Into which region remote from men do you wish to fall?'

Rostam heard the words and realized that he was in the clutches of the accursed Div.

'Whatever he says,' the elephant-bodied warrior communed with himself, 'my one course lies in cunning. If I say one thing, he will do the opposite; he knows nothing of oaths and will bind himself with no promise. Should I bid him cast me into the ocean and make a shark's maw my grave, this despicable Div will at once deal with me by dropping me on to the mountains, where I shall be dashed to pieces, so that Resurrection will begin with me. I must employ some guile that his thoughts may be led into casting me into the ocean.'

He therefore replied,

'A Chinese sage has composed a discourse on this subject which declares that if a man yields up his life in the ocean his soul will not behold the angels in heaven but will remain in abasement where it lies; he will find no entry into the next world. Do not therefore cast me into the sea or make the fishes' belly my grave. Rather cast me on to the mountains, so that the tiger and the lion may experience the grip of a brave man.'

On hearing Rostam's speech, Akvān the Div uttered a roar like that of the ocean.

'I will cast you into a place,' he bellowed, 'where you will remain hidden somewhere between the two worlds.'

As he spoke the words the malign Div seized the valiant Rostam and flung him out of his hand into the depths of the ocean. While falling out of the aether towards the sea, the hero quickly drew his keen sword from his girdle, so that the monsters which attacked him when he descended withdrew affrighted from his onslaught. He swam with his left arm and leg while with his other limbs he sought ways of fending off his attackers, ceasing not a moment from active motion, as is the way of men inured to war. Determining on a certain direction in the water, he at last reached dry land and caught sight of the plain. There he gave thanks to the

Creator, who had delivered His servant from that malign being. When he had rested and loosened his girdle, he laid down his leopard-skin cloak by the side of a spring, cast aside his saturated bow and other weapons and clad himself once more in his coat of mail. From there he went to the spring where he had fallen asleep and the malevolent Div had snatched him up.

Rakhsh, however, with his resplendent coat, was nowhere to be found on the pasture-ground, and the world-conqueror roundly imprecated his ill fate. With energy he roused himself, caught up saddle and bridle and despondently followed the horse's footprints. At a walking pace he went forward, his eyes meanwhile searching for game, when suddenly a pasture-ground came into view. It was well-wooded and watered by flowing streams and everywhere partridges and turtle-doves called. While the herdsman who held charge of Afrāsiyāb's horses had laid his head down in the woodland to sleep, the fiery Rakhsh had come amongst the mares like a Div, neighing loudly in the midst of the herd. There Rostam caught sight of him and with a swing of his royal lasso entangled his head in the noose, then rubbed the dust from him, put on the saddle and grasped his sharp sword.

That done, he began to drive off the whole herd, having pronounced the name of God over his sword. The tramp of the horses as it fell on the herdsman's ears roused him from his slumbers. He raised his head and shouted to his companions, each of whom seized a bow and lasso. Mounted on their speedy coursers they rode out to discover who the evil miscreant could be that was bold enough to enter that pasture-ground, where so many horsemen were on guard. Swiftly they rode off on their task of rending the skin of any such prowling lion.

As Rostam espied the hasting men he quickly drew the sword of wrath from his girdle. Like a lion he roared and called out his name, saying, 'I am Rostam son of Dastān son of Sām.' With his sword he slew two men out of three of them, and the herdsman on beholding this turned his back in flight, with Rostam, hot on his heels, fitting a string to the bow on his shoulder.

(iv) Afrāsiyāb inspects his herd of horses

[Each year Afrāsiyāb had been accustomed to looking over his herd of horses, but he now found none in the places where he expected them to be. The herdsman told him how Rostam had single-handed driven off the herd and slain a number of the guards. This information stirred him to wrath and he went off in pursuit, only to be put to flight by Rostam, who returned to the spring.]

When Rostam once more in his gallop came back to the spring, his battle-thirsty heart was eager for still more. Once again Akvān the Div encountered him.

'Are you still not surfeited with combat?' he inquired. 'You escaped from the ocean and the monsters' clutches, yet you have come on to the field impatient for more strife. Now you are to see that day following which you will never more seek a battle.'

Tahamtan heard the demon's words and with the roar of a lion enraged he loosed his writhing lasso from his saddle-trap, cast it and encircled the other's waist in a knot. Turning in his saddle he raised his heavy axe as a blacksmith does his hammer and brought it down on the demon's head with the strength of a wild elephant, crushing his head, brain and shoulders into one mass. Then, dismounting, he drew his gleaming dagger and severed his head from his body. Now he called for blessings on the Creator, through whom he had beheld victory on the day of wrath.

[In this story] you must recognize the demon as the man of evil, he that displays ingratitude towards God; for you must reckon anyone who transgresses the ways of humane conduct as a demon rather than a man. If your reason refuses to believe these tales, it may be that it has not accurately understood this inward significance.

My aged master, what say you, who have tasted much of the heat and cold in the world? Who knows what ups and downs the long day will bring forth? The gallop of time, in spite of its length, will exhaust all the material at my disposal. Who knows what number of feasts and battles this swift-revolving dome may contain?

X

The Adventure of Bizhan and Manizha

(i) Introduction

It was a night that might have been a ghost which had washed its face with pitch. Mars, Saturn and Mercury were invisible. The Moon had changed her accustomed behaviour; having seated herself on her throne in preparation for her journey, she had darkened herself in the abode in which she lingered; her waist had diminished and her heart was oppressed. Of her diadem two parts had turned azure and the aether she traversed was rust-begrimed and dust-laden. The army of black night had cast over plain and pasture a covering dark as a raven's wing; like rusty iron was the corroded sky, or you might have imagined its surface overlaid with pitch. On every hand Ahriman appeared to my eye as a black serpent with wide-open mouth. Whenever he drew an icy breath it was as though a negro had stirred up the dust with a finger. Garden and streamlet's brim were blackened as if a river of bitumen had overflowed. The revolving sky halted in amaze; Sol remained incapable of movement, in hand and foot. As for the earth, under that pitch-black canopy you would have said it had fallen into deep slumber. The heart of the universe was overwhelmed with terror of itself; the night-watchman had stilled his bell. Yet there was neither the cheep of a bird nor the cry of a beast anywhere; destiny had bound its tongue against uttering good or ill. Nothing was visible, below or above, and my heart was clutched with dismay at the long quietude. In that mood of dismay I sprang from where I lay—I had a loving companion in the house—and, calling out, I asked her for a lamp. She came out into the garden to inquire why I had need of a lamp. Was it that sleep would not come to me in the darkness of the night? I answered,

'My beloved, I am not a man for sleep. Bring a lamp as bright as the sun. Set it down before me and make preparation for a feast. Bring a lute with you and get ready to drink wine.'

My love quitted the garden and fetched a lighted candle and a lamp. She also brought wine, pomegranates, oranges and quinces, together with a polished royal goblet. From time to time she poured wine and played. You would have thought the angel Hārut was exercising his witchery, bestowing on my heart exultant satisfaction of its longings and turning black night into bright day. Listen to what my beloved said after we had mated with the wine. She said, that bright-visaged beloved one,

'May Heaven rejoice in your existence! Pour out a beakerful of wine and let me tell you a story from the records of ancient time, so that when your ear has caught something of what I tell, wonderment may seize you at the workings of destiny. It is a story full of guile and love, of magic and battle, and concerned with men of learning and gravity.'

To that cypress stature I said,

'O moon-cheek, tell me the story tonight,' and she replied, 'When you hear this tale from me, set it out in verse from the Pahlavi book of legends.'

That beloved and beautiful friend recited the story to me out of that book written long ago, and now hear my poetic narrative, keeping mindful of reason and retaining good sense in your heart.

(ii) *The Armānis petition Khosrow*

[The inhabitants of the Armān region came to petition Khosrow over the losses they were suffering from the ravages of wild boars. He offered a rich reward in advance to any of his warriors who would undertake to extirpate the beasts.]

None in the company made any reply except Bizhan son of Giv the happy-starred warrior. He prepared himself for the journey, girding his waist and setting a diadem on his head. He was accompanied by Gorgin son of Milād, his comrade in battle and his adjunct when succour was required. From the king's palace he set forth with panther and falcon with which to hunt game on the long road. So they passed their time on the journey, which seemed in their eyes to traverse nothing but gardens. They came at last to where the forest lay and, as Bizhan cast his eyes upon it, his blood stirred within him in a ferment. Wild boar were everywhere, unwitting that Bizhan had come to drive them away. He alighted close to the forest and scanned the scene to discover how he could attack the beasts. To Gorgin son of Milād he said,

'Enter and clear a place for yourself in some corner. When I begin shooting arrows at the beasts approach the pool there, and as soon as a clamour arises in the forest, lay on your battle-axe but keep ever on the alert, so that if one escapes my clutches you may sever its head from its body at a blow.'

Gorgin the militant, however, retorted to Bizhan,

'My compact with the new king was not on those terms. You bore off the [reward of] jewels, silver and gold and it was you who undertook this onslaught. Ask no more aid from me than my guiding you to the place where I shall station myself.'

Bizhan was astounded at such words and the world seemed to go dark before his eyes. He rushed into the wood as a lion might, and hotly he affixed a string to his bow. Like Spring thunder he rumbled forth and like the rain he beat down the leaves from the trees; while, tempered-steel dagger in hand, he pursued the swine like a raging elephant. One boar charged at him like Ahriman and with its tusks pierced Bizhan's armour; for, as though they were steel files on hard stone, the boar had ground its tusks against a tree. But he thrust a dagger into its chest and cut its mammoth body in twain. [The rest of the herd were similarly exterminated.]

(iii) *Gorgin leads Bizhan astray*

The malevolent Gorgin, his wits perturbed, in the meanwhile had come stealthily to a certain part of the forest, all of which had seemed dark in his eyes. There he greeted Bizhan with a show of pleasure, but there was rancour in his heart at Bizhan's feat and apprehension that ill repute might befall himself, [so that he lusted to do Bizhan an ill. He said to him,]

'Pahlavān, you who have a heart devoted to war and a spirit given to wisdom, many adventures such as this will, through divine influence and your own high destiny, come into your path. Let me recount now certain things that must be said, since at various times I have visited this region with Rostam, Giv and Gostaham, with Nowzar's son and Gozhdaham. What feats of valour we performed on this wide plain while the heavens revolved above us, feats whereby our repute waxed great and we acquired merit in Khosrow's eyes.

'Not far removed from here there is a festal spot whence in two days' time one may reach the land of Tur. A plain all green and gold you will there see, enough to gladden the heart of any generous-minded man. All is woodland, gardens and flowing streams; it is a place fit for a Pahlavān. The ground is silken, the air perfumed with musk and you would declare what flows in the brooks to be rose-water. The branches of the jessamine are bent double under their load of blossom, the rose has become an idol and the nightingale its priest. In amongst the flowers the pheasant proudly steps, and lustily the nightingale sings from the branches of the cypress.

'From this day for nine days more the streamlet's brim will be like a Paradise. There you will see over all the plain and hill fairy-featured maidens seated in merry companies; in their midst will be Afrāsiyāb's daughter Manizha, who will make the garden brilliant as the sun. Accompanied by a hundred serving-maids, each a picture, she will pitch her pavilion in the meads. All the maidens are the veiled daughters of Turks, all are cypress-statured and all fragrant with musk. Their cheeks are rosy, their eyes languorous, their lips wine-filled and redolent of rose-water. You will see the whole plain as ornamental as a Chinese idol-house full of treasure. If we go to that delectable spot, but a single day's ride, we shall be able to capture some of these fairy-cheeked maidens and take them to Khosrow, whose favour we shall thus secure.'

So Gorgin spoke, and, since Bizhan was young, the fibres in the youthful champion stirred. Fame was once the spur to eagerness, but now what he sought was pleasure. He was young, and youthfully he set forth.

(iv) *Bizhan voyages to behold Manizha, daughter of Afrāsiyāb*

The twain set out on their long road, the one urged by nature, the other by the lust to sate his rancour. After a day's journeying, Bizhan the warlike, greatest resource of his army, called a halt between two stretches of forest, and there, in the pasture-grounds of the Armān, they remained for two days disporting themselves with falcon and hunting-panther. When Gorgin learnt that the [future] bride had come there, the whole plain now as brilliant as a cock's eye, he disclosed to Bizhan all he knew, speaking to him of the festivities and the music. Bizhan remarked,

'I will continue this adventure and make my way to the feasting-place to view from afar how Turānians prepare their banquets. Thence I will turn my reins about, raising my polished spear to the sky. We can then take counsel together, being better informed and our wits sharpened by what we shall have seen.'

To the keeper of his treasure he said,

"That diadem which was my father's, which he used to wear on his head at feasting-times thereby illumining the whole banqueting-hall, bring it to me, for I desire to visit the place where the festivities are to be. Bring me also the collar of Key Khosrow and his ear-rings, and further, Giv's jewelled bracelets.'

He donned a robe of gleaming Greek brocade and to his crown attached a feather of the Homā, the royal bird. On the back of [his charger] Shabrang they put a saddle, and he called for his seal-ring gained as a Pahlavān. Then, throwing his leg across the horse, he rode off at a gallop to the appointed place. As he neared it his mind dwelt upon the outcome of his emprise, and, coming to a cypress tree, he stretched himself out under it for protection from the fierce sun while, keeping his horse by him, he covertly viewed the young women. In his sight they were as pretty as the dolls of Qandahār and lovely as glad Spring. The whole plain resounded with the music of stringed instruments, and with the world in song, it was enough to gratify the soul of any man.

That most lovely of maidens beheld the face of the warrior champion on his way, his cheeks bright as Canopus in Arabia Felix or as a violet encircled with jasmine leaves, on his head the world-Pahlavān's diadem and his breast resplendent in Greek brocade. Secretly within her tent she felt her virgin passion aflame for her [coming] suitor, and so she sent her nurse as messenger to the place where the branching cypress stood, to discover who the high-born warrior was who rested there beneath it.

'Is he perhaps Siyāvosh come to life, or else a peri?' she wondered, telling the nurse to inquire how he came to be there and who had guided him to that spot, whether he was born of a peri or was indeed Siyāvosh. Her heart was finding solace in affection for him. Had Resurrection Day dawned in the world that the fire of passion had so fiercely blazed up? Year after year she had made merry at Springtime in that meadow and never before beheld a stranger at the festivities. She had now seen his cypress form, but never anyone else. What was his name and what the place of his origin?

The nurse came to Bizhan, greeted him and called down blessings on him. When she delivered Manizha's message he blushed as red as any rose and answered he was not Siyāvosh, nor peri-born, but had arrived from Iran, the land of free-born men.

'I am Bizhan son of Giv,' he said, 'and I have come as a warrior to combat the wild boar with sharp weapons. I have cut their heads off and flung them to be trampled under passing feet, but their tusks I will carry to the Shah. When I was given tidings of this festive spot I refused to return in haste to Giv son of Gudarz, in hope that happy fortune would show me Afrāsiyāb's daughter's face in my dreams. Also I had conceived the desire to see this meadow adorned like a Chinese temple filled with precious rarities. If you will advise me soundly I will make you a gift of a golden crown, earrings and girdle. Bring me but to that lovely maiden and mate her heart with mine in love.'

Thus spoke Bizhan, and the nurse returned to deliver the secret into Manizha's ear.

'His face,' she reported, 'is such and such, and thus and thus is his figure. So did the World-Creator fashion him.'

At once she sent the reply,

'All you imagined is within your grasp. Come to me in your majesty and illumine this dark soul of mine. Let my eyes be brightened by the vision of you; let valley, plain and encampment become a flower-garden.'

The messenger also acted as his guide; Bizhan's heart and ear had turned into music at the reply he had received.

(v) Bizhan comes to Manizha's tent

No need was there now for words. Bizhan strode forward out of the cypress-tree's shade towards the noble-spirited maiden, hasting on foot in eagerness. As he entered the tent, looking like a tall cypress with his middle girt in a golden belt, Manizha approached him and took him into her embrace. She loosed his royal girdle, then questioned him about his journey and all his adventures, inquiring who had accompanied him in his battle with the wild boars and why he, who possessed such handsomeness, had subjected so fine a person, face and form, to the fatigue of wielding a mace.

They washed his feet in musk and rose-water, then hasted to prepare a meal. Soon they set down a tray covered with viands of every kind to which they pressed him ever and anon. Afterwards they seated themselves for music and wine, having cleared the pavilion of all others. Slaves stationed themselves with lute and harp to make melody. The floor had been given the colours of a parrot, or, with gold coins and brocades appeared like a leopard's hide. The pavilion itself had been perfumed and adorned with musk and amber, ruby and gold. Old wine in crystal goblets put strength in Bizhan and for three days and nights he and she made merry together until sleep and intoxication overcame them.

(vi) *Manizha bears off Bizhan to her palace*

The time for departure arrived, but Manizha needs must have Bizhan in her sight; therefore, seeing him with downcast visage, she summoned her slaves and bade them mingle with honey a draught that would bereave him of sense. This they administered to him and he had no sooner drunk than he swooned and laid down his head in unconsciousness. They had got ready a litter and laying the unconscious man on it they set forth; she being seated in comfort on one side while the other was for his repose. As they approached the city she covered the sleeping man with a curtain and entered the palace at night in secret, opening her lips to none who were not in her confidence. Within the palace she made a sleeping-chamber ready for him.

On Bizhan's waking, Manizha came in haste and poured into his ear a drug to revive his senses and restore them to their accustomed state. When he was fully awake and become alert again he found in his embrace a jasmine-breasted maid of gorgeous beauty. He perceived that he was in the palace of Afrāsiyāb and that on his pillow was this lovely woman. Perturbed in spirit by his situation he sought refuge in God from Ahriman and said,

'Lord, there will be no escape for me from this place. Exact vengeance for me from Gorgin, hearken to my plaint and to the curses I pronounce against him. He it was who led me into this evil plight by chanting a thousand spells over me.'

Manizha answered him,

'Keep your heart in tranquillity. Reckon as nought what has not occurred. Men may indulge in activities of every kind; at times they go to feasts, at times to war.'

So the two made the chamber ready for their supper, prepared to face either the gallows or the marriage-pulpit. From every tent they invited a rosy-cheeked girl, whom they decked in Chinese brocade, and these fairy-visaged maids played on the lute. Thus day and night passed in merrymaking.

A hint of it came to the chamberlain, someone speaking in jest having stirred the tree of destruction. He sought out all these hidden secrets and deeply probed into the matter, tracing it to its beginnings. He looked into the man's identity, inquired what his country was and his purpose in thus coming to Turān. All this he ascertained and then began to fear for his own life. In haste he departed to find some way of deliverance, apprehending that nought availed but to tell the truth. With running steps he emerged from behind the veil and into the presence of the Turānian king, to whom he said,

'Your daughter has chosen a spouse from Iran.'

The king called on the name of the Ruler of the world—you might have thought him a willow bending under the blast of the wind. He wiped away the blood from his eyelashes, where it had dropped on the way from his eyes to his cheeks, and in fierce choler he exclaimed,

'Any man that has a daughter behind the veil is ill-starred, even though he wear a crown.'

Outraged at Manizha's conduct he summoned Qarā-khān, the palace chamberlain, to whom he said,

'Give me clear-minded counsel with regard to the behaviour of this unchaste woman.'

Qarā-khān answered the king thus,

'Inquire more closely into the accusation. If it be true, no room remains for speech; yet hearsay is not the same as seeing with one's eyes.'

On receiving this answer Afrāsiyāb began hurriedly to put into action the suggestion of Qarā-khān. Looking at Garsivaz [his brother] he said,

'Much have we suffered at the hands of Iran and shall again suffer. Who else in the whole world has suffered ill-fortune such as this—the misery inflicted by Iran and by an evil daughter? Go with keen-minded horsemen and keep a watch on the palace, both roof and door. Have a care that you fetter anyone you see on the roof, drag him along and bring him here.'

(vii) *Garsivaz carries Bizhan into the presence of Afrāsiyāb*

As Garsivaz approached the door, loud voices issued from the hall and the sounds of revelry and feasting intermingled with the strumming of harps and the plucking of lutes. (The cavalry had occupied the gateway and roof of the royal palace and closed the paths on every side.) Finding that the gate of the palace was barred within and the sounds of wine-bibbing, festivity and merrymaking continued, Garsivaz stretched out his hand and lifted the bar from the gate, through which he leapt into the midst of the palace. Swiftly he moved to the chamber into which the stranger had intruded, and as from the door his eye lit on Bizhan, his blood boiled with choler against him. Three hundred slaves were present there, all of them engaged in strumming, drinking and singing. In the midst of the women sat Bizhan, red wine in hand, making merry. Garsivaz roared out at him in exasperation,

'Impudent fellow, base villain, you have fallen into the claws of a raging lion. How will you escape from this with your life?'

Bizhan was wrung with uneasiness, thinking how he was to fight with his body unprotected. He thought,

'Shabrang [his horse] is not here with me, nor have I any other horse to ride. The sun has indeed turned against me today. Where is Giv, son of Gudarz the Keshvadi? I shall be compelled to surrender my head for nothing, and I see none in the whole world to aid me; only God is my deliverer.'

In his boot on one leg he carried a dagger of tempered steel. Stretching out his hand he drew the weapon from its sheath, leapt to the door and called out his name.

'I am Bizhan,' he cried, 'a son of the Keshvad stock, chief of all champion warriors and free men. Let no man try to pierce the skin of my breast, or his body is likely to make a journey without his head. Even if Resurrection were to appear in the world, none should see my back in flight.'

He then turned to Garsivaz and shouted,

'Ill-fortune has treated me thus scurvily. You know who my kinsmen are, who my king is and what my standing is amongst warriors. If you seek battle, I am ever ready to steep my fists in blood in the cause of war. With this dagger I could decapitate many a Turānian. But carry me before the Turānian monarch and I will explain this affair from end to end. Ask him to grant me security for my life; it would be conduct worthy of you if you were to be his guide to mercy.'

Garsivaz perceived his intention and saw also how sharp his claws would be in combat. He was aware that the other's aim was hostile and his hand prepared for battle, so he swore an oath to be honest with him and with a pretence of friendship gave him good counsel. By specious promises he parted him from the dagger and by smooth speech beguiled him until he could put him into fetters. He then bound him tight from head to foot as though he were a wild panther. What availed his powers once his fortunes were reversed? That is the way of this revolving hump-back of a sky; where you have shown mildness you will get savagery in return.

Thus they bore him pallid-cheeked and with streaming eyes into the presence of Afrāsiyāb. Fettered and with head uncovered they brought him before the king, whom he greeted and said,

'It would be fitting on your part to inquire where the truth lies. Not of my own will was it that I came into your palace and no person is to blame for this occurrence. I came from Iran for the purpose of destroying wild boars, when I happened upon this Turānian festival. I had sent my people in pursuit of a hawk that had gone astray and went to lie down under a cypress-tree to find shelter from the sun. A peri came, and, spreading out her wing, took me to her bosom as I slept. She parted me from my horse but we set out on the road, where we met the escort of your Majesty's daughter. On the plain round about horsemen were scattered and many a palanquin went by me. From out of the distance an Iranian parasol approached surrounded on all sides by Turānian cavaliers. In the midst of them was a new palanquin over which a silken curtain was drawn; in it was a fairy form asleep, with a crown set on the pillow. Suddenly the fairy called on the name of Ahriman and came forward amongst her cavaliers as swift as the wind. Without warning she set me in the litter and there this beautiful creature chanted a spell over me, so that until we were in the halls of Afrāsiyāb my eyes did not awaken from sleep. In all this there was no fault of mine nor was Manizha dishonoured by it. Doubtless the peri was smitten by ill-fortune in endeavouring to overcome me by magic.'

To this Afrāsiyāb returned,

'Your ill fate overtook you. You are the man who came from Iran with mace and lasso in search of war and high fame. Now you stand before me, like a woman with hands tied, and talk of dreams as a man in intoxication would. By attempting the use of deceitful words you hope to snatch my head from me.'

Bizhan said to him,

'Listen to a word from me and take it to heart. Wild boars can anywhere only fight with their tusks, and lions with their claws. In the same way warriors can only combat their foes with sword, arrow and bow. Here you have someone with his hands tied and

his body naked, whereas others are clad in coats of steel. How can
a lion fight without his sharp claws, however full his heart may
be of martial ardour? If your Majesty desires me to display my
courage before this company, command that I be given a charger
and a heavy mace; then select a thousand chiefs from among the
Turks. If I leave one of the thousand alive on the field of combat
then count me not a man.'

Hearing this speech from Bizhan the king threw him a glance
and became drunk with wrath. Looking at Garsivaz for an instant
he said,

'You told me it would not be right to cut him in two. Can you
not perceive that this vile miscreant is plotting even greater mischief against me? Not content with the evil he has wrought he
now looks to battle and combat in order to display his prowess.
Carry him away as he stands, bound hand and foot, and rid the
place of him at once. Give orders that the gallows be set up in
front of the gates, where men can pass by him on all sides. Hang
the wretch alive on the gallows and report nothing to me that he
utters, so that in the future no Iranian will dare to cast a glance at
Turān.'

Out of the presence of Afrāsiyāb Bizhan was dragged, his heart
tormented with grief and his eyes streaming tears. As he came up
to the gallows his feet trod in the mire formed by his blood-
stained tears. He said,

'If the Lord has written it for me that I must die in wretchedness, then I fear no gallows or execution. I suffer for all Iranian
warriors. O wind, blow onwards to the land of Iran and bear a
message from me to our mighty king. Tell him that Bizhan is in
sore straits, that his body is gripped in the claws of a lion.'

(viii) *Pirān begs Afrāsiyāb to spare Bizhan's life*

God now took pity on Bizhan's youth and brought Afrāsiyāb's
evil designs to nought. From out of the distance by happy chance
Pirān appeared just as the gallows was implanted in the ground,
and when that son of Visa came nigh and beheld the road lined
with Turks, their waists girt for action, and when he saw the
gallows erect with a writhing noose dangling from it, he demanded of the Turānians the reason for the scaffold and against
whom it was that the king's heart was incensed. Garsivaz replied
that it was Bizhan, a man who came from Iran and was the king's

foe. At that Pirān put spurs to his horse and rode up to Bizhan, who, he saw with a sore heart, was stript naked, both arms tied firm as a rock behind his back, his mouth parched and all the lustre and colour fled from his cheeks.

[Pirān heard Bizhan's story] and pity for him stirred the son of Visa, who commanded that he should not be immediately put to the gallows but be held where he was until he [Pirān] should have beheld the Shah's countenance and indicated to him where the star on the path of felicity was situated. He said to the Shah,

'My request is nothing for myself; no one who is your subject stands in need of aught. Under your rule I prosper and our foundations rest on the contentment of our great ones. Yet I am in distress, O King who adorns the throne, though not for the sake of treasure or cattle or diadem. Have I not in former days often given your Majesty counsel on divers affairs? As nought was done in accordance with what I said, I have refrained from anything more of the kind. I counselled you not to slay the son of Kāvus lest you should make enemies of Rostam and Ṭūs. Yet you slew Siyāvosh, who was of kingly stock and had his loins girt up out of affection for you while from Iran they were trampling on us with elephants and rupturing all the links in our chain. You mingled venom in the potion that he drank. You can surely not have forgotten Giv, the mightiest champion in the train of the warrior Rostam? Did you not experience the evils which the Iranians brought on the land of the Turānians? They stamped down two of Turān's three provinces under the hoofs of their horses so that the waters of its fortunes turned bitter. The sharp scimitar of Dastān son of Sām still finds no rest in its scabbard; Rostam still scatters heads with it and still makes blood drip on to the sun with it.

'Although we are at peace, you look for strife. Why without cause do you continue to smell the poison-blossom? If you shed Bizhan's blood for what he has done, the dust of war will settle on Turān. You are a wise king and we are your subjects; open the eye of wisdom and be percipient. See what profit has accrued to Iran's king from the evils you have disseminated. Yet you are now eager for more; eager to make the tree of disaster bear fruit. If war is renewed, we shall not have the power to oppose, O King and master of the world.'

After he had thus poured quenching water on that fire, Afrā-siyāb replied to him in these words,

'Are you not aware of what Bizhan has done to me in making me stand with shamed face before Iran and Turān? Do you not see what dishonour has fallen on my hoary head through this shameless daughter of mine? The name of each of my closely-guarded women has been disclosed and she is thus unveiled. Because of this infamous thing my country and army will laugh at my gates for evermore. If Bizhan finds security for his life at my hands, tongues will be loosed at me from every side. I shall exist in ignominy and torment and shed tears stained yellow with blood.'

Calling down many blessings on the king, Pirān thus addressed him,

'King of happy star, utterer of verities, as your Majesty claims you seek for nothing but your good name. Yet ponder deeply, my lord, on this opinion of mine, namely that we should shackle the culprit firmly with heavy fetters; he would prefer death on the gallows to it. The Iranians will take warning from his fate and never again gird themselves for evil-doing. Once a man is left fettered in a dungeon-pit, his name is no longer called out from the muster-rolls.'

The monarch did as Pirān advised, perceiving that his heart was at one with his tongue.

(ix) *Afrāsiyāb casts Bizhan into a pit*

The king then commanded Garsivaz to have heavy fetters and a dark pit got ready. He said to him,

'Fasten Bizhan's hands firmly to his neck by a chain with a Greek knot such as is employed to secure a bridge. Join all together with heavy rivets and have him enclosed within, from head to foot. Afterwards cast him head downwards into the pit, there to languish deprived of the light of sun and moon. Take elephants then to get possession of that boulder belonging to Akvān the Div which the Lord of the world wrested from the depth of the ocean and cast into the China forest. Bring it here and cover up the pit with it; there he is to remain until he is in misery restored to his senses.

'From there go to the palace of the unchaste Manizha, through whom our line now suffers dishonour. Take horsemen with you and let all be plundered. Leave the wretch with crownless head. Drag her naked to the pit, there to see him whom she had before seen on a throne. Say to her,

'Once you were his Springtime; now be his companion in woe. Be the only one to visit him in his narrow dungeon.'

Garsivaz strode out of the king's presence and executed his cruel design.

[Manizha with grievous toil collected poor morsels of bread with which she fed her lover entombed in the pit. Meanwhile Gorgin, whose treachery had brought about Bizhan's misfortunes, tried to find him, but was compelled to return to Iran without success. Hearing of his arrival there, Bizhan's father, the warrior Giv, came to Gorgin in the hope of receiving news of his son and was told the lying story that he had disappeared while in pursuit of a marvellous wild boar. Giv disbelieved this and, seizing the treacherous Gorgin, drove him into the presence of the Shah, who, turning to Giv, said,]

'I will send mounted men in number, all valiant warriors, into every region in the hope of getting news of Bizhan, and will set about this action with all speed and with mind alert. If there is any delay in my receiving news, do not leave the place of wisdom vacant. Stay until the month of April arrives, when the Sun of our faith shines bright, at the season when the garden rejoices in flowers and the breeze scatters petals over men's heads, when the ground covers itself with a veil of green and the air murmurs softly over the roses. Then will my pure devotion be submitted to Hormazd [Ahura Mazda, Spirit of Good] in the worship demanded by our God. I shall call for that world-revealing Cup, and, going into God's presence, shall stand there and look into it to gaze at the seven climes—every country and region. I shall call down blessings on my ancestors, the chosen lords of the world and on my own pious fathers. I shall then reveal to you where Bizhan is, for it will be shown to me in the Cup.'

Giv heard the words and rejoiced, being freed from anxiety about his son. The king, after Giv had left his presence, at once sent men mounted on swift horses into every region. Eagerly they sought Bizhan about the world in the hope of finding some trace of him. But though they traversed all the territory of Iran and Turān, no trace of him came into view.

(x) *Key Khosrow sees Bizhan in the world-revealing Cup*

When joyous Spring arrived, the king demanded the felicitous Cup and to him then came Giv the Champion with hopeful heart, but with his back bowed in sorrow for his son. Seeing Giv's withered cheeks and perceiving his heart was sore with grief, he clad himself in Grecian robes and went to stand in the presence of God. To the World-Creator he made his orisons and invoked blessings on the refulgent luminary, imploring the universal Helper's aid and begging for justice against the evil Ahriman. Thence he came in majesty to his palace, where, placing the royal diadem on his head, he took the Cup in his hand and within it surveyed the seven climes. He uncovered the workings and Signs of high heaven; its quiddity, its quality and its quantity. Over the whole firmament he ranged within the Cup, from the Sign of the Fishes to that of the Ram, beholding Saturn and Jupiter, Mars and the Lion, Sun and Moon, Venus and Mercury. All things yet to be the wonder-working emperor beheld in the Cup. Into every clime he looked in the hope that he would find a trace of Bizhan.

Coming to the territory of the Wolf-heads, by divine decree he espied him there, fettered in the pit with heavy chains and praying in misery for death, while ready in attendance on him stood a maid of kingly stock. At seeing that spectacle the king turned his face to Giv and smiled in such fashion that the whole throne-room was illumined.

'Bizhan is alive,' said the king. 'Let your heart rejoice. See that you grieve not over prison or bonds, for hereafter no danger threatens his life. He is held captive in Turān, but waiting on him is a maid of famous family. The twain pass their days in weeping and shed tears as abundant as Spring rain. Of kith and kin he has lost all hope; he is dissolved in woe and trembles like a willow-twig. Who will leave home to succour him and go with loins girt to aid him? Who is ready to enter the dragon's maw and carry him out of his hardships to deliverance? Only Rostam the sharp-clawed is fitted for the task, for he can bring up the monster from the ocean depths. Gird up your loins and turn your reins towards the South, resting neither night nor day on the road. Carry my message to Rostam, but breathe no word of this matter on the way. I am summoning him to give him warning of this task. Now will I reduce your sorrows, Giv, to nought.'

[Khosrow indites a letter to Rostam demanding his presence. As soon as he arrives he receives a petition from Gorgin, who asks him to intercede with the Shah for his life, which he has forfeited for leading Bizhan into a trap. The Shah agrees to pardon him and allows him to join Rostam, who is to lead an expedition to rescue Bizhan.]

The king then said to Rostam,
'How will you order your affairs for this campaign? Demand any stores or any men you need to accompany you on your way. I stand in fear of Afrāsiyāb's evil disposition, for he may be avid to spill Bizhan's blood, being an arrogant and malevolent Div to whom have been given powers of magic, enchantment and spellbinding. Should his instinct so move him at any time, he will cut down that warrior where he stands.'

Rostam answered the king of the world,
'I will make my preparations for this campaign in secret. The key to fetters such as these lies in cunning; there must be no haste in a matter such as this. Here is no occasion for mace, sword or lance; we must turn our reins differently in this undertaking. We need an abundance of jewellery, gold and silver; travelling hopefully but ever in apprehension; proceeding in the guise of merchants going with great deliberation to Turān. We need carpets also and robes of price and other gifts too.'

Hearing these words from Rostam, Khosrow gave command to his treasurer to bring him all that his counsellor bade him out of his long-accumulated stores. Accordingly the royal treasurer opened the purses and covered the chamber floor with money and jewels, from which Tahamtan [Rostam] made his choice and took all that was suited to his emprise. He made up ten camel-loads of coin, while a hundred more camels were laden with his gear and baggage. Rostam then commanded the palace chamberlain as follows,

'Select from among the troops a thousand knights, proud and noted warriors, of whom some must be ready-girt for action— such men as Gorgin, Zanga son of Shāvarān and Gostaham, the sword of men of war. A fourth must be Gorāza, leader of troops, guardian of warriors, throne and crown. Rahhām must come also, and Farhād that bold champion, and Ashkāsh, a fighter brave as a male lion. These seven men of war I must have, fully equipped to be guardians over this force and treasure.'

All was efficiently got ready and assembled as he required.

(xi) *Rostam goes to the town of Khotan to meet Pirān*

[The main body of the expedition marched to the Iranian frontier
and there halted, while Rostam and his seven picked men dis-
guised as merchants cross into Turān.]

The warriors undid their silver belts and Rostam made them
dress in coarser cloaks. They then advanced into the Turānian
land as a caravan, full of colour and perfume. In the caravan
were eight valuable horses, one being Rakhsh and the rest the
warriors' own chargers. There were also ten camels laden with
jewels and a hundred more with military equipment. Because of
the great clangour and jingling of bells, loud as the blare of
Tahmurathi trumpets, the whole plain re-echoed with noise as
they advanced on Pirān's city. When the caravan was near to the
city of Khotan, men and women came out to admire it; but the
warrior Pirān was not in his residence and before his gate no
sentinel was stationed. He was on his return from the hunting-
ground when Tahamtan espied him on the road. At once Rostam
entrusted to his attendants a golden vase studded with jewels and
covered with a suitable brocade, and also a pair of costly horses
whose golden saddles were adorned with jewellery. With them
he hastened as fast as he could to Pirān's residence.

[There he presented himself to the Turānian commander, who
asked him whence he came and for what purpose. Rostam answered,]

'I am your servitor and God has brought me to your city to
refresh myself. It is for the purpose of trading that I have journeyed this long and hazardous road from Iran to Turān. I am a
vendor and a purchaser too, and I sell and buy wares of every
sort. I have soothed my spirit by thinking of your splendour, and
now hopefulness prevails in my heart. If you, the Pahlavān, take
me under your wing I shall buy horses and sell precious stones.
Through your justice none harms me; indeed out of the cloud of
your grace jewels rain down upon me.'

With that, Rostam proffered the nobles as largesse the magnificent cup filled with jewels, and he caused to be brought in those
valued horses of Arab blood on whose [shining] coats the wind
had never lodged dust. Many compliments he lavished on the
king as he tendered these gifts, and the whole affair was crowned
with success. After gazing at the jewels within the gleaming cup,

Pirān paid him compliments and seated him on a turquoise throne.

'Welcome to our city in happy mood and in security,' he said, 'for I will make a place for you close to myself. You need have no concern for your goods; none will assail you on their account. Now go and bring all your valuable wares; let all who desire them, far and near, be purchasers. Lodge yourself in my son's house and be as my own kinsman to me.'

Rostam answered,

'Let us rather remain here, Pahlavān, with our caravan. Our wares are entirely yours; but as for our lodging hereafter, any is agreeable to us.'

To that Pirān replied,

'Depart then, and let your lodging be where you will. I will station sentinels for you.'

Rostam accordingly chose a certain house and made preparation for his plan, after depositing his gear and baggage in a storehouse. The rumour now was spread abroad that from Iran a caravan had arrived for the famous Pahlavān. Buyers everywhere opened their ears when tidings came to them of a merchant selling precious stones. They and purchasers of brocades, carpets and gems set their faces in the direction of Pirān's palace, and, by the time that the sun was lighting up the world, a bazaar had arisen about the storehouse.

(xii) *Manizha appeals to Rostam*

Manizha, too, got report of the caravan and came in haste to the city. With head uncovered Afrāsiyāb's daughter approached Rostam, her eyes wet. She inquired after his well-being and said,

'You have enjoyed the fruits of life and your treasure; may you never have regrets concerning your labours! May high heaven so revolve as to accord with your hopes, and may you never suffer harm from them who would cast the evil eye on you! May wisdom be your instructor ever! May the land of Iran be ever cool and its fortunes happy! What tidings have you of the Shah's warriors, of Giv and Gudarz and the Iranian troops? Has no report of Bizhan come to Iran? Are prayers of no avail? This noble son of the Gudarzi family has his body broken by iron; heavy shackles wear away his feet and his hands are pierced by blacksmith's nails. He is dragged down by chains and compressed within bonds; the hapless man's clothes are soaked in his blood. Because of my anxiety for him I find no sleep; in grief for him my eyes are ever filled with tears.'

Rostam was seized with fear at her words. He repulsed her with a cry, saying,

'Remove yourself from me. I know nothing of Khosrow or any warring heroes. I have no acquaintance with Gudarz and Giv. You empty my mind of all thought with your words.'

[She appeals to him in distress and by discreet questioning he discovers who she is and where her lover is imprisoned. He is moved to send to Bizhan by her hand a turquoise seal finely engraved with a message which inspires him with new hope. They arrange that on an appointed night Rostam should attempt to rescue the captive. Manizha lights a beacon fire, by the light of which Rostam is guided within the frontiers of Turān.]

There Rostam addressed his seven warriors and said, 'We must now traverse the land and you will then perform your task of removing the stone from the pit's mouth.'

After their journey those champions alighted [at the spot] and exerted their strength mightily to remove the stone from the mouth of the pit. But although those heroes exhausted themselves the stone remained in its place unmoved. Those notable men had poured out their sweat and the stone had not yielded. Then it was that the heroic male lion [Rostam] dismounted from his steed and, lifting his skirts from the ground, fastened them about his waist. With a prayer to the Creator of strength to be granted strength, he stretched out his hand and without a moment's delay lifted the boulder, which he threw into the forest in the land of China, thus causing the whole surface of the earth to quake.

He then, bitterly sobbing, asked Bizhan how he had fallen into such misfortune. He said,

'You had a full share of the world's sweet joys, how came you to receive the cup of poison from it?'

From out of the dark pit Bizhan in return demanded how the Pahlavān had endured the perils of the road. 'When report of you came to my ears,' he said, 'all the poison in the world turned into a pure sweet draught for me. My whole realm has been such as you see; the ground of iron and a stone the sky.'

[Rostam draws Bizhan up out of the pit, releases him from his chains and unites him with Manizha. Gorgin humbles himself and begs forgiveness for his treachery. The camels are then loaded and Rostam tells Bizhan to take Manizha and depart with the caravan. He himself remains behind to raid the palace of Afrāsiyāb.]

(xiii) *Rostam makes a night-attack on Afrāsiyāb's palace*

The seven warriors now accompanied Rostam after committing their gear to the quick-witted Ashkash [the caravan leader]. They let fall their reins on to the front of their saddles and drew the swords of vengeance, riding on till they reached Afrāsiyāb's palace at the hour of repose and the time for sleep. With one blow of his fist Rostam shattered the bars and fastenings of the gate and threw himself forward like a lion in fury. As he entered, turmoil broke out on every side, swords flashed and arrows hailed thickly. In the forecourt, Rostam called out,

'May. your sweet sleep turn into a nightmare. You, while Bizhan was in the pit, slept in your bed. Did you see no wall of iron marching towards you? I am Rostam the Zāboli, son of Zāl, and this is not the time for sleep or the place for repose. I have broken open your gates, your fetters and your prison, seeing that your only warden was a heavy stone. Bizhan's head and legs are liberated from their bonds. No man but you could have inflicted such torment on his own son-in-law. The fight and vengeance for Siyāvosh should have sufficed you, and on this plain the dust from the hoofs of Rakhsh should have been enough [warning]. But you were in haste to take Bizhan's life; I observe that your mind is rash although your head is sunk in sleep.'

Bizhan too raised a cry, saying,

'Ill-conditioned and reckless Turk. Have a care for that throne and that fortunate position of yours. You placed me on foot before you bound in chains when I was as eager for battle as a leopard and you fastened my hands as firmly as a rock. Now behold me at liberty here on the open plain, where not even a raging lion would dare confront me in battle.'

Meanwhile Afrāsiyāb inside his palace was calling out,

'Has sleep fettered all my warriors? Let all those champions who wish for a ring and a diadem hem them in on every side.'

Everywhere the tramp of hurrying feet was heard and through the gate flowed a deep torrent of blood. Should any man come out of the palace on to the road, fate at once emptied the place he had occupied. The Iranians ever more eagerly pressed on the fight and Afrāsiyāb at last fled from his palace. Into the hall then rode the master of Rakhsh, trampling underfoot all the brocaded carpets. The peri-faced slaves who had till then attended upon their lord took the [invading] heroes by the hand.

XI

The Latter Days of Key Khosrow

(i) Key Khosrow and Afrāsiyāb

[Once they had looted the palace, Rostam and his troops prepared to continue the battle against Afrāsiyāb, who had rallied his forces. Rostam was victorious and returned in triumph to Iran, although his enemy was spared to resume the war later on. Gudarz leads the next Iranian invasion of Turān. The heroes from each side are paired in eleven single combats with Iranians triumphing every time. Pirān, the Turānian commander, is slain but given a hero's burial.

At this point in his history of Key Khosrow, Ferdowsi inserts one of his highly flattering eulogies on King Mahmud of Ghazna (A.H. 388 = A.D. 998–A.H. 421 = A.D. 1030), who ruled over a vast area covering much of East Persia, Transoxiana, the Punjab and Gujerat.

Then come, after the present complimentary discourse, descriptions of numerous warlike incidents in the war between Iran and Turān. Key Khosrow personally leads the final great war against Afrāsiyāb, who once more calls the Emperor of China to his aid. But the Iranians rout the combined forces of the enemy and pursue the fleeing Afrāsiyāb. He is ensnared and brought into the presence of Key Khosrow and the two hurl accusations at each other.]

The emperor [Khosrow] approached, a sharp sword in his hand, his head teeming with hatred and his heart filled with venom. Unwisely Afrāsiyāb said [to himself,]

'I foresaw this day in a dream. The sky has brought many vicissitudes over my head and it has now rent the veil of secrecy.' Aloud he said,

'You evil pursuer of vengeance, tell me why it is that you desire to slay me, who am your grandfather.'

Khosrow replied,

'You evil-doer, worthy of denunciation and obloquy, I will mention first your brother, who sought no well-born man's harm; then Nowzar, that worthy prince, an emperor himself and a memorial to Iran. You severed his head with a trenchant sword and roused the world to turmoil. Thirdly there was Siyāvosh,

173

whose peer as horseman or warrior lives not, nor girds up his loins. You cut off his head as though it were that of a sheep, thereby committing a crime that pierced through heaven's high vault. For what fault did you destroy my father? The day you did so you were unmindful of your wickedness and hasted to your evil deed, for which now you are to receive the evil requital.'

[Afrāsiyāb's appeal for mercy was rejected by Khosrow, who cut off the Turānian king's head, but gave him an honourable burial and magnanimously pardoned the Turānian prisoners.]

No long time elapsed after this event before Kāvus [who had lived in retirement] died, leaving his fame behind as a memorial in the world. From his capital the emperor Khosrow came and seated himself on the dark and gloomy earth and every Iranian worthy of note came unceremoniously on foot with raiments blue and black for two weeks to hold mourning for the king. As his tomb they erected a lofty cupola of a height of ten noose-lengths. His nobles brought brocade and black Greek silk, in which, having poured over him a mixture compounded of sandal-wood, camphor and musk, they wrapped his body up. Under him they placed an ivory throne over which was hung a crown of musk and camphor.

When Key Khosrow emerged from the presence of the throne the gates of the resting-place were shut fast and none ever more beheld Kāvus the king in the place where he had repose from strife and conflict. Forty days the king held mourning for his grandfather, keeping himself aloof from all pleasure and away from his bediademed throne. On the forty-first day he seated himself on his ivory throne and placed the heart-kindling crown on his head, the troops being assembled about the palace and also those nobles entitled to wear the golden helmet. With rejoicings they saluted him, scattering jewels over the throne. From end to end of the world there was festivity to celebrate the emperor's accession, from which moment until sixty years were numbered the world remained submissive to the king.

(ii) *Key Khosrow despairs of the world*

The time came when the noble mind of the king sank into contemplation about the passage of time and his hold upon the sovereign power. He said,

'Wherever there is territory inhabited by man, from India and innermost China even unto Greece, from the West to the gateway of the East, lands mountainous or desert, arid or rain-swept, I have denuded them of my enemies; command and sovereignty are mine and the entire world has ceased to fear any malevolent foe. Many a long day has passed over my head and from the gods I have received all my desires. Yet I have turned my mind to war, my spirit finds no defence against lust, against the contemplation of evil or the belief in Ahriman. I shall become a malefactor like Zahhāk and Jamshid and be the equal of Tur and Salm. On one side my line stems from Kāvus, on the other from Turān, which is full of rancour and false pride. I shall without warning turn ungratefully away from God and bring terror into the serene souls of men. The divine *Farr* will break away from me and I shall turn to crookedness and unwisdom, after which I shall pass away into darkness and my head and diadem will enter into the dust. In the world, all that will remain of me will be ill repute; an evil end will await me in the presence of God.

'I have now exacted vengeance for my father and adorned the world with prosperity. I have killed all who deserved death, all whose way was crooked and who behaved in barbarous fashion towards the pure gods. There remains no land, whether cultivated or waste, in which the proclamation of my sword is not recited. The great ones of the world are my vassals, though they be possessed of throne and diadem. Praise be to God, who granted me the *Farr*, this phase of the stars, my foothold and my power to give protection. It were best now for me to seek the road and to appear before God, who is clothed with honour. Mayhap, that with the grace that has been vouchsafed me as a servant of the Lord of the world, He will carry my spirit to the resting-place of the virtuous, seeing that this crown and royal throne must pass away. No man will achieve greater fame and success, power and fortune, peace and satisfaction, than I have done. We have heard and seen the secret of the world, its evil and its good, whether revealed or hidden. But whether a man be peasant or prince, he must in the end pass over into death.'

To the commander of his guard the king gave the order that should any man seek to gain audience he must be turned away with courteous words, all civility being shown him and no harshness used. Having done that he went tearfully towards his garden, his loins being ungirt. He laved his head and body for worship and with the lamp of wisdom he sought the path to God.

(iii) *The Iranians call out for Zāl and Rostam*

When a week had gone by and the king had not shown his countenance, there arose great rumour and gossip. The Pahlavāns all
assembled, with the nobles, the sages and the counsellors, who
were such men as Gudarz and Ṭus the son of Nowzar. Much
talk there was of wrong and right, of the doings of mighty kings,
of God-serving men and of evil-doers. To Giv his father said,

'My felicitous son, ever dutiful to crown and throne, you have
lifted many a burden from Iran, having departed from land, home
and kin. A gloomy task has now presented itself, one which we
cannot disregard. Someone must go to Zābolestān, to the ruler of
Kābolestān; it will therefore be your duty to go to Zāl and Rostam
with the tidings that the king has turned aside from God and
strayed from the path, that he has closed the door of his audience-
chamber against his nobles and of a certainty holds conclave
with the Divs. I have made many searches and inquiries and have
demanded the truth from him, but although he has listened with
care he has made no answer. We regard his mind as distraught and
his head stuffed with vain ideas, and we fear that, like King Kāvus,
he will become warped and the demons will wrest him from the
path.

'Those twain are Pahlavāns and men of high wisdom, able most
effectively to deal with any eventuality that may arise. There are in
Qannuj, Donbor, Margh and Māy various clear-sighted men,
and others learned in the stars in Kābolestān. When they return in
dignity to Iran, let them bring with them a company of these
people. Since the time that Khosrow has concealed his counsel
and his visage from us, this realm has become filled with rumours
and we have built up fancies of all kinds. The difficulty can now
be solved only by Dastān [Zāl].'

When he had heard these words of Gudarz, Giv chose out
from amongst his troops a numerous group of valorous men,
bestirred himself to action and deep thought, and marched out
from Iran on the road to Sistān. As for the emperor of the
world, he stood in adoration for seven days. On the eighth, when
the world's luminary lit up, the chamberlain in charge of the hall
of audience raised the curtain and the monarch seated himself on
his throne of gold. The Pahlavāns presented themselves with the
priests before the king of the world, and for long they stood
before him, those noteworthy men, wise and ready in counsel,

while he paid them regard, gave them greeting and allotted them regal positions. Of those noble Khosrow-servitors none would be seated and none released his hands [from the attitude of humility]. Then they opened their lips to say,

'Sovereign of your priests, exalter of heads, dispenser of justice, luminous in spirit, you are all-powerful and the royal *Farr* is yours; from the Sun down to the back of the [primeval] Fish is all yours. We who stand in humility before you are all your slaves, all we Pahlavāns of prosperous counsel. Let your Majesty tell us what fault we have committed and why he has closed his door against us; for this long period of time has passed during which our hearts have been filled with grief and anxiety. Let your Majesty reveal the secret to us, lords of the marches, of how we have gone astray.

'If the source of your care is the ocean, we will turn it into dry land, and drench the tabernacle of earth in musk. If it be the mountain, we will dig it up from its foundations; and we will break the hearts of your enemies into pieces with our daggers. If the remedy can be provided by treasure, your Majesty need have no care either concerning goods or money. We are the guardians of your treasure and we suffer grief, weeping at your apprehensions.'

In reply to these words the Emperor said,

'I am not sufficient in power without the aid of my Pahlavāns; but neither do I keep my heart in a state of anxiety, for I am rich in strength, in men and treasure. In no region has any foeman shown himself, about whom any trepidation need be felt. My clear mind seeks fulfilment of only one wish, which will never remove itself from my heart. I set my hopes on that wish and I dream of it all night long until the morning light appears. When I discover truly what it is, I will tell you my secret and give utterance to my hidden voices. As for you, return home in triumph and happiness and let no anxious thought enter your hearts.'

(iv) *Key Khosrow in sleep beholds the angel*

When the warriors had taken their departure, the alert-minded sovereign ordered that the curtain of the audience-chamber should be drawn down. A sentinel was seated at the gates, but he was in despair at the destiny of that once-victorious king. The monarch had stationed himself in the presence of the Almighty and prayed for His guidance, saying,

'Creator of heaven, Giver of light to virtue, justice and love, for me there lies no profit in empire if Thou, O Lord, are discontented with me. Whether good has come from me or ill, grant me an abiding-place in Paradise.'

Thus imploring, the king stood for five weeks, remaining in the presence of God the Almighty. One night, in the darkness, he could find no rest from anxiety until at last the moon rose in the sky, and then, although he slept, his bright spirit, which on earth was linked with wisdom, refused to sleep. In a dream he saw how a holy angel spoke secretly in his ear and said,

'King of felicitous star, monarch of happy fate, you have been accustomed for long to the collar of kingship, the crown and the throne, and now you have achieved all you have sought. If you depart immediately from this world, you will find an abode in the shade of the pure Lawgiver. Linger no further in this darkness. When you dispose of your goods, let it be to them who are deserving; surrender to others this transient world; you will gain true riches when you benefit the poor and your own people. For the throne select a king under whom even the ant on the ground will be secure. In Lohrāsp there appear all the qualities needful for this position. To him grant the kingship, the throne and the girdle.'

Many other things did the angel say to him secretly in a revelation that brought him amazement. When he awoke with troubled spirit from his sleep, he perceived that the place where he had worshipped ran with his sweat. With his face to the ground he stayed there weeping and gave praise to the Lord. Then he came and seated himself on the throne, taking in his hand a garment not hitherto touched and which he now put on.

[The Iranian nobles, disturbed at Key Khosrow's long seclusion, assembled at the palace, where their spokesman Zāl demanded to know why Iran had lost his affection. He then told them of his dream and that he was bringing his reign to a close. Zāl rebuked him for this unprecedented proposal, warning him that he would regret it and saying,]

'If you persist in so devilish a course, the Prince of the universe will remove the *Farr* from you. You will be left in tribulation, your body steeped in sin, and men will no longer call you Shah. Let wisdom be your guide, for the road before you is a long one.'

As the speech of Dastān [Zāl] came to an end, the warriors broke into speech and said,

'We agree with what this elder has said. The gateway to the truth must not be hidden.'

(v) *Khosrow replies*

When Key Khosrow heard what they had to say he was perturbed and for a time held his peace. After deliberating he said, softly,

'Zāl, you who have seen so much of the world and counted numberless years of valour, if I speak harshly to you in this assembly, the Lord will not approve of my ill conduct. Also, Rostam will be aggrieved and from his being offended harm will accrue to Iran. Indeed, if I reckon up the troubles he has suffered, they outdo in value all the notable treasure which he has accumulated. He has made his body a shield before me, and because of him the enemy has lost all rest and sustenance. I will take your answer in good part and will not lacerate your heart with cruel speech.'

Then, in loud voice, he continued,

'You proud warriors, over whom fortune watches, I have heard the speech that Dastān poured out before the flock. [I swear] by the all-possessing Prince of the universe that I am far from the religion and commandment of the Div. My spirit ever turns to God, whom I see as the Healer of my pains. My clear spirit has beheld the world, against the evils of which sagacity has become my defence.'

To Zāl he said,

'Do not be angry. It were best for you to speak your words by measure. First as regards your declaration that of Turānian stock there never was a man born who had wisdom or an alert mind. I am emperor and the son of Siyāvosh. I come of Kiyāni seed and I am a king of alert mind. My grandfather was the emperor Key Kāvus, a heart-kindling monarch full of knowledge and of happy fortune. Through my mother I come of the seed of Afrāsiyāb, whose hatred deprived me of food and sleep. For grandfather he had Faridun and he was Pashang's son. I am not ashamed of this ancestry. Understand, lastly, that though one possesses power, one may not upbraid a king.

'Now that I have got vengeance for my father and adorned the world with triumph, have slain those who displayed their enmity towards me or through whom wrong and injustice were brought into the world, no further task remains to me in the world, no power is left to any evilly-disposed person. Whenever I consider deeply my kingship and the extent of my realm I realize that like Kāvus and Jamshid I must take my departure and like them sur-' render my station. Like the unclean Zaḥḥāk also and the reckless Tur, with whose tyranny the world was surfeited, [I must go]. And I fear that when the day comes for me to be dragged to extinction, like them I shall be dragged into Hell. Day and night for five weeks I have been opening my lips in prayer to the end that the Lord God, the Pure, shall deliver me from this torment and this gloomy earth. I am sated with these troops, this crown and this throne, and have therefore speedily returned to pack up my gear. You, happy ancient, Dastān son of Sām, have said that a Div laid a snare for me, that I have strayed in darkness and crookedness from the path, that my soul has lost all worth and that my heart is fallen into ruin. But if I were turned astray by Divs, I would have spread evil in the world.'

[Key Khosrow then dictates his last wishes to his warriors and nominates Lohrāsp as his successor. It was a step which met with the disapproval of the Iranian nobles, but they ended by accepting the new Shah. After bidding farewell to his family and his subjects, Key Khosrow made his way to the frontiers of his realm, where he disappeared in a snowstorm among the mountains.]

XII

Lohrāsp and Goshtāsp

(i) Shāh Lohrāsp ascends the throne

When Lohrāsp ascended the ivory throne and placed on his head the heart-kindling diadem, he gave praise to the Creator of the world and uttered great adulation of Him. The mighty ones of the world applauded him and declared him sovereign of the earth. So the powerful Lohrāsp was granted peace, a store of wisdom and prosperity in abundance. He sent envoys to Rum, India, China and every inhabited land. From every clime men of knowledge or of skill in any goodly craft set forth and made their way to the Shah's court. For a time they remained without employment at Balkh [Bactria], where they imbibed knowledge, though it might be harsh and bitter, for there the king had built a city of many precincts and market-places. In each precinct he established a site for the festival of Sada, and there erected a fire-altar. Later he built a temple, which he named Barzin and which possessed great size, splendour and luxury.

(ii) Goshtāsp leaves Lohrāsp in anger

Lohrāsp had two sons handsome as the moon, and both were fitted for kingship, throne and crown. One was named Goshtāsp, the other Zarir, and both could have held in their grasp the head of a male lion. In every art they surpassed their father, and for valour they could raise their heads above the whole army. They were indeed two splendid princes, both fortunate, grandsons of the emperor Key Kāvus; and Lohrāsp's spirit rejoiced in them. Yet of the two he never made mention of Goshtāsp, at which the prince was aggrieved, declaring that the mind of Lohrāsp was filled with vanities.

Some time passed, during which Goshtāsp remained in a state of displeasure at the Shah. In Fārs one day a throne had been set up under a blossom-scattering tree, under which by Lohrāsp's command the chief of the army's generals presented themselves.

While they were at table, wine was called for and the emperor's heart was enlivened by flattering speeches. When Goshtāsp had drunk he rose to his feet and said,

'Your Majesty, you who are endowed with true justice, may your reign prosper and your name exist for ever! God has bestowed on you the cap, girdle and crown of Key Khosrow the Just. I stand a slave at your door, a servitor to your diadem and your star, but I regard no man my equal for valour or able to confront me on a day of combat except Rostam son of Zāl son of Sām, the knight against whom no man can stand in battle. When Khosrow conceived his apprehensions about the world, he surrendered the crown to you and himself departed. Now, since I am one of the free-born, name me for the royal crown and throne. As ever I will remain your servitor and will acknowledge you as sovereign.'

Lohrāsp replied to him,

'My son, give ear. Haste comes not well from one who bears a great name. I remember the counsel of Key Khosrow. Listen to it, and perchance you will not be turned aside from equitable dealing. That just monarch said that in the Springtime every garden has a little stream which, if it receives the water, may grow in strength until it causes great damage to the garden. You are still young. Seek no such lofty heights. Weigh your words and utter them with due measure.'

Goshtāsp listened and his heart was stirred to wrath. With pallid face he approached his father and said,

'Keep your indulgence for strangers and remain, as you are, having no dealings with your own child.'

In the army under his command he had three hundred knights, all of them picked men accomplished in battle. On leaving the king he summoned these men and to them revealed the secret purpose in his heart.

'Tonight,' he said, 'make all preparation for departure. Shut your hearts and eyes against this court.'

One asked, 'Where does your road lie? When you depart from here where will your resting-place be?'

He answered,

'Amongst the Hindus I shall be kept happy and bright in spirit. I have a letter from the king of India written in black musk on silk, telling me that if I come to him he will be my vassal, never disobeying my command or being disloyal.'

[Lohrāsp sent his other son Zarir in pursuit of Goshtāsp, who after being assured by one of his retinue that he would be king of Iran, consented to return home. No sooner there, however, than he left again, this time for Rum.]

When Goshtāsp reached the sea, he came down from his horse and encountered a gatherer of tolls. This was an old man, Hishuy by name, liberal-spirited, alert of mind, dignified and well endowed with substance. Goshtāsp saluted him and said,

'May wisdom be the ally of your pure spirit! I am a lettered man who has come from Iran to seek a name. I am learned, of sound judgment and retentive memory. If I could cross this sea in a ship, you would burden me with a load of gratitude for ever.' He answered,

'You are of the kind to wear a crown, or else armour and helmet for sudden onslaughts. Now disclose your secret. Tell it me. Do not attempt to cross the sea in this guise. But first I require a present and then a true story. Where are your profound thoughts and your scribe's face?'

Goshtāsp listened to what Hishuy was saying and replied,

'I have no secret to withhold from you and I will begrudge you nothing that I possess, whether it be circlet or seal, money or sword.'

He gave him money, which the toll-gatherer briskly took and then, swiftly hoisting sail on his ship, landed the hopeful youth on the [opposite] shore. Now in the land of Rum there was a city three leagues or more beyond the capital, a place built by the noble Salm and the residence of a powerful Caesar. When Goshtāsp arrived there, he sought for a lodging in the bustling place and for a week wandered in the land of Rum seeking in that well-populated country for employment. Then, after he had roamed about the crowded city for a while, he passed through a hall into the chancery of the Caesar. There he said to the head scrivener,

'My deliverer, I come from Iran as a scribe in search of reputation. In your work I can be of assistance to you, being able to perform to your satisfaction any task in a chancery that is needed.'

The scribes attached to the court there looked in wonderment at each other as though to imply,

'This fellow would make a pen of steel shed tears and scorch the face of the paper. What he needs is to have a tall charger under him, a bow in his hand and a lasso at his saddle.'

Aloud they said,

'We need no scribe here. More than are necessary have come forward, so take note.'

Goshtāsp's heart was overcome by depression as he heard this and he left the chancery with pale cheeks. Heaving cold sighs from the depths of his being he made his way to the guardian of the Caesar's troops of horses. Goshtāsp came up to him and saluted him, paying him compliments, and the guardian dealt with him courteously, giving him a place by his own side. He said,

'What manner of man are you? Tell me. You have the air and manner of a prince.'

'Man of fair fame,' Goshtāsp answered, 'I can drive colts daringly, and ride them too. If you will employ me, I can be of service to you and I can aid you when troubles or ills befall.'

To him Nastār [the guardian] said,

'Tùrn away from this door; you are a stranger and have no footing here. There are deserts and seas, and the horses run wild. How can I entrust the herd to an unknown man?

Mournfully Goshtāsp departed on hearing these words. He said to himself, 'He that wishes his father ill, himself encounters what is worse.' He quickly left that place and took the road leading to the Caesar's cameleers, the chief of whom he saluted and said,

'May you be ever active and bright of spirit!'

The sagacious fellow, viewing Goshtāsp's face, welcomed him and selected a place where he might rest. Swiftly he spread wide a carpet and brought him food to eat, and Goshtāsp said to him,

'My all-conquering friend of the bright spirit, only give me a camel-caravan. Cut off all payment to me.'

The cameleer replied,

'My lion-hearted man, it would not be fitting for you to do such work as that. How would you be content with such things as wc have? It were better if you approached the Caesar. He will free you from all need to speak as you do. Make no endeavour except to go to Caesar's palace, and if the way there is too long, I have an excellent racing-camel for you, and men to be your guides.'

Goshtāsp bade him farewell and after leaving him set out full of anxiety towards the city, the sufferings he had undergone lying heavy on his heart. He entered the bazaar of the workers in iron, where there was a noted blacksmith named Burāb, a man of repute and great prosperity. It was he who made the shoes for the king's horses and he kept for the Caesar a smithy where he had thirty-five men as assistants and apprentices, who laboured hard with hammer and iron. In his smithy Goshtāsp sat for a long while, until the workmen tired of his sitting there. The blacksmith at last said to him,

'My well-intentioned friend, what is your desire in our smithy?' Goshtāsp replied to him,

'Sire of happy fortune, I shirk neither anvil nor heavy labour. If you accept me, I can be of aid to you. I will work manfully with this hammer and anvil.'

Burāb listened to his history and then agreed to take him as apprentice. In the furnace he heated a massive ball of iron, with which, when it was glowing, he hastened to the anvil. Goshtāsp was then given a heavy hammer while the smiths gathered round him. With one blow he shattered both anvil and ball of iron and at once the bazaar was filled with rumour and report of him. But Burāb took alarm and said,

'Boy, no anvil can withstand your blows, nor any hammer, nor iron nor stone nor the wind.'

At hearing these words, Goshtāsp was left desperate. He threw down the hammer and hungrily departed, without prosect of food or of a place for his lodging.

(iii) *A Dehqān takes Goshtāsp into his house*

Goshtāsp remained with vexation in his heart and in ferment against high heaven, his only share of the world's goods being venom. Near to the city he beheld a rural scene in which were trees, flowers and running streams—a fair resting-place for a young man. Over one stream there hung a tree with such thick shade that the eye of the sun was hidden by it, and in that umbrageous spot the youth sat himself down, full of gnawing care and with his spirit in gloom. Now out of the populous town there passed by him a worthy person who was its elder. He saw the youth's tear-stained eyes and how he had made his hand a prop for his chin, and he said to him,

'Noble youth, why are you so grieved and why is your spirit sad? If you will come to my mansion from here you can be my guest in comfort for a while. It may be that the griefs which burden your spirit will be lessened and your eyelashes be freed of moisture.'

Goshtāsp answered,

'Honoured sir, tell me from what family you originate.' To that, the town's chieftain replied,

'What mean you by this question? I come of the seed of the warrior-king Faridun. No man lacks greatness who is of that seed.'

Goshtāsp, hearing this, rose to his feet and accompanied the worthy headman, who, when he had reached home, prepared his hall for the guest, whom he entertained as a brother and left not for a moment with any desire unfulfilled. A period went by in this way until several months had passed over the incident.

(iv) *The story of Katāyun, the Caesar's daughter*

It happened that the Caesar at that time conceived the idea that now that his daughter had matured and was desirous of a mate, the moment had come for her to wed, seeing her star was in the ascendant. In his palace hall therefore he assembled a company of elders of sound judgment and good counsel, men who were his peers in age and were eminent personages of high worth. This company was bidden be seated and the moon-cheeked young princess was summoned. Katāyun emerged with sixty waiting-women, who surrounded her so closely that no person could see even the top of her coronet. In the midst of them she went about until she was wearied, but none in that assembly met with her favour. She therefore returned from the hall to the quarters within the veil, walking in stately fashion, but tearfully and still eager for a mate.

The earth turned to the darkness of a raven's wing and so remained until the greater luminary thrust his head above the mountains, when the Caesar commanded that the elders of substance should bring into the palace at Rum young men from among whom one should be found to be approved for his good appearance. An announcement of this was sent to every noble, every man of repute and every royal prince; whereupon the sagacious town-elder said to Goshtāsp,

'Why should you remain so long concealed? Come forward now; it may be that you will see the palace and high rank and your heart thus be rid of sorrow.'

Goshtāsp listened to his words and accompanied him, going at a good pace to the Caesar's hall. He placed himself in a corner, apart from the great ones, and seated himself careworn and with weary spirit, while slaves went briskly about. Katāyun and her rosy-cheeked retinue walked about the hall, counsellors following her and her attendants in front. From some distance she beheld Goshtāsp and said,

'The dream I dreamed has now put up its head out of the void.' With that she adorned his felicitous head with her priceless world-famous coronet. When the minister who had been her tutor saw this action he ran immediately to the Caesar and told him that his daughter had chosen a man from amongst the assembly, one who was in stature like a slender cypress in a meadow, whose face was like a flower-garden for beauty and who had such magnificent arms and shoulders that all who beheld him marvelled. 'You might think him compounded of godly splendour, and yet we know not who he is.'

The Caesar at that remarked,

'Heaven forfend that my daughter should, coming from beyond the veil, bring dishonour on her birth. Were I to yield her to him, my head would descend with shame into the dust. It were better that her head and the head of the man she has chosen be cut off here in the palace.'

The minister replied,

'This is an affair of no substance. There have been not a few princes before you in like case. You bade your daughter find a husband; you did not bid her find a proud monarch. Now she has found someone who delights her. Do not wrest your wisdom aside from the path of God. This manner of doing things was the habit of your ancestors, who were dignified and pious men. Rum was established on this practice; do not yourself assume a different one in this civilized land. It would not conform to royal behaviour; do not follow a path you have never trodden before.'

[The Caesar succumbed to this argument and persuasion and gave his daughter to Goshtāsp; but without a dowry. For a time they lived with the elder of the town who had once befriended the young prince. Then, in order to assist the suitor of another of the Caesar's daughters he undertook to slay a phenomenal wolf and on behalf of still a third suitor to destroy a dragon which had been devastating Rum. He was successful in both enterprises and was at last received into the Caesar's favour. The time came when that prince began to cast covetous eyes on Iran, and sent an envoy to demand tribute with the threat that if it were not paid a vast army under an invincible general would devastate the land. The Shah

(Lohrāsp) at first was inclined to yield but as the envoy was about to depart, he told him to tell the Caesar to prepare for war.]

(v) *Zarir conveys a message to the Caesar*

For a time Lohrāsp remained in contemplation, then commanded that Zarir should present himself before him. He said to him,

'This man [the Caesar's son-in-law] can be none but your brother. Get ready at speed all necessary means and make no delay here. If you linger overmuch the affair will end in ruin. Do not rest, and reject any horse that is slow. Take with you a throne and a led horse, golden shoes, a crown and, in addition, the Kāviāni Banner. This realm I will surrender to him, without laying any burden of gratitude for it on him. As for you, go to Aleppo from here thinking all the way of strategy and speaking to your troops of nothing but war.'

Zarir, commander of troops, replied to Lohrāsp,

'I will drag this mystery from its hiding-place. If it is indeed he, he rules us all and is chief; all who once held power are now subordinate to him.'

He said this and then went away to make all ready. It was a notable force that he chose out, descendants of the mighty and of free-born men. They traced their lineage to Kāvus and to Gudarz of the Keshvād dynasty and they were such men as those of the seed of Zarasp which survived, Bahrām the lion-queller and Rivniz, the proud grandson of the valiant Giv, the world-ravisher Shiruya and Ardashir, both of them bold lions, proud warriors of pure birth. Each of these noblemen had with him two horses shining like fire-temples.

There was no pausing until the army reached the neighbour-hood of Aleppo, and there the world was suddenly filled with strife, turmoil and discord. The royal standard was raised aloft, pavilions and tents were pitched. Meanwhile the commander Zarir handed over the army to the prideful Bahrām and himself rode on in the guise of an envoy bearing a message of glad tidings to the king. With him he took five comrades, men endowed with brains, who were both alert-minded and stout warriors. As he neared the Caesar's palace, he was espied by the royal chamber-lain, while in the hall the Caesar sat in sombre mood, with him being Goshtāsp the sagacious. When he heard [the arrival] an-nounced, he granted the newcomer an audience and Goshtāsp displayed his pleasure at the stranger's presence. Like a slender cypress Zarir came in and received a place near the throne of the august king, after whose welfare he inquired; and he made excuses for his coming, although he outshone all the Rumis present. The Caesar answered him,

'You address no inquiry to Farrukhzād [i.e. Goshtāsp]. Have you no courtesy in your heart?'

The magnificent Zarir thus replied to the Caesar,

'This slave is one who became satiated with slavery. He fled from the court of the Shah and has now found a refuge in this one.'

Goshtāsp listened to this but made no remark, although Iran truly came into his mind, and the Caesar, hearing a speech of this nature from the young prince, was filled with foreboding, being a man of clear mind. 'It may be,' he thought to himself, 'that these words which he has uttered have nothing hidden in them but the truth.'

Goshtāsp then placed before him the message from Lohrāsp to the effect that a man of equity who turns aside from justice finds tranquillity in nothing else. If the Caesar were to depart from that rule and stray from the true path, then the Shah would come and make Rum his residence, leaving few of the inhabitants of Iran behind him. It was therefore incumbent on the Caesar to depart from his capital or else to prepare for war without hesitation now that he had heard the warning.

'I will always stretch out my claws for conflict if war demands,' the Caesar answered. 'Return now and let me get a place ready for the battle.'

Prince Zarir heard this reply of the Caesar's and was grieved, for long remaining uneasy about it. As the Caesar rose from his place he asked Goshtāsp why he had suppressed his own answer. To that he replied,

'Long ago, when I was with the Shah of Iran, all the king's bodyguard and all his court were familiar with my qualities. My best course now is to return to Iran, to tell them what I have learnt and then hear what is said. I will gain from them all that you require and make your name glorious in the world.'

[The Caesar agreed to the proposal and permitted Katāyun to accompany her husband. On their arrival Lohrāsp resigned the kingship of Iran to Goshtāsp and himself departed to the Balkh province, where he became an attendant priest at the famous temple of Now Bahār.

In this section Ferdowsi inserts an account of a dream of the poet Daqiqi who had originally composed a thousand verses of the Shāh-nāma in which were described the reigns of Goshtāsp and Arjāsp and the coming of Zoroaster.]

XIII

Goshtāsp and Zardosht

(i) Goshtāsp ascends the throne

When Goshtāsp ascended his father's throne—having his father's *Farr* and his father's good fortune—he set on his head the ancestral crown; for a crown is due to a free-born prince. The justice which he dispensed was such that the ewe drank with the wolf at the stream. The time came when the virtuous daughter of the Caesar, that daughter whose name was Nāhid [Venus] but whom the Shah called Katāyun, gave birth to two sons, peers of the moon for beauty. One was the famous and brilliant Esfandiyār, the warrior prince and valiant knight; the other Pashutan, a heroic swordsman, illustrious prince and destroyer of armies. Now the world was securely in the grasp of the new king and he became desirous of being another Faridun. Princes everywhere brought him tribute and the hearts of all who wished him well inclined to him. Apart from them however stood king Arjāsp, lord of Turān, upon whom the Divs stood in attendance. He would not consent to pay tribute, nor would he listen to counsel; and, since he would not hear the good advice, he suffered the chains which were placed on him. (He had himself demanded revenue each year from Goshtāsp; why then pay revenue to an equal?)

(ii) Zardosht [Zoroaster] appears and is acknowledged by Goshtāsp

Time passed over these events. Out of the earth a tree appeared. It sprang up in the hall of Goshtāsp and grew till it reached the dome; a tree with many roots and multitudinous branches. Its leaves consisted of pieces of good counsel and its fruit was wisdom: how shall one who consumed fruits of this kind ever die? Of happy augury was this [phenomenon] named Zardosht [Zoroaster]. He it was who slew Ahriman the maleficent. He said to the king of the world,

'I am a messenger and I am your guide to God.' Producing a brazier of blazing fire he said further, 'I have brought this out of Paradise and the Creator of the world has bidden you to accept this religion, saying, Gaze on this heaven and earth which I have brought into being without earth or water. Observe how I fashioned it and see whether any other has achieved its like. Surely it is I who am Lord of the world; there is none besides. Since you know that I composed it, it is your duty to acclaim me Creator of the world. Accept the goodly faith from me that address you; learn from me the Way and Practice. Observe what I say and do accordingly. Choose wisdom, hold worldly things in contempt. Learn the way of the religion of goodness, for without religion kingship is without worth.'

When the good king heard of the good religion, he received it and the practice of it at his hands. So also did his gallant brother, the fortunate Zarir (he that could bring down a raging elephant), and the old king his father who had retired to Balkh when the world turned bitter in his heart. Then too the great nobles of every clime as well as the sages and the skilled physicians received it. All came to the king's court, bound on the girdle and entered the faith. There then appeared the divine glory, evil disappeared from the hearts of the wicked, tombs were covered by the radiance of God and seed was cleansed of all defilement.

The noble Goshtāsp, after having ascended the throne, despatched troops to every clime and sent priests about the world to establish domed fire-temples according to the ritual. He first laid the foundation of the temple of the bright fire of Mehr. Zardosht planted a noble cypress before the temple gate, placing an inscription on the tree to proclaim that Goshtāsp had adopted the good religion. He thus made the noble cypress his memorial, and thus does wisdom spread right conduct abroad in the land.

Years in number passed over these events and the slender cypress increased steadily in growth. So greatly did it expand that no lasso could compass it, and it put out many branches aloft. At last the king built a goodly dome about it, forty ells in height and forty in diameter, yet in its foundation neither water nor earth was used. To it he added a great hall of pure gold, the interior being silver and the floor of amber. On the outside he caused to be painted a picture of Jamshid, worshipper of moon and sun. He commanded also that Faridun with his bull-headed mace should be represented, and all the highest were similarly portrayed. Think who else could have executed such a masterpiece!

[The narrative of the war is resumed. Turān demands tribute from

Iran, which, on the advice of Zardosht, refuses it. Zarir is slain in battle and Esfandiyār, Goshtāsp's son, sets out to exact vengeance from Arjāsp, king of Turān, who flees from the battlefield. Into the narrative are here inserted accounts of Esfandiyār's seven adventures, which bear a close parallel to those of Rostam before him. To him is ascribed the feat of having slain the fabulous bird, Simorgh. He is drenched in the blood of Simorgh and thus is made invulnerable except in the eyes, which he closes while being immersed. He also kills Arjāsp. These triumphs induced him to lay presumptuous claim to the throne of Iran. All this while Rostam remained in the background, but now the older hero is brought into conflict with Esfandiyār.]

XIV

Esfandiyār and Rostam

(i) The struggle between Esfandiyār and Goshtāsp

I have heard from the nightingale a story which it repeats after an ancient legend. It is that Esfandiyār once returned home intoxicated and in savage mood from the king's palace. His mother, Katāyun, daughter of the Caesar, took him to her heart in the darkness of the night. Half way through the night he awoke from his sleep, called for a cup of wine and gave vent to speech. He said to his mother,

'The king behaves evilly towards me. He told me that the kingship and the army would one day be mine, as well as the treasury, the throne and the diadem, but only after I had boldly exacted vengeance for king Lohrāsp from king Arjāsp and delivered his sisters from captivity. Thus I would exalt your repute in the world, which must be cleansed of evil-doers, rid of defects and be made anew with adornment. When the sky next brings up the sun and his Majesty's head awakens from slumber, I will repeat to him the words he spoke; he will not withhold the truth from me. If he surrenders the royal crown to me, I will serve him as a priest serves his idols. But if no gleam lights up his face, by the God who keeps the sky established, if I do not set that crown on my head, I will surrender the whole country to the Iranians, make you queen of the realm of Iran and violently and fearlessly act the part of the lion.'

His mother was saddened by this speech and all the silk of her bosom turned to thorns, for she knew that the Shah, ever jealous for his name, would not surrender the treasury, throne and diadem. She said to him,

'My much-afflicted son, what does a noble heart demand? You have everything—treasure, command and power of decision— which concerns the army. Seek for nothing further. Your father has the crown, my son, but you have all the troops, the lands and country. What is better than a fierce male lion standing in his father's presence and girt for service? When he passes away, crown and throne will be yours; his greatness, majesty and good fortune will come to you.'

Esfandiyār replied to his mother,
'The wise axiom which told one never to utter secrets before women, hit the mark truly. Once you have spoken a word to her you will find it in the street. In no matter ought you to listen to a woman's behest, for you will never find her counsel to be wise.'

Esfandiyār went to Goshtāsp no more, but spent his time in dalliance with musicians and the maids who handed round the wine. For two days and nights he imbibed, and delighted the hearts of the beauteous ladies. By the third day Goshtāsp perceived that his son was ambitious to take his place, that the thought was growing in his mind that he must possess the crown and throne of the sovereign. He thereupon summoned Jāmāsp [his wise counsellor] together with Lohrāsp's astrologers, who came embracing their star-tables. The king plied them with questions about the hero Esfandiyār, asking whether he would enjoy long life and dwell in happiness, peace and comfort, whether he would place on his head the sovereign's crown and firmly hold to his virtue and greatness.

When the sage of Iran [Jāmāsp] heard the questions he looked into his ancient star-tables and his eyelashes dripped with tears, his eyebrows wrinkling as he uncovered the truth. He said,
'Evil is my fate and evil my star; and evil will come on my head from the truth which I impart. I would that in the presence of the blessed Zarir destiny had cast me into the claws of a lion, or that my father had slain me before a baleful star had been destined for Jāmāsp. When Esfandiyār has rid the earth entirely of his foes, he will have no more fear or concern about war. He will have freed the world from apprehension of any who design evil and he will cut the dragon's body into two.'

'My dear friend,' said the king to him, 'tell me all, and turn not aside from the path of true knowledge. If his fate is to be that of Zarir [who was killed in the war against Arjāsp], the commander of armies, then my life henceforth will be unhappy. Tell me in haste—for out of this knowledge bitterness has invaded my countenance—at whose hand out of the whole world he will meet his death. That will be a loss over which we shall have to weep.'

Jāmāsp replied,
'Your Majesty, may no evil fate devolve on me! His death will come in Zābolestān at the hand of Dastān's heroic son [Rostam].

Then said the king to Jāmāsp,
'Do not reckon this matter as one of little moment. If I vacate

the sovereign's throne and surrender it to him, with the treasury and the crown, he will not need to see the land and soil of Zābolestān and none will know him in Kābolestān. He will be secure against the turns of fortune; his good star will direct him.'

To that the star-calculator answered,

'Who can escape from the turning wheel? Out of it the sharp-clawed dragon springs. Who can find deliverance, either by courage or wisdom? What is to be will be, without fail, and wise men do not seek to know the hour of it. His fate will come upon him at the hand of a mighty warrior, were even an angel lying before him as his shield.'

[Esfandiyār reminds his father of the hardships he has suffered, his past exploits and the ill-treatment he has received in recompense. As reparation he now demands the throne and crown which the Shah had promised to resign to him.]

(ii) *Goshtāsp answers his son*

'There is no way other than that of the truth,' said the Shah to his son. 'Your exploits have been even greater than you have re-counted. May the Creator of the world be your aid! I now per-ceive no enemy in the whole world, whether patent or under cover. Does not anyone who hears your name shake with terror, nay rather, become lifeless? You have no rival in the world save the crafty but unwise Rostam, that son of Zāl. For such time as he continues to exist, the lands of Zābolestān, Bost, Ghazna and Kābolestān belong to him. His bravery out-tops the sky and he reckons himself no man's vassal. He turns aside from my counsel and command, and he will not bow his head in fealty to me. Yet he was servitor to King Kāvus and remained alive in the world only by favour of Key Khosrow. When he speaks of the kingship and Goshtāsp, he asserts that my crown is new and his own ancient. He recognizes no one in the world his equal in combat, whether it be Greek or Turk or free-born Iranian.

'You must now go to Sistān and employ every device of war, cunning or magic, uncovering sword and mace, in order to place Rostam son of Zāl in fetters. By the Lord of the world, who granted me power and gave light to the stars, the moon and the sun, if you achieve the object of my words, you will hear no further argument from me. I will surrender the treasury, the throne and the diadem to you and seat you with crowned head in the place of sovereignty.'

[Esfandiyār rebukes his father for turning against Rostam and suspects that his motive in sending him against the hero is only to be rid of him; he nevertheless sets out with a small force to Rostam's provinces of Zābolestān and Sistān.]

(iii) *Esfandiyār leads an army to Zābolestān*

At cockcrow, the sound of beating drums came from the palace. Esfandiyār, as massive as an elephant, mounted his horse, then swiftly as the wind moved his troops from their position and rode on. In front of him the road divided and there the king halted; for one way led towards Gombadān and the other for a short distance in the direction of Zābol. Suddenly the camel which was leading lay down flat as though it had been levelled with the ground. The driver beat it over the head, but the caravan's progress was halted. This event came to the eager warrior as an evil omen and he ordered the beast's head and forelegs to be cut off, so that any harm might be averted from him and his divine *Farr* remain uninjured. As soon as the soldiers had cut off the camel's head, his star resumed its accustomed position, and although he had been perturbed by the camel, he now began to despise his evil star.

'The man who triumphs,' said he, 'is the one who attains to brilliant eminence and fortune in the end. Good and bad are both from God and a man must ever retain a smiling lip. I will disobey my father. Rostam has saved Iran many a time. What I need now is a stout-hearted envoy who is sage and acute and has a good memory. He must be a fearless horseman, one whom Rostam will not easily mislead. He will tell Rostam that if he will appear before me and shed radiance on this gloomy spirit of mine, graciously extending his hands for my fetters, he will suffer no harm from us. I want nothing but his good if he will only keep his head turned away from mischief.'

(iv) *Esfandiyār sends Bahman to Rostam*

Esfandiyār chose his own son Bahman as a fitting envoy. After instructing him how he was to equip himself for his mission, he said,

E K—P

'Do not make it difficult for yourself. Salute him from me and make my good intentions clear. Have your words ready and speak with the utmost smoothness. Tell him that if he examines this matter in the light of understanding he will see that his conduct has not been just. He has received high rank, treasure, troops, valuable horses, a throne and a diadem from my ancestors when he gave them ready service as a vassal. [Tell him that in spite of the greatness of the Shahs who reigned during his career] he has paid no visit to that world-renowned court since Lohrāsp ascended the throne, nor has ever turned his glance towards the famous men there, choosing rather to keep himself apart in the world and hold himself in seclusion. But how could the great forget him and not forget themselves? He had always wanted the good and been proud to do the bidding of kings. If anyone reckoned up his labours in the world they would be greater than all his treasures in value.

'There were kings, however, who did not appreciate such a record in a vassal. [Tell him that] Goshtāsp told me that Rostam, having too many riches and prosperous lands and a full treasury, had settled himself in Zābolestān and become intoxicated; that he would not stretch out his arm to perform any task of mine; that when a difficulty befell me he was always far from the scene of battle and that I never saw him in the feasting-hall. Moreover say that I became angry and one day swore an oath by the bright day and the azure night that none of my chosen courtiers should ever see him at my palace except bound in chains. Tell him that I, Esfandiyār, have come from Iran for the express purpose of bringing this about, but that once I have carried him a prisoner before the Shah, I will intercede with my father and change his heart. I will let no harm come to Rostam. Such an issue would be worthy of my birth.'

(v) Bahman delivers his message

Ahead of the young man [Bahman] lay a mountain, towards which he urged his horse. As he looked beyond to the hunting-ground there came into view a gallant company, of whom one was as big as Mount Bisotun. In one hand he held a tree, on to which was spitted a male onager, and at his side was a mace and other weapons and equipment. In his other hand he held a goblet full of wine. An attendant squire went ahead of him, while Rakhsh ambled along on the plain, where there were trees and greenery and running streams. Bahman said to himself,

'Is this Rostam, or the sun at the point of dawn? No one ever saw such a man in the world or heard of his like among the famous names of old. The heroic Esfandiyār, I fear, would be powerless against him and would avoid any battle with him. I must kill him with a rock, though I make the hearts of Zāl and Rudāba suffer.'

Thereupon he dug out a granite boulder, which he dislodged down the steep slope. From the hunting-ground Zavāra saw it and heard the roar of the great rock. He shouted,

'Gallant knight, a boulder is rolling down the mountainside.'

Rostam neither moved nor laid down the onager. Waiting till the boulder was close to him, the whole mountain being dark with the dust of it, he gave it a kick that sent it flying far off. Bahman in his heart regretted his deed when he had looked more carefully at the stature and appearance of Rostam. He thought to himself,

'If our Esfandiyār engages this renowned fellow in combat, he will be reduced to ignominy in the battle. It would be better therefore to be patient with him. Yet if Rostam defeats him in the battle, he will get into his grasp all the realm of Iran.'

He therefore remounted his wind-footed horse and, sunk in contemplation, made his way down the mountainside. As he neared the hunting-ground, Tahamtan [Rostam] saw him and advanced to welcome him, and Bahman dismounted and made the inquiries courtesy demanded. Thereupon Rostam, having asked his name [embraced him warmly and invited him to dine with him].

On a tablecloth there was laid out bread, and an onager roasted whole was brought in hot. A servant set a tray before Bahman, and Tahamtan placed his own brother [Zavāra] at his side, but he invited no other nobles. Of the onager, Bahman consumed not a hundredth part of that eaten by Rostam, who laughed at him and said,

'If you have only that amount of food on your tray, how did you undertake your seven famous labours? How do you wield a spear in battle, when you eat so little?'

Bahman answered,

'No one born of Khosrow should be either a babbler or a glutton. His food must be scanty and his efforts in battle abundant.'

(vi) Rostam answers Esfandiyār

Rostam heard all that Bahman had to say and the mind of the ancient man was filled with contemplation.

'Yes,' he said, 'I have hearkened to your message and my heart has been refreshed at sight of you. Take the reply to Esfandiyār that a man whose spirit is endowed with wisdom looks at his undertaking as a whole. When, like Esfandiyār himself, that man has virtue, success and prosperity, a treasury well filled with all good things, lofty rank, martial ardour and high repute with men of standing and of noble status, occupying a place such as his in this our world, then into his head no ignoble thought should come. Let us abide in equity and serve our God, not taking the hand of evil into ours. Any speech for whose utterance there is no basis is a tree devoid of fruit and scent; and if his spirit treads the path of envy, his labour will be in vain, however long drawn out.

'I have now found all that I ever sought, and come at speed to lay my wishes before Esfandiyār. And I will come alone to him, unescorted by troops, to hear all that his Majesty demands. If I am judged guilty I will put a yoke upon myself and bound in leathern thongs I shall come on foot. But first let him be my guest a while. And before he returns to Iran I will open wide the door to my long-accumulated treasure, whose foundation I laid with my sword, and offer it to him and his army. When the time comes for him to depart and the need arises for him to see Khosrow, I will not turn my rein aside from his on the road but rather go at even pace with him to meet the Shah, whose forgiveness I will beg, turning his rancour to mildness, kissing his head and foot and both his eyes. I will question why the mighty Shah can desire to deal unjustly with me, why he demands to fetter my hands with chains.

'Keep in your memory all that I have said and tell it all to the puissant Esfandiyār.'

[Esfandiyār himself meets Rostam at the river Hirmand and tries to persuade him that if he will acknowledge his vassalship to the Shah of Iran by submitting to the symbolical chaining of his hands, all will go well with him and nothing else be demanded. He replies,]

'We are two proud men, one of us old the other young, two Pahlavāns endowed with wisdom and alert minds. I fear that some evil eye may intervene and our heads be turned from their sweet dreams, that some Div may find his way between us and wrest your heart from the way to the crown and the throne. Shame would overwhelm me were I to consent to what you ask, shame that would never be blotted out. No man will ever see me alive and in fetters. My immortal soul insists. And that is enough.'

[Rostam invites Esfandiyār to visit him. He answers that it would run counter to his father's commands to accept.]

'One [of those commands] was that I should engage you in war, bringing fierce tigers against you in combat; [but if I did so,] I should forget what was due to you for bread and salt, thus bringing doubt on the purity of my origins. If I should turn aside from what the Shah commands, my lodging in the next world would be the fire. Since the desire [to invite me] has come to you, let us strike hands [in amity] over wine. Who knows what tomorrow may bring forth? There is no need for lengthy converse in matters such as these.'

To him Rostam returned,

'This now is what I shall do. I shall go and doff the garb that I have travelled in, seeing that for a week I have been in chase of game. Instead of lamb I have been consuming onager. When the time for eating comes, invite me too and seat me with your retinue at table.'

(vii) *Esfandiyār fails to invite Rostam*

When Rostam had gone from the bank of the Hirmand, the exalted prince gave himself up to contemplation. Pashutan, his guide and counsellor, arrived in timely fashion at the royal pavilion and to him the gallant Esfandiyār spoke and said,

'I have embarked on conduct which is harsh and ignoble. With Rostam's palace I will have nought to do, nor can I invite him here. If he should not come of his own accord I will not invite him, even though the life of one of us might thus come to an end.' [Pashutan replies,]

'I have looked deeply into your affairs. The devil ever bars the path to wisdom, but you are aware of what religion and virtue demand, of God's commandments and your father's counsel. I heard all that Rostam said; his greatness was allied to manliness. Your fetters will never fret his ankles and he will not lightly come

into your bonds. One of you looks for a feast, the other for strife
and hatred; examine well which has the greater blessing.'

The prince now called for the laid tray from his kitchen menials,
but he gave no command for Rostam to be summoned. When the
food was eaten he called for wine and spoke at length of the
Brazen Fortress and his prowess there, and he drank to the health
of the sovereign king. Meanwhile Rostam waited in his palace and
considered the matter of the promised dinner. A long time passed
but no messenger came and he began to look frequently at the
road. When the time for breaking bread had gone by, the saliva
rose higher than his brain and with a laugh he called out,

'Brother, set your tray and summon your own free men to it.
If this is the custom of Esfandiyār, he regards his business with
me as of small concern.'

Thus he spoke and they set his tray; the meal was eaten and all
then rose. When the mighty warrior left his place he at once gave
order to Farāmarz that his courser Rakhsh should be saddled
without delay and the saddle decked with brocade of China.

'I shall go and tell Esfandiyār,' he said, 'that if he is a prince he
must remember my words; namely, that he who fails in his promise wipes out his footprints as a man of honour.'

[With those words Rostam went off, mounted on Rakhsh, to the
river Hirmand, where he was met by Esfandiyār. When he was
reproached by Rostam for the slight laid on him,]

Esfandiyār smiled ingratiatingly on Rostam and said,

'Cavalier, son of Sām, you were incensed when no messenger
came. Yet I had desired in conversation with you to attain to
success and a goodly name. The day had been hot and the journey
long; I meant no vexation to you, so do not be aggrieved. I had
said that at earliest dawn I would make the long journey to you
in order to crave your forgiveness, and that I would rejoice at
beholding Dastān. And now my spirit is wholly gladdened. You
yourself have cast away your wrath and have emerged on to the
open plain, having left your own abode. Be at your ease; be
seated; take cup in hand and no longer remember your wrath and
displeasure.'

He gave him a place at his left-hand side, making Rostam the
ornament of the assembly. But that shrewd man said,

'Such is not my place. I will seat myself where I consider it
appropriate for me.' Whereupon Esfandiyār said to Bahman,

'Let his place be got ready on the right hand, as he has demanded.' Bahman arose with a frown and a resentful glance. When Rostam saw that look of hatred he exploded with anger and addressed the prince,

'Regard me well, with open eyes. Think of my powers and my lineage. I come of the stock of Sām the hero, and though I find no worthy place with you, yet I have prowess to my name, royal splendour and good judgment.'

At that Esfandiyār bade his son give the order that a golden throne be set up before him. On it Rostam seated himself, filled with rage and in his hand a bitter orange which he smelt.

(viii) *Esfandiyār disparages Rostam's lineage*

And now Esfandiyār addressed Rostam to say,

'Lion-hearted chieftain of glorious fame, I have recently heard from my counsellors, great men of alert and ripe wisdom, that Dastān [your father] was of evil stock, born of a Div, and that his origins in the world are no loftier than that. Men always concealed it from Dastān, regarding it as a cause of derangement in the world. His body was black, his face and hair white, and when Sām beheld him despair took possession of his heart. He commanded that the child be carried away to the ocean, there to become the prey of the birds and fishes. But the Simorgh came and spread out her wings over him, though she had seen no sign of majesty or *Farr* on him, and bore him aloft to where her eyrie was, before anyone could catch sight of him. She threw him down amongst her nestlings, in order that, when the time came for them to eat, she might be rid of him. But they left him in contempt untouched, utterly turning from him. He consumed the carrion they rejected and his body was miserably bare of all covering. But now the Simorgh cast her pity upon Zāl and became the sky over his head, and after a period when he had been eating nought but carrion she bore him naked to Sistān. There, Sām made him welcome, being childless, but did so out of unwisdom, senility and dullness of wits. Prosperous nobles and my own royal ancestors who cherished my welfare reared him to manhood and gave him endowment. Many a long year thus passed. Zāl became a cypress whose top was ever out of reach, and when he put forth branches Rostam came as his fruit. In valour, sagacity and beauty he reached to the vault of heaven, and so it was that he has attained kingship and achieved greatness. But he has taken to godless ways.'

(ix) Rostam retorts on Esfandiyār

[In his reply to Esfandiyār, Rostam claims that if it had not been for his services, the names of the ancestors whom the other was boasting about would never have been remembered, while his own were at least their equals in repute, in spite of the fact that Zaḥḥāk was one of his mother's forebears. He repeats the familiar enumeration of the services he has rendered the world during the six hundred years of his life. Esfandiyār's response was a youthful laugh. After a Gargantuan meal, in which Rostam displayed his prowess as trencherman and wine-bibber, Esfandiyār renewed his efforts to make him submit to Goshtāsp.]

Rostam's mind thereat became pensive and vexed, and he thought,

'Whether I submit my hands to his fetters or defiantly seek to do him harm, either course will lead to misfortune and evil. From his bonds my repute will suffer and my fate in his hands will be an ugly one. Wherever men converse together around the world, their scorn of me will never disappear. They will say that Rostam did not escape the hand of a youth, that he went to Zābol and there his feet were pinioned. If, on the other hand, Goshtāsp is slain on the battlefield, my face will be yellow in every king's mind. They will say that I slew a youthful monarch for having spoken a harsh word to me. And if I am he that is slain by his hand, no glory will be left for me in Zābolestān; the line of Dastān son of Sām will be broken and the very name of Zābol will not be remembered.' [He ends his speech by declaring that the issue could only be determined by battle.]

To Rostam thus replied Esfandiyār,

'Seeker after fame, you have quickly turned to harshness in your speech. If you enter the battlefield tomorrow you will learn what men of courage can do. I am not a mountain nor have I under me a horse like a mountain. I shall be a man alone, unescorted. If your skull is ventilated by my battle-axe, your mother will weep from the pain at her heart; and if you do not come to be slain on the field of battle, I shall tie you to my saddle and carry you to the Shah to demonstrate that a slave like you should never seek to do combat with a prince.'

(x) Rostam gives battle to Esfandiyār

When dawn came Rostam put on his corselet, over which his squire placed his leopard-skin. He tied a lasso to his saddle-strap and mounted his elephant-bodied charger.

[After crossing the Hirmand river unaccompanied by any troops, he climbed a hill, from which he called out to Esfandiyār to prepare for single combat.]

The two warriors had vowed that none should come to their assistance in the conflict. Time and again they attacked with their spears until the nails in their armour flew widespread. Continuing thus till the lance-heads were shattered, perforce the two men had to take to their swords. They whirled the trenchant blades around, galloping left, right and all about, until from the champions' violence and the horses' charges the edges of the scimitars were shorn away. They then stretched out their powerful arms and seized the maces that lay in their saddles. Each on the other rained down blows heavy as boulders bounding down from a height. In that bout both the maces were fractured and the men's arms wearied.

Next they caught each other by the girdle, while the two swift horses galloped along. Each man hauled the other towards him, mighty warriors, elephant-bodied, but they broke away distressed and with their steeds exhausted. The hands which the men placed to their mouths were filled with blood and dust, their harness and armour all broken in pieces.

[In a battle which broke out uncontrollably, in spite of all prohibition, between the supporters on either side, two of Esfandiyār's sons were killed and news of the tragedy was brought to him in the midst of his own combat.]

To Rostam he said,

'Man of ill omen, can this be the sworn promise of a man of proud rank? You vowed to bring no troops into the battle; have you no heed for your name and repute? Have you no shame before me or before God? Do you fear no question on Judgment Day? Two men of Sagestān have slain two of my sons, without a regret for their iniquitous act.'

Rostam was mightily grieved at the news and trembled like a twig on a tree. He swore by his soul and by the king's head, by the sun and the sword and the field of battle, that he had given no command for this outrage and that he never would grant his favour to the men who had committed it. He said he would bring his brother, who had allowed the crime, before the prince so that he could exact vengeance from him.

Esfandiyār replied to Rostam,

'If I were to shed a serpent's blood in return for a peacock's, it would be neither good nor fitting, nor would it be the custom of princes who hold their heads high. Set your affairs in order, you ill-omened man, for your fortunes have reached a narrow pass. With an arrow I am about to pin together the body of Rakhsh and your thighs.'

'From a speech such as that,' Rostam answered him, 'there results nothing except that one's honour is diminished.'

[Esfandiyār attacks and wounds Rostam, who retreats to his mountain fastness. He admits to his friends that he has found an opponent worthy of serious consideration.]

'Before me lies a task,' he said, 'which will prove hard, and because of it my spirit is filled with care. I have often thrust at Esfandiyār's armour and it was no more effective than spilling thorns on a rock. The corselet on his breast is never pierced, nor is the silken kerchief on his head disturbed. Howsoever I crave forgiveness [for his son's death] in order to bring warmth to that flinty heart, he demands only that which I cannot grant. I thank Almighty God that the night darkened and in the gloom his vision was impaired, so that I was enabled to escape this dragon's clutches. But I know not how I am to find deliverance further.'

Zāl said to him,

'My son, give ear to me. Now that you have made your case clear, take thought. There is some way out of every difficulty on earth, except from death, where the exit is different from that of the rest. I will devise a scheme, with your approval, whereby I will summon the Simorgh to our aid. If she becomes our guide, our land and realm remain firmly based; if not, then our realm is overwhelmed with ruin from Esfandiyār, that malevolent warrior.'

(xi) *The Simorgh devises a plan for Rostam*

Quickly they decided on this expedient. Prince Zāl climbed a lofty mountain, taking with him from the palace three braziers

for fire and three resourceful warriors as escort. When the wonder-worker reached the summit of that height, he drew a feather
from a wrapping of brocade and having lit a fire in one of the
braziers burnt a barb of the feather on it. At once, although only
one watch of the night had passed away, you would have thought
the aether had turned into blackest cloud, and that moment the
bird gazed down from space and beheld the bright flash of the
fire, beside which Zāl was seated in grief and agony. One swoop
and the bird was down to earth. Zāl, seeing the Simorgh alighting, gave her salutations and called down blessings on her. He
filled the three braziers with incense, while his cheeks streamed
with tears, wrung from his heart. The Simorgh asked him,

'What was it, O King, that brought you so urgently to have
recourse to the smoke?'

He answered,

'May the evil which has come on me from an evil one of evil
stock befall my enemy! The body of Rostam the lion-hearted
has been wounded, and in caring for him my feet have lagged.
There is danger to his life, no less, because of his wounds, the
like of which no man ever saw. You might say that Rakhsh too
is almost without life, being tormented by the wounds of arrow-
heads night and day. Esfandiyār has come to this land demanding
all manner of things, on threat of war.'

The Simorgh said to him,

'Do not let your spirits be distressed by this matter, but it were
fitting for you to show me Rakhsh as well as the mighty world-
bestower.'

Over the wounded parts the Simorgh rubbed a feather, and
Rostam was at once restored to strength and robustness. The
bird said to him,

'Elephant-body, you who are the most noted in every assembly,
why did you seek combat with Esfandiyār? He is brazen-bodied
and bears a famous name.'

Rostam answered,

'If report of the fetters had not been put about, my heart would
not have been inflamed. To me death would be more agreeable
than disgrace or defeat away from the battlefield.'

'To lower your head in the dust before Esfandiyār would be
no shame,' the Simorgh returned. 'He is a king's son and is
valorous in battle and, clean-bodied man, he bears the divine
Farr. If now you will make me a promise to forsake all thought

of making war, will seek no triumph over Esfandiyār in any place of vengeance or on the battlefield, will make submission to him in my presence, devoting yourself to him loyally body and soul, then, seeing that his fate will surely come upon him and he spares no thought for the pardon which you crave, I will devise a scheme for you that will raise your head up to the sun.'

Rostam on hearing these words was rejoiced at heart and he was freed from his apprehension about the fetters. He said, 'I will not step aside from what you say, even were the sky to rain scimitars on my head.' The Simorgh then proceeded, 'Out of affection I will reveal the heavens' secret to you. Fortune will sacrifice any man who spills the blood of the hero Esfandiyār; as long as life shall last in that man he will find no deliverance from torment nor will his prosperity endure. This very night I will show you a marvel that will close men's lips against slandering you. Go and seat yourself on your charger Rakhsh, having chosen a dagger with a watered-steel blade.'

Rostam girt up his loins on hearing these words and from where he stood leapt on to Rakhsh. On he rode till he neared the ocean, where he beheld the face of the aether darkened by the Simorgh, and as he arrived at the ocean's edge, with the mighty bird sinking towards the ground, he beheld a tamarisk whose top was in the air. On it the powerful bird alighted and pointed out to Rostam a dry pathway, from which the breeze dispensed the perfume of musk and along which she told Rostam to advance after passing her wing over the hero's skull. She said to him, 'Choose a branch as straight as can be, one whose top reaches highest and whose length is supplest. Upon this shaft depends Esfandiyār's fate, therefore do not regard this piece of wood lightly. Straighten it in the fire and look for arrow-heads which are fine and old. Then fix three feathers on it and two arrow-heads; I have given you a sign of the harm it can do.'

Rostam thereupon cut the tamarisk-shaft to its base and left the shore of the ocean by the path along which the Simorgh had been his guide by hovering steadfastly over his head. The bird said to him,

'If Esfandiyār now comes forward seeking to do battle with you, appeal to him and demand an honourable course of action, paying no heed to anything that implies dishonour. He may thereby be turned to milder ways and remember the days that are past when you were so constantly coursing about the world to labour and endure hardships on behalf of princes. If, when you have pleaded your case, he will grant you no indulgence, still regarding you as his underling, attach the string to your bow and insert this tamarisk arrow after steeping it in the juice of the grape. Direct both arrow-heads towards his eyes, aiming them at the pupils. Fate will carry the arrow into his eyes, blinding him, and fortune will be hostile to him.'

Thence, contentedly, the Simorgh flew away. Rostam, seeing her thus, aloft in the aether, ordered a goodly fire to be kindled in which he straightened out the tamarisk shaft. To it he attached the arrow-heads and set the feathers on it.

[A battle of words ensues between the two warrior champions.]

The hero Esfandiyār donned his harness and made his way towards Rostam the famous. On beholding that warrior's face he roared out,

'May your name disappear from out of the world! Can you, a man of Sistān, perhaps have forgotten the lasso and the warrior who once opposed you? You have been healed by the magic of Zāl; had it not been for that, your body would have sought the corpse-tower. Now you have been concocting magic again and so you ride in haste to give me battle. I will so pound your limbs today that never again will Zāl see you alive.'

Then Rostam answered Esfandiyār,

'You have not yet had your fill of battle. Have a fear of the Lord, of God most pure. Do not bury wisdom together with your brain in the tomb. I do not come for the purpose of war to-day, but to crave your forgiveness for the sake of my name and reputation. It is you who make unjust onslaught on me, keeping the eye of wisdom covered. By the Lord Zardosht [Zoroaster] and the Goodly Faith, by Nush Āzar and the glory of God, by Sun and Moon, by Avesta and Zand, [I adjure you to] turn away from the path of evil, to cease retaining in your mind those things which are past, even though the skin on a man's body was pierced. Now come and for once behold my abode, casting aside your aims against my life. I will open wide the gate to my long-accumulated treasures, which I will pile high on my horses and give to your treasurer to carry away. I will travel the road with you and go as you command me to face the Shah. If the Shah slays me, that will be my due; so also if he bids me to be shackled. All I seek is a means by which destiny will give you satiety of conflict and war.'

Esfandiyār retorted,

'How long will you prate of Iran and home, ever washing over the surface of peace? If you desire to remain alive as you are, let your body first be chafed by my chains.'

Once again Rostam loosed his tongue and said,

'Prince, make no more allusion to an unlawful subject. Neither sully my name, nor degrade your own soul; from this contest nothing but evil can result. I will give you thousands of royal pearls, a crown, a necklace and earrings too. Thousands of sweet-lipped boys I'll give you, to be at your service both night and day. I'll give you a thousand Turcoman girls worthy of coronets and covered with splendour. All things lawful I will collect about you and I will bring you men from Kābolestān who will give loyal obedience and crush your foes on the day of battle. And I will precede you into the king's presence as a henchman to suffer his vengeance.'

To Rostam thus did Esfandiyār retort,

'How long will you utter words which are beside the purpose? You bid me step aside from God's path and reject the commands of the world-dominating king. But any one who rejects the Shah's behest makes wizardry his sovereign. Choose either war or fetters; utter no more of these empty speeches.'

(xii) Rostam shoots Esfandiyār in the eye

When Rostam perceived that soft words availed nothing with Esfandiyār, he equipped his bow with its string and the arrow of tamarisk, whose heads he had steeped in the juice of the grape. As he adjusted it in the bow he turned his head upwards to Heaven and said,

'Lord of the Moon and the Sun, who increaseth knowledge, glory and strength, Thou dost behold this pure spirit of mine, my soul and the things over which I have power, and Thou knowest how greatly I have endeavoured to turn the head of Esfandiyār from thoughts of war. Thou knowest also that he strives ever to do wrong by dwelling on war and rash attack. Visit me not with punishment for this sin, Thou who art Creator of the Moon and the arrow [tīr, which is also the name of the planet Mercury].'

Seeing how Rostam delayed in his action and how slow to proceed to war, Esfandiyār said to him,

'Fabulous Rostam, has your spirit had its fill of battle? Will you now inspect Goshtāsp's arrow, the lion's heart and Lohrāsp's arrow-points?'

At that the elephant-bodied one swiftly thrust the tamarisk into his bow, as the Simorgh had instructed him. Straight at Esfandiyār's eye he shot and the world for that noble man turned to darkness. Bowed became the back of that tall, slender cypress; wisdom and majesty ceased to be his. Down went the head of that God-fearing prince, his Chinese bow fell from his hand.

[The fallen Esfandiyār entrusted the education of his son, Bahman, to Rostam and then died of his wounds and his body was carried back to Iran, where he was long mourned. Later Goshtāsp and Rostam became friends again.]

(xiii) *Rostam and Shaghād*

Now I will relate the story of how Rostam was slain, converting the annals into my own language. Āzād Sarv was an ancient man who lived with Ahmad-e Sahl [the learned chancellor of the Court of the Samanids] at Marv. He possessed a record of the Khosrows which pictured the forms and faces of the Pahlavāns; his heart was laden with wisdom, his head with eloquence and his tongue with legends of bygone days. He traced his lineage to Narīmān's son Sām and he had much to tell of the battles of Rostam. I will tell you the story as I had it from him, weaving his words together one with another. If I continue in this fleeting world, wit and wisdom acting as my guides, I shall carry this hoary legend to its conclusion in order that it may remain my record in the world.

[Here follows a further dedication to Mahmud of Ghazna, to which patron there is given a broad hint that recognition in some material form would be welcome:—
'My expectation in this reminder now is the receipt of the money from his Majesty.']

(xiv) *Rostam goes to Kābol for the sake of his brother Shaghād*

That old man athirst for knowledge, learned, eloquent and of tenacious memory says that, veiled in Zāl's abode, there lived a slave, who both played and sang. To her one day a son was born, between whom and the moon there was little to choose for beauty,

since in stature and visage he was the cavalier Sām. And in him
his noble family rejoiced. To him there travelled men who knew
the stars and learned soothsayers, the greatest and choicest from
Kashmir and Kābol, worshippers of fire and God-worshippers
too, with Hindu star-maps in their hands. Each made calculation
of the heavens to know what was in store for the handsome
child. The star-reckoners beheld an astonishing thing and gazed,
this man at that, that man at this. They said to Zāl son of Sām
the Knight,

'Monument to the lofty stars, we have taken a sight and observed the secret of the sky. It has no love for this little child.
When this handsome boy attains to manhood and touches the
age of courage and martial ardour, he will destroy the line of
Sām the son of Niram and bring this mighty power down into
ruin. Through him all Sistān will fall into perturbation and he
will bring confusion into the land of Iran. Through him a man's
days will decline in bitterness, not enduring for any length of
time.'

[Dastān called his new son Shaghād. When the boy was weaned he
sent him to the Shah of Kābol for training and there he learned of
the prowess of his brother Rostam. Shaghād grew up and married the Shah of Kābol's daughter, siding with his father-in-law
when Rostam came to demand the usual tribute and was refused
it. The great hero overturned the realm of Kābol, embittering his
brother, who, however, made no mention to him of his feelings.]

In secret he [Shaghād] said to the Shah of Kābol,

'I am now wearied of worldly affairs. As for my brother, he
has no shame with regard to me and my dealings with him can no
longer be peaceable. There is no difference now between elder
brother and stranger nor between sage and witless zany. Let us
work together to ensnare him and so become world-famous. To
achieve success in our scheme you must have a feast to which
you will invite the noblest. Call for wine and music and the
minstrels. As we sit drinking, speak roughly to me and make
disparaging comment in your words. Thus dishonoured I will
go to Zābolestān and make complaint there of Kābol's ruler.
My brother's head will be inflamed on my behalf and he will
make his way to this glorious land of ours. Meanwhile look out
the hunting-grounds which lie on his way; in the places where
he may go hunting, there dig pits. Make them of a size for Rostam
and Rakhsh together, embedding long blades in the bottom of

each, spears and lances with heads of watered steel, the points upwards, the shafts buried deep. If you dug ten pits it would be better than five, if you wish to be rid of a pest for ever. Take a hundred men of resource there, cover the head of each pit securely and keep your lips tight against all speech.'

The Shah departed, estranging good sense from his mind, and at the fool's behest prepared a feast, to which he invited the great and small of Kābol and set them down in front of trays that received high compliment. The food having been eaten a symposium was held, and there was a demand for wine, music and minstrels. When heads were replete with royal vintage, Shaghād broke out in a turbulent mood. He said to the king of Zābol,

'Whatever the assembly, I am the noblest in it. For brother I have Rostam, for father Dastān. Who can boast of more famous kinship than that?'

The Kāboli king thereupon flew into a passion and exclaimed,

'Why should I for ever conceal the truth? You are not of the seed of Sām son of Niram; you are not the brother of Rostam, nor his kinsman. Sām's son Dastān has never spoken of you; how should he give tongue to your name as a brother? You spring from some slave at a pauper's door. His mother would not acknowledge you as his brother.'

The words made Shaghād's heart writhe with torment and, springing up in fury, he turned his head from the direction of Kābol. He came to the court of his royal brother, his mind teeming with devices and his head full of vengefulness. The Pahlavān [Rostam] rejoiced at seeing him, regarding him as a man of ripe wisdom and happy spirit. He said,

'Out of the seed of Sām the Lion, surely, there spring none but the powerful and brave? How go your affairs with the Kāboli, and what has he to say to Rostam of Zābol?'

Shaghād gave answer to Rostam,

'Speak no more of the Kāboli king. Till now I have had nothing but kindliness from him and he has proclaimed himself blessed when he saw me. But he has begun to drink wine and talks of war, raising his head above all other men's. He humiliated me before the assembly, pretending I was of ignoble birth, and he asked how long more there was to be talk of tribute and impost, for was he not the equal of all Sistān? Hereafter he would not speak of [the great] Rostam, or admit his own valour and birth to be inferior to his.'

E K—Q

Rostam heard this and was stirred to fury, saying that words could not always be kept hidden, that he would deprive the Kāboli of his life for what he had said and would wring blood from some hearts and eyes in sorrow for him. Further, he would set Shaghād aloft on the Kāboli king's throne. From amongst his forces he chose out those most suitable, men who had achieved fame in battle, and commanded them to prepare for departure and the transference of their abode from Zābol to Kābol.

When the preparations were complete the Pahlavān's heart was content. And then Shaghād came to him and said,

'Have no talk of war with the king of Kābol. If I were but to write your name on the water in Kābol, no man would find rest or sleep there. Who would venture out to give battle to you? Once you moved forward, who would stay in his place? I feel that he now repents of his action and because of my departure he seeks to find a way out.'

Rostam in answer to that said,

'The action to take is this—I need no army for Kābol—to take Zavāra with a hundred noted horsemen and a hundred noted foot-soldiers.'

(xv) *The king of Zābol digs pits for Rostam*

When he left the city of Kābol the ominous prince went swiftly to the hunting-ground, taking with him from amongst his troops sappers famed for their work. These, wherever game might be pursued across the plain, dug out pits and into the ground at the bottom of each drove spears, swords, lances and sharp scimitars. With cunning they covered over the mouths of the pits so that no man's or courser's eye could distinguish it. When Rostam in a passion set out on the road, Shaghād sent a horseman galloping in advance to say that the elephant-bodied hero was coming escortless, and instructing the king of Kābol to come forward and beg his indulgence. He accordingly came out of the city with his tongue full of sweetness and his soul full of venom; and, as his eye fell on Rostam he dismounted, removed his Indian turban and stood bare-headed. Also he removed the boots from his feet and mournfully squeezed tears of blood from his eyes, as he pressed his cheeks on the dark earth, craving pardon for what he had done to Shaghād. Then he approached on naked feet, his head strewn with dust, his heart filled with guile. Rostam forgave him his misdemeanour and even granted him higher degree than he previously had, bidding him cover his head and put shoes on his feet, then mounted his horse and went on his way.

Now in the city of Kābol there was a garden so spread with green that it rejoiced the heart. Waters flowed, trees were abundant and couches were festively strewn about; the king provided lavish dishes and a joyous feasting-place was laid out. Wine was fetched and minstrels summoned and all the great were accommodated on noble thrones. When all was over the king said to Rostam,

'When it suits your taste, let us go hunting. I have a region where over hill and dale game is everywhere to be found in herds. Ibex, gazelle and wild ass are there for anyone who has a galloping courser.'

At his speech Rostam's passion was stirred to boiling for the field with its streams, its gazelles and wild asses. (When the time arrives for a blow to strike a man, his mind is distracted and his senses go astray; that is the way of this unstable world, which never reveals to us what it holds hidden.) The king ordered that the horses be saddled and that hawks and king-falcons be stationed about the plain. He himself had a royal bow and quiver laid ready for him and he rode out with Shaghād riding beside him. Zavāra went with Tahamtan [Rostam] and a number of men from his famous escort. Troops were scattered in the place where the game was, opposite the region where the digging had been done. But it was there that Zavāra and Rostam made their way, because of the fate which lay in the pits.

Rakhsh, smelling the scent of newly-turned earth, rolled his body about as though it were a ball. He plunged in terror at scenting the earth, tearing and ploughing the ground with his hoofs. The speedy courser began to pace the road delicately, till he came to a place between two pits, and there Rostam's heart filled with rage at Rakhsh. Fate covered his eyes and he was maddened, so that he brought out a whip of supple leather with which he lashed at the unnerved Rakhsh and roused him to passion. Being hemmed in between two pits, he sought for a way of escape from the clutch of fate, but his hind legs plunged down into one of the pits, where there was no room either to hold fast or to struggle. The pit's bottom was covered with knives and keen swords; no place there for courage and no means of escape, so that the flanks of the mighty Rakhsh were slashed through, as were the breast and legs of the stout Pahlavān. With fortitude he dragged his own body out and raised his head up out of the pit.

(xvi) *Rostam kills Shaghād and then dies*

When despite his wounds Rostam opened his eyes and beheld the malevolent face of Shaghād, he perceived that the knavery was his doing and that his hostile betrayer was Shaghād. He said to him,

'You man of vile and ill-omened fate, your actions have brought this prosperous land to desolation. For this misdeed sorrow will come upon you; you will be so tormented because of this evil that you will not reach old age.'

The base Shaghād replied,

'The revolving skies have brought just retaliation on you. How have you dared to shed so much blood, raiding and harrying in every direction? The time has come for destiny to bring your career to a close and for you to meet death in Ahriman's trap.'

As he was speaking, the lord of Kābol moved from his path on to the open plain where the hunting was. There he saw the elephant-bodied hero grievously stricken and with none of his wounds bound up. He said to him,

'Most famous warrior, what has befallen you on this hunting-ground? I will go quickly and bring physicians, and for the pain you suffer I will shed tears of blood.'

'You base-born knave,' retorted Tahamtan, 'the time for healers is at an end for me. Squeeze out no blood-suffused tears on my behalf. However long you may exist, the moment for you will come at the last, for no-one living can escape the skies. My *Farr* is no more potent than Jamshid's, whose enemy cut him in twain with a saw; nor is it mightier than Faridun's or Key Qobād's, mighty kings of resplendent lineage. Garovi Zereh slit the throat of Siyāvosh with a dagger when his time arrived. All were sovereigns of Iran, veritable lions in battle. They departed, and we but follow slowly after, like ravening lions we lie by the roadside. My son Farāmarz, dear to me as my eyes, will come to exact vengeance from you on my account.'

Then he addressed the vile Shaghād, saying to him,

'Now that this misfortune has come on me, withdraw my bow from its covering and apply that gift of mine to use. String it and place it before me with two arrows. It must not befall that some prowling lion shall catch sight of me and injury come upon me from him. If the bow is there, it will be of use to me, for no lion will then rend my body while I live. But the time will come when I shall cast my body into the dust.'

Shaghād approached, extricated the bow, fixed the string to it and straightway drew it. With a laugh he placed it before Taham-tan, being rejoiced over his brother's death. In distress Tahamtan took up the bow, his terrible wounds overwhelming him with torment. But now his brother was seized with a great fear of his arrow and went over to a tree which he intended to use as a shield for his body. The tree was hollow within although its branches and leaves were still in place, and behind it this evilly intentioned man took refuge.

Rostam, seeing all this, stretched out his arm and in spite of his wounds loosed the arrow from his thumbstall, pinning the tree and his brother together. In the very moment of his death his heart kindled with joy. Shaghād heaved a deep sigh as he received his wound, but Tahamtan made his agony brief. Thus said Rostam,

'Praise be to God—for I have ever been a man who has known God—that, when my spirit reached the point of departure from my lips, day had not turned to night before I exacted this vengeance. Now, O God forgive my sins and take me unto Thyself.'

As he spoke the spirit departed from his body.

[Farāmarz, Rostam's son, in his turn led an army against the king of Zābol, whom he slew for his part in the death of Rostam.]

XV

Goshtāsp surrenders the Kingship to Bahman

Now that the period of Tahamtan has come to a close, I will relate the story of another episode. When the face of destiny turned black for Goshtāsp, he fetched Jāmāsp before his throne and said to him,

'Because of the fate of Esfandiyār I have been so branded by destiny that no day in my life is sweet to me. Because of my vengeful star I have been deprived of all joy. After me Bahman shall now be king and Pashutan shall be the keeper of his secrets. Do not turn your heads from his command, nor seek to remove yourselves from loyalty to him. Let each of you serve him as a guide on his path, for he is the man worthiest of throne and crown.'

He gave him the key to his storehouses and heaved a cold sigh that came from the depths of his being. Then he said to him,

'My career has run its course; the waters have risen above my head. For a hundred and twenty years I have reigned as king, never finding my peer in the whole world. Strive to ally yourself with justice; when you have brought justice in, you will be released from care. Act ever with honour, for with it no failure can befall anything you undertake. I surrender to you my throne, diadem and treasure, after having myself borne much suffering and toil.'

Thus he spoke and his life ended; the time which had passed over him bore no more fruit.

XVI

The Story of Bahman Son of Esfandiyār

When Bahman ascended his ancestral throne, he bound his girdle about his loins and unloosed his arms for toil. To his army he granted money in sums large or small as well as provinces and border-lands in abundance. He formed a council of wise men, nobles and chieftains well tried in affairs.

[He spoke to them of his endeavour to avenge his father's death, a project in which he was assured of his audience's approval and support. An army of a hundred thousand horsemen set out immediately for Zābolestān, the land over which Rostam had reigned as feudatory king. After plundering the country Bahman returned home.]

Ardashir [Bahman] had a son, a lion-hunter, whom he named Sāsān, and also a daughter, whose name was Homāy. She was a gifted woman endowed with wisdom and perspicuous judgment. They called her Chehrzād [Scheherezade], and wherever she appeared in the world there was gladness. Now because of her beauty her father took her to wife in accordance with the custom which you call Pahlavi, and she became pregnant by him. Six months passed and then she was overtaken with pangs so that Bahman was smitten with illness at what he saw. As he lay on his bed of sickness he commanded that Homāy should present herself before him together with the notables and men of felicitous star. To them he said,

'This pure-bodied Chehrzād has not long enjoyed this world. I surrender to her my crown and exalted throne, as also my army, treasury and sublime destiny. She has been next in succession to me and her sovereignty will pass to the child as yet unrevealed who will be born to her. Whether it be a girl that she bears or a boy, to her or him this crown, throne and girdle will belong.'

Sāsān heard the words and was dismayed. Gloom filled his heart at Bahman's speech. For three days and nights, savage as a leopard, he journeyed away from Iran and for very shame went to another land. Filled with resentment he continued until he arrived at the city of Nishāpur. For wife he sought one of the seed of a noble family whom he cherished, holding her dear as his own life. But he did not reveal his own lineage.

This pure-bodied wife bore him a fine son, born under a goodly star, a boy of splendid birth. His father gave him the name of Sāsān, and soon thereafter came to the end of his life. When the boy grew from childhood into manhood he found nought but poverty in the house. So from the king of Nishāpur he sought and received a flock which roamed freely in search of pasture over mountain and plain. For a time he continued as shepherd to the king, finding his resting-place with his flock.

And now let me return to the career of Homāy, after the death of Bahman had occurred.

XVII

The Story of Dārāb

(i) *Homāy leaves her son Dārāb in a casket on the Euphrates river*

Ardashir [Bahman] died of his sickness, and crown and throne were left unoccupied. It was then that Homāy came and set the crown on her head, establishing a new practice and a new order. She gave audience to her troops, opened the door of the treasury and distributed money. In judgment and equity she surpassed her father and because of her justice the whole world prospered. While she was bearing her child she kept it a secret from the citizens and the army, and when she gave birth to her son [Dārāb] she told of it to no one and kept him affectionately in a place of concealment. She brought a noblewoman to be his nurse, to whom she entrusted her son, telling her that if anyone should speak of him she was to say that the nobly-born child had died.

So matters continued for eight months and her son grew to resemble the Shah who had passed away. She then commanded that a skilled carpenter should seek out a piece of timber suited for a delicate piece of work. Out of the seasoned wood he constructed a handsome casket which was covered with bitumen and musk. It was softly lined within with Greek brocade while the outside was overlaid with varnish and wax. At the bottom of the casket the man placed an easeful bed and the sides were filled in with pearls of finest lustre. Red gold was poured abundantly into the casket and in it were embedded rubies and emeralds. On the arm of the nursling babe a royal pearl was fastened.

Now when the child was overcome with sleep, the soft-handed nurse, weeping tears, came and laid him very gently in the casket and covered him warmly with Chinese satin. The narrow top of the casket they rendered dry with varnish and bitumen, wax and musk. At midnight the casket was carried away, no man opening his lips to another. Swiftly they took it out of the presence of Homāy and launched it on the Euphrates river. Close behind it two men followed to observe how the river would deal with the babe. The timber floated like a ship on the water so that the observers had need to make haste.

When the whiteness of dawn put up its head above the mountain the casket halted alongside the stream at a fulling-place[1]
where there was a stone and where the workers had narrowed
the head of a channel. A fuller caught sight of the little casket,
ran forward and drew it away from the place where his work lay.
When he opened it and took out the materials which were spread
out there he was astounded at its workmanship. He covered it
over with clothes and came home at a run, his joyful heart full
of anticipation and his spirits sparkling while the observers
swiftly ran back to the mother to tell what they had seen of the
casket and the fuller. She bade them to keep concealed all that
they had observed.

(ii) *The fuller rears Dārāb* [*the prince*]

When the fuller came back from the stream before his due time,
his wife said to him,

'This is glad tidings, that you should return with the clothes
half wet. From whom do you expect to receive pay for this kind
of work?'

Now the fuller's heart was saddened with grief because a clever
child of his had died and his wife in sorrow had lacerated her
cheeks and her spirits were gloomy. To her the fuller said,

'Let your spirits be restored; from now onwards tears will be
out of place for you. And now, if what I say can remain hidden,
I will tell my worthy wife something. At the stone on which I
beat the clothes, in the channel where I throw them into the
water when they are clean, I saw a casket with a baby hidden in
it. If I open wide the top of what is now closed, you will have a
longing to see the little child, for the little son we had was given
no long life, and died. Now you have found a son you never
hoped for, all decked in brocade and jewels.'

When he put the clothes down on the ground, he revealed the
casket's narrow top. His wife stood in amaze at what she saw and
called down blessings on the Creator of the world. Amidst the
silk she saw a glowing face, in appearance resembling Ardashir.
His pillow was covered with pearls of the first water and at his
feet were rubies and emeralds. By his left hand were dinārs of
red gold and to his right lay an abundance of corals. The woman
swiftly fed him at her breast, rejoiced at the heart-ravishing child,

---

[1] Where clothes were washed.

through whose beauty and the riches there her heart was purged
of grief. The fuller said to her,
'We shall treasure this child with our lives for ever more. He
surely bears a royal name and is of royal stock in the world.'

She cared for him as though he were her flesh and blood, as
though he were her only son. On the third day they bestowed on
him the name of Dārāb, for they had found him nesting on the
running water [Persian *āb*]. There came a day when this clear-
witted woman, while speaking of this and that to her husband,
said,
'What will you now do with these jewels? Who will be your
adviser to inform you?'

The fuller answered his wife,
'My dear helpmate, the jewels are no better than dust to me
lying hidden. It were best for us to forsake this town and, emerging on to open ground after straits and difficulty, go to a city
where no man knows us. There we can live with hearts at ease
and with means at our disposal.'

Next morn the fuller loaded up his gear, set forth giving no
further thought to his country and his home. They took Dārāb
with them, nestling in their bosoms, and brought nothing in their
loads but gold and jewels. They travelled sixty leagues away from
their home, to settle in another town, where they were unknown.
Here they made their abode in the style of householders of some
wealth. The city was governed by a nobleman of repute, to whom
the fuller made a practice of sending a piece of jewellery, for
which in return he received clothes as well as silver and gold.
This continued until no great amount of the jewels was left. The
man's wife, who was his adviser with respect to his goods, had
one day said to her husband that they had no further need to
toil, because they had become wealthy, without further obligation to seek work. He answered,
'My virtuous and clever wife, you may call anything a trade.
What is better than a trade? Of all pursuits a trade is foremost,
and as for you, your occupation is to maintain Dārāb in a fit and
proper manner. Then see what fate has in store for you.'

The boy was reared with such care that he sustained not even
a caress from a swiftly-moving breeze. By the time that the skies
had revolved over him for a number of years he had become a
fine, broad-shouldered youth, so that when he wrestled with his
playmates on the road none had his sturdiness or strength and

they formed themselves into a group opposed to him, since they had learned to fear him. By now the fuller's prosperity had begun to decline and he rebuked the boy for his idle conduct. He said,

'Beat these clothes on the stone, for it is no disgrace to you to follow a trade.'

Dārāb fled from the task, and the fuller's eyes shed tears of blood. Two parts of every day he spent looking for the youth, whose traces he sought in the open and in the city. One day he saw him bow in hand, with arms outstretched and his hand equipped with an archer's thumbstall. Seizing the bow, he said sharply,

'You wild fellow, you ravening wolf, in spite of being so young you have become perverted.'

He answered,

'Father, you direct my ability into obscure paths. To begin with let me go to some scholar that I may duly learn the Zand and Avesta, and then command me to a trade, which you may seek out for me. But do not make a citizen of me yet.'

The fuller rebuked him at great length but then handed him over to the scholars, from whom he acquired knowledge and became a man of dignity, beyond rebuke and upbraiding. He said to his foster-father,

'No advantage will come to me from the fuller's craft. Rid your affections of any concern about me; for my career in the world let me become a horseman.'

Thereupon the fuller looked about for a riding-master expert with the reins, able in the management of horses and a man of good repute. Having found such a man he entrusted the youth to him for a long period of time. The man gave him instruction in all that was required; how to wield rein, lance, shield and bow and the method of controlling a charger on the battlefield. He taught him also the art of polo-playing, how to exercise skill in archery, how to acquire honour and how to evade an enemy. So well trained did he become in these arts that against him a leopard would have found its claws of no avail in combat.

(iii) *Dārāb inquires about his birth*

Dārāb one day said to the fuller,

'There is within me a secret which I keep concealed even from myself. It is that my affections are not moved towards you and my face bears no likeness to yours. Wonderment stirs me when you call me son, and when you make me sit beside you on the couch.'

The fuller answered,

'Your words, alas, touch on sorrows of long ago. If your station is higher than mine, then seek out your father; and as for your secret, it lies with your mother.'

One day the fuller left the house in some haste to go to the river. Dārāb locked the door securely and taking his sword in his hand came to the woman and said,

'Attempt no crookedness or evasion and speak the truth about every word I ask you. What am I to you? Who am I by birth? How does it come about that I live with the fuller?'

The fuller's wife in terror begged for mercy and called on the Lord the All-possessor to come to her aid. 'Do not demand my head's blood,' she said. 'I will tell you all you ask. Speak on.'

She recounted the story to him in every point, hiding nothing that had occurred and having no recourse to falsehood.

'We were workers with our hands, coming of no well-born stock. It is from you that we have everything we possess, and it is through you that we humble folk became proud. We are your servants and it is for you to command. Consider what you desire; we are yours body and soul.'

Dārāb stood in amazement as he heard the words and set his mind to consideration. He asked,

'Of those riches has anything remained, or has the fuller dissipated all? If there were left only the price of a single horse at this time of my distress and poverty it would suffice.'

The woman replied that there was enough and more, money in abundance, orchards and lands. Of money she gave him the whole sum there was, and showed him that precious jewel untouched. With the money he bought a good horse, a saddle at a small price, a mace and a bow.

Now there was at that time a certain noble lord of the marches, possessed of dignity and judgment, a worthy highly respected who was able to impart guidance. To him Dārāb went with his gloomy spirit full of thought. This Marquis was a man to whom no harm had ever come from the world and he treated the youth as a person of consequence. It was a time when an army was advancing from Rum, to make an incursion into this land of prosperity. The Marquis was slain in a battle and the leadership for that reason went astray. Dārāb heard of all this and, anticipating great pleasure, he presented himself to the new commander and had his name inscribed. The army was ever increasing its strength in its various branches, troops having marched in from every region. From her royal palace Homāy came with the lords of the marches in order that the troops might pass in review before her and that she might count their persons and see the names on the muster rolls. When she caught sight of Dārāb with his *Farr* and splendour he appeared like the whole plain for size, as though he filled the whole earth with his marching stature. When she thus beheld his broad shoulders and heart-captivating face the milk trickled from her motherly breast. She asked,

'Whence comes this knight, with his girth and chest and upright bearing? He seems bold, gallant and warlike, but his weapons are not in keeping with his quality.'

By the stars she selected a propitious time and when the warriors had agreed on their plans they led the army away from the Queen's presence.

(iv) *Reshnavād discovers the truth about Dārāb*

One day a violent storm broke out and gave concern to Reshnavād, the commander. There was thunder and rain, lightning and uproar, the land was covered with water and the heavens resounded with clamour. Men galloped away from the rain in every direction and set up tents in the open. Dārāb too was disturbed by these happenings and sought a way of escape from the downpour. As he looked about him he beheld a desolate piece of ground in the midst of which stood a vaulted hall, lofty, ancient and dilapidated, which had once been erected by some ancient king. There he was compelled to spend the night, a man entirely alone, without comrade or companion.

The commander of the army, for his part, had gone about amongst his troops and in the course of his perambulation he had passed by that dilapidated arch. Out of the ruins a cry came to his ears, a voice came from that place of terror, saying,

'Broken vault, rouse to wakefulness! Keep watch over this king of Iran! No tent had he, nor friend, nor comrade; he entered your shelter and lay down.'

Reshnavād said to himself,

'Can this be the noise of the thunder or the raging wind?'
A second time the cry issued from within,
'Vault, do not cover over the eye of wisdom. Within you lies the son of King Ardashir. Do not fear the rain, but take these words to heart.'

A third time also this voice reached his ears, at which he wondered, his heart being made anxious by the cry. To his counsellor he said,

'What can this be? Someone must enter the ruins to see who is lying there asleep, so unmindful of his own safety.'

When they entered they saw a youth of intelligent countenance and the appearance of a Pahlavān. His clothes and his horse were wet and soiled, for he had made the black earth his resting-place. The commander was told what had been seen and his heart beat fast at their words.

'Summon him immediately,' he commanded. 'Who would dare to linger, hearing a cry such as that?'

They went in again and said, 'You that lie there, awake from your sleep upon this ground.'

At the same moment that Dārāb mounted his horse, the vault collapsed. The king's captain, seeing this marvel, looked Dārāb over from head to foot, then swiftly entered with him into his pavilion, exclaiming as he went,

'Oh Lord, unique God, no man else in the world has beheld a marvel such as this, nor has anyone heard the like from the most experienced of the great.'

He commanded that clothes should be brought and a place was got ready for Dārāb in his own pavilion. Then they lit a fire mountain-high in which they burned sandalwood in abundance, musk and amber.

When the sun struck up his head above the mountains, the captain made his preparations for marching on. He commanded the priest who was his counsellor to procure a set of garments complete from head to foot, an Arab steed with golden trappings, a coat of mail and a sword with a sheath of gold. These he gave to Dārāb, to whom he said,

'Lion-hearted man, eager for battle, what are you, and what is your birthplace and country? It were best that you should tell me all truthfully.'

Dārāb hearkened and related everything, bringing all his past out of concealment. At once Reshnavād dispatched a messenger with instructions to bring the fuller and his wife, together with the jewel.

'Bring both Mars and Venus,' he said.

[Reshnavād now wrote a letter to Queen Homāy informing her of Dārāb's history, of the voice he had heard in the ruined vault and how the vault had fallen. This letter, together with the great jewel that had been found on Dārāb's arm, he sent by a swift runner to Homāy, who now perceived that the handsome youth she had seen when she reviewed her army was none other than her own son.]

(v) *Homāy enthrones Dārāb*

When she had placed Dārāb on his golden throne, Homāy approached him with a kingly crown in her hand. She kissed him and laid it on his head, thus proclaiming to the world the tidings of his coronation.

[From every province she summoned the priests, counsellors, commanders of armies and other nobles, who, in a great assembly, acknowledged Dārāb as their sovereign, showering jewels on him as a sign of their approval until he was entirely covered. The fuller and his wife, who came to offer their loyal greetings, were rewarded with purses of gold and other gifts, the man being told to return to his trade, in the course of which he might again find a casket containing a Shah.

The war against Rum, over which Filicus (Philip) reigned, was resumed.]

Two heavy battles were fought within three days. On the fourth day when the world illuminator was kindled, Filicus and his army fled in defeat, no man keeping even his helmet or Greek cap. Their wives and children were taken captive and many were slain by sword and arrow. The remnant fled into a fortress in Ammuriya, amongst them being many who had pleaded for mercy. From Filicus there now came a messenger, astute, alert and possessed of qualities of various kinds, some agreeable, some harsh. Purses, slaves and largesse in abundance he brought and two chests filled with jewels fit for a king. His message ran thus,

'To God I pray that He be my guide. I am preparing festivities as the conclusion of this conflict; may we never turn our hearts to battle again! If you desire to come to Ammuriya, which is my capital, and wish to take possession of it, my heart will be in turmoil for the sake of my name and repute. Even in the moment of feasting I will enter into battle again. Therefore behave as befits a monarch, for your father was a king and your son is a prince.'

Dārāb summoned his nobles on hearing these words and imparted the whole history to them.

'What say you to all this palaver?' he asked. 'Filicus seeks to preserve his honour.'

These great men in answer said,

'Let him select for action what he knows to be best. That famous monarch has a daughter of cypress stature and beautiful as the spring. No idol-adorner in China ever saw her like; she shines forth like a jewelled ring amongst other beauties. If your Majesty saw her you would approve of her. Let this lofty cypress be transplanted to your garden.'

The Shah summoned the messenger from Rum and repeated to him what he had heard. The messenger listened, departed like the wind, and recounted to the Caesar what had been said. Filicus and his courtiers rejoiced that he should have a son-in-law like the Shah, but discussion ranged back and forth about tribute and taxes and how much the king of Rum should bear. It was agreed that each year the Shah should be paid a hundred thousand eggs of molten gold, in each of which there was to be a royal gem, each of the gems a jewel of price. The Caesar then commanded that all the learned men and men of substance prepare for the road and accompany the royal lady to the Shah.

They had prepared a golden litter and demanded slaves worthy of a royal personage. With them went ten camels laden with Greek brocades, in which all the patterns were outlined in jewels while the background was gold, and three hundred camels laden with carpets and other wares fit to be presented to the Shah.

(vi) *Dārāb returns the daughter of Filicus*

One night, as the princess lay by the king's side, bejewelled, perfumed and gloriously beautiful, she suddenly exhaled a pungent breath at which the monarch conceived disgust. He twisted about and turned his face aside into the bedclothes. When he perceived this unpleasant odour, he was apprehensive about what it might mean; his mind filled with uneasiness and his brows were twisted into frowns. Wise physicians were summoned

EK–R

and seated themselves beside the princess. One perspicacious and shrewd physician pursued researches until at last he produced a remedy. He pounded up a herb which burned the mouth—in Rum it bore the name of *Sekandar*—and applied it to the mouth of Nāhīd [the princess], who shed tears. The evil odour departed, though her mouth was burned, and once more her cheeks resumed their glowing colour.

Yet although the lovely princess was now as fragrant as musk Dārāb's affection had turned into distaste. The king's heart turned coldly away from his bride and he returned her to Filicus. She was sad and pregnant, but spoke to no one in the world of the matter. After the nine months had gone by for the beauteous princess there had come into the world a child splendid as the sun. Because of his stature and glorious appearance his mother named him Sekandar [Alexander], for she held the name to be auspicious, on the ground that she had obtained a remedy for her illness through it. To all his nobles the Caesar announced that a new Caesar had appeared of his own stock. Dārāb's name went unmentioned; Sekandar was the son and Caesar was his father. He was ashamed to say that Dārāb had repudiated his daughter.

[Sekandar in due course became heir to the Caesar's throne. Meanwhile Dārāb had married again and by his wife had a son named Dārā, who at the age of twelve succeeded his father.]

The Reign of Dārā Son of Dārāb

When Dārā had put the mourning for his father out of his heart, he elevated the crown of sovereignty to the sun. He was a quick, youthful and impatient man, against whose tongue the edge of a sword blunted itself. Being established on the throne he made proclamation saying,

'Chieftains, proud warriors, valiant nobles, I desire no one to fall into the pit, and I will summon no one out of the pit to assume the coronet of high office. He that transgresses my command need not reckon his head as part of his body; if there is any defection in his heart I will cut out his heart with the sword. I desire no one possessed of wealth to use it to my displeasure, nor do I require anyone to be my guide. I am my own guide and I am my mind's enlightener. In the whole world, enjoyment and good fortune proceed from me and all loyalty is to me; greatness, sovereignty and power of command—all are mine.'

He removed the coverings from his father's stores of treasure, mustered his army and distributed supplies. Where a stipend had been four dirhams it was raised to eight; to one man he gave in a cup, to another on a platter. Lavishly he gave dirhams and dinars and horse furniture, corselets, swords and heavy maces. When a man was a chieftain experienced in affairs he granted him a district; to one of his proud nobles he gave a border province and to each of his troops he made gifts of value. From every region envoys arrived, from every man of note and every ruler; from India and China, from Rum and every other land. All came in veneration with gifts, tribute and impost, for none could stand in opposition to him or claim equality with him.

The History of Sekandar

(i) Sekandar accedes to the throne: Arestātalis

Filicus died and for a time there was trouble in Rum. Then Sekandar ascended to the throne of his fathers. He pursued goodness and fettered the hands of evil. Now at that time there lived in Rum a certain man of repute, because of whom all that land and realm lived in happiness. His name was Arestātalis the Sage, and he was sagacious, alert and widely talented. This clear-minded man presented himself before Sekandar, made his tongue ready for eloquence and assumed his own place for himself. He said,

'Triumphant prince, if you follow your present way of life you will lose all repute. The throne of kings has seen many like you and never continues for long in anyone's possession. Whenever you say, ' "I have attained the highest station, and I need no guide in the world," ' know that you are the most ignorant of men. We are of the dust and are born destined for the dust; whether we will or not we surrender our bodies to it. If you are virtuous, your fame will endure and you will continue triumphantly on your kingly throne; but if you do evil you will reap nought but evil and never a night will you rest happily in the world.'

Sekandar listened and approved it all, regarding the speaker of the words as a man of profound sense. Thereafter all his actions were regulated as the philosopher commanded, whether at feasting or fighting, struggling for repute or making war. One day an envoy, eloquent of speech, clear-minded and of noble birth, came from Dārā to Rum in order to demand tribute from that fertile land. As he disclosed his business to Sekandar, the Caesar became enraged at this talk of bygone tribute and impost. He said,

'Go to Dārā and tell him that all the glory has now departed from our tribute, for the bird which laid the golden eggs has died and so our tribute is made valueless.'

The envoy heard the reply and at its tenour became panic-stricken and vanished from Rum.

[Sekandar now called up his forces and marched against Egypt, which he overthrew in eight days. He then turned his attention to Iran.]

When Dārā heard that an army had marched from Rum and was coming to his own land and home, he despatched from Estakhr [Persepolis] an army so numerous that by their spears alone they barred the way to the wind. Leaving Fārs his object was to attack Rum and set all ablaze in that fertile land.

(ii) *Sekandar visits Dārā as his own envoy*

Sekandar, on hearing of this army's approach, set out upon the road to encounter it. While two leagues still remained between the two forces he called his captains together and with them discussed every aspect of the situation. When he was gorged with his advisers' words he said,

'My own plan is nothing but this—that I should go to him as an envoy from myself and so penetrate into all his plans.'

He called for a girdle studded with royal pearls and a kingly robe, a fine courser with trappings of gold and, at his saddle, a sword with a golden scabbard. From among the Greeks he chose out ten cavaliers who could speak and understand everything spoken and heard, and at early dawn he issued forth from his camp with these famous ten interpreters. On his arrival in Dārā's presence he dismounted and gave him salutation. Dārā the world-possessor called him forward, inquired concerning his wellbeing and gave him an envoy's place beneath his own throne. But having taken his seat he immediately rose up and delivered Sekandar's message in due form. He said,

'Sekandar says,

' "Bearer of a goodly name, you who have spread your triumphs over every place in the world, my desire is not for conflict with the Shah nor to remain on the territory of Iran for long. My only object is to go about the land for a brief period and for once to see the world. All I desire is to act honourably and with good intent, more especially as you are the ruler of Iran. If you refuse me a passage it will not be possible for me to traverse the air as though I were a cloud. You have come here to bar my way with your army, being unaware in any respect of my plans. If you make war, I will make war on you, and I will not leave this country without conflict. Choose then a day for a battle and hold steadfastly by it, not turning aside from what you desire. As for me I do not avert my purpose of warring against any prince, however numerous his army may be." '

Observing his courage and determination, his manner of speech, his *Farr* and his appearance—it was as if Dārāb himself was seated on his ivory throne, arrayed in his armlets, collar, *Farr* and crown. He said to him,

'What is your name, and what your origin? In your *Farr* and features there are the marks of kingship. You hold a rank higher than that of a subordinate. Methinks you are Sekandar himself.'

He answered,

'There are not a few eloquent men at Sekandar's gate who are the very diadem on the heads of sages. How should so mighty a monarch, greatest prince of all, bring a message in person from himself? Sekandar's wisdom is not of the kind which would let him transgress the practice of the ancients. The great commander entrusted his message to me in this fashion, and I have repeated to your Majesty what he said to me.'

A splendid lodging was prepared for him such as was suited to his high rank, and the Emperor of Iran, when his own repast was set before him, commanded his chamberlain to invite the ambassador. The repast being consumed, a symposium was got ready; wine, music and minstrels were called for. As soon as Sekandar had drunk of the delicious wine he put the goblet into his bosom. The butler came and reported to Dārā that the Greek had mated himself with the goblet, whereupon he commanded that the guest be asked for what purpose he had retained the goblet in his bosom. Sekandar replied,

'The cup is an ambassador's perquisite. If the custom of Iran differs from this, I will return the cup to the Shah's treasury.'

The monarch laughed that this should be the custom and commanded that a goblet filled with royal pearls be placed in the envoy's hand, with a red ruby on the top. Now it happened that the men who had been out of the realm demanding tribute from Rum, at that juncture returned from abroad and entered the banqueting hall. When, with due ceremony, they were approaching the king, one of them caught sight of the face of Sekandar, and as he approached the Shah to deliver his salutations, he said,

'The prince seated there on the throne with mace and diadem is Sekandar. When in accordance with your Majesty's command we went to him to exact tribute from him he treated us contemptuously and in his speech disputed with your Majesty. We fled from his realm at dead of night, spurring our horses to the utmost. In Rum we saw no man that resembled him, and it is out of sheer bravado that he has entered this land of ours. He covets your army and your treasure, your throne and your crown.'

Having heard what the envoy had to say, the Shah gazed more keenly at Sekandar, who realized what was being said in secret to the king of the world. He remained in his abode until the day declined and the sun had sunk in the west. Coming then to the palace gateway he boldly mounted his horse and, telling his escort of knights that their lives now depended on their horses, they sped away from the world-conqueror. Dārā sent mounted men in pursuit, to the number of a thousand brave warriors eager for battle. Like the wind they pursued him, but when night turned black they no longer recognized the road and when they saw a sentinel they returned on their traces, all they had gained being the hardships of the long journey.

[Dārā, having determined to destroy Sekandar, now led an army against him where he lay at the river Euphrates. After a week of fighting a dust storm arose, blinding the Iranians, who fled back, with the triumphant Rumis in pursuit. Sekandar marched to Persepolis, capital of the Shahs, while Dārā and his nobles fled to Kermān, where for some time they remained lamenting their fate and declaring they must wait until Destiny's revolving wheel brought an improvement in their fortunes. Approaches which the Shah made to Sekandar were disregarded, and when he invited the Emperor of India to come to his aid Sekandar attacked the Shah, whose reluctant troops were easily routed.]

Two ministers Dārā had, both men of substance, who had been with him on the field of battle. One was a priest named Māhyār, while the other's name was Jānusiyār. When they saw that the struggle was unavailing and that Dārā's ascendant star and his fame had waned, one said to the other,

'This ill-fated fellow will never more see crown and throne. A dagger must be thrust into his heart or an Indian scimitar launched at his head. Sekandar will surely grant us a province and we shall be a diadem resting on the head of our own realm.'

To Dārā, then, the two men who had been his counsellors and treasurers went as the night grew dark. Jānusiyār was holding a dagger and he thrust it into the bosom of the monarch, whose head fell forward, after which his army to a man deserted him.

[The two assassins informed Sekandar of their deed and at his request led him to where the Shah lay wounded to death.]

He looked to see if the wounded man could still speak, and he rubbed his face with his hand. From the royal head he lifted the diadem and he eased the Pahlavi armour on his breast. Shedding tears as he gazed on the wounded body so far from a physician's help, he said to him,

'This pain shall be alleviated for you, and the hearts of your enemies shall be smitten with fear. Arise and seat yourself in this golden litter, or mount your horse if you have the strength. I will have physicians brought for you from India and Rum and I will cause tears of blood to flow for the pain you have suffered. I will surrender the kingship and the throne to you and when you recover I will depart from hence. The men who have outraged you I will at once hang head downwards on the gallows. My heart bled and a cry issued from my lips when yesterday I heard from my elders that we two are of one stock and share a single shirt. Why should we extirpate our seed in rivalry?'

On hearing this, Dārā said in a strong voice,

'See to my children and my kinsfolk and my loved ones whose faces are veiled. Marry my pure-bodied daughter and maintain her in security in your palace. Her mother named her Rowshanak [Roxana] and with her provided the world with joy and adornment. It may be that by her you will have a noble son who will restore the name of Esfandiyār to glory, bring lustre to the fire of Zardosht [Zoroaster] and elevate the Zand and the Avesta. He will treat the great as great and the lesser men as lesser, and the Faith will flourish and prosper.'

(iii) *Sekandar ascends the throne of Iran*

[Dārā gave up the ghost and Sekandar called on the princes of Iran to acknowledge him as their sovereign.]

'Know that today I am Dārā. Though he has departed I remain. Iran remains what it has been from the start; rejoice in this and come and go in safety. My heart is heavy with grief for Dārā and I shall endeavour to abide by his will. Anyone who desires to remain in his own halls had better not turn in flight away from his loyalty to me. Bring to my treasury what is due and thereafter you will suffer neither pain nor annoyance. Strike coins only in the name of Sekandar; endeavour not to break your covenant with him. Maintain the capital of your sovereigns in the state to which they have been accustomed in the past. Do not allow your lands to remain unguarded, thus you will make your own dignity clear. Do not allow your bazaars to lack watchmen, who must ever have my name on their tongues so that no harm may be wrought by robbers and you may ever remain tranquil at heart and be the gainers of profit. Also from every city send a beautiful serving maid or slave, modest and of alert mind, who may be suited for our golden apartments, and who knows how to observe our religion, one who does not object to coming (for one should not be unjust with a slave). Let these be sent to my harem. If strangers pass through our realm, men of worthy demeanour and unbabbling lips, whose hearts are innocent of guile, men who bear the designation of Sufi [members of Islamic mystical orders],[1] who meet poverty with contentment—reckon such men as religious mendicants and inscribe their names at the head of the registers. If any of you is in misery from having received an injury at the hands of an official, let him break the heart and spine of the oppressor, let him destroy him root and branch.'

This missive, once it had gone forth, bore fruit and the whole world lived at peace.

[Sekandar reigned over Iran for fourteen years. Into the record of his reign Ferdowsi inserts an incident in the life of Sekandar's contemporary in India, Keyd, King of Qannauj.]

(iv) *Keyd of India beholds visions*

This is something the Pahlavi narrator told me—amazement will come to you when you hear it. There was a monarch named Keyd in India, a man of wisdom, perspicacity and happy fortune. He had the mind of a sage, the brain of a philosopher, the manners of a king, the brilliant intelligence of a Mobed [chief priest]. Ten nights in succession he beheld visions—mark this wonder!— and he commanded that all men in Hindustān possessed of wisdom and having skill in language and philosophy should assemble to form a council. To them he related his dreams, bringing into the light all that had been concealed. But no man there could provide an interpretation, so that their hearts were filled with

[1] One of many anachronisms in the Shāh-nāma.

concern and their faces paled. Then out spoke a man who said
to the Keyd,

'Oh King, most sage and most memorable of the great, there
exists a certain man of note, Mehrān by name, who in this world
has reached the goal of philosophy. But he cannot abide in the
city and his only dwelling is with the beasts. He lives upon the
seed of the mountain herbs and he regards people like us as other
than human. His own existence is with the wild asses and gazelles
and he stays remote from settlements and men. Nothing in the
world causes him harm, for he is a pious worshipper and a man
of high destiny.'

Keyd the king in his wisdom replied,

'It cannot be our way that we should neglect this talented man.'

Without delay he mounted his horse and, drawn by the report
of Mehrān, he departed from the city, accompanied by a number
of learned doctors. When he arrived at the place where Mehrān
was, he made appropriate inquiries of the sage, to whom he said,

'Pious worshipper of God, you who dwell on the mountain
with the wild sheep, listen profoundly to these dreams of mine,
interpret them, giving them all your mind. One night when I was
asleep and at rest without fear or apprehension, I beheld an abode
like a lofty castle, in which there raged an immense elephant. No
door was apparent in this lofty castle, but in the front of it there
was a narrow hole. Through this the furious elephant passed
without its body receiving the least harm from the restriction,
except that, although the vast body came through, the trunk remained behind within the building.

'The next night I beheld in that abode a throne, which had been
vacated by some personage of high estate. Someone ascended
that ivory throne and there placed on his head a heart-kindling
crown.

'On the third night the vision came to me speedily. I beheld in
my sleep a piece of fine-spun linen to which four men were cling-
ing, their cheeks purple with the effort of pulling it, one against
the other. In spite of their efforts, the linen was nowhere torn
and the men themselves remained unexhausted.

'On the fourth night this is what I saw. A man athirst stood by
a stream and a fish poured water towards him, but he turned his
head away. Suddenly he sped away and the water pursued him.

'My spirit on the fifth occasion saw the following in dream:
close by a lake there was a city, all of whose inhabitants were

blind. Yet I saw not one of them troubled by his blindness, for from their commerce, their buying and selling, you would have said the whole city flourished.

'On the sixth night, worthy master, I saw a city in which all the inhabitants were suffering from disease. They went to inquire of the one healthy man amongst them and asked him how he could endure so much pain and disease. Imagine, those ailing on the brink of death tending to the healthy!

'When half of the seventh night had passed, I saw a horse grazing on the open plain. It had two hindlegs and two forelegs but also two heads, and with its teeth it swiftly cleared the grass. It kept a mouth grazing on either side, but its body had no aperture for evacuation.

'On the eighth night I saw three vats standing facing me on the ground. Two were full of water, but the middle one was empty, as though years of drought had passed over it. Out of the two which held water two charitable men were dispensing the cool contents, which despite their efforts never diminished, although the lip of the dry jar was not moistened.

'On the ninth night I saw a cow lying asleep in the sunshine on the grass by a lake. By her stood a little calf, its body lean, withered and lacking all comeliness. Yet the cow, although she was of rounded body, sucked milk from the emaciated and feeble calf.

'I hope you will not be wearied before you come to the end of my history and will listen to my tenth dream. In the midst of a vast desert I saw a fountain by the side of which a lofty hall and dome had been built. The desert was covered with water and moisture from end to end, yet the lip of the fountain had crumbled away from dryness.'

(v) *Mehrān answers Keyd*

When Mehrān had heard this history from Keyd he said,

'Do not let your heart suffer anxiety because of these dreams. Your lofty repute will not be lowered nor will any harm befall this land. From Rum and Iran Sekandar will bring a mighty force, with chosen captains. If you wish your glory to remain undiminished, ally yourself with wisdom and do not seek to enter into war against him. In this world you have four possessions never yet seen by men either of the lesser or the greater breeds. First, like topmost Paradise, is your daughter, through whom your crown receives lustre throughout the world. Next is the sage [*feylasuf*, i.e. philosopher] you keep in concealment and who informs you of the world's secrets. Third is your skilled physician, who has won high repute for his science. Fourth is the cup into which you pour the water that can never be warmed [lose freshness] either through fire or sun.

'By these four you can allay the heat of Sekandar. When he comes, remain steadfast as you are. Do not contemplate war if you desire him to make no long stay here. You will be unable to resist his forces, his strategy, his stores or his land. If you wish me to provide fruitful advice about what you are to do, I will give you an answer to your dreams.

'First you saw a house with a narrow entrance from which an elephant suddenly emerged. You must recognize that house as the world and the elephant as an impious king who acts with injustice, utters falsehoods and has nothing of majesty but the name.

'Second, the crown and throne which you saw vacated by one and then by destiny's will occupied by another. That is the perverse vengeance taken by the world, which carries one man away and quickly brings another in. He may be mean at heart and feeble of body, eager in lust and dark in spirit. When his subjects are glad, that sort of king has his heart full of rancour and his lips emit sighs.

'Then the finely-woven linen you saw which was being pulled by four men of sharp wits, yet without the fabric's being torn or the men pulling being overcome by weariness—you must understand, with regard to that, that the linen is the religion of God and the four who pulled are its adherents. One part is the faith of the fire-worshipping elder who without [ritual] silence will not take the sacred *barsam* in his hand. A second part is the religion of Moses whom you call the Jew and who forbids you to worship any God but his. Third is the religion of the Greek, the Christian, who brought justice into the king's heart. Fourth is the pure religion yet to be brought by the Arab, which lifts the heads of percipient men out of the dust. Afterwards shall come one of famous name out of the desert, where men ride bearing lances [i.e. Arabia]. He is of pure and noble spirit, through whom the religion of God shall spread to all four points. Yet the adherents from four corners pull against each other and become enemies in the cause of religion.

'After that there is the thirsty man who turned and ran from the sweet water when the fish drew it for him. The time will come when the pure-spirited man will suffer humiliation after he has drunk the water of knowledge. Like the fish he will sink into the ocean depths while the head of the evil-doer will be elevated to the Pleiades. He will invite all who thirst to enter the water, but none will partake of his wisdom; while fleeing from him whose aim is understanding, they will universally open their lips for evil.

'Fifth. When you saw a city in which there was great traffic, full of consuming and offering, buying and selling, in which, as you said, fate had stitched up men's eyes so that none saw the other because of blindness and none even glanced at another, [it meant that] the time will come when the sage will wait upon the fool. The learned will be unhappy and despised, for the tree of their wisdom will not come to fruiting. They will become the flatterers of the unlettered, before whom they will appear with praises on their lips, although those who lie will be aware that no lustre comes from their servility.

'Sixth was when the sick and feeble went to ask one who was in good health about his miseries. The time will come when the poor man in distress will be treated with scorn by him that has money. He will become a servant earning nothing, not receiving the wage of a slave.

'Seventh. When you saw the two-headed horse through whose body the fodder had no passage, [it meant that] the time will come when men will rejoice only in material things and will never reach satiety. Their own selves is all they will look after; they will succour no one else.

'Eighth. When you saw the three water-jars of which one was empty and two were full to the brim of clear water, [it meant that] the day will come when the indigent man will become faint and humiliated and though the Spring clouds are full of water they will hide the sun from him but will not drop their rain on him. The rich will be generous and affable to one another, but they will leave the lips of the poor parched.

'Ninth. The full-bodied cow which sucked milk from its own lean calf [meant that] when Saturn enters the Sign of Libra the world will be subdued by the power of force. The state of the sick and poor will be enfeebled, yet the strong will make demands on them.

'Tenth. You beheld a fountain in which the water had dried up, whereas all about it were waters sweet as musk. No living water flowed from the fountain nor were the other waters being driven by any urgency into it. There will come a time hereafter when a king will arise possessed of no knowledge, whose gloomy spirit will be overshadowed by wrathfulness. He will constantly be renewing the armed forces wherewith a man desirous of fame acquires a crown for himself. In the end neither army nor king will remain; a new order will come about to make the world secure against evil and the divine glory will be made to shine afresh. Today is the era of Sekandar's prosperity; he is the diadem on the head of the great. When he arrives, surrender those four possessions of yours to him; in my belief he will demand no more. If you satisfy him with them, he will pass on, for he is a seeker after knowledge and possesses wisdom.'

When Keyd heard these words from Mehrān, his sere fortunes seemed to be refreshed. He kissed his head and eyes and returned home contentedly, triumphant and rejoicing.

[Keyd then sent Sekandar a message informing him of his four exceptional possessions, which Sekandar sent a delegation of nine wise men to inspect. They sent back such glowing accounts that he immediately required them to be brought to him. All were tested and met with his approval.]

XX

The Adventures of Sekandar

[In some detail Sekandar's campaigns against India, Fars and Egypt are then described, there being inserted the episode of his pilgrimage to the sacred Black Stone of Mecca. It was from Jidda, the port of Mecca, that he launched his expedition against Egypt. After that, attracted by reports of Andalusia, he went as his own ambassador to Qeydāfa, queen of that land. She, however, had previously sent a skilled painter to make a portrait secretly of the Caesar, and she recognized him when he presented himself before her. Then follow adventures in a variety of lands. The names of some are recognizable from our geographies, but others exist only in the realms of legend and phantasy. Some of the most characteristic of these adventures, and the best known from the works of the Persian writers of romances and painters of miniatures, are those which follow.]

(i) *Sekandar goes to the sea of the west*

From the realm of the Brahmin he came to where he beheld a sea boundless and deep. Men went about like women, their faces veiled, in female garb, painted and perfumed. Their language was not Arabic, nor Pahlavi, nor Chinese, nor Turkish, nor the Persian royal tongue. All they ate was fish, and there was no road by which anything else might be brought. Sekandar was astounded at their appearance and he called upon the name of God when he contemplated the spectacle. As he stood there, a mountain rose up out of the waters, gleaming with moisture and yellow as the sun. Promptly he sought out a swift ship in which to go and inspect it accurately with his own eyes. One of his philosophers told him that it would not be possible for him to voyage across that sea and that he must be patient until someone endowed with science should inspect the mountain. In the ship there embarked thirty men, some of them Greek and some Persian. That mountain was in fact a yellow fish, and the moment that the crew came close it swallowed up the whole ship and the mountain disappeared into the waters. The army and Sekandar were struck

243

with amazement at the sight and every man called out the name of God.

From there the army marched on until a new piece of water came into view. Scattered about it were reeds as large as trees, whose wood you would have said was so hard that it was like that of the *Chenār* [the Oriental Plane]; their thickness was ten cubits and more and their height forty cubits. The houses there were all built of the wood of the reeds, the floors too were of reeds trampled down by the foot of man. But the army could not linger in that reedy place for, because of its brackishness, none could drink the water there.

From that lake they marched onward until they came to where a mighty river appeared. In that spot the whole world lived pleasurably, the water was crystal clear and the soil was fragrant as musk. The men supped and were making preparations for sleep when out of the water there emerged writhing serpents and out of the forest came fiery-coloured scorpions, so that the world became gloomy and cramped for the men lying there. On all sides many died, noble and wise men and warlike heroes. Wild boars also descended from all sides by hundreds, their long tusks gleaming like diamonds. Furthermore there came lions more enormous than bulls, against which the men had not the strength or skill to fight.

The troops departed from the riverside and going into the reedy ground set all on fire. So many were slain that the path became impassable because of the corpses.

(ii) *Sekandar leads his army to the west*

After Sekandar had made all inquiries and observed the ocean he led his army towards the west. In his path there appeared a great city, inhabited by men of enormous size. All had red hair and pale faces and all were trained for war in time of conflict. They presented themselves before him at his command, but like men distracted they beat themselves on the head. Of their chieftain Sekandar enquired whether they could point out any marvels to him. An ancient replied,

'Oh King of auspicious star, conqueror of many lands, on the further side of this realm there is a lake and we have never understood that the shining sun can pass beyond it, for it disappears into the depths. On the far side of the water the world becomes dark and the known parts of the earth end and the hidden begins. Concerning that place of darkness I have heard some rumours which never reach to the basal truth, but there is a man well acquainted with the sciences and a fearer of God who tells me that in that place there exists a spring and that man of good sense and discretion has called it the Water of Life. Furthermore, that clear-minded and sagacious man says that anyone who drinks of that Water of Life never dies. The water flows through Paradise and if you lave your body in it your sins are washed away.'

Sekandar enquired whether a horse could make its way to that place of darkness and was told by the pious man that only colts could be ridden on the road to it. He thereupon ordered the herdsman to bring into his encampment all the horses freely grazing round about, and of them he chose ten thousand mounts all four years old and fit to be ridden.

(iii) *Sekandar goes in search of the Water of Life*

In high spirits he set out thence with his troops and travelled on until he reached a city, the middle and boundaries of which were beyond his ken. All things needful were there in plenty, for it abounded in gardens and open spaces, palaces and mansions. There he alighted. Next morning he made his way unescorted to the stream and there remained until the sun paled and sank into the azure water. By God's grace he saw the marvel of how the blazing luminary disappears from the world and then returned to his encampment with his mind full of profound thoughts.

When night fell he called on the name of God and set his mind once again to thinking of the water to which the ancients had given the name of Water of Life. He then chose out from among his troops those whom he held to be the hardiest, and having collected provisions for forty days and more he set forth eagerly to discover what marvels he might see. Having found a lodgment for his escort in the city he sought about for a guide, whom he at last found. This was Khezr, who became his counsellor in this undertaking, and he was chief of all the men of note in that community. Sekandar submitted himself to his orders, having surrendered heart and soul in a compact with him. The king said to him,

'If we bring the Water of Life into our possession, we will long continue in the service of God. No one will ever die who nurtures his soul on God and wisely makes God his refuge. I have in my possession two seal-rings which at the sight of water shine in darkness like the sun. Take one and go in advance, being ever watchful over your soul and body. The other will act for me as a lamp on my path when I march on with my escort in the darkness. By its light we shall see what the Lord of the world has kept concealed. You are my guide as He is my refuge. He will reveal the Water and the Path to me.'

They went along for two days and two nights, not a man uttering a word to ask for food. On the third day two different paths appeared in the darkness and then the king disappeared from Khezr's ken. The prophet [Khezr] himself went onwards to the Stream of Life, with the head of his vitality reaching high as Saturn. In the limpid water he bathed his body and head, seeking no beholder but God the Pure. He drank and rested, then turned back at speed with loud praise for the Creator.

(iv) *Sekandar builds the dam of Gog and Magog*

Sekandar had seen the East and now went towards the West, having conceived the notion of traversing the whole of the world. On his way he saw a fine city, which was so large that neither wind nor dust could have passed across it. When the sound of Sekandar's drums was heard from the backs of his elephants, the elders came out a distance of two leagues to welcome him. He asked them if in that region there existed marvels greater than could be equalled elsewhere. But when they loosed their tongues to the monarch it was to lament the manner in which fortune's wheel had turned against them. They said,

'We are confronted by a difficult task of which we shall speak to your fortunate-starred Majesty. From that mountain there, whose summit reaches into the clouds, something comes which fills our heart with torment, anguish and blood. From Yājuj and Mājuj there descend on our city creatures through whom our lot becomes one of sorrow and suffering. Their faces are those of camels, their tongues are black and their eyes the colour of blood. In their black faces are teeth like boars' tusks and none dares to encounter them. Their bodies, covered with bristles, are the colour of the Nile; their chests, bosoms and ears resemble those of elephants. When they lie down to sleep one ear forms their bed, with the other they make a covering for their bodies. Of each female a thousand young are born; but who can tell their number more or less? They come upon us in herds like horses and they charge down like the wild boar. In the Spring, when the turbulence from the clouds arrives, that green sea is stirred to effervescence, the clouds raise up serpent-like creatures out of the waves, and the aether roars like a lion. The clouds cast those serpents down onto the mountain and then great multitudes of these people appear whose food consists of these serpents, which last from one year to the next. When the weather turns cold, they become emaciated and their voices then are as weak as those of pigeons, whereas in the Spring, because of the serpents, they roar aloud. If your Majesty could devise some means of ridding us of this trouble, you would receive the blessings of us all and thereafter live long in the world.'

Sekandar was left marvelling at their story and being disturbed by it set himself to consideration. At last he said,

'Treasure will come from me but labour and other help must come from your city. I will devise a plan of cutting off this road of theirs.'

Sekandar then came to inspect the mountain, bringing with him a company of his philosophers. He commanded that smiths be brought and that copper and bronze, together with heavy hammers, should be fetched, as well as mortar, stone and timber beyond reckoning, which were to suffice for all that was required in the town. When all was ready and his ideas precise, masons, smiths and such as were masters in their trades in the world over flocked to Sekandar and worked together in that honourable task. On two sides of the mountain they built walls, the thickness of each from base to summit being a hundred ells. There was one ell of charcoal and one of iron, between them being copper. Into the middle of all the layers sulphur was poured according to magical ideas of past kings. Thus they commingled layers of every element. When all was compact from ground to summit, naphtha and oil were mixed together and poured over these elements. Onto this again charcoal by the ass-load was thrown, and then Sekandar gave the order that all was to be set alight. The flames were fanned by a hundred thousand smiths, working at the command of the all-conquering king. From the mountain there issued an explosive roar; the very stars were overcome by the heat of the flames. For long the smiths fanned the flames and toiled, fusing together the elements which had been rapidly smelted in the fire.

So was the world liberated from Yājuj and Mājuj and the earth became a place of repose and tranquillity. Because of that famous Alexandrian barrier the world was delivered from evildoers and tyranny.

[There follow accounts of adventures in which Sekandar is depicted as a sight-seeing traveller. He visits a topaz palace enshrining a corpse, comes to the Talking Tree which warns him that he has not long to live and will never see his homeland of Rum again. He goes to China, whose king, the Fāghfur, rebukes him for his proud ambition, and to Sind, where he routs an army sent against him and acquires rich booty consisting of elephants, golden crowns, scimitars and slaves in abundance. After marching thence to the Yemen, where he was received with lavish gifts, he advances on Babylon.]

(v) *Sekandar marches to Babylon*

To Babylon then Sekandar led an army so numerous that because of its dust the world became invisible. For a whole month he and his troops rode on without finding a place to rest, and continued so until they reached the mountain whose summit lay beyond the range of sight. On it hung a black cloud which you would have said approached to Saturn. No way across the mountain appeared, so that the king and army were in difficulty about what they should do. But with great toil they at last crossed this mass of granite, which caused even the lightest-footed of them to despair. When wearily they had climbed to the other side they beheld a mighty river. As the air became clear the army's spirits were gladdened, for there they beheld not only the river but the plain and the road beyond. They drove on towards the great stream singing praises to God, seeing that on all sides were creatures wild and tame beyond counting and the troops now had an abundance of game for their victuals. As they continued their march there appeared in the distance a man of great size, covered with hair and having immense ears. Under his hair his body was blue as the Nile, while his ears were as large as those of an elephant. On seeing the man with these strange qualities the warriors dragged him into the presence of Sekandar, who was filled with amazement at the sight. He enquired of him,

'What man are you and what is your name? What do you find in the river there and what do you need?'

The man replied,

'My father and mother bestowed on me the name of *Gush-bastar* [Bed-ear].'

The king asked further,

'What is that object in the middle of the river, on the other side of which the sun is rising?'

To that the man returned,

'It is a city like Paradise and you would say that no particle of earth entered into its composition. There you will see no palace or mansion that is not built and roofed with bone, and on their walls you will see the battles of Afrāsiyāb depicted more brilliantly than the sun. There is also there the portrait of Khosrow, that martial king, in all his greatness, valour and wisdom, clearly limned. In the city you will see neither dust nor earth. The people's nurture is nothing but fish; they have no food other than that.'

'Go,' said Sekandar to the man with the ears. 'Bring me someone from the city to tell me what novelty I can see.'

Without delay Gush-bastar departed and brought back with him a group of men, eighty in number, who had crossed the river with him. The elders amongst them held in their hands a golden goblet encrusted with pearls, while the young men held diadems. The night passed. At the time of cockcrow the roll of drums came up from the royal camp and Sekandar marched on to Babylon.

On the following night there was born to a certain woman a child whose appearance caused all who saw it to marvel. Its head was that of a lion, it had hoofs for feet, its shoulders were human and it had a cow's tail. This monster died at the moment of its birth—let no one claim origin from that woman! They brought it to the king, who gazed on it with wonderment but took it as a portent of evil. Astrologers in number were called and there was much discussion concerning the dead child. These men who told the stars were greatly troubled and concealed their uneasiness from the king, who, at their attitude, was stirred to fury and threatened that if anything was kept hidden from him he would at once sever their heads from their bodies and their only grave would be the lion's maw. Seeing the king thus roused, one of them said,

'Glorious monarch, you were in your beginnings born under the constellation of the Lion. That is established by the priests and the nobles, and you see that the child's head resembles that of a lion. It means that the head of the realm will be brought low. For a time the world will be filled with turmoil which will not cease until a new monarch ascends to the throne.'

All the astrologers in his presence said the same and showed what pointed to the truth of it. Sekandar heard and was smitten with grief. He said,

'From death there is no escape, and I feel no apprehension in my breast at the prospect. My life will continue no longer; fate grants no less than what is allotted, but also never adds to it.

(vi) *Sekandar counsels his mother*

[Sekandar dictates a letter to his mother in which he warns her that he is about to die. He continues,]

'Bury my body in the soil of Egypt; let nothing of my behest go astray. Should a son be born to Rowshanak [Roxana], without dubiety his father's name will be thus kept alive. Let none but that son become king of Rum, for he will cause that land and realm to flourish again. But should it be, in an evil moment, that a daughter is born, then betroth her to a son of Filicus, whom you will call my son, not my son-in-law.

'Of the goods which I brought from India, China, Iran, Turān, and the land of Makrān, keep what you need and bestow on others what is in excess of what you can enjoy. Of you, my dear one, my request is that you shall remain thoughtful in spirit and clear in mind. Do not let yourself be troubled by your body, for no person exists eternally in the world. Without any doubt my spirit will behold yours when the appropriate time arrives. Endurance is a nobler virtue than love; the impatient are men of a lower degree. Your love watched over my body for years; now pray to God for my pure soul.'

[Sekandar died in Babylon. His corpse, after some argument, was carried to Alexandria, a city which he had founded. While recounting the words of grief he places in the mouths of Sekandar's mother and wife, Ferdowsi is reminded of his own miseries and addresses a lament to Fate complaining in particular of his old age. To this, Fate is made to reply that it acts only as God commands.]

XXI

Rule of the Ashkāni [Arsacid or Parthian] Kings

Now, singer, ancient in days, turn back to the time of the Ashkāni kings. What said the old book concerning them? What of their story did the narrator remember? After the days of Sekandar, to whom does he say that the world and the throne of the mighty reverted? The Dehqān of Chāch, who knew of these matters, says that after Sekandar's death the ivory throne was for long unoccupied. The chieftains who were of the seed of Āresh were bold, rash and headstrong. In each corner of the world there was one who had seized some fragment of a clime and those who seated them with rejoicings on the throne called them the Kings of the Tribes. Two hundred years so passed and it was as if there were no king in the world. You would have said the earth's surface enjoyed repose. This resulted from the plan devised by Sekandar whereby Rum's prosperity might remain for everlasting.

First of the Kings of the Tribes was Ashk of the line of Qobād, then came the warrior Shāpur of happy birth. After him followed Gudarz of the Ashkānis, and Bizhan who was of Keyānid stock, then men such as Narsi, Ormazd the Great and Āresh, holder of a mighty name. When you have gone beyond them there comes the famous Ardavān the Sagacious, endowed with good judgment and clear mind. When Bahman of the Ashkānids ascended the throne he distributed his treasure amongst his nobles. Men called Ardavān great because he kept the sheep safe from the claws of the wolf. In his possession were Shiraz and Esfehan, which the understanding call the Land of the Noble. On his behalf Bābak ruled in Estakhr [Persepolis]. Since their branch and root were cut short, the learned narrator holds no record of their annals. I have heard nothing of them but their name, nor seen anything in the Book of the Kings.

XXII

The Dynasty of Sāsān

(i) Bābak dreams about Sāsān

When Dārā was slain in the midst of battle, the fortunes of his whole line were reversed. He had a son of happy destiny, clever and warlike, whose name was Sāsān. When this youth saw his father slain and how fortune had turned against the Iranians, he fled before the army of Rum and would not be caught in the toils of destruction. He died miserably in Hindustan; but a young son of his was left. Matters continued thus until the fourth generation, each father in turn naming his son Sāsān. All were shepherds or camel-drivers, inured to pain and heavy toil the whole year round. The youngest Sāsān left his home and laboriously sought for work, hoping to receive a wage for his toil. He came at last to where Bābak's shepherds had their being, and on a pasture-ground he saw the head shepherd, to whom he said,

'Can a wage-earner be of use to you, passing here in ill-fortune?'

The head shepherd engaged the unhappy youth and kept him toiling day and night. Since the young man was industrious he found approval, and from being a simple shepherd he became the head shepherd in charge of the flocks.

Bābak, son of Rudyāb, lay sleeping one night when his illumined spirit beheld in a dream how Sāsān rode astride a wild elephant, his hand holding an Indian scimitar. Men who came towards him saluted him and called down blessings on him. By his benefactions he caused the earth to flourish and he swept away the unhappiness from every gloomy heart. The next night also as Bābak lay asleep his mind was occupied with thought. In the dream he saw a fire-worshipper bearing three blazing fires in his hand, like the fire altars of Azargoshasp, Kharrād and Mehr; all flamed before Sāsān, sandalwood burning in each.

When Bābak's head was roused from sleep his spirit and mind were full of cares. Men who were understanding in dreams or had ability in like sciences came flocking to Bābak's palace, together with nobles, sages and counsellors. He disclosed his problem and told them of his dreams from beginning to end, while the men

252

who were to provide him with his reply gave ear. The counsellors were overwhelmed with thought at the problem. At last one said,

'Proud King, the interpretation of this dream needs careful scrutiny. The man whom you thus saw in your dream will raise his head in sovereignty above the sun; and even if this dream should not be relevant to him, he will have a son who will enjoy the world.'

Bābak rejoiced at hearing this reply and gave to every man gifts suitable to his rank. He then ordered that when next day dawned the head shepherd should come to him. The man appeared before him wrapped in his felt cloak, the woollen garment covered with snow and fear tormenting his breast. Bābak cleared the place of all not in his confidence and out of the door went slaves and counsellors together. He then enquired after Sāsān's well-being and flattered him, seating him close beside himself. He asked him of his origins and his birth. At first the shepherd was afraid, and gave no answer, but then he said,

'Your Majesty, if you will grant a shepherd security for his life, I will tell you all there is to know about my origins; but that is only if you will clasp my hand in yours and swear an oath that you will do no ill to me in this world, either openly or in secret.'

Bābak opened his mouth and, pronouncing the name of God, he said,

'I will bring no harm on you in any respect; indeed I will maintain you in happiness and worthy state.'

At that the shepherd said to Bābak,

'Pahlavān, I am Sāsān's son, descended from the emperor King Ardashir, whom men call Bahman, as you may remember. He was the proud son of the warrior Esfandiyār, himself the monument in the world to Goshtāsp's existence.'

Bābak heard the words and shed tears from those clear eyes which had beheld the dream. He said to the youth,

'Go to the baths and there remain until a new robe is brought to you.'

Royal garments were brought to him and a charger with Pahlavi trappings. A mansion filled with rich material was got ready for him and from having been a head shepherd his head was raised to lofty rank. When he had taken up his abode in the mansion, slaves and servitors were stationed before him. In all matters he was given high rank and freed of all cares where material provision

was concerned. And then Bābak gave him his daughter, by him
beloved, and crown of all his kin.

(ii) *Ardashir son of Bābak is born*

Nine months passed over this gracious young woman and then a
son as glorious as Phoebus was born to her. He had the very
likeness of the monarch Ardashir and he grew to be large, handsome and heart-captivating. Upon him his father bestowed the
name Ardashir and whenever he beheld him he found happiness and
contentment, fondling him at his bosom whenever there was need.

(A long time elapsed and today men of sharp wit call him
Ardashir-e Bābakān.) He was taught skill in every art, and merit
grew within him until you would have said that he illumined the
world with his knowledge, stature and beauty of countenance.
Tidings came at last to [the Parthian emperor] Ardavān of the
skill and knowledge of the youth and he thereupon wrote a letter
to Bābak, that notable Pahlavān, saying,

'I hear that your son Ardashir is a cavalier, one well-trained also
in speech and quick to acquire knowledge. On receiving this letter
send him immediately to me in happy spirit. I will free him of all
care concerning the things needful to him, and will grant him
precedence among my warriors. When he is with my children I
will never say that he is not my kinsman.'

As Bābak read that letter from the king, he rained many a blood-
stained tear down on his cheeks. He ordered that a scribe be sent
to him with the youth Ardashir newly come to manhood, and to
him said,

'Read this letter of Ardavān's and consider it with your clear
mind. I will write a letter to the Shah which I will send by a well-
disposed messenger and in it I shall say that I am sending him my
heart and eye, namely this heart-engaging and delectable youth,
whom I have advised well. When he arrives at that exalted court
let the treatment of him be such as conforms with the behaviour
of kings, so that not even the breeze shall blow harmfully on him.'

Swiftly then Bābak opened the door of his treasury and gave
the youth gifts of all kinds, grudging his son nothing, neither
golden horse-trappings, mace or sword, money or brocades,
horses or slaves, Chinese silks or royal cloth of gold. All these
were brought and set before the youth, who departed to become
courtier to Ardavān.

(iii) *Ardashir-e Bābakān arrives at Ardavān's court*

When Ardashir arrived at the palace the Shah was told of this visitor demanding audience. Graciously he summoned the youth before him and set aside a lodging for him within the walls. To him there he sent victuals of every description, garments and furniture, and to the place that Ardavān had allotted him the youth proceeded with notables of the court.

When next the sun planted his throne on the dome of the sky and the world was white as the face of a Greek, Ardashir called a servitor and sent to Shah Ardavān the gifts which custom demanded.

Ardavān saw these things with approval, felt the youth would be of value to him and treated him as though he were his own son, not leaving him for a moment in discomfort. Whether it was to wine-drinking, feasting, or hunting-field, the king never went unaccompanied by the young man, entertaining him as though he were his own blood and making no distinction between him and his own sons.

It occurred one day on the hunting-ground that the king's courtiers and sons were distributed round about and Ardashir rode with Ardavān. In the distance wild asses appeared on the plain and a furore broke out in the numerous company of hunters. Every man put spurs to his wind-speedy courser, and the dust was mingled with their sweat. Ahead of all galloped Ardashir, and as he neared the game he fixed an arrow to his bow and shot a male onager in the rump, so hard that the arrow passed through the creature point and feather. At that moment Ardavān rode up to inspect the wild ass thus pierced.

'Who shot this onager in this way?' he asked. 'The blowing wind must be allied with his hand.'

Ardashir made answer,

'It was I who shot this onager down.'

But Ardavān's son said,

'I shot this onager down and am now looking for its mate.'

To him Ardashir retorted,

'The plain is wide enough and there are onagers and arrows in plenty. Shoot another in the same way. Lying is regarded a fault in high-born men.'

Ardavān broke into a rage at Ardashir and uttered a shout at him, saying to him roughly,

'The fault is mine, for your upbringing and conduct are due to me. Why should I have taken you with me to feasts and to the hunting-ground or as part of my retinue? Was it in order that you might surpass my sons, seek to excel them and show your prowess? Go! Look after my Arab horses and keep your place in the stables. Be a groom in the stalls and assistant to any man at any task.'

Ardashir, his eyes running tears, thus came to be the groom of the Arab horses. He thought to himself,

'What is this that Ardavān has done to me? May his body be racked and his soul tormented!'

With his heart full of rancour and his head filled with schemes he wrote a letter to his grandfather recounting what had occurred and wondering why King Ardavān had been so greatly roused. When the letter came to Bābak he revealed nothing of it to a soul, but his heart was filled with wrath and anguish. Out of his treasury he brought a sum of golden dinars, ten thousand of which were to be sent to the young man. That sum was loaded onto a swift dromedary with a man mounted on it. At the same time he ordered a scribe to write a letter to Ardashir, saying,

'My newly-matured youth of little sense, when you went hunting with Ardavān, why did you thrust yourself ahead of his sons? You are his attendant, not his kinsman. He did not treat you as he did offensively or out of wickedness; you brought the harm upon yourself in your folly. Now have regard to where your success and happiness lie; do not in any matter turn your face from his bidding. I send you a little money and here in my letter give you certain pieces of advice. When you have put the sum to proper use, demand more, as long as time continues.'

The galloping dromedary with the experienced elder mounted on it went at full speed to Ardashir, who, on reading the letter, felt appeased. His mind now turned to guile and scheming. He had taken a lodging near to the horses and though he regarded his abode as unworthy of his birth, he furnished it lavishly with carpets of every kind, with garments and food. Pleasure became his occupation day and night; wine, music and players were his adjuncts.

(iv) *Golnār sees Ardashir*

In Ardavān's possession there was a lofty palace, in which lived a slave-girl whom he valued greatly. This glorious maiden's name was Golnār ['Pomegranate blossom'] and she was like a picture brilliant with jewels and beauty. To Ardavān she acted as counsellor and held charge also of his treasury. Dearer she was to him than his own life, and he broke into smiles when he saw her. It happened one day that from the palace roof she caught sight of Ardashir and at that pleasing spectacle her heart was gladdened. As Ardashir looked up with smiling lips he found a lodgment in the lovely woman's heart.

In this state the matter remained until the day turned to darkness and the next day approached the night. The girl then made fast a rope to a pinnacle, having tied several knots in it and tested it with her hands. Now she boldly descended from the wall, giving praises to the Benefactor, and adorned with brilliance and perfumed with musk and amber she gracefully approached Ardashir. From his brocaded pillow she lifted his head and when he was awakened took him closely to her bosom. The youth gazed at the lovely maid, at her hair, her face and perfumed splendour and said to her,

'Whence did you spring? You have brought solace to my distressful heart.'

She answered,

'I am your slave. My heart and soul overflow with love for you, and if you desire it I will come to you to enliven the gloom of your dark day.'

Some time passed and then disaster fell on Sāsān's guardian; the much experienced and alert-minded Bābak died and left his ancient home to another man. The world darkened for Ardashir in sorrow for that prince of illumined spirit who had come to his aid in the past. He detached his thoughts from Ardavān and after receipt of these tidings began to devise a different scheme of life. His heart was rancorous at the wrongs he had suffered and on all sides he sought for a way to escape.

During the following days Shah Ardavān brought a number of men learned in the stars and of perspicuous mind to the palace and questioned them about his star and his future career. He then sent them to consult with Golnār, that she too might study the stars. For three days, until three watches of the night had passed, the girl remained without ceasing in the company of the astrologers. She was agitated and disturbed yet she retained her memory of their conversation. On the fourth day those men of clear mind went to reveal their secret to Ardavān. With their sky-charts at

their bosoms they left the maiden's palace for the king's. There
they revealed the secret of high heaven; namely his future—what,
when and how it would be. Within no great time from then, they
said, the sovereign's heart would be afflicted by certain happenings. A lesser man would flee from a greater one. He would be
one who came of warrior stock and his prowess was mighty.
Moreover he would in the future rise to lofty monarchy; he would
be a world conqueror, of felicitous star and prosperous.

At what they said the heart of the renowned and well-fated king
was greatly downcast.

(v) *Ardashir flees with Golnār*

When the face of the land took on the semblance of pitch, the girl
came to Ardashir, and she found that youth as greatly disturbed
as the ocean. Not a day usually passed without her seeing Ardavān
and she related to Ardashir what those sagacious men had disclosed.
Hearing the words he determined to be patient and keep his own
counsel. His mind however set quickly to work and thereafter
he sought more eagerly than ever for a way of escape. He said
to her,

'If I depart for Iran and go from Rayy to the Empire of the
Brave think you that you would accompany me on the journey,
or would you remain here with the Shah? If you accompany me
you will become powerful; you will be the diadem on the country's
head.'

She replied,

'I am your slave. As long as I live I will not be parted from you.'

She said this with her lips breathing cold sighs and with blood-
stained tears pouring from her eyelashes. Ardashir then said to her
that they must without fail depart on the morrow. The maiden
returned to her own palace, having placed her head and her life in
her hand. When the world's face had been yellowed in the sun
and azure night had entered the firmament, the maiden opened the
door to the treasure-houses and began to choose out jewels of
every description, rubies and royal pearls, and as many gold coins
as she might need. She then returned to the place which was her
dwelling, keeping the treasure close at hand, and there she
remained until night came over the mountain. Ardavān had fallen
asleep and the whole palace was deserted when swift as an arrow
she left and brought the jewels to Ardashir. This ambitious youth

when she arrived was holding in his hand a beaker, and the guardians of the horses lay about in drunken sleep. He had picked out two valuable steeds and had them in the stable there ready saddled. As soon as Golnār appeared he set down the beaker and bridled his Arab steeds, donned his cloak and mounted, having a finely-tempered scimitar in his hand. On the other courser the girl rode, and now they at once set forth with their faces turned from the palace towards Fārs, travelling with joyful hearts and picking out their path.

(vi) *Ardavān gets wind of the flight*

Ardavān was never content either by day or by night to be deprived of the presence of that lovely maid. Never did he raise his back and shoulder from his embroidered pillow without looking on the face of Golnār and finding it of goodly omen. Now, although the time came for him to rise and adorn his throne with his brocaded presence, the maiden did not come to his pillow. He was angry and lay tormented by wrath, while in his audience-chamber his courtiers stood ranged, and his crown, throne and hall were all ready bedecked. From the hall of audience the chamberlain arose and coming in to the monarch he said,

'Proud nobles stand at the gate, all of them lords of provinces.'

To his courtiers the king thereupon said,

'Why has Golnār not kept to her accustomed practice and habit? Why has she not come to my pillow? Can there be any anger in her heart against me?

To him came the chief of the scribes to say,

'Last night without warning Ardashir departed, carrying off a white horse and a black one which were your Majesty's coursers. At the same time your Majesty's favourite, the one that was your treasurer, went away with Ardashir.'

The warrior's heart bounded from its place; he flung his leg across a bay horse and with a numerous escort of mounted men he raced along that road scattering fire. Along the way he came to a notable city crowded with men and beasts and there he made enquiry whether, after set of sun, they had heard the sounds of coursers' hoofs. Two persons, he said, had passed along that road at a gallop, one riding a white horse, the other a black. A man replied that two persons had indeed passed through the city on horse-back and gone on to the plain outside. At the tail of the riders a fine ram as big as a horse had galloped, stirring up the dust.

Ardavān asked his counsellor why a ram should thus be running behind. He answered,

'It is his *Farr*. In his kingliness, through the blessedness of his star, it acts as his protection. If this ram keeps pace with him, pursue no further, for this matter is like to prove a lengthy one for you.'

At that very spot Ardavān dismounted and took repose; but then galloped on again in chase of Ardashir. Meanwhile the youth and the maiden like the stormwind had not for a moment ceased from their rushing progress. At last Ardashir became distressed by this swift course. From an eminence he beheld a pool and as he galloped he said to Golnār,

'Now that we are linked with weariness we must alight at this spring, because we are both, horse and rider, shaken to pieces. Let us stay by the water and drink; then, when we have rested we can continue.'

The pair arrived at the water, their cheeks pale as the setting sun, but as Ardashir was on the point of dismounting he beheld two youths at the pool. In a loud voice they cried out quickly to him,

'Use your reins and stirrups. You have escaped the dragon's maw and fiery breath and you would not benefit at all by halting now. You must not dismount to drink and you must bid farewell to your body.'

Ardashir listened to what his young counsellor said and told Golnār to take it well to heart. His stirrup became heavy again, he left his rein slack and raised his gleaming spear to the sky. Behind him, rushing like the wind, Ardavān came galloping, his soul black with rancour. When half the day had passed and the world-illuminator had traversed half the sky, he beheld a city full of splendour. There men crowded about him. He said to the priests there,

'When was it that those two riders passed this way?'

One who directed him made answer,

'When the sun turned pale and azure night drew its pall around, two persons covered with dust, their mouths dry with lack of water, passed through this city. At the tail of one of the riders there came galloping a ram, the like of which I have never seen, even in paintings on palace walls. It had wings like the Simorgh's,

a peacock's tail, and a head, ears and hoofs like those of fiery
Rakhsh. In colour it was purple, its pace that of the hurricane. No
man remembers a ram of that kind.'

His chief counsellor said to Ardavān,

'It were perhaps best to return from here to your own place,
there to muster an army and make preparation for war. This
contest has taken on a different aspect; since fortune is firmly
settled in his favour, we should achieve nothing by pursuing him.
Write a letter to your son telling him this story from beginning to
end. It may be that he will find some trace of Ardashir. He must
not profit from that wild sheep.'

Ardavān on hearing these words perceived that his fortunes
were on the decline. He alighted in the city there and paid homage
to his Benefactor. At early dawn he gave the order to his retinue
for the return. On reaching home at Rayy, after night had fallen,
his cheeks the colour of the reed, he wrote a letter to his son
[Bahman] saying,

'Treachery has raised its head amongst our affairs. Ardashir left
my pillow with a speed never attained by an arrow, and made for
Fārs. Seek for him covertly, telling this matter to nobody on
earth.'

Ardashir for his part had reached the river and there rested.
Then he called out for the sailor, speaking much to him of what
he had undergone. The crafty old ferryman scrutinised the stature,
face and chest of Ardashir and knew that he was nought if not of
royal stock, and he was gladdened by his *Farr* and splendour.
Coming in haste down to the river he launched ships from far and
near upon the water. At the news of famed Ardashir an army
formed itself at the stream. Every man at Persepolis who was of
the stock of Bābak spoke proudly at the news of the king. Furthermore, those in any country who were of the seed of Dārā could
scarcely contain themselves, and when news came of King
Ardashir the heart of every ancient turned youthful in joy. Men
came from river and mountain, company on company, to join the
young prince. Sages and counsellors from every city crowded
about him. The youthful Ardashir thus addressed them,

'Bearers of great names, men of pure spirit, there is no one in
this notable assembly of sages and men of understanding who has
not heard what base deeds the evil-natured Sekandar perpetrated
in the world. He slew every one of my ancestors and got the
universe into his grasp by working injustice. I am of the seed of

E K—T

Esfandiyār, yet Ardavān rules in the land. It is not right that we should call it justice or acknowledge this state of affairs to be equitable. If you will be my allies I will permit no one but myself to use my title or possess my lofty throne. What say you to this? What answer do you give? Let me have your felicitous counsel in this matter.'

Every man present in that assembly, whether wielder of a sword or a counsellor, on hearing that call leapt to his feet and each spoke truly what lay nearest to his heart. They said,

'Each of us that is of Bābak's line is rejoiced at beholding you; those of us who are Sāsānians gird up our loins for vengeance. Body and soul we are at your service; our joy and sorrow hang upon what happens to you. By your double origins you are of higher degree than any of us; kingship and sovereignty are your right. At your command we will reduce the mountain to the level of the plain and with our swords turn the ocean into blood.'

At hearing the reply couched in such terms, Ardashir's head rose higher than Venus or Jupiter. He lavished blessings on those noble men and let his heart be suffused with thoughts of war. Near to the sea he founded a city which became his arsenal.

[Ardashir began his war against his old master by defeating Ardavān's son, Bahman, and marching on his capital Persepolis. Ardavān in his turn attacked, but fortune was against him. A violent dust-storm which arose threw his army into panic because they thought it was sent by God. The Shah himself was captured and by Ardashir's command put to death. Thus was the Āreshi (Arsacid) line brought to an end.

Ardashir married Ardavān's daughter, who brought him a rich dowry and an additional claim to the sovereignty of Iran. He made his capital in Fārs, the ancient heart of the realm, and from there led forays against the Kurds.

To lighten the tale of wars and bloodshed Ferdowsi now tells the legend of the fabulous worm (*kerm*), from which by popular etymology the city of Kermān takes its name.]

XXIII

The Story of Haftvād and the Worm

(i) Haftvād's daughter

Attend to this wondrous story which the Dehqān [one of Fer-dowsi's authorities for his folklore] related, at the time when he was disclosing his hidden stores of knowledge about the city of Kojārān on the sea of Fārs, while discussing the affairs of Fārs in height and breadth. It was a tightly-filled city, its inhabitants numerous, and all earned their bread by toil. In it were many young women who worked for their bread. Close by was a mountain, to which the girls used to go in groups, each carrying a certain weight of cotton, and each having a spindle-holder of poplar-wood. At the gate the girls assembled and walked out of the city to the mountain. They used to put all their food together, none asking for herself more or less than her share. Their conversation was not of sleep or food, for all their pride and rivalry concerned their cotton. At night they returned home again after their cotton had been converted into long thread.

Now in the city there lived a man, poor but of happy disposition, whose name was Haftvād. This was his name and designation for the reason that he had seven (*Haft*) sons. And he had one daughter, no more, whom he loved dearly although he reckoned daughters of no account. It happened one day that all the girls in company were seated with their spindles on the mountainside. When the time came to eat, they laid aside their spindles and mingled together all they had of food. This fortunate young woman had on the way espied an apple blown down by the wind, and she had swiftly picked it up. Now list to this wondrous tale! When this fair-cheeked maid bit into the fruit she saw a worm lying snug within it and lifting it out with her finger she placed it gently in her spindle-holder. When next she took the spindle and cotton out of the holder, she said,

'In the name of God, the Unassociated and Unmated. Today through the felicitous star of this apple-worm, I will show you at what speed I can spin.'

All the girls made merry and laughed, displaying wide open

mouths and silver teeth. She spun twice as much as she used to spin in the day and wrote the reckoning of it on the ground.

[When the time came] she departed thence with the speed of smoke to show her mother what she had spun, and her mother lovingly applauded her, saying,

'You have done well, my lovely sunny-cheeked maid.'

Next evening when she reckoned up her toll of thread she again brought home twice the quantity of her daily stint. The whole company used to gather round this industrious girl, who now devoted heart and soul and body to her spinning. She said to those honest girls,

'Dear friends of happy augury, through the felicitous star of the worm I have now spun so great an amount of thread that I shall never again suffer want.'

She had indeed spun as much as the sum total of her previous spinning and she could usefully have had twice as much. Again she brought home the thread she had spun and her mother's heart was made as glad as happy Paradise. Each dawn the peri-cheeked maid gave a morsel of apple to the worm, and the more cotton she brought the more that enchanting maid was able to spin. One day her parents said to their skilful daughter,

'You spin so much, it must be that you have acquired sisterhood with a peri.'

Swiftly the silver-bodied maid now related to her mother the story of the apple and the little worm concealed in it. Indeed she showed her parents the felicitous worm, thereby increasing the contentment of the woman and her husband. He, Haftvād, took all this as a happy augury and had no thought in his mind of any other matter, and he ever conversed of the blessed star of the worm. His once outworn fortunes were now renewed again.

Some time passed, their fortunes becoming brighter with each day. Never for a moment did they neglect the worm, which they kept well supplied with food. It became powerful of body and acquired strength; its head and back assumed a shining spendour. The spindle-holder became too tight for its body; its skin turned as black as musk but its body was saffron-hued on breast and back. The girl now fashioned a handsome casket in which she made a nest for its repose.

In the city, matters reached the point where no one uttered a word either of advice or judgment without Haftvād, so greatly had he increased in esteem, dignity and wealth. Those seven sons also had become prosperous. But there was a prince who ruled the city, a proud man possessed of an army and of great name, and he concocted a pretext for exacting money from the base-born Haftvād. A group of noted personages leagued themselves with Haftvād and the seven sons, so that in the city of Kojārān the sound of trumpets arose and men came forth with spears, swords and arrows. At the head of his men Haftvād marched to do battle and give full scope to his manly virtues. He was able to seize the city and slay the prince, and there fell into his hands a large quantity of jewels and much other booty.

Now men gathered thick about him and he departed from the city to the mountain, on whose summit he built a citadel. For it he made a gateway of iron, so that it became both an abode of security and an arsenal of war. There had been a spring on the mountain and by good fortune it had been included within the citadel. Round about the fortress he built a wall so lofty that even a man with good vision could not scan its top.

In course of time the casket became too straitened for the worm and a pool was constructed for it among the rocks on the mountain. When the lime and stone of which it was constructed had been warmed by the air, the worm was gently deposited in it. And now each dawn the custodian of the worm came at speed from Haftvād's mansion and prepared for its sustenance a potful of rice, which the creature ate.

A number of years passed and the worm grew to be the size of an elephant, with great limbs and back. Time also passed over Haftvād, who had now given the citadel the name of Kermān. The fortunate young woman had become the worm's custodian and her father a warrior, commander of the worm's army; a scribe and a vizier waited upon it and its provender now consisted of rice, honey and milk. At its court Haftvād ruled as its army-commander and to him were referred questions concerning all manner of things, just or unjust. From the Sea of China to the confines of Kermān, across every sea his armies were distributed under the command of his seven sons, and any king who was disposed to lead an army in war against the worm was shattered when he heard of Haftvād's strength. His citadel had become so powerful that the very winds did not venture to stir about it.

(ii) *Ardashir goes to war with Haftvād*

[Haftvād's rise to power awakened Ardashir to the danger of his
becoming a rival to himself and he marched out to suppress him,
but was driven back.]

When tidings came of Ardashir's departure and of his being delayed by the side of the ocean for lack of food, since the roads
had been barred against him, a certain low-born fellow named
Mehrak issued forth from Jahrom [in Fārs] accompanied by a
numerous rabble to attack the palace of the Shah. He gave up all
the stores to plunder and distributed purses and coronets amongst
his men.

Ardashir, on receiving news of this, plunged into thought at his
encampment on the ocean brink. He asked himself why he had not
set his own house in order before setting out on an expedition
abroad. Summoning his troops he questioned them at great
length about Mehrak and said,

'Our position has become difficult. I have tasted enough of
fortune's bitterness, and this trouble from Mehrak did not enter
my reckoning.'

With one voice they answered,

'Since Mehrak has secretly turned out to be your enemy, why
seek in travail for new conquest in the world? You hold a mighty
rank and the earth is yours; we are your slaves and the command
is yours.'

At that he ordered that trays be decked for a feast, and there was
a call for wine, goblets and musicians. On each tray a roast lamb
had been laid, and the men set themselves to feasting. As Ardashir
picked up his bread and was about to eat, a swift arrow plunged
into the fine fat lamb before him and was entirely embedded. Hot
with rage those astute and martial warriors withdrew from their
feasting and one of them drew the arrow out of the lamb. A
writing was deciphered on it and a lettered man amongst them
read it out. On it was inscribed in Pahlavi,

'Wise king, if you will but hearken, this swift arrow came from
the roof of the citadel, which, by the worm's good fortune, is the
citadel of peace. Had I aimed at Ardashir, the arrow's feather
would have passed through him. It will never happen that a prince
of your kind will bring the worm to submission as long as its
present fortune holds.'

The monarch repeated the writing on the arrow to the priests who were there. Between the citadel and him a distance of two leagues intervened, and the minds of the captains occupied themselves with the occurrence.

(iii) *Ardashir is informed of the worm's history*

That night Ardashir was engrossed with thoughts about the worm. When the sun replaced the moon, he withdrew his troops from the ocean's brim and returned at a gallop to Fars. In pursuit of him went the worm's army, which held the roads against him on every side and slew many a notable man. But the king with a few intimates galloped to safety.

[After an encounter with two youths who advised him about the strong position held by the worm and its forces, but nevertheless encouraged him to attack it, he came upon the traitorous Mehrak. He was killed, with all his family except one daughter, who had hidden herself away.]

After that he set forth to make a renewed onslaught on the worm, against which he directed all his forces. Now there was a man named Shahrgīr ['Empire-taker'], King Ardashir's astute chamberlain. To this Pahlavān the Shah said,

'Remain on the alert, keeping sentinels stationed night and day, men of ready understanding and resource. Post look-out men and guards to watch over the army by day and night. I am now maturing a scheme like that of Esfandiyār's, my ancestor. If the look-out man should see smoke in the daytime or a fire as bright as the sun in the night, then you will know that the worm's career is at an end and that its ascendant star and the briskness of its market have passed away.'

Out from amongst his captains he chose seven men of courage, lions on the day of combat, every man fully in his confidence, who would not whisper his secret even to the wind. From his treasury he selected a great number of pearls, brocades, golden dinars and stuffs of every kind, for with the eye of wisdom he looked upon material goods as things of nought. Two coffers he included in his load filled with lead and solder, and also a brazen cauldron, since he was a master in cunning. Then, when everything he was to take was fully assembled, he called for ten asses from his stable-master. He himself was clad like an ass-driver in a cloak of felt, although his load had in it silver and gold.

All now with willing hearts and eagerness for the road set out
from their encampment towards the worm's fortress. The two
rustic youths who had become attendants at his table he took with
him from his retinue, for they were not only friends to him but also
his guides. After some travel they at last came near to the fortress
and there on a mountainside they rested and took breath.

In attendance on the worm there were sixty men, not one of
whom was ever remiss in his duty. A watcher amongst them cried
out aloud,

'What have you concealed in your coffers?'

The Prince answered him,

'In my load I have goods of every kind; jewellery, robes, silver
and gold, brocades and gold dinars, satins and pearls. I am a
Khorāsāni come to trade and I never rest in the tasks I undertake.
By the worm's blessing I possess many treasures and have now
come at a felicitous moment to the worm's capital. I should regard it a privilege to enter its service, for through its goodly
influence all our affairs have gone well.'

The worm's servitors heard what he said and immediately
opened the gates. He drove the loads into the fortress and there
this noteworthy prince began to carry out his scheme. He quickly
removed the covering from his bales and distributed the gifts
which custom demanded. Then he spread a table before the
servitors and stood there to wait upon them. Having opened the
locks which fastened the coffers, he brought out wine, and with
it filled goblets. Those whose task it was to bear food to the worm
—the milk and rice which were its nurture—turned their heads
away from the wine-cups, for this, being their turn of duty, was
no occasion for wine-bibbing. Hearing about the food, Ardashir
leapt to his feet and said that he had a great quantity of rice and
milk and, if the head-servitor would permit him, it would warm
his heart to feed the worm for three days.

'It may be that thereby,' he said, 'I may attain to renown in the
world and acquire some of the felicity of its star. Drink wine with
me for three days; on the fourth, when the world's luminary rises,
I will erect an extensive storehouse, the summit of whose dome
will reach higher than the palace walls. I am a trader and am looking for custom, and my esteem with the worm will gain increase.'

With these words he achieved all that he desired. They told him
to attend on the worm, and the ass-drivers thereupon brought
provender of every kind. Meanwhile the worm's attendants re-

mained seated, wine in their clutches, drank in abundance and became intoxicated, being now worshippers of wine. When their very souls were soaked in wine the monarch came with his two table-attendants bringing the solder and the brazen cauldron under which, as the day dawned, they lit a fire. When the time arrived for feeding the worm, its viands now consisted of boiling solder. They brought the heated metal to the pool just as the soft worm raised its head. They saw its tongue, the colour of a brazen cymbal, working as it used to do when it had been accustomed to eating rice. The youths poured in the metal to where in the pool the worm lay grovelling. A rumble burst forth from its throat so heavy that it shook the pool and the whole region about it. Meanwhile Ardashir and the two youths departed as swiftly as the wind, drawing their swords and with mace and arrows ready. As for the servitors lying there drunk, not one escaped alive from their hands. The black smoke rising from the roof of the fortress proclaimed the valiant deed to the army commander, and at a run the sentinel came to Shahrgīr to inform him that King Ardashir had triumphed.

[It only remained for Haftvād to be defeated and slain and then Ardashir ascended the throne.]

XXIV

The Reign of Ardashir

(i) Ardashir ascends the throne

At Baghdad Ardashir seated himself on the ivory throne and on his head placed the heart-kindling crown, with his waist girdled and the royal mace in his hand he adorned the place where he was to dwell. Thereafter he was called Shāhanshāh [king of kings], and none could have distinguished him from Goshtāsp. When he set the crown of greatness on his head, he thus addressed the multitude from the throne of triumph and joy,

'In this world my treasure is justice and the whole universe has been revived through my efforts. None can take this treasure from me; evil comes to any man who evil does. From end to end this world is under my protection and my habit is the justice which all men approve. Let there be no man who lies down hungry through the fault of any of my officers, my captains or warrior knights, whether the man be a wrong-doer or a man of excellent virtue. This Court of audience is open to any man, whether he is my ill-wisher or a friend.'

To every region he sent troops and, if the ruler proved hostile, they brought his head down level with the road when he chose the path of the sword and the battlefield.

(ii) Ardashir's adventure with Ardavān's daughter

When Ardashir had killed King Ardavān and shed his blood, he brought the whole world into his grasp and married the dead king's daughter in the expectation that she would tell him where his treasure was. Two of Ardavān's sons had gone to Hindustān, where they were companions in toil and misery; two others lingered here in the king's prison, their eyes befouled with tears and their hearts rent with anguish. The eldest son was in Hindustān, a noble youth whose name was Bahman. He sought out a messenger of ready wit and sense and one who could retain what was told him. Now since he himself saw no hope of receiving a share in the kingdom he handed to the messenger a venomous

potion with instructions that he was to go to his sister and say
to her,

'Seek for no mercy from the enemy. You have two brothers in
Hindustān, companions in exile, and two in King Ardashir's
prison. Your father was slain and his sons wounded by arrows,
yet you have thus broken off your affection for us. Can the Creator
of the skies approve such conduct? If you wish to become queen
of Iran and win the approval of every gallant man in the world,
take this Indian bane and use it upon Ardashir.'

The envoy arrived one night at dusk and handed his message to
the young woman, whose soul and heart burned for her brothers,
and her breast was set aflame. She accepted the rare poison that he
held out and determined to have her own share of the satisfaction
that was to be taken. One day King Ardashir went out hunting.
When half of the long day had passed he decided to turn back
from the hunting-ground and was about to leave the road to go
in to Ardavān's daughter when that beauteous maid came running
towards him. She brought him a goblet of yellow jacinth filled
with sugar and barley meal, all steeped in cool water, but with
the sugar and the meal she had mingled the poison in the hope
that Bahman might now perhaps get his quietus from fate. As
Ardashir took the goblet in his hand it fell and was irretrievably
broken, at which the princess in her fear was seized with trembling and her heart broke in two.

Beholding her thus trembling the monarch's suspicion was
aroused and he was filled with misgiving about the way in which
the heavens might revolve for him. He gave orders that four
domestic fowls should be brought to him by a servant. Until these
birds were loosed on the barley-meal the bystanders thought his
suspicions were vain; but as soon as the fowls ate the grain they
died immediately and it was seen that his suspicions were justified.
He then commanded that a priest and a minister should come to
him. He inquired of his counsellor,

'If you place an enemy in a high position and he becomes so
drunk with flattery that he treacherously lifts his hand to threaten
your life, what would be the punishment of that presumptuous
act? How shall we remedy the ill which we ourselves create?'

He answered,

'If an underling stretches out his hand to threaten the life of the
sovereign, his sinful head must be cut off. And if anyone advises
the contrary he should not be listened to.'

Thereupon he commanded that Ardavān's daughter should be reduced to a corpse which should never again experience life. The priest took his departure, with the princess going in front of him trembling and her heart filled with sin. She said to the priest,

'Man of wisdom, time passes over us both, you and me. Even if you must inexorably put me to death, I bear a child by Ardashir. If I deserve to have my blood shed or to be hanged from a high scaffold, at least let the matter rest until the child is parted from me and then do whatever the king has commanded. This is not a fate which I can avoid, and it is better for me to be wise than foolish.'

The wise priest turned back on his footsteps and told Ardashir what he had heard, but the king bade him refuse to listen to her words and to carry out the command which had been given. The priest said to himself,

'It is a misfortune that a command such as this should have been given by the king. We are all destined for death, young and old, and King Ardashir has no son. However many years he may count upon, when he passes away the throne will go to an enemy. It will be best to abandon this profitless deed and with courage plan some nobler scheme. I will save this lovely woman from death, and it may be that I can make the Shah repent of his decree. If he will not, then when the child is separated from her I will carry out the royal behest.'

In his own mansion he caused a place to be got ready where he might cherish her as he did his own body and soul. And to his wife he said,

'I will not permit even a breath of air to behold her.'

He considered that he had many enemies and that all men had thoughts which were evil as well as those which were good, and so decided to devise a plan which would prevent any slanderer from sending foul water down his channels. He accordingly retired to a room and cut away his testicles, then cauterized the place, applied a liniment and bound all up. Over the testicles he quickly sprinkled salt and, swift as smoke, deposited them in a casket, upon which he immediately set his seal. Groaning and with pallid cheeks he departed from his home. When next he came to the sublime throne he laid down the casket, with its seal and fastenings intact, and said to the king,

'Let your Majesty have a care for this and entrust it to the keeping of his treasurer. Let the date be written on the casket and let it be made clear whence it came and who brought it.'

(iii) *The birth of Shāpur, son of Ardashir*

The time of parturition came—but the secret was not disclosed even to the wind—and to Ardavān's daughter a son was born, a boy of royal mien and clear spirit. The priest kept all men at a distance from his mansion and gave the child the name of Shāpur. For seven years he kept him concealed, during which time the boy assumed the presence of a king, possessed of *Farr* and broad shoulders. One day the minister went into the king and beheld tears on Ardashir's face. He said to him,

'May your Majesty rejoice! Brooding is evil food for the spirit. In this world you have attained every ambition and you have wrested your enemy from the throne. The time has now come for rejoicing and wine-drinking; it is no time for brooding. The world in all its seven climes is under your sovereignty; yours are the army, the throne and the dominion.'

The monarch answered him,

'My pure-hearted minister, keeper of my secrets, fate has been accommodated to me by my sword; anxiety, toil and unpleasantness have passed away. My years have reached fifty-one, the musk [blackness] has turned to camphor [hoary-headedness] and the roses have vanished. I should now have a son standing before me, to comfort my heart, fortify me and guide me on my path. A father without a son is like an orphaned child who must be taken to the bosom of strangers. After me my throne and crown will pass to an enemy; the dust will be all my profit after my pain and toil.'

The old quick-witted priest told himself that the time had now come for him to speak. He said to the king,

'Your Majesty, if I am assured of safety for my life I can remove this sorrow from your Majesty.'

The king replied,

'My sagacious friend, why should any fears for your life assail you? Tell me what you know and speak freely. What can be nobler than the speech of sages?'

The minister thus answered him,

'King of clear mind and pure reason, I gave your Majesty's treasurer a casket, and it would be good if you were now to call for it.'

To his treasurer the king said that the man who had once given him a certain article to hold in trust had now come to retrieve it.

It was to be restored to him and inspected. The treasurer accordingly brought the casket and surrendered it to the minister, whom the king questioned about what it contained and whose seal it was that had been placed on the fastenings. He answered,

'It is my own warm blood, and the burden of my modesty, cut from the root. You surrendered Ardavān's daughter to me in order to receive back a lifeless corpse. I did not slay her, for she had a child concealed within her and I stood in awe of the Lord of the world. Yet, by reason of your command, I sought no easy path for myself but cut off my manhood in order that none might slander me or wash me in the sea of accusation. Now seven years have passed since your son has lived with me, your minister. No other king has a son like him; he resembles nought so much as the moon in the sky for beauty. Out of affection I have bestowed the name Shāpur upon him; may the heavens rejoice by virtue of his happy fate! His mother too lives, as well as he, and she is counsellor to her ambitious son.'

The king was left in amazement at this and began to conceive ideas about the boy. After a while he said to the minister,

'My friend of illumined mind and pure counsel, you have suffered greatly in this matter and I will not permit your sufferings to endure any longer. But now go and seek out a hundred boys of like age with him and at one with him in height, face, breast and shoulder. All are to be clad as he is; there must be no difference, great or small. Send all these boys out with polo mallets, provide balls and send them all out on to the open ground. When that comely child appears on the ground, my soul will be moved to affection for my son, my heart will be witness to his genuineness and will grant me acquaintance with my own offspring.'

At dawn the king's minister took those children on to the ground, all being so alike in dress, face and stature that none could be in the least distinguished from another. On the ground, you would have said, there was a festival, at the centre of which was the prince Shāpur. When the boy turned to strike the ball he carried it further than all the rest. Ardashir had come to the ground with a company consisting of young men and elders, and looked about him. As he saw those children a cold sigh came up from the depth of his being and pointing with his finger he said to his minister,

'Look, that is an Ardashiri standing there.'

His counsellor replied,

'Your Majesty, your heart is true witness to his sonship. Stay until these fresh-cheeked children bring the ball near to you in play.'

To a slave the king said,

'Go and bring their ball here with a mallet so that I can see which of those boys will approach, boldest of the bold, lion-like, and carry off the ball under my very eyes, taking account of no one. The one who does that will indubitably be my own pure son, of my seed, my stock, and my kin.'

The king's slave departed at his command, struck the ball and bore it ahead of him while mounted on horseback. The boys galloped after him swift as arrows but as they neared Ardashir they stopped short and remained where they stood, having failed to overtake the ball. Shāpur the Lion advanced, took possession of the ball before his father's face and carried it off, passing it to the other boys when he had gone some distance away.

In pure pleasure at this, Ardashir's heart was brought to the state of an old man turned young. His knights raised the boy from the ground and passed him from hand to hand to the king, who, reciting praises to the Lord, took him to his bosom. He kissed the boy's head, face and eyes, and said,

'A marvel such as this may not be concealed. Even the thought of it had never been admitted to my heart, for I imagined him slain. God has magnified my empire and therefore has provided me with someone who shall be a memorial to me in the world. His command may not be disregarded, though one may raise one's head higher than the sun.'

He called for jewels from his treasury, golden coins and precious jacinths in abundance. These coins and jewels they poured over the boy, and over all they sifted musk and ambergris. His head disappeared under the gold coins and none could see his face for the jewels. On the minister also the king lavished jewels and seated him on a golden throne; and so much treasure did he grant him that it filled his hall and palace. He then commanded that Ardavān's daughter should be fetched, now rejoicing and her spirit unclouded. He forgave her the fault she had once committed and cleansed away the corrosion from her silvern glory.

From the city learned men were brought who taught the boy the art of writing Pahlavi, and noble and kingly etiquette. Further they instructed him how to manipulate his reins in battle and how to point down his spear at a foeman. Concerning the drinking of wine also they taught him, how to distribute largesse and the ordering of a feast, how an army is led and all about the toil and business of war. He then made alterations in the dies for the stamping of his dirhams and his dinars in all their detail. On one side there now was the name of King Ardashir and on the other the name of his distinguished minister.

After further honouring his minister, the king looked about for a place where before nothing but thorns had grown and on it he built a fine city, that which you now call Jondi-Shāpur, for you know no other name for it.

[Ardashir sends a messenger to an astrologer in India to inquire what the stars foretold about his empire. He received the answer that it will continue to prosper if his son marries the daughter of Mehrak, who had once revolted against him. This rouses Ardashir to anger. Remembering that Mehrak had left only one daughter he sends everywhere to have her killed. She, however, had found safety in the house of a village headman.]

(iv) Shāpur's adventure with Mehrak's daughter

Some time passed and the sovereign's reign grew more resplendent that ever. One day at dawn he set out for the hunting-ground accompanied by the keen-witted Shāpur. Horsemen rode hither and thither until the whole plain had been cleared of game. In the distance there appeared a spacious village with many gardens, open grounds, palaces and domes, and Shāpur galloped ahead until he arrived there, alighting at the house of the village headman. Within the mansion's wall a pleasant garden was laid out, and into its verdant depths the young prince entered. There he glimpsed a moon-lovely maiden who had just lowered a bucket hanging from a pulley into the depths of a well. When the girl saw Shāpur's face, she came up to give him salutation.

'May you be happy!' she said. 'May you be glad and smiling, perennially amongst those who never encounter harm! Surely your charger is thirsty. In the village the water is everywhere brackish except here, and in this well the water is cool and sweet. Let me be your drawer of water.'

Shāpur answered,

'Why should you suffer the toil of doing what you say? I have men to attend on me; let them draw the cool water from the well.'

The girl turned aside, walked a little way off and seated herself by the rill which flowed there. The prince meanwhile ordered one of his attendants to bring a vessel and draw up the water, and he departed at a run. Fastened to the bucket was a rope moving on a pulley. When the bucket was filled with water, the servitor's face twisted into frowns, for the heavy vessel would not come up out of the well. At that, Prince Shāpur came forward, impatiently vituperating the man, to whom he said,

'You half-woman, did not this maiden handle the bucket, with pulley and rope? She drew abundance of water up from the well, yet you have become overwhelmed with distress and must call for help.'

Coming forward he took the rope from the servitor; but the task proved difficult for the prince, who, finding the lifting of the bucket so heavy a task, expressed admiration of the maid, for she had been able to bring the weighty bucket up on the pulley. He thought that she must surely be descended of royal stock. As he thus drew up the bucket, the maiden approached and in kindliness lavished compliments on him. She said,

'May you live in felicity as long as time lasts and may wisdom ever be your instructor! Surely by the blessedness of Shāpur son of Ardashir the water in the well will be converted into milk.'

'Fair maid,' he said in answer to her flattery, 'how do you know that I am Shāpur?'

She returned,

'A story which I have often heard from the lips of veracious people is that Shāpur is a warrior of elephant strength and that he overflows with generosity like the river Nile. In figure he is a cypress, his body is composed of bronze and in all things he bears the likeness of Bahman.'

He said to her,

'Answer me truly what I ask. Disclose to me what your origin is, for there are the signs of royalty in your visage.'

She answered him,

'I am the daughter of the headman of the village. That is why I am so trained and skilful.'

Said Shāpur,

'Lies never confer lustre on royal personages. No peasant ever had so lovely a daughter, one with such a face and such enchanting qualities.'

She answered,

E K—U

'Prince, if I am given security for my life, I will tell you everything about my origins.'

To that Shāpur retorted,

'Suspicion between friends grows in no garden. Speak to me and harbour in your heart no fear either of me or of our renowned law-giver and sovereign.'

The girl then said,

'In truth then I am the daughter of Mehrak son of Nushzād. A virtuous man brought me as a child to this decent village elder, into whose charge he entrusted me. Through fear of our noble sovereign I became the drawer of water and household servant that I am.'

As Shāpur departed from the village, the elder stationed himself before him and to him the prince said,

'Grant me this handsome maiden, and call on Heaven as witness [to the marriage].'

At his behest the elder granted her to him in accordance with the rites of his fire-worshipping people.

[Of this marriage a son named Ormazd is born to Shāpur and Mehrak's daughter. The child grows to boyhood and by his prowess at polo is recognized to be of royal stock by his grandfather Ardashir, who becomes reconciled to his son's having married Mehrak's daughter. Being now assured of the continuance of his line, he draws up a charter to ensure the good governance of his empire.]

(v) *Ardashir's charter for the welfare of his realm*

Now hear the words of Ardashir's wisdom and lay all to heart! He strove to establish a firm order of government, disseminating benevolence and justice in every direction. When he desired an increase in his army at his capital he sent a counsellor to every region demanding that those parents who had sons should not permit them to grow to manhood without education. All should learn horsemanship and the methods of warfare with battle-axe, bow and poplar-wood arrow. When a boy had by his training acquired strength and achieved perfection in every pursuit, he proceeded from his own district to the king's capital. The mustermaster there inscribed his name and record and furnished him with a hall and a residence. If war broke out, the newly matured youth set out from the capital with a Pahlavān [army commander]. An intelligent adviser well acquainted with affairs and eager to know what was happening in the world went with every thousand youths and watched the doings of each. If a man of them proved slothful in battle and was shown to be unfitted for combat, the counsellor wrote a report on him to the king; this he did both for the unskilled and the doughty in battle. When the sovereign had the report, he stationed the subject of it before him. To the meritorious he gave a robe of honour and anything valuable he might request. If his eye lit on someone without merit, that man never again girt his loins for war.

Thus he proceeded until his army was so vast that no star could perceive all of its extent. If any man had ability to be a counsellor, he promoted him above the multitude. A herald went about among the troops proclaiming that any man who sought the king's pleasure and had washed the ground in the blood of brave men would receive a robe of honour from him and his name would be commemorated in the world. With his troops he set the whole world to rights; he became the shepherd and the warriors his flock. He brought into his council men expert in affairs, allotting no task to anyone lacking knowledge. They were watchful over their skill in speech and their penmanship, being men who excelled in subtlety with regard to the finer points. The more successful these counsellors were the higher did the Shah advance their fortunes. Those less well endowed with art in script or in subtlety did not go to the court of Shah Ardashir. They joined his agents, but the good scribes remained with the king. He was full of praises when he saw a truly lettered man at his court. 'A writer,' he said, 'accumulates treasure for me and his reasoning powers dispel trouble. My capital and army and any of my subjects in need of help prosper through him. Scribes are the sinews of my spirit; they are aware of what is hidden within me.'

When a governor proceeded to a district the Shah said to him, 'Hold money in contempt. Sell no man for gain, for this fleeting world lasts for nobody. Seek ever for honesty and wisdom; let greed and folly be remote from you. Take none of your associates or kinsmen with you; the escort which I give you will be sufficient to come to your aid. Each month distribute money to the poor but give nothing to any man who wishes you ill. If you maintain your district in prosperity by justice, you too will remain prosperous and happy thereby. But if any poor man lays him down in fear, then you must be selling a life for silver or gold.'

If a man went to the king's court for some urgent need or to
seek justice, the king's trusty officers came to him and questioned
him about the governor of that province, whether justice was being
done or whether the governor was covetous for wealth. Furthermore they inquired who were the learned men in the province
and who, because of their poverty, were in distress. Next they
wished to learn what people were attached to the governor's
court, inquiring whether they were elders of experience and men
of piety.

[The officer said to such visitors,]

'His Majesty declares that no man shall enjoy the king's wealth
or the fruits of his toil except one endowed with understanding
and capable of learning. What can be better than an old man of
wisdom? I am eager to have about me men of ripe experience as
well as young men of outstanding talent and ability. Nevertheless
learned and receptive young men may sit in the places of the
old.'

When his army was about to set forth for battle he made
wisdom and long deliberation his associates, always choosing out
some lettered man as ambassador; someone who was wise, well-
instructed and of retentive mind. It was someone who could
deliver a message in suave language, so that, lacking a true cause,
wars might not come about. Such an envoy would go to the
enemy in order to learn the secret of his circumstances. Being
wise he listened to all that was said and shirked no toil or other ill.
Thus he acquired royal robes of honour, made alliances and got for
himself patents of nobility and lasting memorials.

Even at times when the king's head filled with heat, his heart
with rancour, and an effervescence of the blood stirred in his liver,
he overcame it by distributing pay to his army from the highest
to the lowest, so that no man might be left with a grievance. Also
he appointed a Pahlavān eager for repute, wise, alert and a seeker
after good order, who, further, had to be a lettered man experienced in practice and skilful in his art, able to observe any injustice
committed by the army. In addition he appointed a man to be
mounted on elephant-back whose call carried for a distance of two
leagues. This man called out,

'Noble warriors, men of courage, name and fame, let harm
assail no poor man, nor yet anyone of repute and wealth. At every
place where you alight, distribute food when you yourselves eat,
laying under an obligation all who are my subjects. Let none of

you stretch out a hand towards people's goods especially if they are worshippers of God. Should any one of you show his back to the enemy, his existence thereafter will be a hard one, for either he will dig his grave with his own nails or ropes will saw into his breast and shoulders. Once his name is removed from the roll, dirt will be his food and his bed will be the dark earth.'

To the Commander he said,

'Be not dilatory, but neither be too swift and over-hasty. Always have elephants posted in front of you and sentinels spread out at a distance of four leagues. When the day of glory and combat arrives make a tour of your troops and say to them, "Who are these fellows [the enemy]? For what purpose are they on this battlefield? Let a hundred of their horses be overthrown for every one of ours; even a hundred for one are too few. For each of you, whether callow youths or veterans, I will procure an Ardashiri robe of honour."

'Once you have secured the victory, shed no more blood; that is to say, once the enemy are in full flight. If any of the foe asks for quarter grant it and exact no vengeance. But if you see the enemy's back in any action, neither gallop after him nor abandon your own position. Never feel secure against an ambush, but leave your army in safety on the battlefield.'

If an ambassador came from any land, whether Turk or Rumi [Greek] or noble Persian, the Warden of the Marches took note of him, not regarding such matters as being of small importance. Lodgings were prepared along the highway, a task which the governor performed. Clothing and food were provided and there was no lack of carpets and bedding. When the governor was informed of an arrival and had ascertained why the ambassador came to the king, a fine racing-camel and a scribe were despatched to Shah Ardashir in order that an escort should be sent out to welcome the envoy. The Shah adorned his turquoise throne, his courtiers were drawn up in their ranks on each side with all their robes embroidered in thread of gold. The ambassador was then summoned into his presence and given a place near the throne, where all his story was elicited from him. Afterwards the Shah escorted him to his palace in ambassadorial state, having provided for him all that he would need; and he invited him to table and wine, seating him near to the throne. When he went hunting the ambassador accompanied him and when the time came for his dismissal the envoy was presented with a royal robe of honour.

Now give ear to the utterances of that renowned Ardashir, whether you be old or young.

[Here follow a series of aphorisms and advices to a king on how to govern his realm and keep his subjects contented.

At this stage Ferdowsi leaves the realm of legend and romance and enters the period when Iran's history impinges on that of Rome.]

XXV

The Reign of Shāpur,[1] Son of Ardashir. His War with the Romans

The time came when the news was divulged that the royal throne was vacant. Ardashir, that wise king, had died and left the throne and diadem to Shāpur. Revolt broke out in every land and region from Cappadocia to Rum, and when tidings of this came to Shāpur the Shah he paraded his drums and banners and troops. As far as Pāluina he despatched a light-armed force without full supplies or impedimenta. Out of Cappadocia there marched an army from whose dust the sun itself grew dark, and another army marched out of Pāluina, in command of which was a prince named Bazānush [Valerian].[2] He was a proud knight of illumined spirit and much valued by the Caesars, a lasso-thrower, great in fame and of lofty dignity.

As the clamour of the drums arose on either side, that noble warrior stepped forth from the heart of his army, while from the foe there came out a gallant nobleman whose name was Garshāsp the Lion. He was a brave knight who, on the day of combat, feared nothing, whether it was a raging elephant or a man that stood opposed to him. The two warriors wrestled together in their struggle and their dust dropped onto the stars. Many were the devices by which they attempted to satisfy their rage but neither man could be overcome by the other. At last the entire armies on either side clashed together like mountain against mountain. From the great clamour caused by trumpets and Indian gongs you would have thought the sky dislodged from its place. In the midst of his army the warrior Bazānush was taken captive with bleeding heart, and of the Rumis in Pāluina ten thousand were killed among the battling ranks, a thousand and twice three hundred were made prisoners and panic seized the hearts of the remaining warriors.

[1] Sapor I, A.D. 244–272. He is here confused with Shāpur son of Ormazd (Sapor II, A.D. 309–79). Also Iran's two wars with Rome are confused.

[2] The Emperor Valerian was captured in A.D. 258 and carried about in chains by the Persians. Hence the legend.

To Shāpur son of Ardashir the Caesar sent a man of intelligence to inquire how long he would continue to shed blood for the sake of money? What would his answer be to God the All-wise when on the day of reckoning he was asked what excuse he could make? He, the Caesar, would send all that he possessed if no further pain was inflicted. He would obey any command concerning tribute and send numbers of his kinsmen as hostages. As for the Shah, it would be a just act on his part to retire from Pāluina. Shāpur stayed till the Caesar had sent him as tribute and tax ten oxhides filled with gold and Caesarian dinars, to which he added many valuables more.

For the sake of the captives of Rum, Shāpur built a citadel in a prosperous territory. That region now holds the gate to the Khuzis and every traveller must pass through it. In Fārs he raised a lofty citadel, magnificent and rich, and he built the fortress in the city of Nishāpur which is rightly named Shāpur-kard. Wherever he went the Shah carried Bazānush with him and listened to his counsel on all matters. At Shushtar there was a river so wide that even the fish could not traverse it, and to Bazānush Shāpur said,

'If you are an engineer, you will build me a bridge as continuous as a cable, such a one as will remain everlastingly in position as a pattern to the wise when we have turned to dust. The length of this bridge, reckoned in cubits, shall be one thousand; you may demand from my treasury all that is required. In this land and region apply all the science of the philosophers of Rum, and when the bridge is completed, you may depart to your home or else remain as my guest for as long as you live.'

In gallant fashion Bazānush undertook the task and brought the bridge to completion within three years. When it was done he departed from Shushtar and speedily set his face towards his own home.

[No further events are recorded in the life of Shāpur, who left his throne to his son Ormazd. He and a number of his successors reigned for only short periods and Ferdowsi has little to say of them except to applaud their virtues. Only when he comes to the long reign of Shāpur 'Zu'l Aktāf' (? the Man of the Shoulders) does Ferdowsi once more have a story to tell worthy of his epic theme.]

XXVI

The Reign of Shāpur Zu'l Aktāf

(i) Ṭā'ir and Māleka

For a long period the throne was vacant and the heads of the rulers were laden with cares. Then in the royal ladies' quarters one of the ministers espied a tulip-cheeked girl as glorious as the moon. The tips of her eyelashes were pointed as Kāboli daggers and her two tresses were as intertwined as Bāboli script. Now this peri-cheeked girl had concealed within her body a child, and her whole world rejoiced at her beauty. When it was discovered that she was pregnant the chief priest led her to the throne. Over her head there was suspended a diadem on to which golden coins were poured. Soon a child was born to that pretty creature, a boy handsome as the sun in glory (my poetic Dehqān of priestly stock recounted this version of the story to me).

The minister gave the boy the name of Shāpur and he held a great feast [at which the child was crowned as Shah]. Some time passed over the head of that king, and the crown which illumined the world shone with his brilliance. It then came about that a beleaguering army approached Ctesiphon led by Ṭā'ir, the lion-hearted lord of the [Arab] Ghassānids, and composed of men from Rum and Fārs, from Bahrain, Kurdestan and Qādesiya. The army was immensely large and plundered all that land and region; for who could have had the power, the stamina and the agility to resist it?

Now Ṭā'ir had become aware of the existence of the king's aunt, a beautiful woman fresh as the Spring, whose name was Nusha, and to her palace this prince came. Thereupon Ctesiphon became full of rumour and report and this gracious creature was abducted from the palace and imprisoned by those debased and ignorant people. For a whole year she was kept by Ṭā'ir and her heart was now sore with anxiety. She bore him a daughter beauteous as the moon and you might have thought from her presence that she was another Narsi [her grandfather] crowned and enthroned. Her father, on beholding her, called her Māleka ['Queen'], for this daughter was fitted to rule an empire.

285

Now by the time that Shāpur had reached the age of twenty-six years he was as glorious as the sun. One day he came on to his parade ground, inspected his army and picked out twelve thousand warriors, each of whom was to be mounted on a racing-camel swift as the wind. In advance went a hundred men as guides. [In the battle which followed] Shāpur slew may of the Arab foe and Ṭā'ir, on beholding this, showed his back in flight. Many of the Arabs were taken captive, the rest took refuge in a fortress in the Yemen, against which Shāpur led so vast an army that it blocked the way even to ants and gnats. He found Ṭā'ir and the Arab army in the fort and wrested from him both the gate leading to war and the path of escape.

(ii) *Māleka daughter of Ṭā'ir becomes enamoured of Shāpur*

One early morn the heroic Shāpur mounted his horse and rode out effervescent with eagerness, a bow in his hand, on his breast a royal cuirass and above his head a shining black ensign. From the palace wall Māleka looked down and beheld the standard of the captain of those famed warriors. Her cheeks were like rose-petals, her hair black as musk, her musk-breathing lips the colour of the red willow. Sleep and repose departed from the lovely maiden and, her heart overwhelmed with love, she went to her nurse, to whom she said,

'This prince, with his sun-like visage, who comes here seeking vengeance, is all-powerful and he is the blood which flows in my veins. I will call him "World", for he is my world. Bear a message to him from me. He has come to make war; nevertheless offer him a wedding feast on my behalf. Tell him that I am a princess of like birth with him and that I am of the seed of the mighty warrior Narsi. Say also that I side with him in this war and that I am of his kin, being Nusha's daughter. If he will ask me in marriage, the fortress shall be his, and when he receives the palace, its beautiful ornament (myself) is his. Let him swear you an oath and give you his word in pledge.'

[The nurse at dead of night delivered the message, to which he gave answer promising 'by sun and moon, by Zoroaster's girdle, by *Farr* and crown', that he would grant the princess's every wish.]

(iii) *Māleka betrays Ṭā'ir's fortress to Shāpur*

When the sun showed his crown in the East and the yellow flowers of the earth took on the hue of teak-wood, the princess took from the minister of the treasury the keys of the larders and of the store where the wine-vats were kept. Then to every captain in the fortress, to each warrior champion and war-scarred veteran she sent food and wine as well as perfumes such as narcissus and orange blossom. Summoning the butler she spoke to him for long, saying to him in flattering words,

'Tonight you are he that will serve the wine. Give Ṭā'ir the purest. And do not leave them till they have the wine well in hand, so that when they lie down they shall be intoxicated.'

'I am your slave,' replied the butler, 'it is by your command that I live in the world.'

When the sun yellowed in the West and dark night commanded it to turn aside from its path, Ṭā'ir called for the royal wine in a goblet and began by drinking to the health of the Ghassanids. A watch of the dark night had passed when Ṭā'ir sought repose from tumult and uproar, and all went to their bedchambers. Then the maiden commanded that none should speak except in a whisper when the fortress gate was stealthily opened. Shah Shāpur had kept an expectant eye upon it and had within his heart been nursing anger at the drunkards' voices. When the lamp shone out at the fortress gate, he told himself that fortune was now alertly on his side. He commanded that a pleasant apartment should be got ready for Māleka while he himself entered the fortress and set about the slaughter which would satisfy all his old hatreds.

Now, within the fortress, a great number of the troops which Ṭā'ir had with him lay drunk. The rest who had been sleeping awoke and made resistance everywhere, no man turning his back in fear, and of these the Shah of Iran slew a great many. Ṭā'ir fell a prisoner into his hands and was made to walk away naked without a hope of evasion.

[When Ṭā'ir was confronted with his daughter enthroned, he understood that she was the author of his discomfiture. He failed to impress the Shah when he told him that she would betray him in like fashion and he ordered that Ṭā'ir's head should be cut off. As for the other Arabs held captive, their arms were by his command torn from their bodies at the shoulder, whence he received the name of 'Shāpur of the Shoulders'.]

(iv) *Shāpur travels to Rum*

[Disguised as a merchant Shāpur gains access to the Caesar of
Rum but is unmasked and cruelly maltreated.]

They carried Shāpur drunk to the apartment of the woman and
tied his hands, so that by no act of courage could he escape from
the net of ruin. (When important foreknowledge of this kind is
not taken to heart, what avails the calculation of the astrologers?)
A candle was lit in front of him and cruelly they stitched him into
the skin of an ass. Without delay then they carried the hapless
prince into a narrow, dark chamber, the key of which was handed
to the châtelaine of the palace. The Caesar said to her,
    'Give him sufficient bread and water so that his life shall not
hasten away too soon. If he remains alive for some time, he may
perchance realize what value to set on throne and crown. He will
nevermore dream of the Caesar's throne as possible for one who
is not of the Caesar's line.'
    The Caesar's wife kept the door of that chamber locked, for her
own residence was in a different mansion. A handsome maid was
her treasurer and chosen counsellor in every business, a woman
of Iranian birth, who could trace back her ancestry from father
to father. To her the queen entrusted the key of the door of the
chamber where Shāpur the warrior lay imprisoned in the skin of
the ass, and that very day the Caesar led an army out of the country
[in order to devastate Iran]. Much of the land was depopulated
and many Iranians became Christians.
    Time passed and meanwhile the Roman army departed from
Iran. All this time the woman who had charge of Shāpur in Rum
left him not for a moment in solitude, night or day, and day and
night she wept over the skin and her heart burned for Shāpur.
One day she said to him,
    'You handsome creature, what man are you? Have no fear, tell
me; for with your slender body in that ass's skin, your sleep and
repose are being destroyed. You were like a cypress-tree having
at its top the circle of the moon crowned by musky locks and now
your cypress figure has become rotund and your body, which once
had elephant's strength, is feeble as a reed. My heart burns for you;
day and night my eyes pour out tears. What do you seek by continuing thus to suffer and refusing to tell me your secret?'
    Shāpur said to her,
    'Beauteous maid, if any love for me stirs within you I desire a

promise from you, an oath from which you will never depart in the slightest, neither revealing my secret to my enemy or paying any consideration to my woes and suffering. I will then tell you what you ask, and my words will reveal the truth to you.'

'By the Lord, by the priests' girdle of seventy-two intertwined cords,' the girl swore, 'by the soul of the Messiah and the mourning on the Cross, by the lord of Iran, by love and dread, I will not repeat a word of what you tell me to anyone and will seek no advantage from your words.'

Then Shāpur told her all his secrets, leaving not a word of good or ill in concealment. He continued,

'Now, if you will do what I command, having given your heart in pledge to me in return for this secret of mine, your head shall be raised higher than that of any princess, and the world will submit itself to your footsteps. When the time comes for my bread, bring me also hot milk. Keep this matter hidden; go very gently to work. Soften this ass's skin with the milk. It is something which will become a legend in the world. Long years will go by after me and people of understanding will speak of this.'

Stealthily and in whispers the maiden asked all her friends for milk, and when her vessel was full she set it on a hot fire and took it secretly to Shāpur. Over this [daily] proceeding the sky revolved for two weeks and at last the ass's skin was soft; from it Shāpur emerged woeful at heart and with bleeding body.

[The two then discussed how they were to escape. The girl said,]

'Tomorrow from the time of dawn all the nobles will be setting out for the place where the festivities are held, for there is a feast being celebrated in Rum; men, women and children will all come forth. When the queen departs from the city to the assembly-place outside, this house will be empty and I will contrive some device without fear of any mishap.'

[She picked two of the best horses out of the stables and on them the two escaped from Rum. After the hardships of a long journey they entered Iran, and took refuge in the house of a gardener, who recognized Shāpur as a person of consequence. By this man he sent a message embossed with his royal seal to his old Chief Minister.]

(v) *Priest and Pahlavān get tidings of Shāpur's arrival*

The minister, as the gardener spoke, perceived that the lion-hearted newcomer was none other than the Shah and that the description of him could be fitting to none but a man of the highest rank. He therefore sought out a messenger of good intelligence, whom he sent to the Pahlavān with the information that the *Farr* of King Shāpur had appeared and that he was to recruit an army from every district. The commander rejoiced at the words, for his heart was full of ardour and his lips of sighs [for the Shah]. As night led in its black banner and the stars and the moon's disk appeared, an army that came from every region assembled at the place where the great personage was in hiding. They advanced to the house in which the gardener lived and went joyfully to meet the king's host, the Shah himself having ordered that though the court was being held in a humble spot the way to him must be kept open. Every man who came into the presence of that seeker of fame bowed his face down to the ground. The Shah took each to his bosom, complained of the ills he had suffered, told how he had been tormented in the ass's skin, and repeated the words he had heard from the Caesar. Also he spoke in high praise of the handsome slave-girl and recounted the affection she had shown him. He said,

'In every region where my troops now are and where my sovereignty and my road penetrate, send men to give warning and to put sentinels out on the paths. Bar the road to Ctesiphon [the Persian capital held by the Rumis], for no information of me must reach the outside. If the Caesar gets news of me and hears that the royal *Farr* has appeared again, he will come and destroy my army and will break the heart and the spine of the Iranians. At this moment we have not the ability to resist him and we must suffer, while his abounding good fortune continues. When our counsellors come accompanied by troops we shall be able with our army to block the ways even to the gnats. We will work to establish a new order of things and in secret perhaps make our garden faultless. Let scouts go into every corner of the land, and place sentinels who shall be on guard both by day and by night. Henceforth let no man lie down with loins ungirt feeling secure against the Rumis.

(vi) *Shāpur captures the Caesar*

[The Shah's scouts reported that the Caesar had no care for anything but hunting and wild living and that his troops were scattered in all directions. Seizing his opportunity Shāpur with 3,000 armoured knights made a sudden onslaught on Ctesiphon, where the Caesar lay overcome by wine. He was seized, together with a large number of his retinue, kinsmen and other nobles, whereupon Shāpur wrote proclamations of victory which were to be read out in every province of the empire. The Caesar is brought before him.]

To him the Shah said,

'You man compounded of evil, you who are a Christian and an enemy of God, you attribute a son to Him that has no partner, to Him that has neither end nor beginning in the world. You know not how to utter a word that is not falsehood, and falsehood is a fire that sheds no light. If you are indeed the Caesar, where are your generosity and sound reason? And how do you give guidance to virtue? Why did you clew me up in the hide of a vile ass and cast me ignominiously to the ground? I came, as merchants do, to a festivity and not with drums and troops to do battle. You thrust your guest into the interior of a vile ass and now you turn towards Iran accompanied by an army. You will see how men who are men behave, so that you will never more seek conflict with Iran.'

[The Caesar appeals for his life to be spared and says he will surrender all he possesses in return. Shāpur agrees, but demands in addition hostages from the Caesar's own family to the number of the Iranians who had been killed by the Rumis. Though the Caesar's life was spared for the time being, he was cast into prison with his ears and nose mutilated and there died. In his place the Rumis set up Bazānush (Valerian) as Caesar. In Iran Shāpur now reigned in triumph.]

(vii) *Māni [Manes] appears as prophet*

There now came from China a man of eloquent tongue whose like as an artist the earth never sees. By his skill he had attained all his desires, although he was a man full of ambition. His name was Māni. In addition to his being an artist, he claimed also to be a prophet and one superior to all others who had brought religions into the world. From China he arrived before Shāpur, demanding audience with the object of making the Shah an ally in his prophethood. He was a man of ready tongue and he spoke such words that the king was converted to evil doubts. His head thus becoming active with ideas, he summoned the priests, with whom he remained for long in discussion, admitting to them that through this Chinese of ready tongue he had fallen into doubt concerning his own faith. He desired them to debate with the man and hear what he had to say; it might be that they themselves would believe in his doctrine. They replied,

'This man is a painter; he has not the substance of our Chief of Priests in him. Listen to our priest's words for a moment, then summon Māni and see in what fashion he will open his lips.'

Accordingly Shāpur commanded that the priest should present himself and discuss with Māni. He did so on matters numberless, arguing in the presence of the Shah about all things white and black. Māni was in the midst of his discourse confounded by the speech uttered concerning the ancient faith by the priest, who said to him,

'You idolator, why do you so recklessly stretch out your hand against God? He it was that created the high heaven, within which He created space and time and within which are light and darkness. His essence is more sublime than that of all else. The lofty sphere revolves both night and day; within it lies your refuge, but also your danger. Why do you believe in the arguments of the idol and refuse to hearken to the counsel of our faith? I that speak to you declare that God is one, you have no recourse but to worship Him. If you endow the image that you fashion with power to move, is it possible for you to use this moving thing as an argument? Do you not understand that such argument can be of no avail, that nobody holds it to be effective? If Ahriman were the associate of God, dark night would be as bright as day. All the year round night and day would be equal; in their succession neither would be longer and neither shorter. The World-creator cannot be comprehended in an image, being above all space and time. What you maintain is the doctrine of madmen, and nothing else. No one can associate himself in it with you.'

Many such words he spoke linked with understanding and humanity, and Māni was overwhelmed by what he said. His flourishing market faded away. For a time thereafter the sovereign was in a state of perturbation, and Fate's revolution hemmed him closely in. In the end he commanded that Māni be taken and expelled with ignominy from the court, with the words,

'This idolator can no longer be accommodated in the abode of human beings, for the tribulations of the whole world are due to him. Let his skin be flayed off him from head to foot and stuffed with straw so that no other may presume to take his place.'

He further commanded that the man's body be hanged at the gateway of the city or else from the wall of the hospital. The whole world called down blessings abundantly on the king and poured dust upon the dead man.

(viii) *Shāpur makes his brother Ardashir his heir apparent*

Under Shāpur the world burgeoned so happily that not a thorn was seen on the rose tree in the garden. Through his justice, good planning and wisdom, his striving, generosity and warlike campaigning, there was none who remained hostile to him throughout the realm. But then, when he harboured no further hopes from the lofty wheel, his years having reached seventy and more, he commanded into his presence a scribe accompanied by the Chief Priest and Ardashir, who was still a youth, the youngest of the king's brothers, and on whose head rested the diadem of justice and sagacity.

Now Shāpur had a son, also named Shāpur, who had not yet reached maturity. In the presence of the nobles and of the scribe the king addressed Ardashir as follows,

'If in honour you will swear an oath to me, giving me your tongue in pledge, that you will, when my son reaches manhood and the wind of maturity blows over him, surrender to him my treasure, throne and army and be his counsellor ever desirous of his good, then I will entrust to you this royal crown and moreover will pass to you my treasury and my army.'

In the presence of the nobles, old and young, Ardashir accepted these terms.

[A long deed of covenant was drawn up and in due course Shāpur received the throne from his uncle. Ferdowsi at the end of the document indulges in some melancholy reflections on his own life, saying, 'Bring me ruby wine, Hāshemi (his servant), from the vat that never fails, for my years now are sixty and three and my ear is deaf. Why should I continue to seek fame and splendour in the world? I will go on to tell you the tale of Shah Ardashir. Remember what I have to say.'

Ardashir 'the Beneficent' reigned for twelve years and then, in accordance with his oath, surrendered the throne to Shāpur, whose reign lasted for only five years and four months. He was succeeded by Bahrām, son of Shāpur, whose reign lasted for fourteen years. He was succeeded in his turn by his brother Yazdegerd 'the Sinner'.]

XXVII

Yazdegerd the Sinner

(i) The birth of Bahrām, son of Yazdegerd

Seven years passed of the reign of Yazdegerd, during which time all his ministers suffered pain and outrage. At the beginning of the eighth year, in the month of Farvardin [March–April], when the Sun reveals his religion anew to the world, a son was born to him on the day of Ormazd, under a goodly star and world-brightening omens. On him his father bestowed the name Bahrām, rejoicing in the little child. To the Court there flocked all the astrologers—those men whose speech was deserving of attention. Amongst them was a greatly honoured man of dignity and understanding who was chief of the Hindu star-gazers and whose name was Sorush. Another was one named Hoshyār, who came from Fārs and who by his science could fit a bridle on the stars.

These men were commanded to appear before the king and they did so with keen minds and eagerness to find the true paths. With their astrolabes they observed the stars and with Rumi tables they investigated the true courses. One seeker observed that the secret of the stars was that the child would one day be a monarch in the world and would be king over the seven climes. Moreover he would be of cheerful heart and pious disposition. With their findings they hastened into the Shah's court, with their astrolabes and star-tables at their bosoms, and told the royal Yazdegerd that they had surveyed the whole field of science and discovered in their calculation of the sky that it was favourable towards this child, into whose possession the seven climes of the earth would come, and that he would be a mighty king enjoying the blessings of all men. When the astrologers departed from the palace, the warriors and the priests, honourable counsellors of the Shah, seated themselves to investigate plans of every kind in order that some scheme to suit the circumstances might be discovered. [They said,]

'If this boy does not inherit his father's nature he will be a just king, If, however, he does possess the character of his father, the whole world will be overturned from top to bottom; neither priest nor warrior will be contented nor will he himself be happy or serene of spirit.'

All these priests, sincere of heart and of good intent, came to the king and said,

'This child, so full of merit, is remote from any taint of blame. Now the whole world is under your command and in every land tribute and loyalty are owed to you. Look about therefore for some place where learning is fostered and which favours its scholars. There choose out men of dignity to be tutors, men on whom praise will be bestowed in our land. So shall this prince of happy disposition acquire talent, and the world will rejoice in his authority.'

Yazdegerd gave ear to the priests and sent envoys abroad, some to Rum, some to India and China and others to every other civilized realm. A man of note also departed for the land of the Arabs to spy out the advantages and defects there. So it was that lettered men came from every clime, men of experience in the world who had lived good lives and were sagacious. All these came to the court, aspiring to office under the king. He questioned them closely, paid them compliments and gave them lodgments within the city precincts. Amongst them from the Arabs went No'mān, accompanied by a troop of noted spearsmen.

When all these men of distinction were assembled in Fārs, they presented themselves before royal Yazdegerd. Each in his turn said,

'We are your slaves, hastening to come at the bidding of the Chosroes. Who among the great ones will find the good fortune of taking the brilliant son of the king of the world to his breast and so illumining his mind as to clear it of all darkness? All of us here, whether we come from Rum or India or Fārs, whether we are astrologers or geometers, many-sided philosophers, rhetoricians, or skilled craftsmen, are without exception the dust at his feet. Seek out those of us who meet with your approval and will be of value to you.'

For his own part, however, Monzer [the Arab Prince of Yemen] said to the Shah,

'We are your slaves and live in the world only for the sake of the Shah. He knows all our qualities, for he is the shepherd and we are the flock. As for us, we are cavaliers, warriors and tamers of horses and we have power to destroy any masters of learning.

Not one of us is a star-gazer or has any endowment of geometry. But our souls are devoted to the Shah and under us we have Arab steeds. We all stand in attendance on his son and we adore his greatness.'

(ii) *Yazdegerd entrusts his son Bahrām to Monzer and No'mān*

Yazdegerd listened to this speech from Monzer and gathered in his wit and wisdom; and so, with his eye on the outcome from the very beginning, he entrusted Bahrām to him. An order came that a robe of honour was to be made and presented to him and his head was exalted to the skies. From the palace of the king of the world and far out on to the open plain there extended a procession of horses and of camels with howdahs. Servants and female attendants without number stretched from the bazaars to the king's gate and thence into the king's audience-chamber, while all the bazaars were festively decorated.

When Monzer returned to the land of Yemen, every man and woman came forth to welcome him. Then, when he had reached his capital, his first act was to seek out a large number of his finest cavaliers, both owners of estates and Bedouins, men of substance, rich men, whose protection was sure. From the families of these notables he picked out four women, whose character was patent from their lineage. Two were Bedouins and two of land-owning families of royal seed who were prepared to act as nurses. They maintained Bahrām as a suckling for four years, and although he was sated with milk and his body had become stout they found difficulty in weaning him, so they kept him softly at their breasts. When he reached the age of seven years, what said he, with the reason associated with maturer years? He said,

'Noble prince, do not treat me any further as a nursling. Hand me over to learned teachers, for the time has now arrived for men to instruct me.'

'My noble youth,' said Monzer to him, 'the need for instruction has not yet arrived for you. When the time comes and you determine to acquire knowledge, I will not leave you to play in the palace hall or to make a boast of your sport.'

Bahrām answered,

'Do not treat me as a babe unfitted for work. I possess understanding even though my years are few and I have neither the chest nor shoulders of a warrior. You have the years, but your comprehension is too small to understand that my composition is different from what you imagine. Do you not understand that he who is seeking for the right moment decides which out of all tasks must come first? Having found that moment, you wash your mind free of care. A task performed at an inauspicious time is fruitless. Teach me those matters which are appropriate to a king; it is proper that I should know them. Amongst the principles of truth what stands first is knowledge; happy the man who from the outset looks to the end.'

Monzer gazed at him in astonishment and under his breath called on the name of God. He immediately sent a hard-riding counsellor on a racing camel to Shursān to seek out three scholars who were held in honour there. One was to teach Bahrām the art of letters so as to cleanse his mind of obscurities, one to give him an understanding of the habits of hawk and hunting-panther that kindle the heart, moreover to teach him polo, the use of bow and arrow, how to wield the sword in face of the foe, how to manipulate the reins to right and left and how the head should be kept proudly raised among warriors. The third was to teach him the ways of kings, and the speech and conduct of men experienced in affairs. These learned men presented themselves before Monzer and their discourses ranged over all the sciences. He entrusted the person of the prince to them, for he was himself a man eager to increase his knowledge as well as a warrior.

Bahrām of the line of Khosrow steadily grew until he could give a good account of himself in skill amongst any men. When he reached the age of eighteen years he was a bold warrior, brilliant as the sun. In no pursuit now did he have need of an instructor, either in letters or at polo or in handling panther and hawk, in the manipulation of his reins on the battlefield, in the taming of horses or training them. He requested Monzer, therefore, to dismiss the skilled instructors to their homes. To each he gave many gifts and they departed in felicity from the court.

One day the young prince said to Monzer,

'My wise and clear-minded patron, it is without true reason that you watch over me as you do, never leaving me for a moment in anxiety. And yet amongst all the people you see in the world there is not one heart which does not have its secret. Men's faces become pallid with anxiety but the body of the warrior flourishes in happiness. Now the person of a beauteous maid increases man's happiness greatly, for a woman is man's refuge from pain.

The young man requires to achieve his happiness through woman, whether he be the wearer of a crown or a Pahlavān. Through woman, moreover, God's religion keeps its hold and she is the young man's guide to the good life. Command therefore that there shall be brought here five or six slave-girls who shall be beautiful and sunlike in their splendour. It may be that if I make my choice of one or two of them my thoughts will be directed to God's praise. Perhaps also a son will be born to me to bring comfort to my heart, the emperor too deriving pleasure from me, while I shall be complimented in every assembly.'

Monzer heard the young man's speech and he, the elder man, applauded him. In all haste he despatched a messenger to the warehouse of a slave-dealer, who brought out forty Greek slave-girls, all desirable and fitted to bring solace to the heart. Of these pretty maids he chose out two whose bones of ivory were clad in skin of roses. Their figure was cypress-like and they were compounded of all that was desirable, colourful and glorious. Of the two, one played the lyre, while the other was tulip-cheeked and beautiful as Canopus in the Yemen. She too was of cypress stature and her tresses were lassos. Monzer approved of them and paid their price, while Bahrām smiled and applauded and his cheeks blushed the colour of a ruby in a ring.

(iii) *The adventure of Bahrām and the lyre-playing girl*

Polo and the hunting-ground now were Bahrām's sole occupations. It happened one day that he went out hunting accompanied by the lyre-player and without his retinue. The Greek girl's name was Āzāda and the colour of her cheeks was that of coral. She was the solace of his heart and she shared all his tastes. Her name was ever on his lips. One day when he went hunting he had asked for a racing-camel, the back of which he adorned with brocade. From the saddle four stirrups hung down and the twain galloped together over hill and dale. Under his quiver the gallant Bahrām had a bow with which to cast pebbles, he being proficient in every kind [of skill]. Suddenly there came running towards them two pairs of gazelles, and the young man smilingly said to Āzāda,

'My pretty one, when I string the bow and put the knot in my thumbstall, which gazelle do you wish to see shot? The female is young and her mate very old.'

Āzāda gave answer,

'My lion-hearted prince, men of war do not go in chase of gazelles. Convert yonder female into a buck with your arrow and with another arrow let the old buck become a female. Then spur the camel on to a sharp trot as the gazelles try to escape your arrow. Shoot a pebble at the ear of one so that it will lay its head down on its shoulder. The pebble will cause the creature to scratch its ear and for the purpose it will bring its hind leg up to its shoulder. Then, with your arrow, pin head, foot and back together, if you would like me to call you the most brilliant [archer] in the world.'

Bahrām Gur ['The Wild Ass'] strung his bow and raised a shout in that silent waste. In his quiver he had an arrow with two heads, which he kept for hunting on the plain. As soon as the gazelles were in flight the prince shot away the horns on the head of the fleeting buck, using the arrow with the double head, whereat the girl was filled with amazement. The buck's head being shorn of its black horns at once came to look like a doe. Then the hunter shot two arrows at the doe's head at the places where horns might grow. Instead of horns there were now two arrows, the doe's blood reddening its breast. Now he urged the camel towards the other pair while he placed two pebbles in the bow. One he shot into the ear of one of the gazelles, greatly to his pleasure, for which he had reason, seeing that the gazelle immediately scratched its ear. At that moment he fixed an arrow into his bow and with it pinned together the creature's head, ear and hind leg. Āzāda's heart burned with grief for the gazelle, and Bahrām said to her,

'How is it, my pretty one, that you release such a stream of tears from your eyes?'

'This is not a humane deed,' she replied. 'You are no man; you have the spirit of a demon.'

Putting out his hand Bahrām dashed her from the saddle headlong to the ground and drove the camel over her, bespattering her head, her breast and her arms and the lyre with her blood.

'You silly lyre player,' he called out to her. 'Why did you try thus to ensnare me? If my aim when I shot had gone astray it would have brought disgrace on my birth.'

The girl died beneath the camel's feet and never again did he take a girl with him when hunting.

[Some time elapsed and Bahrām Gur returned home to his father Yazdegerd. By some misdemeanour on his part he offended the

Shah, who confined him as prisoner in his own house. In the end he found release, whereupon he immediately returned to the Yemen. When in due course the Shah died, Iran's powerful princes, priests and other notables declared themselves unwilling to be ruled over by a man of the same family as that of his evil predecessor. They therefore placed on the throne an elderly nobleman named Khosrow. He was incapable of protecting Iran from the enemies surrounding it, and appeals for help were sent to Monzer in the Yemen. Bahrām learned of his father's death and the conditions prevailing in his country and was persuaded by Monzer to set out with an army to win the throne for himself. A group of Iranian nobles came out to meet him.]

(iv) The Iranians come to welcome Bahrām

Bahrām addressed the nobles thus,

'Dukes, experienced and venerable princes, by inheritance from ancestor to ancestor the kingship is mine. Why should you now contest it?'

The Iranians retorted,

'We will not let you prolong our misery and we are entirely unwilling to have you for our king. Our land and home are ours, in spite of your having an army. We have been afflicted with outrage by your dynasty and suffered grief and torment; day and night we live in agony and the cold winds blow upon us.'

'Is that indeed the truth? The wish is king over every man's heart. Even if you do not desire me, why do you seat a man in my place without having consulted me?'

A priest answered,

'None can escape from the path of justice, whether he be a subject or of royal birth. Be one of us and choose a king whom all men shall bless.'

Three days were spent in argument, during which they sought to choose a sovereign for Iran. They wrote down the names of a hundred noblemen who could bring lustre to crown, throne and girdle. Of this number Bahrām was one, for he was a prince who charmed the heart. The hundred names were reduced to fifty, those of resourceful men who were also, however, full of demands. First among the fifty was Bahrām; and if he demanded his father's place it was only equitable that he should do so. Then out of the fifty they wrote down thirty names, the choicest in Iran for fame and achievement. Amongst those thirty also Bahrām led, for he was both worthy of the crown and youthful as a prince. Of the thirty the priests picked four, and of those four Bahrām was sovereign.

When the appointment of the king became imminent, the elders in Iran declared that they did not desire Bahrām, as being rash, frivolous and over-ambitious. A clamour arose amongst the princes there, for they had set their hearts on their own decision. Monzer thereupon addressed the Iranians, demanding to know where the advantages and defects in this lay and why they were so aggrieved and wounded in spirit over this young and untried king. The chieftains set out their replies at length and summoned many a man of Fārs who had a grievance, gathering on that plain all the many in Iran on whom Yazdegerd had inflicted injuries. One man had had his arm and both feet cut off by him and another had been left alive with neither hands nor feet. Still another one he had deprived of hands, ears and tongue, leaving him like a body without a soul. No'mān was stunned at sight of these mutilated men and burst into anger. Bahrām too was profoundly saddened. He called out against his father's tomb,

'You man of dark fate, why did you stitch up the eyes of your happiness? Why did you destroy my spirit in the fire?'

Monzer the world-seeker then said to Bahrām,

'All this may not be hidden from the princes. You have heard their words; give them an answer. Dull wits are not suited to a prince.'

(v) *Bahrām replies to the Iranian nobles and offers to submit to an ordeal*

In answer to the princes, Bahrām replied,

'You have all spoken truly but there is something worse, and it is proper for me to charge my father with it. There is tribulation within me because of it and my delicate reasoning has been clouded thereby. His castle was my prison and my palate was pierced by his hook. I escaped and made Monzer's deserts my refuge, for I had never enjoyed the Shah's favour. I have prayed God till this last to be my guide in His goodness and permit me to wash away from my soul and heart all the sins which the Shah committed towards mankind. From one ancestor to another the kingship descends to me, and I have understanding and goodwill.

'I will make a compact with you giving my tongue as pledge to God. Let us bring out the ivory throne of the king of kings and on it place the most precious crown. Then let two fierce lions be brought out of the forest and, the crown being placed between them, let them be tied one on each side. Then shall the man ambitious for the kingship advance and seize the crown from the ivory throne and lay the illustrious diadem on his head. He will seat himself as king between the two lions; he being in the middle with the diadem on him and the throne beneath. If you turn your backs from what I propose, choose some proud fellow who is my equal. I and Monzer with our battle-axes and sharp swords— for Arab warriors know nothing of flight—will pound the life out of your chosen king of kings and slice off your heads as high as the moon. I have spoken; give me an answer. Let me have your felicitous consent to this trial.'

After making that speech he departed and entered his tent, leaving the world stunned at what he proposed. The warrior champions, priests and all others in Iran, when they heard those words, said,

'This is divine magnificence; it does not derive from self-delusion or folly. He speaks no word but what is true and we ought to rejoice at the truth. Now, as for his proposal about fierce lions and the throne and the royal crown to be placed between them, if the male lions tear him to pieces, the just Lord does not demand his blood from us. Since he himself spoke of this plan and proposed it we shall be able to rejoice at his death. If, on the other hand, he carries off the crown, he will surpass Faridun with his *Farr*. We shall not ask for any other monarch and we shall have justified his words; nothing more than that.'

[After swearing a solemn oath before the chieftains and priests that he would rule justly, Bahrām is promised the kingship on condition that he submits to the ordeal he has proposed. With his bull-headed mace he slays both the lions, seats himself on the ivory throne and crowns himself king of Iran with the royal diadem. Thereafter the usurper Khosrow swears allegiance to him and all goes well during his reign of sixty-three years. Ferdowsi's narrative is little more than a selection of popular tales describing Bahrām Gur's amorous adventures and his prowess as a huntsman. In the tale here selected as representative of the rest there is a touch of grim humour not often encountered in this generally solemn work.]

(vi) *Bahrām Gur's priest destroys and rebuilds a village*

At early dawn one day Bahrām went out hunting on the plain accompanied by his retinue. On his right was his minister Hormaz and on his left his keen-witted priest. They told him stories, speaking much of Jamshid and Faridun. Ahead of them ran hounds and panthers and over the plain king-falcons and hawks were being sent up all day long, yet when the blazing sun had reached the zenith not a trace of wild ass or gazelle had been seen. Wearied by the fiercely blazing sun, the king despondently turned back from the hunting ground. There came into view ahead of them a verdant hamlet full of houses, men and animals, and out of it on to the road there emerged a numerous crowd to view the spectacle of the cavalcade. The monarch himself was in ill-humour, being heated and desirous to rest himself in the place. But no one there saluted him. It was as though the earth had petrified those asses, until the king became enraged at the stu-pidity of the people there, and he cast no kindly glance upon them. To his priest the Shah said,

'Let this ill-starred place become the resort of wild beasts and may the water in its stream turn to pitch.'

The priest understood what the king's words implied and turning away from the road he addressed the inhabitants, to whom he said,

'This flourishing town, full of fruits and men and animals, has greatly pleased Shah Bahrām, and he desires to establish a new order here. Every one of you is promoted to be an elder so that this fine village may be turned into a city. In this place even women and children are now elders, needing to obey no one's command; here no one is a hireling and no one master, but all walk the same path. Women, men and children—all are elevated to the headship; each single one is chieftain of the town.'

A great shout arose in that rich town out of joy that now all equally were elders. Women and men, servants and hirelings thereafter declared their opinions as heads of the town, and since the youths of the place had lost their awe of the elders they at once cut off their heads. Every man attacked his fellow and blood flowed in every direction. The inhabitants felt that Resurrection Day had arrived in that rural spot and took flight from it. Only a few ancients were left, helpless and crippled; for now all means of cultivation, work and carriage had vanished. The aspect of the whole town declined into one of desolation, the trees having withered because there was no water in the stream. The plain became a desert and the houses fell into ruin, now that all the people and animals had fled away.

A year passed and springtime arrived. Again the Shah went hunting in that direction and came to that place which had once been flourishing and happy. Now when he looked he saw it no longer existed in its old form; the trees were withered and the houses in ruins, in the whole region there was neither man nor beast. The king's cheeks paled at the sight; he felt the fear of God and was tormented with sorrow. He said to the priest,

'How sad that so pleasant a village should have become a desert. Quickly set about restoring it; spend money so that they shall no further suffer misery.'

The counsellor left the king's presence and swiftly moved about the desolate place, hastening from one empty house to another. At last he came upon an old man sitting idle. He dismounted from his horse, greeted him, made room for him by his side and said,

'My elderly master, who destroyed this once flourishing place?'

The man replied,

'One day our sovereign passed through this district of ours and a foolish priest came with him, one of those great ones whose deeds bear no fruit. He told us that we were all nobles and that we were not to pay reverence to anyone; we were all headmen in the town, even women and men were all superior to the elders. As soon as he said it the whole of the town was in turmoil, filled with looting and killing and beating. May God requite him in due measure! May grief and pain and hardship ever renew themselves upon him! The affairs of this place go from bad to worse; we are an object over which to shed tears.'

At the old man's story the good man [the priest] was grieved. He asked who the village headman was and was asked in reply who could be headman in a place where grass-seed was the only fruit. The good man said to him,

'You be the elder. In every task you are to be the diadem on the head. Demand money from the monarch's treasury as well as seed and oxen and asses and food. Drag anyone you find idle into the town; all are subject to you and you are the chief. Call no curses down on that priest; it was not of his own desire that he uttered

those words. If you require aid from the royal treasures I will
send it to you. Demand as much as you need.'

[The newly-appointed headman rejoiced and by the following
spring the village was enjoying greater prosperity than it had ever
had before. The moral of the story is then given to the king;
namely, that when two conflicting ideas come into a man's mind
or when a town has two chiefs, confusion and ruin are the result.]

(vii) *Bahrām Gur and the four sisters*

A week later the lord of the world went out to the chase accompanied by his priests and nobles, purposing to remain hunting
and drinking wine with his retinue for a whole month. The time
passed in the taking of great quantities of the game which roamed
both on the mountains and on the plain; and then the monarch
turned happily back to the town with his retinue. Night was falling and the whole world darkened as these noble men rode on
reciting to each other the adventures of the kings. Suddenly a fire
appeared burning in the distance, bright as the fire which the
Shah kindled at the feast of Bahman [January]. As the king of
kings gazed at the illumination there came into view at one side
a prosperous village, in front of which he saw a mill with some
men seated here and there. Beyond the fire were girls, who had
made themselves a festal place apart. Each wore a wreath of roses
on her head, and all about were seated musicians who sang odes
of the battles of Khosrow, each in turn reciting a new one. The
faces of these girls were beautiful and they wore curling tresses;
all were elegant of speech and they were redolent of musk. Close
to the door of the mill and somewhat in front of it they had
formed in line on the grass for their minstrelsy; each holding a
nosegay of flowers and being in part bemused with happiness and
wine. At one point a shout went up from the festal spot, and
someone then called forth,

'This is to the health of Bahrām the Shah, who has the *Farr* and
fine shoulders, a handsome face and great affection. It is through
him that the revolving firmament continues its existence. You
would say that wine trickles from his cheeks and the perfume
of musk is exhaled from his tresses. All he will hunt is the lion
and the onager, whence men call him Bahrām Gur ["The Wild
Ass"].'

When the emperor heard their voices he turned his rein and

went in their direction, and, as he came near to the girls and looked about him he saw that the plain from end to end was peopled with lovely maidens, by whom the path of his approach was barred. He therefore ordered that the cupbearers should bring wine from the provision made for the journey and let the people there drink it. A crystal cup was brought and placed in Bahrām's hands while from among the maidens there, all bearing noble names, four presented themselves to him. One was Moshk-nāz [Pure Musk], the second was Meshkanak [Partridge], the third was Nāzyāb [The Fondled] and the fourth Susanak [Lily]. They came forward to the Shah holding each other's hands, their faces like the spring and their stature tall. They recited odes in honour of Bahrām the king of kings, the wise and triumphant. Turmoil possessed his heart because of them and he asked,

'Rosy-cheeked maidens, who are you and what do you celebrate with those fires?'

One of them replied to him,

'Our father is an old miller who is now hunting game on these mountain slopes. He is on his way home, for the night is getting dark and his eyes will be puzzled by the gloom.'

At that moment the miller with a company came down from hunting on the mountain and, catching sight of Bahrām, he rubbed his face in the dust and then came forward in awe and reverence. The Shah commanded that a golden goblet be offered to the old man just returned from his journey and said to him,

'These four sunny-cheeked maids, why do you keep them? The time is ripe for them to have husbands.'

The old man called down blessings on him and said,

'There are no mates to be had for these girls. They have reached their present age as virgins, and they are pure in their virginity. Of possessions they have nought, neither gold, silver nor anything of any good at all.'

Thereupon Bahrām said to him,

'Give all four of them to me and you will never more need to maintain your daughters.'

The old man retorted,

'Cavalier, do not insist on that which you have said, for I have neither raiment, nor estates, nor land, neither silver nor mansion, neither oxen nor asses.'

Bahrām answered,

'All that is agreeable to me; I have no need of possessions.'

To that the answer came,

'All four are yours to be wives or servants or the dust of your inner apartments. Your eye sees them with all their defects and merits. Do you approve what it has seen?'

Bahrām answered,

'I accept all four of them from their excellent parent.'

Thus saying he rose to his feet. Out in the open the neighing of led horses was to be heard and he ordered the attendants in his retinue to take the lovely maidens to the royal women's quarters. The escort filed out of the plain and all night long troops were crossing it. Meanwhile the miller remained in a state of bewilderment and in the darkness of the night he fell into thought. He said to his wife,

'That distinguished man, handsome as the moon, with his fine presence and majestic bearing, how was it that he came to this place in the night?'

His wife answered,

'He saw the fire in the distance and hearing the sound of the girls' music he seated himself amongst them bringing wine and minstrels.'

Again the miller said to her,

'Wife, give me your opinion. Will this matter end in good or in evil?'

She replied,

'This is of divine ordering. When the man saw them he asked nothing about their birth nor was there any thought of wealth in his mind. He was merely looking about in the world for a beautiful woman and he sought neither money nor a king's daughter. If the Buddhist priests in China saw anything like them the adoration given to the idols would soon cease.'

When night turned into day again the headman from the village came and said to the old man,

'My blessed champion, good fortune came to you in the darkness of the night. The green branches of that tree of yours have come to fruiting. In the darkness of last night Bahrām the Shah came from the plain where he had been hunting, and seeing the festivities and the fire he turned his rein and drew in to you. Now your daughters are his wives and are safely in his women's quarters. The king of kings is now your son-in-law; in every region hereafter men will speak of you. He has granted you this province and fine estate. Pine no more, for you can turn aside from all care and fear. We are all now your vassals; nay more, we are all your slaves.'

(viii) *Bahrām slays a dragon: his adventure with the gardener's wife*

For a long time the Shah lingered with his nobles, occupied with wine, goblets and minstrels. Spring arrived and the ground displayed itself a veritable paradise; the air planted tulips everywhere on the surface of the earth. The whole region was covered with game. In the channels the waters flowed as though they were wine and milk; onagers and gazelles roamed the mountain slopes and pastured in herds everywhere among the herbage. Someone said to Shah Bahrām Gur that the time for hunting the onager was being overlong delayed, whereupon he commanded that a thousand men be picked from amongst his mounted troops, that hunting panthers and hawks were to be got ready as well as kestrels and proud falcons. All were to journey to Turān in search of game and the chase was to be continued for a month.

Now the king set out for the land of Tur in pursuit of game and beheld the world full of colour and perfume. They cleared the land of onagers, wild sheep and gazelles and lingered for two days over their exploits, Bahrām ever with the wine-cup in his hand. On the third day, when the sun lit up his throne and the world became white, mountain and sea taking on the hue of ivory, the valorous king of kings set out once more to hunt. He espied a dragon having the appearance of a male lion, on its head a mane as long as the creature's own height and on its chest two breasts like a woman's. He affixed to his bow a cord and a poplar-wood arrow which he let fly at once at the dragon's chest. Another arrow he shot through the creature's head while the blood and venom came spurting from its chest. Alighting now from his horse he drew a dagger and slit the dragon's body from end to end. It had swallowed a young man who had been congealed in the blood and venom.

Bahrām wept bitterly over the dead man, but his eyes became obscured because of the venom. Bemused and staggering he went on his way, longing for sleep and water, and so continued until he reached an inhabited village. There on the plain he came to the gate of a house where a woman stood with a jar on her shoulder hiding her face from the king. He said to her,

'Will you give me a resting-place here, or must I continue onwards in suffering?'

She answered,

'Gallant knight, regard the house as your own.'

When he heard her reply he rode his horse into the garden and
the hostess summoned her husband, whom she told to bring
straw and to rub down the horse. If he had no comb, he was to
use a woollen saddle-cloth. She herself went into her private
apartment, and when she emerged she swept the house clean. She
spread out a reed mat on which she laid a cushion, all the while
calling down blessings on Bahrām. Then she went to the tank
and brought water, meanwhile quietly scolding her husband.

'This old fool,' she said, 'stands there immovable even though
he sees that there is someone in the house. This is not the work
for womenfolk, for I must wait on the warrior.'

Shah Bahrām now went away to wash his face, for he felt unwell after his combat with the dragon, and the woman brought
in a tray on which she had carefully set out chives and vinegar,
bread and sour milk. He ate a little and lay down groaning, covering his face with a silken kerchief. When he woke from his sleep
the woman said to her husband,

'You ugly fellow with your unwashed face, you have a lamb
to kill. This cavalier is a great man and must be of royal seed. He
has the chest of a warrior and the splendour of the moon; he
resembles no one so much as Bahrām Shah.'

The wretched husband replied to his wife,

'Why must you talk so much? You have nothing salted, nor
fuel, nor bread, and you never spin thread at night as other
women do. When you have killed the lamb and this cavalier has
eaten and departed, what profit will you have from this action?
Nothing but winter and cold and raging winds will come to you,
all together, and that without a doubt.'

Thus did her helpmeet speak. But the woman gave no ear, for
she was kindly and full of good sense. In the end, at the woman's
bidding the lamb was killed for the knight, and when it was
slaughtered she cooked a pot of wheaten meal, having made a fire
of half-burnt wood. Then she brought a tray for the royal guest
on which were laid eggs and water-cresses which she followed
with a roasted leg of lamb and the comestibles with which to
garnish it. When Bahrām had washed his hands after his food he
still remained sleepless and unwell so that when night came up

to meet the sun the woman brought him a jug of wine and some jujube fruits. The Shah said to her,

'Woman of few words, recite me some ancient story. While you are talking I shall drink the wine and chase the unhappiness out of my heart. I give you full liberty in telling your story and you may freely make complaint about this Shah of yours.'

'That is well,' said the woman of few words. 'He is the beginning and end of all things.'

Bahrām inquired,

'Only that, and nothing more? Do people see no justice or kind act from him?'

That woman of stout character said to him,

'Clear-minded man, there are many people and houses in this village and there is constant coming and going of horsemen, and the agents of the Shah's revenue are many. Let anyone call one of them a robber and the end of it will be trouble in abundance for him. The agent seeks after five or six pence and for them makes a man's life a misery to him. Or he gives a pure-bodied woman a vile name and then tries to avail himself of her modesty. Great harm is done, for the reason that the money taken does not come into the treasury. That is the trouble which comes to us from the lord of the world.'

The monarch fell into musing as he heard these words, and realized that because of his agents' deeds he was acquiring an evil name. The God-fearing king said to himself that a just ruler does not inspire fear. He determined that for a time he would control all rigorously, so that beneficence and justice could be distinguished from harshness. Tormented by his gloomy thoughts he felt unable to sleep and all night long his mind was occupied with the methods of strict government. When the sun rent its musk-perfumed veil and showed its face in the sky, the woman emerged from the house and said to her husband,

'Bring the cauldron and some fire from indoors; throw grain of all kinds into the water but without letting the sun see it. Now I will go and milk the cow. Do not neglect this matter of the cauldron.'

She brought the cow from where it had been pasturing, carried in a bundle of grass and set it down. Now she pulled the teats, uttering the words, 'In the name of God who has neither companion nor peer.' But she soon saw that her cow's udder was empty of milk, and so the heart of that young hostess became old. She said to her husband,

'Master, the mind of the king of the world has changed its purposes. The king has become a tyrant; his heart last night was secretly tormented.'

'For what reason do you say that,' he inquired. 'In what do you find an evil omen?'

'My dear husband,' she answered him. 'I do not say this without cause. The milk has dried in the teats, the musk in the pod is no longer perfumed. Fornication and hypocrisy will be openly practised; the gentle heart will become hard as granite. On the plain the wolf will eat men, and the wise man will flee before the fool. Eggs will addle under the hen when the tyrannous man becomes king.'

The monarch heard these words and quickly repented of his purposes. Now when once again the happy, chaste and pious woman touched her cow's udder, uttering the words 'In the name of God who produces milk from the hidden source', the milk poured out of her cow's teats. When the milk was boiling in the cauldron and the woman with her husband had completed their preparations she went over to her guest, the man following her with a tray. The king, having partaken of the milk, said to his worthy hostess,

'Take this whip to the gateway and hang it up in a place where men pass by. Look for a stout branch of a tree, where it will receive no damage from the wind; then see who comes in from the road.'

Quickly the master of the house ran out and hung the king's whip from the tree. For a time he watched it. Then, men without number appeared on the road and everyone who saw the whip called down blessings on Bahrām. The woman said,

'This man can be none other than the Shah; that face is fitted only for someone of high rank.'

[The pair ran to the Shah, begged mercy for their meagre hospitality and were rewarded by the man's being granted the province for his own.]

(ix) *The Khāqān of China invades Iran*

After a time the tidings came to India and Rum, to Turkestan and China and every populous land that Bahrām's heart was set only on amusement and that he disregarded all mankind. He posted neither sentinel nor watchman and in his land there was no warden of the frontiers. He was ever engaged in sport and he let the world go by, knowing nothing either of what was public or hidden. These circumstances came to the hearing of the ruler of China and he mustered an army of chosen troops from China and Khotan. He paid them and set out for Iran without any man sparing a thought for Bahrām.

Then from Rum, from India, from China and every populous land the rumours came to Iran that the Caesar had mustered an army and was bringing troops. Furthermore that armies had appeared from China and Khotan. All men that held leadership in Iran therefore, whether elders or young men bearing great names, came in a body to Bahrām Gur; they came filled with wrath and resentment and turbulence and they spoke many a harsh word to the king.

'Your brilliant fortune,' they said to him, 'has turned its back on you. The minds of those kings are intent on war, while your heart is fixed on sport and feasting. In your eyes the treasury and the army are things to be despised in the same way as the land of Iran, the throne and the crown.'

The monarch said to the priests, his counsellors,

'The Lord of the world is my ally, loftier in his knowledge than even the highest of you. With the majesty of a great king I guard Iran from the claws of the wolf; by my good fortune, my troops, my sword and my treasure I will avert this trouble and grief from the land.'

[He nevertheless clung to his frivolous ways of life and the Iranians were defeated. In the end, however, Bahrām was able to summon up sufficient strength to regain all that had been lost and also to make new conquests. Although he continued to remain addicted to women and the pleasures of the chase, he did attend to the affairs of the state. Near the end of his life he invited ten thousand gypsies from India so that even the poor could enjoy music and dancing with their wine.]

(x) *Bahrām Gur's life comes to an end*

So he consumed sixty-three years and no one was his equal. At the beginning of the new year his vizier came to him—namely that wise priest who was his scribe—to tell him that the royal treasuries were empty and that he had come to ask for his commands. Bahrām answered,

'Do nothing further, for we no longer need to continue our activities. Resign the world to Him that created it; it is through Him that this revolving wheel is made manifest. The wheel goes on, but God remains in his place as my guide and yours to what is good.'

That night he slept. Next morning at dawn an army without number came to the palace, and an assembly in like numbers gathered about it. There his son Yazdegerd approached him, and to him in the presence of the nobles the Shah gave the crown, the necklace and collar and the ivory throne. Now he resolved to devote himself to the worship of God, for he had surrendered the crown and vacated the throne and so he hastened away from the world's affairs. When the night darkened he laid himself down to sleep. Next morning, when the sun displayed its head from below, the heart of the Shah's counsellor was stricken with fear. The king of the world could no longer be roused.

[The part of the Shāh-nāma which now follows consists of a number of annalistic accounts of the reigns of the kings who followed Bahrām. There is little in them to hold the attention except a poignant description of a famine which occurred in the reign of Piruz, son of Yazdegerd.]

XXVIII

The Famine in the Reign of Piruz

In the second year [of the reign of Piruz] the air dried up and water in the channels became scarce as musk. So was it also in the third year and the fourth and because of the drought no man was left with sufficient food. The mouth of the atmosphere became dry as the dust and in the channels water was rare as theriac, until, because of the multitude of dying men and cattle, there was not room to set foot on the surface of the earth. When the king of kings of Iran beheld this portent he lifted all tax and levies from the world, and wheresoever he had a hidden granary in a town he gave away what it contained to small and great. Then from the royal court a mighty proclamation was issued, saying,

'Bearers of name and all holders of authority, distribute such grain as you possess and in return stuff your treasuries with golden dinars struck in the name of Piruz. Let any man who has corn in secret, or cows, or sheep pasturing at large, sell them at such rate as he wishes, because there are living beings deprived of all food.'

To every governor and independent ruler he sent letters at speed bidding them open all their granaries wide to anyone in the world who had need. If anyone should die, young or old, man or woman, through being unable to find bread, the Shah would spill the blood of the hoarder who held God's handiwork in contempt. Every house must be vacated and men were to come out on to the open plains and raise their hands aloft. To Heaven now there arose the great clamour of many voices in lament weeping in anguish, pain and distress. On mountain and plain, on open lands and in caves, men prayed to God to be merciful to them. For seven years no man, small or great, beheld any green herbage in the world; in the eighth year in the month of April clouds came as a blessing and pearls rained down on the thirsty land so that from the gardens once more issued the perfume of musk. The calyx of the rose held dew to overflowing and from the arch of heaven the rainbow shone out. For a time the land was delivered from the evil of the malevolent men who had beset it with their bows ready strung.

[When that peril was over, Piruz resumed the war against Turān but was routed in battle and slain, being afterwards avenged by the general of the young son who succeeded him on the throne. Internal quarrels and political rivalries impoverished the land, which was still further weakened by religious dissensions. In the troubled reign of Qobād, there appeared a certain Mazdak, who claimed to be a prophet bringing reforms into the old faith. He was naturally denounced as a heretic by the Zoroastrian hierarchy.]

XXIX

The Reign of Qobād

(i) Qobād adopts the faith of Mazdak

Now there appeared a man, Mazdak by name, who was eloquent, learned, endowed with good reason and the desire for success. He had profundity and scholarship and the valiant Qobād lent ear to him, so that he became the counsellor of the king of kings, warden of his armoury and also his treasurer. It had happened that because of drought food became scarce in the land, both for high and low. Clouds had disappeared from the sky and in Iran neither snow nor rain was seen. The great ones of the world at King Qobād's court spoke of nothing but water and bread until Mazdak told them that the Shah would point out to them a path for hope. He himself went to the king and said,

'Pious king, I would make certain requests of you, if you would vouchsafe me your reply.'

Qobād told him to speak on and enliven him with his words, and Mazdak then said,

'One man, being bitten by a serpent, is in danger of his soul's departing from his body; at the same time another man has an antidote. The stricken man, however, receives no advantage from the antidote. What is the punishment, say you, for the man who owns large quantities of the antidote?'

The monarch replied,

'The possessor of that theriac is a murderer; he must be slain in the gateway for the death of the man bitten by the serpent, as soon as the accuser can get him into his clutches.'

Mazdak arose on hearing this reply and came to the people who were calling out for help. To them he said,

'I have spoken to the Shah and made enquiry of him concerning every side of this matter. Be patient until tomorrow's dawn, when I will show you the path by which you may gain your just due.'

The people departed with apprehension in their minds and filled with anxiety, while from a distance Mazdak beheld these aggressive men and went running to the Shah, to whom he said,

'Yesterday I placed a certain case before you and you gave me the reply, thereby opening a closed door for me. Now if it be permitted I will put another case to you.'

'Speak on,' said the king, 'and do not keep your lips closed, since what you say is of profit to me.' Mazdak returned,

'Noble king, suppose you bind a man in strong fetters; in his helplessness he would surrender his life for a crust of bread. But food is withheld from him, so that he dies. What is the requital for someone having bread who leaves the fettered man in his misery? Let the king tell me whether that someone is wise and God-fearing.'

The king replied that such a man was a vile wretch whose life was forfeit for his not having done something to aid. At that reply Mazdak kissed the ground and left the Shah's presence to go to the palace gate, where he said to the assembly,

'Go to every place where grain is hidden and take your measure of it. If a price is demanded, pay it.'

He delivered over to be raided all there was to be had in the town, so that every one that came received some benefit. Hungrily they rushed in and plundered the grain both in the city's granary and in that of the Shah Qobād. The custodians saw what occurred and ran to the emperor to inform him that the royal granary had been plundered and that Mazdak was deserving of the blame. Qobād summoned that eloquent man, whom he accused of plundering the granary.

[Mazdak's excuse was that he had laid his case in the form of parables before the king, who had indicated what action should be taken.]

Qobād was made unhappy at the speech of Mazdak and at his words; although they were equitable, his mind went sharply to work. He questioned the other further and received his replies, observing that the man's heart and soul overflowed with argument on such topics as the prophets had discussed as well as those which veracious priests and princes had dealt with. The king was convinced by Mazdak's eloquence and a great multitude gathered about him, many a one being led astray into irreligion. He told them that an empty-handed fellow was the equal of any rich man, that no one person should claim superiority over another, since the rich were the warp and the poor the weft. In the matter of possessions, he said, the world must be made equitable; it was unlawful and an evil thing for the rich to have excess. Women, houses and material goods were all to be equitably distributed; the empty-handed were one with the rich. He proposed to bring this about by means of his pure religion, in which the heights would be clearly distinguished from the depths. If anyone persisted in any faith but that, God's curse would lie on his path.

All the poor, young and old, became one with him. He took from one and gave to the other, and all reasonable men were stunned. When he had heard all, Qobād attached himself to the faith, believing that the world would be made happy by what Mazdak said. He seated him joyfully at his right hand, although his court did not know who the new counsellor was. His religion now flourished throughout the world and no man dared incur his wrath. The rich abandoned all thought of felicity and surrendered their possessions to the poor.

Then one day Mazdak told the King that many grandees were resisting his religion, and that above all Kasrā, the heir apparent, refused to accept it. He was confronted and asked to sign a declaration to yield and to cease from his wayward path. Mazdak proclaimed before Kasrā,

'There are five things which turn wise men from the truth. They are envy, anger, hatred, and needs which are usually followed by greed. If you overcome these five Divs, the path of the Lord of the universe will emerge clearly before you. The incitements to these five are worldly possessions and women. It is because of this that the Good Religion [Zoroaster's Faith] has waned in the world. If you wish to avert harm from the Good Religion, women and possessions must be shared in common.'

(ii) *Kasrā hangs Mazdak on the gallows*

[Kasrā demanded five months' respite before he decided, declaring that in the sixth month he would refute all Mazdak's claims and arguments. In the meantime he gathered his advisers together from all parts of Iran, heard what they had to say and in due course appeared before the Shah.]

'The time has now arrived,' he said, 'when I can pursue my questioning of "The Good Faith". If the truth lies with Mazdak and consequently the religion of Zoroaster has failed, then I will accept his pure faith and give his laws control over my own life. If the practice followed by Faridun was wrong, then Zand and Avesta are no longer needed in the world. Instead of them there will come the words of Mazdak, and no guide is needed in the world but him. Should he however have uttered falsehood, his aim not being how to find the path to God, then you must turn inexorably away from his practice and beliefs and banish his unhappy religion from you. Surrender him to me, together with all who adhere to his faith; let neither pith nor skin abide for any of them.'

He called to witness [the Fire Temples] of Rāzmehr, Kharrād, Farā'in, Bandui and Behzād, and thence departed to his own palace in order to consider how he might best accomplish what he had truly sworn. When Sol showed his crown at night's departure and the world became white as ivory, the emperor's eloquent son rode forth with his counsellors and nobles and came to a halt in front of the royal palace. All there were ready to hear argument and eager for the truth. The Chief Priest came forward to the king and opened his speech in the presence of the assembly there. Addressing himself to Mazdak he said,

'Seeker after knowledge, you have created in the world a new religion making women and possessions common to all. How shall a son know who his father is, and how shall a father recognize his son? When men are all alike in the world, subjects not being distinguished from rulers, who will choose to be a subject and how will it be possible to create a ruler? Who will be servant to me and you, and how will the good be divided from the wicked amongst mankind? When a man dies, who will inherit his abode and his goods, when the Shah and his labourer stand on equal footing? The world will be laid waste by this creed. Such evil should not issue from Iran. All will be masters and none will be hirelings; when the treasure is held by all, who will be treasurer? None of those who have brought religions into the world ever spoke like you; you kept your insanity secret. You will lead mankind to Hell, since you do not regard evil deeds as being evil.'

Qobād on hearing the Chief Priest's utterance was aroused and gave approval to all he had said. Kasrā also spoke on his part and the heart of the misbeliever was filled with perturbation. The whole assembly now gave tongue, crying out,

'Let not Mazdak stand by the king's side! He destroys God's religion! Let him not remain at this noble court!'

The monarch renounced that faith, and his head was filled with repentance for what he had done. He handed Mazdak over to Kasrā, together with all who had adhered to that religion and practice.

Kasrā owned an estate with high walls. He ordered holes to be dug there and had the followers of Mazdak implanted, heads in the ground and feet upwards. Then to Mazdak Kasrā said,

'Go to that magnificent garden and see how the seed that you planted in this world has borne fruit. You shall see trees that no one has ever seen or heard of before.'

Mazdak went and opened the garden gate. As he saw what was within he uttered a cry and fell unconscious. Then Kasrā ordered a tall gallows to be erected and strung the unfortunate man up alive, later killing him with a shower of arrows. (If you are wise, do not follow the path of Mazdak.)

XXX

The Reign of Kasrā Nushirvān

(i) Kasrā's land reforms

[Kasrā succeeded his father with the title of Nushin Ravān or
Nushirvān ('Happy Soul'). Some years after his accession he re-
formed the revenue system of Iran.]

The kings who had preceded Kasrā, whether their estate was
greater or less than his, had demanded their share of what was
sown and harvested and none of their subjects escaped untaxed; a
third or a fourth part having been for the king. But when Qobād
came to the throne one-tenth became the rule. He had considered
making it even less than one-tenth, endeavouring to make the
lesser man equal to the greater, but fate granted him no respite to
achieve his aim. When Kasrā in his turn ascended the ivory throne,
he magnanimously remitted the tax of one-tenth.

Then the expert and the warriors, the nobles and keen-minded
priests, assembled together with the princes to distribute the land
after measuring it with the cord. They levied an impost of one
dirham on all, being on their guard that no villager should be reduced to distress. He that had no seed or cattle when the time came
for cultivation was provided with them from the king's treasuries
and no ground was left to lie without being tilled. On such ground
as went untilled there once was no word of tax; on that point the
ancient rules were abrogated. The levy for a fruit-bearing vine
was set now at six dirhams and the same sum was paid for date
groves. From olive and walnut trees and those which in the
autumn had branches laden with fruit, a dirham came into the
treasury for each ten trees, but the levy was not exacted until
the next year. Those fresh vegetables that come to market in June
were no longer taxed. From men that had money and were not
farmers, who did not suffer the cares and toil of sowing and
reaping, the tax-gatherer took each year according to their means,
from ten dirhams down to four. The head of the household was
not oppressed and the money was taken in three instalments each
year. One-third of this revenue the tax-gatherer carried to the
royal register every four months; and the scribes and royal

servitors in the register were not innumerable. The Shah covered the face of the earth with his justice; wherever land was deserted he brought it into cultivation. Any man, small or great, could lie down to sleep in the open, and to the water-hole there came the ewe as well as the wolf.

(ii) *Kasrā's Christian wife bears him a son*

[Kasrā built up a great army which he employed not only to keep unruly provinces in order but to assist his allies and make numerous raids on his hostile neighbours, a good many of whose strongholds he was able to capture. On one of his expeditions abroad he acquired a Christian wife who bore him a son, afterwards named Nushzād. The boy was reared and educated to the splendour of a princely career.]

He learned about Hell and the way to Paradise, about the Almighty and the Messiah and about the religion of Zoroaster. But in his sight Zand and Avesta were untrue and he laved his cheeks in the water of the Messiah. By thus forsaking his father's religion for that of his mother he left the whole world amazed and his father was made so unhappy that for him the rose produced nothing but thorns. The doors of the prince's abode were closed and made into a prison for him. Thereafter Gonde Shāpur was made his residence, away from Iran and his father.

Now when that Shah returned from Rum he complained of the disturbances and hardships of the journey. So great was his weakness after it that he despaired of his body and because of illness gave no further audience. A rumour was brought to Nushzād that the monarch's *Farr* had become tarnished, that the alert-minded Kasrā had died, and that destiny had entrusted the realm to another. Nushzād ['Happily Born'] rejoiced at his father's death (May he never enjoy the name of happiness!).

[He came back to the capital only to find that the rumour was untrue. He nevertheless reopened his palace and gathered the Christians of the land about him, while his mother helped him with money. After various struggles he was killed in battle.

A new figure, afterwards to become famous in the Iranian saga, is now introduced by the poet.]

XXXI

Bozorgmehr[1] the Wise Vazir

(i) Kasrā has a dream and Bozorgmehr comes to the palace

Now in my words about Bozorgmehr I will reveal a fresh face. Beware lest you look on dreams as being of no significance; realize that they are a part of prophecy, especially when it is an emperor who beholds them and his bright spirit encounters them.

One night Shah [Kasrā] Nushirvān lay asleep, but his soul was alert, wise and clairvoyant. He beheld in his sleep how in front of his throne there sprang up a majestic tree, which rejoiced the king's heart so greatly that he called for wine and music and minstrels. But seated with him on that couch of ease and luxury was a sharp-tusked boar. There it sat and indulged in wine-bibbing, demanding to drink from Nushirvān's own cup. And when Sol put up his head in the Sign of Taurus there was heard on all sides the melodious lament of the lark. The king sat upon the throne moodily, his heart full of presentiment because of the dream.

An interpreter of dreams was summoned and the warriors were given places at an audience, at which the Shah told his counsellors and guides what he had seen in his vision. The interpreter of dreams made no response, for he had no recollection of any similar story.

[The Shah sent about the land for other interpreters, offering rich rewards for anyone who could explain the significance of the vision. One of the messengers came to Marv.]

Arriving at Marv he sought about and beheld a priest with the Zand and Avesta, teaching boys the book in harsh and angry tones. There was an elder boy who sat by the master, his mind full of zeal for the Zand and Avesta. They called him Bozorgmehr and in his eagerness he had put his face close down on to the copy-book. The envoy turned his rein and left the road and approached the teacher to ask about the matter of the Shah's dream. The cleric replied that such was not his subject and that of all science he was

---

[1] Sometimes found in the Arabicized form of Buzarjomehr.

familiar only with the Zand which he taught to the boys. Outside of that he could speak of no subject. When Bozorgmehr heard what the envoy was saying, he listened and raised his face. To the master he said,

'This is game for me. Interpreting dreams is my subject.'

The man of the Avesta shouted out to him,

'Have you corrected your copybook? You boast wildly. Have you ever interpreted a dream?'

At that the envoy said,

'My learned man, perhaps he knows something. Do not attempt to subdue him. It may be that destiny has illumined this boy and that he has learned from fortune rather than from you.'

Angry at Bozorgmehr, the master told him to tell the envoy what he had in mind. He answered that he would speak to nobody save the Shah, and only then if he gave him a place before the throne.

[The envoy provided all that was necessary for the journey to the capital. On the way, one night, as the boy lay resting, a serpent approached his head but drew away without touching him, a fact which greatly impressed the courtier. On arrival at the court he related how he had found the boy and the adventure with the serpent.]

The emperor Kasrā summoned him into his presence and for long discoursed on his dream. The boy in reply said,

'In your house, among the women of your seraglio, there is a young man who goes about garbed as a woman. Clear the place of all strangers so that no one may give a hint of what I am about to advise.'

[The king's eunuchs were commanded to parade the occupants of the seraglio naked before him and a youth was discovered who was claimed by one of them to be her brother. As a warning to others who might be tempted to offend similarly, the two were hanged within the precincts of the seraglio. Bozorgmehr was taken into the Shah's favour and was soon set on the course towards high rank.]

Each day his fortunes improved and the king's heart rejoiced in him greatly, for his heart was filled with equity and his mind and brain were well furnished with knowledge. At his court he kept well-read men, men equipped with every science, so that there were always seventy men of eloquent speech at the palace, where

they slept and ate. When the Shah was at liberty from his occupations of dispensing justice, giving largesse, wine-drinking or
waging war he was constantly demanding fresh discourses from
each cleric there, thus furnishing his mind with knowledge.

At that time Bozorgmehr was still young, of good voice, clever
and handsome, and from those clerics of fame, familiar with the
stars and otherwise learned, he acquired wisdom in such degree as
to surpass them all. High above all those sages he could raise his
head; none was his equal for knowing the secrets of the stars and
he lagged behind nobody in the practice of physic. In administra-
tion, law and the provision of judicious counsel men's opinion
of him was everywhere good.

[In a series of seven festive sessions held at weekly intervals by
Kasrā Nushirvān, Bozorgmehr propounded in didactic form his
views on religion and his political philosophy. During his term of
office war broke out between China and the Hyātalis (Ephthalites).
Iran became involved and her troops were sent to assist the
Chinese. In the course of his duties Shah Nushirvān became
acquainted with the fact that the Khāqān, or ruler, of China had
a beautiful daughter and he sent an envoy to demand her in marriage if he could be assured that her mother was a princess and
not a slave-girl. The envoy arrived at the Khāqān's court and
delivered the Shah's letter to him.]

The Khāqān of China read the missive and laughed at the offer
made and at the demand that only the best should be chosen for
him. He gave the envoy the key of the seraglio and told him to
investigate who was present in those living-quarters. With him
went four servitors in whom the Khāqān placed his trust. After
they had opened the door of the apartment these attendants told
him specious tales, such as that the maiden whom he had seen as
he entered had never been gazed upon by star or sun or moon.
The seraglio was indeed a very paradise adorned, and it was filled
with maidens lovely as the moon and the sun and decked with
treasures of every kind.

Seated on thrones were five beautiful maidens with coronets on
their heads and precious things all about them. But the Khāqān's
daughter herself wore no diadem and she had neither necklace,
collar nor jewels of any kind. She covered her bosom with a single
garment and wore a cap of refined musk on her head. No embel-
lishment had she on her cheeks and no adornment but the
Creator's. She was a cypress topped by the moon, her new throne

reflecting the glory of her appearance. As he gazed on her the envoy knew that he had never before seen her like, and, being of perspicacious mind, he understood that the Khāqān and the princess were not acting with honesty. He said to the attendants, 'The Khāqān has an abundance of necklaces, crowns and thrones, yet I choose that one who is without a crown or an adornment, for she far surpasses all the rest. I came here with travail in order to make the best choice. I did not come for Chinese brocade.'

[On returning to the Khāqān's presence the envoy informed him what had occurred and he, after making the astrologers take the omens, consented to send his daughter to be Nushirvān's wife. Under this mighty Shah, guided by the good counsel of the sage Bozorgmehr, Iran for long enjoyed peace.]

(ii) *The Rāy [Rajah] of India sends the game of chess to Nushirvān*

[While the Shah was in ceremonious conclave one day,] he received information from his vigilant spies that an envoy had come from the ruler of India with elephants, parasols and Indian cavaliers. With him also were a thousand laden camels and he sought audience of the Shah. On hearing this the monarch sent a numerous body of troops to welcome the mighty king's envoy who, on coming into the presence of the Shah, lavished on him those compliments which are customary among the great and called down blessings on him. He brought as a gift a great number of pearls, parasols, elephants and earrings. The Indian parasols were adorned with gold and into their fabric was woven a variety of jewels. In the presence of the court he opened up the caskets bound on top of the camel-loads and set all down before the king. The loads themselves held an abundance of silver and gold, musk, amber and fresh aloes-wood, jacinths, diamonds, and Indian scimitars completely damascened. Kasrā inspected these articles over which the Rāy had taken such care, and sent them all to his treasure houses.

The envoy now presented a message on silk which the Rāy of India had sent to Nushirvān. Accompanying it was a chequer-board so carefully constructed and with such art that a treasure-house had been emptied for it. The message which the Indian brought from the Rāy was to this effect,

'May you live as long as the skies endure! Bid those who have been most engaged in the pursuit of science to place the chequer-board before you and let each man express his opinion as to how this subtle game is played. Let them identify each piece by name, declare how it must be moved and upon which square. They must be able to distinguish the foot-soldier [pawn], the elephant [bishop], and the rest of the army, such as the rook [castle] and the horse [knight], and the movements of the vizier [queen] and Shah [king]. If they discover how this subtle game is played, they will have surpassed all other sages and I will then gladly send to your court the impost and tribute which you exact. If, on the other hand, the council of notable men of Iran fail utterly in this science and prove themselves to be unequal with us in it, you will no longer be able to exact from this land and territory of ours any kind of tribute or impost. You, on the other hand, will submit to the payment of tribute; for science is superior to any wealth however noteworthy.'

Kasrā gave his ear and mind to what the speaker said, the game of chess was placed before him and for long he contemplated the pieces. On the board there were ivory pieces shaped in exquisite forms, while some were of teakwood. The king questioned the envoy about them and about the finely constructed board and was told in reply that the rules and movements of the game were those of warfare, and that he would see, when he discovered the method of playing this game, that the tactics, strategy and laws were those common on the battlefield. At that the king said that he required a week's delay after which, on the eighth day, he would be able serenely to play the game.

The warriors and the priests who were his counsellors flocked to the king's court, where the chequer-board was set out before them. Each man studied it intensely, casting about to contrive a solution and playing one against another in every kind of way. Sometimes one of them made a statement and asked a question while the remainder listened, but none discovered the rules of the game. They departed at last, their faces covered in frowns, and when Bozorgmehr came to the king he found him in a grave and disappointed mood. The beginning was toilsome, but he foresaw the end.

[For a day and a night he studied the game; then the Shah summoned the Rāy's envoy, who repeated the message given him by his master. It was then, in the presence of the envoy and all the

Shah's nobles and counsellors, that Bozorgmehr provided an exposition of the game. He said,]

'The sage has invented a battlefield, in the midst of which the king takes up his station. To left and right of him the army is disposed, the foot-soldiers occupying the rank in front. At the king's side stands his sagacious counsellor advising him on the strategy to be carried out during the battle. In two directions the elephants are posted with their faces turned towards where the conflict is. Beyond them are stationed the war-horses, on which are mounted two resourceful riders, and fighting alongside them on either hand to left and right are the turrets ready for the fray.'

As Bozorgmehr set the two armies in motion the assembly was left in a state of amazement, while the Indian envoy was deeply mortified at the success of this man over whom fortune so keenly watched. Wonder lingered in the heart of that man of wizardry and he set his mind to thinking in the following manner,

'This man has never seen a chequer-board nor ever heard of it from Hindu experts. How did he hit on the idea contained in it? No one in the world can hold this man's position.'

[As a rival to the game of chess, Bozorgmehr invented the military game of *Nard*, or backgammon. This was sent to the Rāy of India together with two thousand loads of treasure as a gift in return for the chess, with the proviso that if the Brahmins failed to discover how the game was played the equivalent of the treasure should be sent back. The Brahmins were baffled and the Rāy sent the Shah a year's tribute.

There follows a long and fanciful story of the circumstances in which the game of chess came to be invented. A certain king of India named Jamhur died, leaving a wife and young son, Gow. In the king's place the people elected his brother Māy to the throne and he soon afterwards married his brother's widow. She bore to him a son named Talhand. Then Māy died and the doubly-widowed woman was placed on the throne to reign as queen. In course of time the two half-brothers disputed for the throne and Talhand was killed in battle. To explain how her son came to die, the game of chess, which represents a battle, was invented.]

When the sound of the drums came from the meydān, experienced men called for ebony-wood of which two of them constructed a four-square board. This represented a trench and a battlefield on to which armies had been marched. A hundred squares were marked out on the board for the manœuvring of the troops and the kings. There were two forces, of teak and ivory respectively, with two kings resplendent with *Farr* and crown. In addition there were to be seen foot-soldiers and cavaliers marshalled severally in two arrays of battle, and also horses and elephants, in addition to the king's counsellors and the champions to launch the horses against the hostile army. All these figures had been carved in order to represent a battle, one side moving impetuously and the other with deliberation.

The king adorned the heart of the army, having at hand an astute friend. On either side of the king was an elephant, which stirred up dust as blue as indigo. Beyond the elephants were stationed two camels, on which were mounted men of ready resource, and by the side of the camels were horses ridden by men who looked for where the conflict lay on the day of battle. Then again there were the occupants of the turrets, one on each flank, which went out from among the combatants on either side. Before and behind went the foot-soldiers, who were present to give help where danger threatened.

As the king passed on to the battlefield the counsellor accompanied him, not moving more than a single square from him in the conflict. The proud elephant moved three squares and could survey the whole battlefield from two leagues distance. The camels likewise moved three squares on the field, roaring and bubbling with rage. So also the horses moved three squares, though more rarely they moved one square. As for the turret which went out to seek battle, none could oppose it, but it attacked everywhere on the field. Each piece moved in its own area, none departing from it in any wise. If a player saw the king during the struggle he called out aloud, 'King, beware!' and the king then left his square, continuing to move until he was hemmed in. That occurred when every path was closed to the king by castle, horse, counsellor, or the rest of the army. The king, gazing about in all directions, saw the army encircling him, water and trenches blocking his path and troops to left and right before and behind. Exhausted by toil and thirst the king is rendered helpless; that is the decree which he receives from the revolving sky.

(iii) *How Borzūy brought the Kalīla o Demna from Hindustān*

See now what the felicitous Barzīn said when he was elucidating the career of Nushirvān—may his soul continue ever young! He used to call for men instructed in every science, with whom he would adorn his court: physicians, orators, warriors and interpreters of the dreams of notable men. Amongst this group there was a celebrated man of high rank who was the crown on every head. He was an eloquent physician, Borzuy by name, and although he had reached old age he continued to be an eager student, equipped with all the sciences, for each one of which he had a repute throughout the world. It happened one day, at the time when the king was giving audience, that he came in to the sovereign and said,

'Your Majesty, you are one who welcomes knowledge, who seeks after wisdom and is eager to learn. I have today with tranquil mind been reading in a book of the Hindus, in which it was written that on the mountains of India there grows a certain herb which glistens like Greek satin. It is gathered by persons familiar with it and by the application of science mingled into a compound. When sprinkled over a corpse, it is immediately restored to life. With your Majesty's leave I wish to undertake the difficult journey there and, using every science to guide me, I hope I may track down this marvellous thing. And it is fitting that a corpse should return to life, seeing that Nushirvān is lord of the world.'

[The Shah gave his permission, equipped Borzuy fully for the journey and handed over to him a number of valuable gifts, together with a letter for the Rāy of India, whom he requested to assist the physician in his search. On his arrival in Hindustan he was received with high honour and granted all facility for his task.]

When Borzuy turned his face towards the mountain, a company of physicians went with him. With science as his guide he traversed the mountains on foot, on his way gathering herbs both dry and fresh and examining many both withered and in full growth. All kinds of them, whether dry or fresh, were scattered on corpses, yet not one was restored to life by the herbs, and it seemed that their magic powers had evaporated. His heart was disturbed by the thought of the king's displeasure, of the anger of the nobles and anticipation of the travails of the road. Also he regretted those valuable gifts he had presented and he was wounded by the thought that the reports which he had heard were vain. Angrily he inquired why the uninstructed and flinty-minded author had written in his book a thing so false and full of wind, whose fruits were nought but travail and foul language. Turning to the sages present he said to them,

'My experienced and laudable friends, whom do you know who is wiser than yourselves, someone who can raise his head above the throng?'

With one voice they replied,

'There is an ancient sage here who surpasses us in years and wisdom and who in his science is superior to any of the great.'

They guided Borzuy to this man, whose mind was filled with contemplation and whose lips were ever ready for speech. Borzuy laid all his trials before him, speaking of the book which he had discovered and the words which he had heard from men expert in knowledge. When the ancient sage began to speak he discoursed of every branch of science.

'I too have found this thing in books,' he said, 'and have moved eagerly, led by the same hopes. When nothing came to light after all my travails, I had perforce to listen to a different interpretation. The herb is the scientist; science is the mountain, everlastingly out of reach of the multitude. The corpse is the man without knowledge, for the uninstructed man is everywhere lifeless. Through knowledge man becomes revivified. Happy is he who submits himself steadfastly to labour. In the king's treasury there is a book which the well-qualified call Kalila. When people become weary of their ignorance, the herb for them is Kalila, knowledge being the mountain. If you seek this book in the king's treasury you will find it, and it will be your guide to knowledge.'

Borzuy rejoiced to hear this and all his past toil appeared in his eyes as empty wind. He blessed the sage and departed for the king's court, and, traversing the road like fire, he arrived in the Rāy's presence and lavished compliments on him.

'May you occupy your throne as long as India exists!' he said. 'Rāy, you whose triumphs are widespread, there exists a certain book whose title in Hindu is Kalila. In your Majesty's treasury it is sealed as precious and it contains guidance mingled with discernment and wisdom. That herb is a metaphor for this Kalila, nought else. I beg that your Majesty, lord of India, may bid your treasurer consign the book to me, if you will not hold that to be irksome.'

The Rāy's spirit was rendered unhappy by this request and his body was agitated where he sat.

'Borzuy,' he said, 'no one has ever sought this of me, either recently or in times past. Yet were the emperor Nushirvān to demand my body and soul I would not withhold them from him, nor anything else I have nor any person noble or humble here. But read it in my presence here, lest some malevolent person hostile to me should claim that the book was written by a mortal Read, understand and investigate it from every point of view.'

Borzuy replied that he could do nothing other than the Rāy commanded. The royal treasurer brought the Kalila and Borzuy was left with the counsellors. Each chapter that he read of the book he committed to heart the same day, and he never read more of it than he could remember, waiting then till the following dawn. Whenever he had occasion to write a despatch to the Shah of the world he secretly included a chapter of the Kalila. With contented heart and sound body he continued there steeping his serene spirit in knowledge, persevering until he saw the reply to his despatches, which said,

'The sea of knowledge has reached us.'

When that came he left his abode and approaching the Rāy asked leave to return to his own country.

[On his return he was received by Nushirvān, who gave him the key of his treasure-house, asking him to take from it anything he wished. All that he took, however, was a suit of royal robes, modestly disclaiming any desire for more. But he had, he said, a certain ambition.]

'I have one request to make of your Majesty,' he said, 'so that some memento of me may endure in the world. It is that Bozorgmehr should transcribe this book and make patent the toil which Borzuy suffered over it. Let him name me in the first chapter, if it be your Majesty's command, so that after my death the travails I underwent shall not remain hidden from the learned of the world.'

'This is a large request,' said the Shah, 'of the true measure of a man who seeks glory. Yet it accords with your labours, although your words are loftier than your station warrants.'

To Bozorgmehr the Shah then spoke, saying that this request should not be forgotten and that when the scribe turned his reed into a pen the chapter at the head of the book should commemorate Borzuy. The book was transcribed from the royal copy

—and in those days there was no script but Pahlavi. Treated with veneration it remained in the royal treasury and no person unqualified ever beheld it. So matters continued until people [in Iran] began to speak Arabic, before which time it was always read in Pahlavi.

When [the Caliph] Ma'mūn of the illumined spirit revived the world, transforming the sun and the day—for he had the heart of Mobeds and the mind of Kiyānis,[1] and his loins were girt up to acquire every science—the Kalila was translated from Pahlavi into Arabic, as you nowadays hear it. It remained in Arabic until the reign of Naṣr [the Sāmānid ruler of Khorāsān], who became king of the age and ruler of the world. His vizier was the powerful Bul Fazl, who was his treasurer and controlled his affairs, and he commanded that it should be rendered into the Persian Dari [i.e. New Persian as spoken at court], thus putting an end to controversy. Afterwards as he listened to the work he conceived the idea—wisdom being his guide, and his ambition, both expressed and concealed, that this should be his monument in the world—that translators should be seated before Rudaki [the blind poet laureate] and recite the whole work to him. That poet turned the scattered prose into ordered verse and strung those pearl-filled words in line.

> [At one point in his career Bozorgmehr is accused by his master of having stolen a valuable bracelet; though it had in fact fallen from his wrist while he was asleep, broken, and the jewels which composed it been swallowed by a bird. The distressed vizier made no answer to the accusation and was imprisoned and tortured, being later released and taken back into favour when he guessed the contents of a locked casket sent to him as a gift.
>
> After relating this trivial incident Ferdowsi inserts a list of aphorisms and wise decisions made by Nushirvān in answer to a variety of problems. These are followed by a report of a debate between the vizier and the priest concerning the phenomena of the universe and the principles of religion and morality.
>
> War breaks out anew, this time between the Shah and the Caesar, ending in the foreign king's agreeing to pay tribute to Iran. When the Shah reached the age of seventy-four years he nominated as his successor Hormazd, eldest of his six sons, and died a year later. Rather surprisingly Ferdowsi prefaces his record of the new Shah's evil career by a short lyrical passage addressed to an apple-tree in fruit.]

[1] An allusion to the alleged Persian sympathies of Ma'mūn.

The Reign of Hormazd

(i) Hormazd kills Izad Goshāsp

All continued as before until Hormazd was established in authority and all things were accomplished as he desired. He was then stirred to display a spirit of evil and he turned aside from the path of law and religion. One by one he destroyed innocent men whom his father had respected, people who had lived happily and been secure against the threat of harm. And that became the practice and the habit of the new king. Thus, there were three men who had been scribes to Nushirvān; one was an aged savant and the other two younger men. The eldest was named Izad Goshāsp. Of the others one was Borzmehr, an accomplished scribe brilliant and handsome, and the other, whose name was Māh Āzar, was gifted, clear-minded and prosperous in all his undertakings.

The heart of Hormazd was ever in a state of apprehension that these three men would some day become ingrate towards him. So on a certain day he stretched out his hand against Izad Goshāsp and for no sin had him fettered and cast into prison. At that the heart of the Chief Priest was stricken with anxiety and his cheeks became colourless with apprehension, for he was himself a lettered man of unspotted character and great wisdom, and his name was Zardohesht. A day passed, during which no visitor came to Izad Goshāsp and he had neither food nor covering nor anyone to comfort him in his grief. Then he sent the Chief Priest a message from the prison in which he [Izad Goshāsp] said,

'I am in the Shah's prison without anyone to visit me. My belly hungers, my pangs increase. Of your kindness send me something, and if I die get my shroud sewn and send me some linen.'

Grieved by this message the priest's heart lost all repose. In his reply he urged the prisoner not to lament over his bonds, if danger was not in fact threatening his life. As for himself, he mourned over the conduct of Hormazd and his cheeks became pallid in his anxiety. He said to himself that the news would now reach that ungenerous and ignoble king of the Chief Priest's

having sent something to the prisoner and that his life therefore
was not worth a moment's purchase. Harm would assuredly
befall him from that monarch, who would turn a grim face in
wrath towards him. Yet his affection for the scholar Izad Goshāsp
wrung his heart and made his cheeks pallid, so he bade his cook
carry some viands to the prison and he himself went there to visit
the prisoner.

So filled with terror did the gaoler become at sight of him that
all colour vanished from his cheeks. He dared not forbid him
entrance, although he feared the Shah who was irascible and
youthful. Weeping tears the old man dismounted and was admitted to the dungeon where Izad Goshāsp lay. They embraced
one another, overcome with woe, their eyes raining tears fast as
the clouds of Spring, and they discussed the king's ill-nature until
all was said. Then a tray was laid before Izad Goshāsp, they
observed the ritual silence and took the sacred *barsam* rod in their
hands. To the priest Izad Goshāsp said,

'When you depart from here, tell Hormazd that though he may
avert his head from what I say, let him give a thought to the
labours I undertook for his father and the reverence I paid him
and how I nurtured him himself in my bosom. For all those
labours my only reward is to be fettered, with the fear of torment
to follow. On the Day of Reckoning I will display to God a sinless
heart filled with the grief caused me by the king.'

When the priest departed for home a spy who had heard all
went at full speed and repeated this to Hormazd, whose soul
linked itself with evil. Savagely he turned against Izad Goshāsp
and sent to the prison a man who slew him. He heard many reports meantime of what the priest had been saying but revealed
nothing of it to him, turning over in his mind ideas good and evil
as to how he might slay Zardohesht. At last he gave orders to his
cook that with the food which the priest was to eat he was to
mingle poison. When the priest at audience-time arrived to inquire what his royal master's orders were he said to him,

'Do not depart from here today, for we have found a new cook.'

When the priest was seated and the tray set before him, the
colour at once drained from his cheeks; he knew that it held his
fate and that the truth lay in what he suspected. He ate whatever
the cooks brought in to the king to the last morsel, but when the
poisoned bowl was presented the priest looked and gazed at it
closely, his clear mind now rid of all doubt that in this bowl pre-

sented to him the poison lay. Hormazd watched him, tightened his lips and stretched out his hand towards the bowl, as kings do when they are extending courtesy or when they wish to show kindness to their servants. Putting out his hand with dignity towards the bowl he took from it a piece of the marrow of a bone and said to the priest,

'I set aside this good and tasty morsel for you. Open your mouth and take this delicacy. In the future you will demand such food as being indispensable.'

'By your life and head,' replied the priest, 'may your head and diadem exist for everlasting, do not bid me eat such rich morsels as these! I have reached repletion; do not command me.'

'By Sun and Moon,' said Hormazd to him, 'by the purity of the soul of the world-possessing Shah, take this rich morsel from my fingers. Surely you would not humiliate me over this request?'

The priest answered,

'The Shah's command has come. I can have no further opinion or course of action.'

He ate, and from the tray departed in misery and torment, riding speedily to his own house. To no one did he speak of the poison but cast off his clothes and lay down, giving an order that a bezoary be brought either from his own ancient store of such things or from the city. But no antidote was a remedy against that venom and he complained bitterly concerning Hormazd. The king sent a trusty man to see how the priest was faring and whether the venom was taking effect on his body, or if his scheme had failed to bear fruit. As the priest's eye alighted on the messenger the tears trickled from his lashes on to his cheeks and he said,

'Go to Hormazd and tell him that his fortunes have begun to decline. I will take this cause before the Judge in the place to which we shall both go together. Let him sleep no longer in security against evil, for divine retribution is coming to him. Bid him farewell from me, that man of evil thoughts; evil will come upon him for the evil he has wrought.'

The trusty agent grieved at what he had heard but conveyed the words to the Emperor, who repented of what he had done and writhed at the priest's blunt words.

[After the removal from his path of possible rivals and of servants whom he regarded as opposed to his wishes, the king returned to the path of equity.]

(ii) *Hormazd returns to the path of justice*

Hormazd thereafter no longer lived as he had done, but fear thrust lances deep into his heart. Out of the year he spent three months at Estakhr [Persepolis] while the dark nights were brief, for the city there was cool and the air limpid; moreover it was not possible for anyone to pass close by there unobserved. For three months of the autumn he remained at Esfahān, where the air was good; also it was the residence of the great. In the winter his abode was at Ctesiphon, with his army, priests and counsellors, and in the Spring he was on the plains of Arvand [the Tigris].

In this fashion a period of time went by, his heart ever in a state of awe. Three watches of each night he spent in prayer and he neither shed blood nor committed injustice nor did his soul even contemplate evil. When the azure tent of night was hidden and the mountain of yellow coral [the sun] appeared, a herald announced in a loud voice,

'If any sown land is trampled down so that the cultivator is led into distress by the loss so incurred, or if a horse intrudes on any sown ground, or if anyone trespasses in a fruit-bearing orchard, the horse's tail and ears must be cut off and the thief's head must be drawn up on the gibbet.'

For months and years he roamed about the world and nothing either good or ill was hidden from him. In every region he acted with justice that brought him praise from the villagers. Now he had a son whom he held dear, one who could scarce be distinguished from the moon for his beauty. His father had named him Parviz, but he sometimes called him 'Khosrow the self-willed'. Once, from the stable a horse escaped which happened to be the mount of Prince Parviz. The horse being young made for some sown ground, with the horse-keeper in hot pursuit. The owner of the cultivated land complained bitterly to this man, asking whose horse it was and demanding that its tail and ears should be cut off. The horse-keeper replied that the animal belonged to Prince Parviz, who had little regard for underlings. But he then went to the Shah and reported what he had heard in the sown field. Hormazd said to him,

'Pay attention now! Cut off the horse's tail and ears and let a reckoning be taken of how much loss has been suffered by the cultivator. The amount must be claimed from Khosrow, whether it be one hundred or seven hundred. Pour the money out in treasury dirhams on to the field in the presence of the owner of the crop.'

When Parviz heard of the heavy retribution he invoked the nobles everywhere to request his father to forgive him the offence and not to cut off the black horse's tail and ears. But the monarch was incensed about it and dismissed all those experienced men with contempt. The horse-keeper ran in terror from the king to the ploughed field where the young stallion was and with a dagger severed its ears and tail, on the very field into which it had plunged its hoofs.

[Further examples are then enumerated of the Shah's stern methods of administering justice.]

(iii) *King Sāva leads an army against Hormazd*

When the years of Hormazd's reign had been completed there arose in every province rumours of enemies at hand. Along the road from Herāt there came marching Shah Sāva, with drums and elephants, stores and troops. If you wish to take the reckoning of his army, count a thousand times four hundred, while of war elephants there were twelve hundred. You would have said that there was no passage left on the earth. From the plain of Herāt to the bank of the Marv river the army was as tightly fitted in as warp and weft. To Hormazd the king wrote a letter saying,

'Call together your troops in every clime and repair the bridges and roads for this army of mine. Provide fodder, bearing in mind my swords, for I desire to pass through your realm. My troops lie at the river, they cover the mountains and the plain.'

The Emperor read the letter and blanched at that numberless army. And now also from the side of Rum the Caesar advanced and covered the land with his forces. Of these Rumis there were a hundred thousand warlike horsemen of renown. The Caesar took back at the edge of the sword all the towns which had once been seized by Nushirvān, at whose name the Caesar still trembled. Then along the Khazar road another army came which blackened the whole land and countryside. Leading them was a warrior of great experience accompanied by stores and a large personal escort. Force upon force from Armenia to the gates of Ardabil his troops were distributed. Furthermore, from the desert there advanced an army of spear-wielding cavaliers in numbers beyond compute having men like 'Abbās and 'Amr as their leaders, knights and warriors of newly-found pride.

By their ravages the whole country was laid waste, including the cultivated lands from which Hormazd received his revenues. As the armies advanced to the River Euphrates, no room was left for any cultivation. When the days of his prosperity darkened and news came to him of the state of his army, Hormazd paled at the reports of his spies. Now he regretted how he had slain his priests and the disappearance of the wise men from his court. No longer did he see those thoughtful counsellors, and in an agony of fear for himself his body writhed. He sent out envoys to summon the Iranians and filled his hall with them. Having seated them before him he disclosed to them the secret he held concealed and told those notables of Iran that armies were now advancing on their land in such numbers that no person in the world remembered the like. Those lords of the marches were downcast and became tormented with fears of every kind. The priest who was his vizier now spoke and said,

'If the Khazar army comes into battle our warriors will not be given any respite. We can parley with the Rumis and extirpate the Arabs, but the gravest threat to you comes from Shah Sāva and our prospects are darkest from his direction. Our danger will approach from the Khorāsān road, for he will destroy our troops and stores. When the Turk advances from the Oxus to make war we shall not have a moment of respite.'

[Troops, mounted and foot, to the number of a hundred thousand were mustered and these, after he had dealt with the other enemies, he proposed to despatch against Sāvah. Before doing so, however, in the presence of his council he consulted Mehrān an aged sage, who had a prescience of what was likely to happen and gave the name of a man he believed worthy to lead the Iranian army.]

A certain noble, bearer of a great name, was groom of the king's stables. He approached the Shah and said,

'The hint that the worthy sage gave to the proud nobles could refer to none but Bahrām Chubina, son of Goshasp, a proud knight who is able to quell any horse. You have granted him Barda and Ardabil and he has become a warden of the marches, entitled to drums and elephants.'

At once the Shah despatched a swift dromedary to Bahrām, bidding the messenger not to delay on the road even for time to scratch his head.

(iv) *Bahrām Chubina presents himself before Hormaҙd*

When dark night had cast off its black and musky veil and the sun once more displayed his countenance, the Lord of the Marches [Bahrām] came to the court and into the king's presence. The exalted nobles there made way for him and the sovereign called him forward, seating him on a throne higher than that of the men of note there present. He then asked him whether he was to make peace with King Sāva or to send an army against him. The warrior's reply to this was that there was no way of making peace with Sāva. Since Sāva was desirous of war, to ask for peace would be admission of defeat. It would mean that Sāva would become emboldened when he saw the Shah's horses in retreat. When Hormazd then asked if he was to delay or to set himself immediately in motion, the answer was that it would be a good omen if the enemy should commit some act of transgression which turned him aside from the path of rectitude.

The experienced men who had been with the Shah warned Bahrām, as with anguished hearts they departed, not to act over-rashly at the king's request, for King Sāva had so many troops with him that they blocked the way for ants and gnats. Who would command the troops if there was to be war? In reply Bahrām said that the king had appointed him to take command.

(v) *Hormaҙd allots the command to Bahrām*

As for the king of kings of Iran, he rejoiced at what had occurred, for he was now relieved of his anxiety about the enemy. He had made Bahrām commander of his army and the warrior's head touched the clouds. Every hero who sought for fame saluted Bahrām as commander-in-chief. That warrior presented himself in full array before the king and begged leave to summon the muster-master to make a reckoning. He wished to see which of the troops were ready for war and which of them held back when their names were called. The king told him in reply that he was commander and hence responsible for good or ill. Whereupon he proceeded to the Shah's parade ground and ordered the army to be drawn up. Out of the Iranians he picked out a force each man of which was a chief among horsemen, and the names thus inscribed reached the number of twelve thousand, all being cavaliers fully armed and possessed of horse armour. A force larger than that would be unwieldy, he said, and furthermore only men of forty should be enrolled.

As commander of this force Bahrām appointed one Yalān Sina, whose breast was ever filled with martial ardour. He used to go about in front of the army on the day of combat, turn his horse about, call out his own name and remind the warriors of the causes of the war. A second man he chose was the one named Izad Goshasp who would not deflect his horse's gallop from a raging fire. Him he commanded to have charge of the impedimenta and to keep the left wing in line with the right. At the rear of the army came Kondā Goshasp, who from horseback could seize lions by the tail. Bahrām addressed his men as follows,

'If you wish God to be on your side and make this dull market of yours brisk, you will refrain from cruelty and do little harm, never girding your loins for evil. If the trumpet sounds in the darkest night, you will immediately spring from your place and drive your chargers on so that the clamour re-echoes in the darkness. Take no thought for the health or rest of either man or horse on the day of battle.'

[When Bahrām presented himself before the Shah, he was asked why, knowing the strength of the Turks under Sāva, he had restricted his numbers to twelve thousand and instead of taking youthful warriors had picked on men forty years old. His answer was that when fortune was favourable it did not matter what allies one had, and in support of his argument he cited Rostam and other heroes of the past who had triumphed over far more powerful enemies than themselves.]

'As for the men forty years old, who you say will not be more eager for the fray than young ones, they have acquired experience and surpass the young in manly qualities. They remember the loyalty produced by bread and salt [i.e. hospitality] over which the skies have long revolved. They fear the slanderous tongue and have a care for their own honour and repute and therefore do not desert the battlefield. Furthermore, for the sake of his wife and children and kin, the spirit of the mature man is more steady. The young man looks for plunder and is liable to be led astray and if the time comes for deliberation he is impatient. He has neither wife nor children nor farm nor tilth and where goods are concerned he cannot distinguish what is of value from what is worthless. Being without experience he nevertheless does not acquire knowledge, and does not look towards the final end of an action. Once he is victorious in war, he makes merry, laughs and causes delay; but if there is no victory for him, the enemy sees nothing but his back.'

(vi) *Bahrām goes to war against Sāva*

The army marched off from the region of Ctesiphon. Led by a commander of the quality of Bahrām it was an army sagacious, warlike and brave, with a general proud as a male lion. When he had gone the Shah returned to his palace and in a confidential discussion with his chief priests he said,

'That man [Bahrām] is happy; he laughs on the day of battle. But what say you is likely to occur hereafter? It is a matter we must discuss.'

The priest replied,

'This Pahlavān, with his magnificent stature, ready speech and clear intelligence, can surely not be anything but happy and triumphant, making fertile what before was barren? What I fear is that he nevertheless might in the end turn against the king, who has been his patron. He displayed great boldness in his language and behaved like a lion in his conversation with your Majesty.'

To that Hormazd replied,

'Do not pollute the antidote with poison, you malevolent wretch. Let him gain the victory over King Sāva and I will deem it right for me to hand over the crown and the throne to him. Let things remain as they are, and may nothing occur but that he should become king, to the blessing of all.'

The priest blanched as he heard this speech from the Shah and bit his lip. For some time the monarch kept this conversation in mind and then sought out a confidential agent at his court whom he could employ to ascertain the truth of the matter. This man he sent to follow the Pahlavān [Bahrām] and return with the report of what he saw. While Bahrām, lance in hand, was marching out of Ctesiphon at the head of his troops, there came towards him from some distance away a seller of sheeps' heads. He had a good covered basket filled with them and several were left outside the cover. Strangely, the commander put spurs to his horse and picked up one of the heads on the point of his lance; then he rode on, cleared the lance and threw the head away. Continuing on his road he took a reading of the stars and interpreted the incident

of the head as foretelling that he would cut off the head of King
Sāva, which he would cast on to the roadway in front of his army
and bring confusion on all his troops.

Hormazd's envoy saw all this and took a horoscope in due
form which told him that this man of blessed augury would after
his labours secure the throne and then, having attained his
ambition, he would revolt from the Shah, who would find
difficulty in overthrowing him. On his return the man reported all
this to the Shah, who became mated with grief and anxiety, for
the words were more bitter to him than death. He withered; his
green leaf sered. At a gallop he despatched a young messenger
from his court bearing an order for the commander of the army
not to move from where he was encamped that night and to
return to him at dawn. Then, the message continued, the Shah
would have his chamber cleared of all others and give him all
necessary advices, for certain advantageous details had entered his
mind.

The messenger overtook the commander, to whom he reported
all he had been told. His reply was that an army was never recalled
once it had begun its march; to turn back now would be taken as
an ill omen, which would be nothing but an encouragement to the
enemy. He would come to the Shah, he said, when he had secured
the victory, after which the land and the troops would be covered
with glory.

[For the time being the Shah was placated and Bahrām led his
army forward against Sāva, king of the Turcomāns, with whom he
exchanged a long series of threatening and vituperative missives.
Meanwhile Hormazd also sent messages to Sāva, declaring that
the army which was advancing against him was not that of Iran but
merely an advance detachment. By this piece of treachery he meant
to persuade the Turcomān king to attack and kill Bahrām, whom he
had once again come to regard as a possible rival. Bahrām however
evaded the trap set for him and defeated and killed Sāva, whose
head he sent to Hormazd, accompanied by a proclamation of victory. Not long afterwards, on the pretext that Bahrām had behaved
dishonestly over some of the spoils, the king allied himself to the
Khāqān of China against the triumphant warrior.]

The sovereign wrote a letter to Bahrām to this effect,
'You maleficent demon, you no longer realize who you are,
holding yourself thus independent of the great. Do you see no
virtue in God? Are you seated on heaven's wheel? Does no

thought occur to you of my cares, my army and the treasures I have expended? You do not tread the path of other commanders; you raise your head to the heavens, turning aside from my behest and plotting schemes. Here now is a token of honour worthy of you, a thing of value suited to your exploits.'

When the Shah had attached his seal to this missive he ordered that a black box should be brought containing spindles, cotton and various other undignified articles such as hair shirts of blue and red, female pantaloons and a yellow veil. To convey this worthless robe of honour a messenger of suitably mean status was picked out.

(vii) *Bahrām dons the women's garments*

Bahrām, when he beheld the present which accompanied the letter, chose the path of self-control and silence.

'Is this my recompense?' he asked. 'Why is this attack which the Shah makes on me? Wickedness of this kind does not originate in the mind of the Shah; it must come from the mean suggestion of some enemy. The emperor is lord over his servants; if he subjects me to ignominy it is his right. Yet I did not imagine that such malevolent creatures could find admittance into the Shah's presence. Everyone has seen what I have accomplished and what I have suffered in the way of anxiety, toil and hardship. If the reward for all that is this insult, if indeed it proceeds from malevolent fate, then I will lay my complaint before God against this revolving sky which has thus patently cut off all favour from me.'

With the name of the Lord, Giver of all good, on his lips, Bahrām donned the red and yellow garments and placed before him the spindle-holder and other articles which the Shah had sent him. He then commanded all the princes and notables distinguished by the Shah to come to him from the camp. His gloomy soul while he waited for them was occupied with thought. When the nobles arrived, young and old, and saw their commander attired in that guise they were stunned at the spectacle and their minds were active with conjecture. Addressing his audience he said,

'This is the kind of robe of honour which the Shah has sent to me. The Shah is our sovereign and we are his vassals and our hearts are full of affection for him. What is your view, looking on this? What shall we say to the king of the world?'

As one man they loosed their tongues and said,

'If this is your worth in the eyes of the Shah, then his troops
are no more than the dogs at his court. What was it that the
ancient sage at Rayy said when he was cast into despair by
Ardashir? He said that if no regard was paid to all he had accomplished, then he had no further care for priest or royal throne.
Here is someone who cares nought for your welfare. How then
can you hope to obtain true honour from him?'

Bahrām answered,

'Do not speak in such terms. It is from the Shah that the army
derives honour. He is the giver and we are the people who receive.'

The retort which came from the Iranians was,

'We will no longer keep our loins girt. We neither desire him as
Shah in Iran nor Bahrām as Pahlavān of the army.'

With that they walked out of the commander's palace and out
on to the open plain.

(viii) *Bahrām foresees his fate*

Two weeks passed and then the commander went out into the
open country. Before him there appeared a thickly-timbered
forest, worthy setting for a happy wine-bibber, and there he
espied a wild ass grazing. It was better game than anyone could
have imagined, and very gently Bahrām rode up to it, without
even making his courser warm. Within the forest, before one
came to the hunting-ground itself, there was a narrow defile
through which the onager passed, coming out on to a wide plain,
part of which was desert, part garden-land and part soil left un-
cultivated. As Bahrām stood gazing across this plain he beheld in
the distance a fine castle, towards which he set his face, the wild
ass moving ahead of him. He rode on until he came to the front
of the castle and there handed over his reins to Izad Goshasp who
had been following him. With none to guide him and on foot
Bahrām entered the portico of the castle.

[For some time Izad Goshasp stayed holding the reins of the valuable steed, and then sent his comrade Yalān Sina in to discover
what had become of their general. He found him in a vast and
lofty apartment in attendance on a beautiful woman seated on a
throne. She told him that his presence there was inadmissible and
that his master would shortly follow him out. Meanwhile a feast
for them all was being prepared in a garden.]

When Bahrām emerged from that garden you would have thought that the tears raining from his eyes were of blood. His demeanour had changed, his speech and replies were different from what they had been before and you would have thought he carried his head aloft in the skies. At that juncture the male onager arrived once more and acted as guide to the commander, who drove his bay courser after it until they emerged from the forest. From the hunting-ground he came into the town but of what had occurred in the castle he uttered no word to his escort.

(ix) *Bahrām Chūbīna assumes regal garb*

[The next day Bahrām ordered that a throne was to be erected on which he seated himself, putting a sovereign's crown on his head. His retinue understood that before them was a bold and determined man eager to avenge the insult which had been laid upon him and to wrest the throne from Hormazd. His chief scribe, with a companion, deserted him and fled to inform the Shah of what was happening. They were pursued and the scribe was captured, but the other man, the astute Kharrād, son of Bazin, escaped and reached Hormazd's palace. There he told the king what he had seen.]

Not long afterwards there arrived from the Pahlavān a mounted man bringing a basket filled with swords that had their edges blunted. When the Shah saw them he commanded that they were all to be broken, rendered useless and flung back into the basket to be returned to Bahrām. Without a word being spoken the meaning of that message was patent. When Bahrām uncovered the basket and saw the long swords with their mutilated edges and all now broken in half, that man of contumacious mind began to consider. Summoning the Iranians he seated them about the basket and thus addressed them,

'Look on this gift of the Shah's and hold it no matter for contempt. He is declaring that this army of ours is useless, and the points of these swords give witness to what he says.'

This act of the Shah's filled the troops with apprehension as did the speech of the army commander. They said,

'One day the Shah's gift to us was a spindle and some coloured robes, and now come these broken swords. All this is something worse than blows and scorn. Even if Bahrām son of Goshasp rides his horse into the dust of the royal court, may Bahrām vanish marrow and skin, together with him from whom Bahrām springs!'

The commander heard their words and perceived that the hearts of the troops were turned against Hormazd. He said to his army, 'Remain on the alert with your minds awake. Kharrād son of Barzin has revealed all those things which we had kept hidden. Now look to your lives and swear an oath of loyalty to me. A detachment of you must be despatched along the road, for we are being observed by the enemy.'

This was what he said, but the true purpose he had in view was something different. Round about his army he set mounted men at intervals to prevent any letter from the Shah reaching the Iranians who might gird their loins to do battle against him, the commander. Some time passed and no man received a letter from the monarch.

[As part of his campaign to secure the throne, Bahrām had coins struck in the name of the Shah's son Khosrow Parviz, hoping by this device to enrage the Shah against the young prince and have him put to death, thus removing a strong rival from his path. But the plot went astray and Parviz was able to escape the danger threatening him. At the same time Hormazd sent an army against Bahrām, who routed it after its commander Āyin Goshasp had treacherously been slain.]

When the king learned of the fate of Āyin Goshasp, that famous warrior, he closed his gates in sorrow against the granting of audience and none ever saw him now with wine in his hand. All his tranquillity and desire for food and sleep departed and he was ever with tears in his eyes. At the gates men spoke of the Shah and of his having let down the curtain against the giving of audience. At such conduct the warriors were in amaze and each man drew his own conclusions. At last rumours began to spread over Ctesiphon and all lustre departed from the realm. The heads of the king's retainers were filled with grief and anger and they began to curse where once they had blessed; about the court the troops diminished in number and the world became a narrow place in the mind of the king. To his brothers Banduy and Gostaham report came that the royal throne had become tarnished and that the prisoners had all cast off their bonds. They therefore sent men to discover what truth there was in the rumours and which men of war were left at the king's gates.

In truth when men learned how destiny was working they revolted against the Shah's authority and went astray. They broke the prisons, raising such clamour that the very desert burst into turbulence and within the city the soldiery were left destitute and without sustenance. It was now that Banduy and Gostaham came forward clad in armour, with their own troops and equipment. Utterly washing shame from their eyes they advanced boldly on the palace and displayed themselves in the market-place before the troops, while some of their men entered the palace gate on horseback. Addressing his force Gostaham said,

'This cannot be reckoned a slight matter. If you will side with me, no further regard need be paid to the cause of the Shah. If you will prepare yourselves to exact vengeance for the great Iranians against whom Hormazd has turned despite their innocence, as he has done against a god-fearing prince deserving of the crown and the throne, then you, who stand by your beliefs and religion, will cease henceforth to acclaim him Shah. Set your hands to retaliation against him; let loose on him the waters of Iran which he has dammed up. We will be your leaders in this deed and set up a new Shah in his place, and, if you are not dilatory in your actions, we will surrender the land of Iran to you. As for ourselves, we will make some corner of the world our own and there make our refuge accompanied by our friends.'

At Gostaham's words the troops with one accord denounced their allegiance to the Shah, declaring that no man who stretched out his hand to slay his own son was worthy of the crown. Further emboldened by his speech they set fire to the royal gates, entered the palace and approached to where the Shah sat in majesty. From his head they removed the crown and cast him headlong from the throne. Then with hot irons they branded his eyes, so that he resembled a candle-wick that was black having once been bright, but they spared his life after carrying off all his treasure.

XXXIII

Khosrow Parviz comes to the Throne

(i) Khosrow meets Hormazd

With all speed Gostaham and Banduy sent off a mounted messenger with a spare horse to go to Āzar Goshasp and report at
night to Khosrow the events which had newly taken place in
Iran. He related what he had seen of the turmoil, whereat the
young king's cheeks grew pallid as fenugreek. He said,

'If there be anyone who from rashness or folly departs from the
path of wisdom, recking nought of the workings of the lofty
Wheel, that man's life shall be profitless. May my sustenance and
sleep turn to fire if this misfortune of which you tell me can
please me. When my father sought to shed my blood I could not
continue to make Iran my abode; yet I stand before him as a slave
ready to obey any word he says.'

When the report came to Baghdad that Khosrow came as a
claimant to the throne of greatness, the whole city rejoiced at the
news and the ambitious prince found satisfaction in their pleasure.
The city notables and all who possessed authority went forward
to welcome him; an ivory throne was set up on a dais, where they
placed on him a collar and a precious crown. Yet it was with pain
that Khosrow entered the town and went to his father with deep
sighs. At seeing him he wept and paid him due honour, remaining
with him for a long while. He said,

'You know that had I been there to support you no one would
have dared to prick your finger with a needle-point. Now consider what you would have me do. Sorrow has come to you and
a bleeding heart to me. I seek no crown nor do I desire an army;
for your Majesty I would cut off my head.'

Hormazd replied to him,

'Son of great wisdom, this period of distress will pass by for
me also, where he that caused me this pain will not long endure.
All will pass away from us, whether it be grievous or pleasurable.
I have three wishes to make of you and I will demand nothing
more. One is that at dawn each morning you will gladden my ears
with song. The second is that you will send me some proud

350

cavalier who has memories of wars long ago and will speak to me of battles and of his exploits in the chase; let him also be a veteran who can converse about kings. With him let him bring some written chronicle wherewith to divert my mind from pain and hardship. My third wish concerns your uncles. They are your vassals, not your equals. Let them no longer be able to gaze on the world with their eyes. Sate my wrath against them for this affliction.'

Khosrow replied to him,

'Perish anyone who does not grieve for your eyes! Yet with your clear mind reflect that Bahrām Chubina has become a Pahlavān and that on his side he has an immense army, both of cavalry and sword-wielding warriors. Once we stretch out our hand against Gostaham we shall find no resting-place in the world. As for the old and well-read men who can recite past events to your Majesty, cavaliers nurtured on war and acquainted with the customs of feasts, I will send a fresh one regularly to you. May you not grieve in the slightest over your sufferings.'

(ii) *Bahrām learns of Hormazd's blindness*

In time Bahrām learned of the fate which had befallen that notable monarch and knew that his son had ascended the throne. He therefore ordered his drums to be brought forth and his great banner displayed on the open plain. His impedimenta were got ready and his troops mounted and he made all preparations to wage war on Khosrow, who, being informed of what was afoot, began to suffer uneasiness at his foe's activities. He therefore despatched wideawake spies to discover whether the army was at one with Bahrām over the war and whether the campaign would be an extended one. These men moreover were to discover whether Bahrām marched in advance of the troops or in the midst of them, how he placed himself when giving audience and whether while on the road he indulged in hunting.

The spies departed from the gate but his retinue were left unaware of his action. The men went, saw, returned and came in to him in secret. They reported that Bahrām's troops were at one with him in all things, both the men of note and those of low rank. Whenever the army was on the march, he went in their midst, being sometimes on the right flank, sometimes on the left and at times also in the baggage train. He took all his men into his

confidence, never requiring to have strangers about him. He sat in
audience as kings do and went in pursuit of game with hunting
cheetahs. He followed no practice except that of kings and he was
continually reading the book of [Kalila and] Dimna.

(iii) *Bahrām wrangles with Khosrow*

[On hearing this report, Khosrow got his forces together and led
his army out of 'Baghdad'. Banduy and Gostaham were ordered
to arm and the king with his troops marched on as far as the source
of the Nahravān river. So the two armies, the one led by Khosrow
Parviz and the other by Bahrām, faced each other, with the river
between them. A long battle of argument and vituperation now
began over the question of which of the two had the greater right
to the throne of Iran. Bahrām said that Khosrow was no more
than a king of the Alān Turcomāns, therefore could not claim to
rule the Persians. In reply to that Khosrow, after praying to the
sun for victory, accused the other of being a miscreant appointed
by the Divs to be their king, whereat Bahrām retorted that
Khosrow had shamefully usurped the throne of Hormazd his
father. It was he, Bahrām, who should be on the throne, for had
not his ancestors the Ashkānids held royal powers at the time
when Bābak's daughter gave birth to Ardashir? And did not
Ardashir become king after slaying Ardavān? Since then five
hundred years had gone by, the Sāsānian power had declined,
and the day had come for him, Bahrām, to take possession of the
throne. Thereupon Khosrow said that none could hold the kingship but a member of the line of the Keyānids, and Bahrām could
not claim to be one. Who was now the master of this unstable
world? Bahrām retorted, 'I am, for I will extirpate the Keyānids.'
He continued,]

'The truth is, you man of vile race, that you are of the seed of
Sāsān. He was a shepherd and the son of shepherds. Did not
Bābak grant him the work of a shepherd?'
Khosrow's answer was,
'When Dārā died he was unable to leave the crown of greatness
to Sāsān. Fortune having failed him, of what value was birth? No
justice will come from unjust words.'
He smiled as he spoke, turned away from Bahrām and went
towards his own encampment. But there rode out one of three
brutal Turks, men of the Khāqān's force, ravening as wolves, who
had told Bahrām that on the day of battle they would, for the
glory that would accrue to them, bring the Shah's body alive or

dead to him in the presence of the whole army. That vile horseman who was wild, unrestrained and without reverence, rode
out grimly seeking combat, with a rope of sixty loops over his
arm. As he approached the Shah's ivory-hued charger, he took
aim at the precious crown, cast the writhing rope and caught the
crown in his noose. Gostaham however at that moment thrust his
sword at the rope so that no harm befell the king's head. Swiftly
the Turk put a string to his bow and loosed an arrow brighter
than the aether. At that Bahrām turned on the malevolent Turk
and said,

'May you have no abode but the dark earth! Who bade you
attack the Shah? Did you not see me standing [humbly] before
him?'

He returned to his camp with his spirit grieved and his body
melting in sorrow.

[Bahrām's sister Gordiya met him on the way and after hearing
what had passed rebuked him for his ambition and his ingratitude
towards Hormazd, to whom, she said, he owed many favours.
After an interval, hostilities were renewed. Bahrām attacked first
and Khosrow fled before him, taking refuge with his father
Hormazd at Ctesiphon.]

(iv) *Bahrām routs Khosrow*

When Khosrow beheld his father's face he blessed him and for
long stood in his presence. Addressing him he said,

'That Pahlavān, the horseman whom your Majesty yourself
chose out, is advancing like a king possessing a *Farr*, and he
brings a numerous army. I gave him all the counsel that occurred
to me, but it was of no avail with him. All his desires are for battle
and strife; may his name never live! A great battle was fought
unsuccessfully and many men were lacerated by fate. The army
deserted me; you might have said they did not see me except as
they passed me on the road. They nominated Bahrām to be king,
not being able to foresee the end from the beginning, and then he
brought up an army like a moving mountain as far as the bridge
of the Nahravān. Since the situation was hopeless, I fled, in order
not to be caught in the trap of destruction. I am now looking to
see where I gain or lose; it may be that the Arabs will come to
my assistance. If your Majesty will grant it, I will bring Arab
horsemen into play.'

To that Hormazd answered,

'There is no reason in that, for you now have no established footing. Your going there would be nothing but labour lost for they have no armour for their body nor any supplies. The Arabs will be of no aid to you, since they can hope neither for profit nor loss from you. And they will pay no regard to your lineage, but will hand you over to your enemies for money. In this affair God is your support and Fortune will laugh in harmony with you. If you desire to leave your land and home, then swiftly go from here to Rum and tell the Caesar what I in my hard-pressed condition seek from him as aid. In that place there are men and provisions, he is well equipped with weapons and troops. The descendants of Faridun [in that land] also are your kinsmen; when your affairs are in difficulties they will come to you.'

Khosrow heard the words and kissed the ground, calling down many blessings on Hormazd. He then said to Banduy, Garduy and Gostaham,

'We have become associated with grief and toil. Get yourselves ready and load on your baggage, for you must surrender the homeland of Iran to the enemy.'

As he spoke a cry came from the sentinel that black dust was rising from the road and that there was a shining emblem in the midst of the advancing troops. On hearing this Khosrow mounted his horse quickly as smoke and galloped out with an azure banner at his back. (It was a banner in the form of a dragon, which Bahrām Chubina had caused to be made for the battle of Nahravān.) Turning his shoulders round and facing backwards he saw Gostaham and Banduy. They were riding at the slowest pace and he called out to them hotly,

'You ignoble men, what has happened to you? You run from the enemy as if he were your kinsman. Why else is this slow pace of yours? Bahrām is almost upon you.'

Banduy replied,

'Prince, do not let your heart be troubled over Bahrām. He will not see our dust, for his black banner is far distant from here. What your friends are saying to each other is that there is no need for haste, for as soon as Chubina arrives in the Shah's palace he will hand over to Hormazd the crown and royal office, sitting as his counsellor by his side and casting his hook with good result into the sea. Together they will write a letter to the Caesar as coming from the Shah, saying that that base slave [yourself] has departed in flight from his land and home. Let him [they will say] find no peace in Rum, for as soon as his plans are ready all his guile and trickery will be employed against us. They will say, "When he arrives in your country at once imprison him; fill his over-confident heart with wounds. Return him to this court, not permitting him to raise his head again." So they will immediately put fetters on your legs and send you back weeping to this court.'

Khosrow's mind was bewildered at what he heard and his face darkened at their words. He answered,

'Because of the evil of destiny it is fitting that things should be of this nature even though they befall me. Much remains to be said and the task before me is a difficult one. I place my reliance on God.'

He rode off, exclaiming,

'Everything whether good or ill has been inscribed upon my head by the law.'

As he rode away those two evildoers turned back, with their heads full of vengeful thoughts. Immediately from the road they entered the king's palace, fully charged with rancour and with sinful hearts. Passing through the gate and approaching the throne they swiftly removed the string from a bow and flung it suddenly about his [Hormazd's] neck. And so they hanged that revered body of his. Gone now were that crown and imperial throne; you might have thought that Hormazd never existed in the world. The throb of drums ascended and the faces of the murderers became red as sandarac. At the same time Bahrām Chubina's banner appeared in the midst of the army on the march. Swiftly the assassins Gostaham and Banduy escaped from the place and continued their flight until they rejoined Khosrow. That monarch with a single glance at their faces understood why they, with their hearts holding a secret, had deserted the king of the world. His cheeks turned pale as the flowers of fenugreek but he revealed nothing of what he thought to those violent men. To his troops he said,

'Turn away from the main road, for a pursuing army is pressing hard. Take the way of the desert and the long detour. Do not slacken for a moment.'

(v) *Khosrow goes to Rum*

[Bahrām selects six thousand of his warriors to go in pursuit of
Khosrow.]

Khosrow had taken to the desert in order to save himself from his
enemies, and he continued his flight until he came to a monastery,
the tops of whose walls were out of sight. They called it God's
House, and it was a sacred place of worship, the abode of peni-
tents, and the residence of a bishop and a metropolitan. One of the
worshippers there was asked by Khosrow what food was to be
obtained, and received the answer that there was only unleavened
bread and water-cress, since only that food could be eaten there;
no viands would be available of the kind to feed him. He quickly
dismounted from his horse, as did his escort of two cavaliers, and
after a Magian ritual silence they took the sacred *barsam* in their
hands. Then they seated themselves on soft sand which was blue
in colour and hurriedly ate what was put before them. The king
inquired of the bishop if there was wine, and was told that they
made wine from dates in the month of July when the weather was
hot. A little of it was still left, clear as rose-water, and resembling
a coral in the sunshine for redness. A goblet and liquor were now
brought, by the side of which the sun lost its colour. Khosrow
drank three goblets full and ate some barley bread, then, his brain
being warmed by the red wine, he fell asleep on the soft sand, his
head resting on Banduy's thigh.

[Pursuers appeared unexpectedly on the scene, and Khosrow only
escaped capture by exchanging clothes with Banduy, who remained behind with the chief priest in the monastery. He was
taken before Bahrām Chubina, who reviled him for the trick
whereby Khosrow had been enabled to elude him, but did not put
him to death. He now called together a council of his elders to
decide who should be king of Iran, he or Khosrow. In the argument which followed he declared that he would destroy any
pretender to the throne, and he caused a declaration to be written
down that he, Bahrām, and none other was the rightful king of
Iran.]

XXXIV

The Reign of Bahrām Chubina

(i) Bahrām ascends the throne

When the azure curtain of night had vanished and the world became yellow at sight of the sun, a man came forth and placed in Bahrām's hall a dais for a throne. The hall was swept as clean as ivory and over the throne a crown was suspended, a seat was placed on the dais and the hall was opened. Bahrām Shah then seated himself and on his head placed the royal Keyāni diadem. Now the scribe brought the declaration of royalty, which had been inscribed on a piece of valuable silk. On it all the nobles subscribed their affirmation that Bahrām had become lord of the world, and when all had added their names to the document a golden seal was placed on it. Bahrām then spoke and said,

'This realm is mine; the pure God is witness to it. For a thousand years let there ever be someone of my seed who shall be sovereign here, for generation after generation. Let there ever be some worthy man of my stock endowed with the crown and lofty throne.'

[Still held in Bahrām's prison was Banduy, by whose stratagem Khosrow had escaped. After seventy days' detention he persuaded his gaoler that Khosrow would soon be arriving from Rum with an army and would capture the city. In return for a promise that he would be granted an amnesty when that occurred, the gaoler agreed to remove Banduy's chains and so bring about the downfall of Bahrām.]

(ii) Banduy escapes from Bahrām

To Banduy the gaoler said,

'If only my courage does not fail me! Today Chubina plays at polo and yesterday I thought out with five companions a scheme to bring destruction on his head.'

Calling for a coat of mail he donned it under his cloak and then rode off from the palace. This fellow had a dissolute wife who wished him underground, for secretly she was in love with

Bahrām Chubina and full of hatred for her husband. She sent a messenger to Bahrām warning him to look to himself, for her husband had secretly put on armour and tied it down tightly. She did not know what evil he plotted but it would be well for Bahrām to keep at a distance from him. Chubina having received the woman's message, telling him not to play polo with the gaoler when he arrived at the ground, touched each man who was to play with him gently on the back while he addressed him agreeably in friendly tones. This he did until he came to the son of Siyāvosh [i.e. the gaoler] on whose body he had clearly perceived the armour. He said to him,

'You viler than serpent, who wears armour underneath his cloak on the polo ground?'

So saying he drew the sword of vengeance and cleft him from head to foot.

[The news came to Banduy, who at once fled the city, accompanied by the nearest kinsman of the dead gaoler. Khosrow meanwhile was continuing his secret journey by way of the desert to Rum. As he approached the Christian town of Karsin with his escort, the inhabitants who happened to be outside the walls fled home in terror and barricaded themselves in. In the night, however, a thunderstorm broke out and the walls crumbled when they were struck by lightning.]

The whole city was in a state of consternation and the bishop prayed to God for forgiveness. In every street fodder was provided. Then three aged priests came forth in haste and, bearing into the presence of the king those things which grew in that fertile land as well as garments originating in Rum, they declared it was evident to them that they had been at fault. Khosrow was young and of a noble disposition and he therefore refrained from admonishing them for their conduct.

[Continuing his journey towards Rum he passed through a city where there was a Christian monastery. One of the monks in residence there recognized him and foretold a blessed future for him, although he would have to meet opposition from his enemies. While he was in the city, Khosrow engaged in a long correspondence with the Caesar, whom he alternately cajoled and reviled and who, after consultation with his astrologers, generally replied in terms similar to his own. In the end, a treaty of friendship and alliance was concluded between the two monarchs, one of the conditions being that Khosrow was to receive the Caesar's daugh-

ter in marriage. Amongst Khosrow's retinue was the famous
Kharrād son of Barzin, a philosopher and savant of ready wit,
with whom the Caesar debated on a variety of subjects, one of
them being that of theology.]

(iii) *Kharrād explains the Hindu religion*

The Caesar said to him,
'May you live for ever! You are fitted to be counsellor to kings.
I have in my palace a wondrous chamber which is beyond all
imagining. You will not comprehend on beholding it how it could
have been constructed and whether it is a work of magic or
divinely created.'

On being apprised of this Kharrād went to behold the ancient
structure and there he beheld [the figure of] a man on horseback
suspended in the air. On returning, Kharrād said to the Caesar,

'This mounted figure is made of iron and the dome above it is
composed of a well-known substance that the learned have called
Maghneyātis [magnetic ore], which figure the Greeks erected over
an Indian horse. Anyone who has read in the works of the Hindus
will be gladdened and enlightened by them.

The Caesar then asked Kharrād,
'How far have the Hindus advanced on the path of learning and
how far has that reached? How do they stand with respect to
religion and worship? Are they idolators, or what are they?'

Kharrād replied,
'In India the Cow is king. They do not believe in God or in the
revolving sky and no one cares for his own body. They disregard
the sun in its course and they do not reckon people like us as
being possessors of knowledge. Anyone who kindles a fire then
casts himself into it and is consumed, believes that there is a
[corresponding] fire in the air, which the Hindu philosophers call
the aether. They speak of the process in smooth and comforting
words, declaring that fire comes to fire and that by his act of self-
immolation a man's sin vanishes. They regard the kindling of the
fire and burning of themselves as the attainment of truth.'

(iv) *Kharrād rebukes the Christians for straying from Christ*

Kharrād continued,
'It is not the truth, and the Spirit of the Messiah bears witness

to this. Do you not see what Isā son of Maryam [Jesus son of Mary] said when he was revealing the secrets which had been hidden? He said, If someone takes your shirt, do not contend too fiercely with him, and if he smites you on the cheek so that your vision darkens because of the blow, do not put yourself into a rage nor let your face turn pale. Close your eyes to him and speak no harsh word. In your eating be content with the least morsel of food, and if you lack wordly possessions do not seek about after them. Overlook the evil things and pass meekly through this dark vale. But for you now lust has become dominant over wisdom and your hearts have gone astray from justice and honour. Your palaces soar up to Saturn and camels are needed to carry the keys to your treasure-houses. With the treasures you have arrayed many armies in resplendent proud armour. Everywhere you fight as aggressors, destroy the peace with your swords, and turn the fields into pools of blood. The Messiah did not guide you along this path.

'He was a poor and contented man who lived by his own toil. He lived humbly and subsisted on meagre food. (When the Jews captured him, they found him friendless and helpless and so slew him and put his body on the gallows.)

'Father to him was his temple and mother his church. He was the keeper and the seeker of truth and the detector of evil. His spirit became illumined and ready to receive wisdom, so that he was eloquent, wise and learned, and in time he also attained prophethood, and while still young became known for his discernment. You say that he was the son of God and that He died on the gallows with a smile. But a wise man laughs at such things, and if you are a man of reason you will concern yourself solely with God, for He needs neither son nor wife and to him all secrets are revealed. Why do you turn aside from the faith of Keyumars and the path and creed of Ṭahmuras, who declare that the Lord of the world is one and that to serve any other is without reason?'

[Here follow some details of the characteristics of a good Zoroastrian, the last of which is the alertness of a king who is doughty in battle and who keeps a close watch on his enemy. The whole speech of Kharrād received the Caesar's approval and he despatched a great army partly to support Khosrow but also to act as escort for the daughter he was sending to the Shah.]

(v) *The Caesar sends his daughter to Khosrow*

The Caesar had a daughter, whose name was Maryam. She was wise, of good sense, dignified and prosperous in all her undertakings. He bethrothed her to Khosrow with due form and religious ceremonial, invoking God's blessings on her. So vast was the wedding array which he sent with her that the swift steeds that were to convey it were greatly delayed. It consisted of golden vessels and royal jewellery, jacinth, and garments of gold cloth; in addition there were carpets, bedding and Greek brocades patterned with cypresses on a background of silver. Furthermore, there were bracelets, necklaces and earrings, and three bejewelled crowns of the greatest value. Four golden palanquins were got ready, the housings adorned with royal pearls, and there were forty other litters in ebony, flashing like the cock's eye with jewels. Then came pretty slave-girls to the number of three hundred, accompanying the princess in her ravishing glory, and three hunded male slaves, erudite and alert-minded, and they brought horse-trappings of gold and silver. Forty Greek eunuchs also were there with faces like peris; these were personages of note, who captivated the heart.

With them too came four Greek philosophers, wise, learned and distinguished men, to whom he confided all that needed to be said. In secret he instructed Maryam how to maintain her poise, how to achieve her aims and her duties in the distribution of largesse, the etiquette of eating and all things proper. For three stages on the way the Caesar escorted her and on the fourth he stepped forward in the presence of her retinue and commanded that Maryam should come forth. To her he gave counsel in abundance, saying to her,

'Until you reach the land of Iranians be on your guard, not loosening the girdle about your waist. Khosrow must not see you unveiled, so that an unexpected adventure may not befall you.'

Having said this he took leave of her with affection.

[When he had welcomed his bride and the Rumi reinforcements, Khosrow made an expedition to Āzar-Abādegān (Āzarbāijān), where he received the welcome of the populace. To Bahrām Chubina the news of Khosrow's newly recruited strength meant a setback to his own hopes and he wrote to the Iranian chieftains reminding them of his own claim to the throne and warning them not to place their hopes on the Sāsānian Parviz. The messenger who was carrying the letters, instead of delivering them to those chieftains, treacherously handed them over with the accompanying gifts to Shah Khosrow. His comment was that he had no quarrel with Bahrām and invited him to come with his army to Āzarbāijān, where he would receive amicable welcome. But Bahrām when he set out was in hostile mood and he launched an attack which routed the Rumi allies of Khosrow. He then went out with a handful of men to give combat to his rival. But at a critical moment his escort deserted him.]

(vi) *Khosrow does battle with Bahrām*

To Gostaham the king then said,
'Fate hems me in. Why should I have entered on this useless warfare, now that I have been seen with my back turned in flight?'
Gostaham answered him,
'Horsemen are approaching; how can you give battle alone?'
Glancing behind him Khosrow saw that it was not Bahrām alone that came but four cavaliers. To save himself from the foe and escape, he cut away his horse's armour, and then saw that of the vengeful enemies at his back three were now left, far behind. In front of him appeared a narrow defile and the three horsemen were riding like leopards in pursuit. The defile narrowed into a cave, the end of it barred by the mountain. The monarch, now isolated from his escort, thereupon dismounted and went running towards the mountain, sore at heart. It was no time for delay and there was no place of rescue, with Bahrām coming swiftly on while shouting to Khosrow,
'You treacherous fellow, your ascent has now brought you to a precipice. Why did you cast your fate into my hands by turning your back on me in this way?'
In this desperate plight, with a sword at his back and a rock in front of him, he prayed to God and said,
'Oh Lord, Thou art above the revolution of Fate. Come to my aid in this place of despair. Thou dost exist; I will not therefore lament to Saturn and Mercury.'
No sooner had the words left his mouth than from the mountain there issued a roar, and the blessed Sorush appeared, clad in a green robe and mounted on a bay horse. At sight of him Khosrow's courage was restored. Sorush took him by the hand, and, since this came from God the Pure it cannot be regarded as cause

for wonderment, removed him out of danger from his enemy, bore him off with ease and set him down. Khosrow said to him,

'What is your name?'

The angel replied,

'My name is Sorush. You are now secure, therefore cease your alarm. You will hereafter be king in the world, so never be anything but a true worshipper.'

With those words he vanished from the sight of Khosrow and no one again ever beheld a similar marvel, save that Bahrām had seen it and in his amazement called aloud on the name of God. To himself he said, 'As long as I fought mortals my courage never was lacking. But now my battle is with the peris, and there is room for tears over my dark fate.'

On the other side of the mountain Khosrow appeared on the road far from all mankind, but when they at last saw him, his renowned army rejoiced and the heart of Maryam was delivered from pain.

[Inevitably after such supernatural intervention Bahrām was routed when Khosrow attacked him again. This time he took refuge with the Khāqān of China.]

(vii) *Bahrām flees for refuge to the Khāqān of China*

When the bright sun once more adorned its throne, a patrol went out on the Shah's behalf and in the encampment of Bahrām found no living man; the tents were standing but no person appeared. When the patrol reported this to the Shah he felt aggrieved, for he had been eager to do battle. Out of his army he selected three thousand warriors, clad in mail and with their horses armoured.

Bahrām for his part was not assured of the loyalty of his troops nor of his country. With his heart full of fear he rode by devious paths, carrying gold and silver with him. Alongside the men rode Yalān Sina and the warrior Izad Goshasp, who guided the troops by untrodden ways, reciting to them the adventures of the kings of old. In the distance there appeared a poor village which was ill fitted to receive personages of high rank. But Bahrām rode into it, his heart wearied by pain and sorrow. The mouths of all the men were parched with thirst so that when they came to the door of an old woman who lived there they covered their tongues with smooth words and begged her for water and bread. She listened to their speeches and brought forward an old sieve, laid down a tattered waterskin and on the sieve placed some barley bread. Yalān Sina handed the sacred *barsam* to Bahrām but he in his distress did not even remember the ritual silence.

When the bread had been eaten they asked for wine and decked their tongues with low murmurings.

'If wine is your desire,' said the old woman, 'there is wine here in an ancient gourd the head of which I have cut in order to make a cup to put over it.'

'Since there is wine,' said Bahrām, 'what better cup can there be than that?'

The old woman departed and fetched the wine, at which Bahrām was greatly pleased. He took a cupful of it so that the old woman too might be gratified and said to her,

'Gracious mother, what news is there of the world?'

'There are a few things I have heard,' she said, 'at which my brain has become addled. A large number of people have come from the city today, all talking of nothing but the war with Chubina. They said his troops had gone to join the Shah while their commander and his escort fled.'

'Virtuous lady,' said Bahrām, 'tell me no fables about this matter. Was this action wisdom on Bahrām's part and will he perchance win his desire from this wisdom?'

She said,

'Illustrious man, why has some Div bedazzled your eyes? Do you not know that ever since Bahrām son of Goshasp [Chubina] spurred his horse against the son of Hormazd, every man of sense mocks at him and no longer regards him as amongst those who can hold their heads up high.'

Bahrām said,

'His one desire is to drink wine from a gourd and to eat barley bread from a sieve, so keep these for him until the new barley is harvested.'

Night came and he lay down in that gloomy spot with his cloak for bedding and with his armour under his shoulders. But no sleep came to him and he found no rest; he sought for some hope but he found none. When the sun revealed its secret in the heavenly vaults, the commander caused the drums to be beaten for the rouse, got together such men as he had and with those valued few set out on the road.

[The poem now returns to follow up the fortunes of Khosrow. He plundered Bahrām's deserted encampment and informed the Caesar of his victory. After a time the Rumi reinforcements, which had provided the escort for the Caesar's daughter Maryam, returned to their own country.

In this part of the story Ferdowsi includes an elegy over the death of his son.]

Ferdowsi's Lament for the Death of his Son

My years have passed sixty and five and no purpose now would be served for me by striving after wealth. Perhaps I should take my own counsel and give a thought to the death of my son. It was my turn to have gone, but it was the younger man who departed and in my agony for him I am a body without a soul. I hasten about dreaming that perchance I may find him; and if I find him I will hasten to him with reproaches, telling him that it was my turn to go and demanding why he has gone, robbing me of hope and tranquillity. He had ever been one to take me by the hand when distresses came and now he has taken a path far from his old fellow-wayfarer. Have you perchance found younger companions on the way, since you have so swiftly gone ahead of me? When this young man reached the age of thirty-seven, the world no longer went according to his liking. He has gone and what remains is my grief and sorrow for him; he has steeped my heart and eyes in blood.

Now that he is departed, going towards the light, he would surely choose out a place for his father? Long is the time that has passed over me and none of my fellow-wayfarers have returned. Surely he awaits me and is angry at my tarrying? May the All-possessor keep your spirit ever in brightness! May wisdom ever be the shield that guards your soul!

Bahrām Chubina in China

(i) Bahrām and the Khāqān of China

[When Bahrām Chubina left his camp to escape from Khosrow he made his way to China, whose Khāqān he delivered from the extortions of a chieftain named Maqāturā by killing him in single combat. His victory caused the Khāqān's wife to engage his services against a lion known as Kappi which was devastating the countryside and had devoured her daughter. He slew the monstrous beast and as his reward was given another of the Khāqān's daughters, and high office.

Khosrow soon learned how his rival was faring and wrote to the Khāqān to demand under threat of invasion that Bahrām be sent back to him. A defiant reply declared that since Bahrām was now the Khāqān's son-in-law he had better be spoken of in terms of respect. At the same time both Bahrām and the Khāqān prepared for war. The Iranians for their part hesitated about the conflict and sent an astute envoy named Kharrād, who had previously been on a mission to Rum, to see what could be achieved by diplomacy and cunning.]

Kharrād made inquiry and found a day when the Khāqān was at liberty and he then courageously hastened to open negotiations with him. He said,

'Bahrām is a man of base origins and more evil that Ahriman the maleficent. His eyes are ever deep in affairs which are not mentioned with propriety. Hormazd the monarch gave him advancement and raised him to rank higher than the sun. No one in the world knew his name previously, but now he has achieved every ambition in the universe. True, he has performed goodly acts for you, yet he will in the end revoke his loyalty to you. That is what he did with the Shah of Iran, for he is loyal neither to God nor to king. If you send him to the Shah, you will elevate that monarch's head above the moon, all China and Iran will be yours and your abode could be in any place that you desired.'

The Khāqān said,

'You should not speak words of that kind, for you seek to tarnish my honour. I am not the man to conceive malice and break my oath. The oath-breaker finds the earth is his shroud.'

Kharrād perceived from these words that his chances which had once been fresh had withered and that Bahrām had imbued the Khāqān with hopes of conquering Iran. Any words of his own were but wind in the willows. In despair of making an effect on the Khāqān, he turned in his search for assistance towards the Khāqān's consort and cast about to discover who was in her confidence and would undertake to enlighten her unsuspecting mind. He made the acquaintance of a certain palace attendant with whom he now associated himself and to whom he imparted Khosrow's words. The impious fellow was filled with satisfaction at the confidence, and to him Kharrād said,

'Help me to approach the queen and become the scribe at her gate.'

The attendant replied to the schemer,

'Your hopes will receive no satisfaction from her. Bahrām Chubina is her son-in-law, and all his existence, both inward and outward, depends on her. You are a well-instructed man; devise some effective plan yourself without revealing the secret of what you do.'

Now there was an aged Turk called Qalun whom his fellow Turks treated with small regard. For clothing he had nothing but a sheepskin and all his food was sour whey and millet. When Maqāturā had on a certain day been so ignominiously slain by the hand of Bahrām, Qalun's heart had boiled with the pain of it; night and day he wept in grief. By blood he was a kinsman of Maqāturā's and his heart was full of rancour and smoke against Bahrām, against whom he harboured thoughts of vengeance, while his tongue never rested from cursing him. This man was summoned by Kharrād and given a place in his own fine mansion. He showered money on him, both silver and gold, and provided him with garments and rich food. When he sat at table he invited Qalun and seated him amongst men of note.

Now Kharrād was a man of great wisdom, patient at heart and experienced, and when he was in the presence of the Khāqān he kept his lips closed, yet when he was with the palace attendant he was continuously asking his counsel about how he was to find a place with the Chinese queen. One day this old man said to the great envoy,

'You are a proud and learned man, if you had any knowledge

of physic and your name abroad had some renown, you would become a diadem for her head, particularly now when her daughter is ill of a malady.'

He answered,

'I have some acquaintanceship with physic. If you tell me how, I will set my hand to the task.'

The attendant went running to the queen and told her that a new physician had come to the town; to which she said,

'Bring him and do not linger long enough to scratch your head.'

The man came to Kharrād and told him he must hold this matter secret, that when he presented himself before the queen he must mention his name to her and then apply himself calmly to his medical treatment. Accordingly the ingenious Kharrād presented himself to the queen and diagnosed the malady as some affection of the patient's liver, prescribing for it pomegranate-juice and a certain water-herb which the herb-gatherers call succory. By these remedies he desired to assuage the fever which raged in her mind. When seven days had passed, by God's command the maid became as bright as the world-illumining moon. From her treasury the queen commanded that gold coins should be brought, together with a purse and fine robes of cloth, and also gold.

'Accept this trifling gift,' she said, 'and demand in addition anything you require.'

He answered,

'Retain these things. I will demand them when I may apply them usefully.'

(ii) *Kharrād sends Qalun to Bahrām, who is slain*

Bahrām had departed for Marv, having equipped his army as colourfully as a pheasant's wing. He asked the Khāqān not to permit anyone, whether Turk or Chinese, to proceed to the land of Iran or to allow any tidings to reach Khosrow, for any word would be a new gift to him. The Khāqān therefore sent out a herald to proclaim that if without his seal any man went to Iran he would be cut in two. And he swore by God that such a man would not be able to redeem his life with money. For three months Kharrād delayed, keeping his purposes secret. Then with some anxiety he summoned Qalun and giving him a favoured seat in his mansion he said to him,

'There is no one in the world who does not harbour some

secret grief in his heart. You once begged barley-bread, millet and a sheep's skin from anyone, when you were in China. Now you eat wheaten bread and lamb, and your clothing is of fine stuff. Your days have long passed the span; much you have seen of days and nights and much of mountains and plains. I now have a task for you that is filled with danger and from it you may receive either a throne or a dark grave. I will procure a seal belonging to the Khāqān of China and with it you may depart as if you were about to traverse the whole world. You must go to Bahrām, exercising the highest courage. Put on your black sheep-skin coat and take with you a knife. Watch for the day of Bahrām (the twentieth) in the month, and on it go to that brilliant man's door. He regards that day as inauspicious—I have observed it over many a year— and does not wish people to assemble at his house then, and he dresses in a robe of Chinese brocade.

'Say [at the gate] that you have a message to deliver to this felicitous nobleman from the queen. Keep the knife unsheathed in your sleeve until someone admits you alone; then when you are close to Chubina you will say that the exalted lady has bidden you to speak the secret close to his ear in order to preserve it from any stranger. When he asks you to tell him what the secret it, hasten towards him, thrust the dagger into him and cut upwards at the navel. Then leap away by whatever means you can find. Someone who hears his cry will run from the commander of the guard either to the stables or the carpet-store or the treasury, so that no trouble from the killing will befall you.

'Even if they kill you, you have after all seen the whole world and tested all that is good and evil in it. But it is likely that no one will show any concern with you so as to do you any harm at that moment. If you escape from being killed, you will have bought the whole world and have the means to pay the price. The triumphant Shah will grant you a city and will add to it some other portion of the world.'

Qalun said to that sagacious man,

'I need no guide. My years have reached a hundred. How long more shall I endure misery? May my body and soul be ransom for you for having been the giver of my bread when I was in poverty.'

Kharrād then went at speed from his house to the queen and said to her,

'The time has come for me to make a request, which I will now tell you, benevolent lady. My family on the other side of the river are being put into fetters. It would be worthy of you to set my own feet at liberty. Procure me a seal of the Khāqān, realizing that you are thereby granting me my life.'

She replied,

'He lies drunk. I may perhaps put clay against the seal-ring on his hand.'

She asked him for some sealing clay, went from her apartment to the drunken prince's pillow and applied the clay to the seal. She then returned to the persuasive Kharrād, who blessed her, then departed to hand over the stamped clay to the ancient Qalun.

[The plot succeeded and Bahrām was assassinated by Qalun, who did not, however, escape retribution, for he was taken by the palace servants and beaten to death, while Kharrād received the reward of his cunning at the hands of Khosrow. The Khāqān of China, who had been Bahrām's friend and patron, wishing to show his sympathy to his dead friend's family, wrote to his sister Gordiya, who was in his territory at Marv, inviting her to become his wife. Her reply requested a delay and made excuses for postponing a decision; but she had in secret determined that the ancient feud between Iran and Turān would not permit her to ally herself with the Khāqān. At dead of night, clad in armour and with a strong escort, she fled to Iran; but he sent his brother Ṭavorg in pursuit of her.]

XXXVII

The Story of Gordiya, Sister of Bahrām

(i) *The Khāqān sends his brother Ṭavorg in pursuit of Gordiya*

On the way a great number of Gordiya's escort, preferring safety, decided to ally themselves with the Khāqān. His brother came to him and said,

'Noble master, a strong force has drawn away to Iran, but many of the men have come over to me for protection. Nevertheless, this is an affront, and your army and country will ever more laugh at your gate.'

On hearing these words all colour fled from the cheeks of the commander of China. He said,

'Hasten, lead a force after her and observe how far her army has gone. However, when you overtake them, do not act with harshness, but first address them with sweet words. None of them knows our ways and it may be that you will be able in this fashion to break our enemy's back. Speak courteously to them, flatter them and make them feel pride in their valour. But if they should attack you, be a man and avoid all hesitation. Dig their grave at Marv, so that the ground shall be coloured like a pheasant's feather.'

The commander set out with six thousand men, all of them picked warrior horsemen from among the Turks. On the fourth day he overtook them, but the lion-hearted woman saw his army without any uneasiness in her heart. Swiftly she turned to her camel-drivers, who put down their loads as a defence, while she looked for ground that was favourable for a battle. Donning her brother's armour then she mounted a speedy courser. The two armies in array taking their lives in their hands confronted each other, while out in front of his troops stepped Ṭavorg, whom the Khāqān called The Old Wolf, and thus addressed the Iranians,

'Is that noble woman not present with this great force?'

The valiant Ṭavorg had not recognized Gordiya, for she was clad in heavy armour and had her loins girt warrior-fashion. Putting spurs to his horse he advanced closer and said,

'That sister of the murdered prince, where shall I find her in the midst of your troops? I have some words to speak to her both of fresh matters and of the events that are past.'

'I am here,' said Gordiya. 'I can send my horse against a ravening lion.'

On hearing her voice and seeing her mounted on that sturdy and spirited charger, Ṭavorg was astounded. He said,

'The Khāqān of China chose you out of all the realm that you might be a reminder to him of the lion-like Bahrām, that excellent knight. If you will listen to what he has to say he promises to reward you for the courtesy. He told me to hasten and say that if what he proposed was not possible for you, you must understand that it was not meant in verity, for he too has withdrawn from his word. You have no chance of leaving this land. You need not marry if you have no desire for a husband.'

To him Gordiya replied,

'Let us go aside from the battleground, away from the troops, and I will give you the answer to all you have said, placing my excellent reasons before you.'

Out before his army Ṭavorg rode and approached this stout-hearted and notable woman. When, seeking for an expedient, she beheld him thus alone, she removed her dark helmet and revealed her face, saying to him,

'You have seen Bahrām and admired the way he rode and fought. I have the same mother and the same father as he did, and now his life is ended. I will put you to the test and try you in combat. If you find me suited to be a wife, tell me; perhaps you may yourself wish to be my husband.'

Thus saying she put spurs to her horse, with Izad Goshasp galloping after her. At the same time the Chinese commander attacked and the two warring lions grappled together. The noble champion's sister came on at the Chinese knight with a spear which she thrust at his waist, piercing his mail and breaking its fastenings. As he dropped from the back of his steed the sand beneath him became a river of blood. Yalān Sina with his body of picked men now spurred his horse on to the battlefield and broke the Chinese army, slaying many and wounding more. Gordiya had gained her victory. Now she made her way towards Iran and into the presence of the sovereign of the brave, first having encamped by the Āmui river, where she stayed for a while with many thoughts working in her mind.

[To avenge the death of his father Hormazd, Khosrow killed his uncle Banduy, who had begun the feud. He now summoned Gostaham back from his station at the frontier but was met by disobedience, for Gostaham realized what was in store for him. He had learned that Gordiya had escaped with a strong force from the Khāqān of China and he came to enlist her aid, on the plea that since she was Bahrām's sister she could expect no mercy from Khosrow. He was a true Iranian and after some persuasion she consented to a marriage with him.]

(ii) *Gordiya kills Gostaham*

Time passed and again the Shah's spirit was aggrieved by Gostaham. Having been stirred to wrath one day he said to Garduy [Gordiya's brother],

'Gostaham has mated with Gordiya. A great party has gone over to him and I opine that he has become leader of their counsels. One of my agents has come from Amol and revealed what has hitherto been kept secret.'

In this tenor he spoke till the night fell and the eyes of the warriors there became too dulled for sight. When the attendants had brought in candles and wine, the hall was cleared of guests so that only Garduy was left with Khosrow, who conversed with him on all matters great and small. He said,

'I have sent a large army from here to Amol in order to satisfy my vengeance. Many were captured or wounded and those who returned were full of laments and in woeful plight. Now I have one device wherewith to meet this case, considering that crown and throne hang on it. When Bahrām Chubina went astray from the path Gordiya ever remained loyal. Now I have a plan of which you must not speak to the court.

'A letter must be written to Gordiya which shall be as a brook full of wine in the garden of Paradise. It will say: Over a long period you have displayed your friendship and been our ally in every task and every circumstance. My tongue has never revealed the secrets of my heart, but now the day has come for speech, for Garduy is to me as my own body. Seek how you may contrive a scheme whereby an ugly misfortune can be obliterated. Put Gostaham under a tombstone and you will get my heart and my household into your grasp. If you do this, your army and all your friends in the world can have my protection and never more suffer humility. I will grant a province to anyone you wish and he will become its governor. You yourself will come into my golden private quarters once you have brought all my feuds to a prosperous end. I will swear many oaths to this and bind myself to many pledges.'

To that Garduy's comment was,

'You know that where you are concerned I hold as nothing my own life and children, my lands, estates and kinsfolk, although I value them greatly. I will send this letter to her by trusty hand in order to brighten her unhappy spirit. I will also send another letter, bearing the king's seal, with script as bright as the shining moon. To my sister I will send my wife as messenger and from that door she will clear away all enemies. A task such as this is one to be accomplished only by a woman and more especially a woman of ready resource. The more I regard your letter the more necessary I see your missive to my sister to be. The matter will fall out swiftly according to your hopes, but nothing great or small must be added.'

Khosrow heard this and rejoiced; all the grievances in his heart turned to a breath of air. At once he called for paper from his treasurer and ink compounded of fine black musk, then wrote a letter like a garden in which the flowers were like the cheeks of the beloved. It was full of promises, pledges, oaths, words of every kind of flattery and good counsel. Once the direction on the letter was dry, a seal of musk was affixed to it. Garduy too wrote his letter giving his sister advices and discoursing of many things. He began the letter by recounting the evils that Bahrām had committed and how he had disgraced his family and his country, for the man whose spirit is lacking in wisdom does not look into the inwardness of his conduct. He continued by saying,

'He has gone and we must follow, believing in the justice of the Lord of the world. When my wife comes to you and illumines your dark vision, turn aside in no particular from what she says, for if you do then the face of our fortunes will become pallid.'

When the lion-woman saw the king's letter, you would have thought she beheld the moon descended on to the earth. She laughed and said that the proposal was a matter of no difficulty to one who had five such allies as she had. To a certain five persons then she read the king's letter, which she kept concealed from the rest of her train. She began when she opened her lips by demanding first an oath of secrecy, after which she took their hands in hers.

The night became black. Quenching every lamp as her husband
lay by her side she suddenly took his mouth in her clutch. At that
moment those five men came to her assistance, advancing to the
pillow of the illustrious man. Hard she strove with her drunken
husband but at last she had fastened securely his speech-uttering
tongue. There in the darkness the warrior died, surrendering his
nights and his bright days. Cries and alarums rang out in the city
and in every ward there was fire and storm. As she listened to the
clamour the intrepid woman was covering her body with a Greek
kaftan. In the darkness of the night she summoned her Iranians
and spoke to them of the slain man, and to increase their courage
and boldness she displayed to them the letter of the Shah.

[Having accomplished her task, Gordiya wrote informing Khosrow of its successful conclusion. In reply he invited her to his
court. There he loaded her with rich gifts and introduced her into
his harem, soon after making this Amazon his wife. In the sixth
year of his reign his previous wife Maryam, who was the daughter
of the Caesar of Rum, bore him a son. At that time, says Ferdowsi,
children of noble families were given in private a name which was
kept secret in addition to another one which was public. The
private name of this child was Qobād and the other Shiruy.
According to the astrologers he had been born under an evil star,
nevertheless the Shah wrote to the Caesar apprising him of the
birth of Shiruy and in return received a vast sum of money as
tribute. In the missive accompanying the money, the Caesar made
numerous flattering references to the Shah's ancestors and exploits
and then said he had a request to make. This was that the true
Cross which had once been captured from Rum and was now held
in the Shah's treasury should be returned. In his reply the king of
Iran, after acknowledging the Caesar's compliments, went on to
say,]

(iii) *Khosrow refuses a request for the true Cross*

'As for what you say concerning your holy religion, the Sunday
fast and the devotion, my secretary has read each detail to me and
all your delicate and touching words. I am not ashamed of the old
religion; there is nothing better in the world than the religion of
Hushang, which is a compound of equity, justice, reverence and
charity, together with a regard for the calculation of the heavens.
I am most convinced of the existence of God and exert myself
ever to think what is right. We do not recognize that He has an

associate, a kinsman or a wife; He is never concealed and will not disappear. God cannot be contained within the compass of the mind, and by His very being He remains your guide.

'As to what you say further about the gallows [Cross] of the Messiah in remembrance of times past, every religion which is established in virtue keeps reason for its guide. What man that adheres to it can mourn that its prophet was placed on the gallows and say that this prophet was the son of God and that he returned to the gallows with a smile? If he were God's son He went to His father. Suffer no more grief over that decayed piece of wood. When the Caesar utters words of folly, every aged man should laugh at him for doing so. That gibbet of Isa [Jesus] was not worth the trouble which the Shah Ardashir took of placing it in the treasury. If I send a piece of wood from Iran to Rum, the whole of my realm will laugh at me; it will seem to my priests that I have become a Christian and that for Maryam's sake I have turned presbyter. But ask any other thing of me that you desire; the way to me is open so far as you are concerned.

'I approve your gifts and the trouble you have taken over each detail. I have granted to Shiruy [Qobād] all the treasure which was brought, thereby laying the foundation of a new treasure for him. I am full of concern about Rum and Iran and thought has become my occupation during the dark nights, since I fear that when Shiruy grows to manhood he will bring calamity on Rum and Iran. The first to do so was the great Salm; then came Sekandar that vengeful old wolf. Shall the world renew talk of fresh wars as well as of ancient feuds?

'You must rest assured about your daughter. She brings lustre to your crown. She remains vigilant in her Christian faith, and seldom listens to our arguments. She is serenely happy and rejoices in her new son.'

XXXVIII

The Romance of Khosrow Parviz and Shirin

(i) *The preface*

This book of ancient tales has itself become old during the narration of the speeches and actions of veritable men. But I will rejuvenate it, making it a memorial to those proud men. It will be twenty-six times ten thousand distichs long, told in fitting language to dispel the cares of men. No one today sees a book in Persian written to contain even a hundred times thirty verses. If you seek out the bad lines from this work you will hardly find five hundred.

A certain royal and bounteous personage, who shines out among the kings of the world, has never glanced at these tales, the fault lying at the door of slanderers and of evil destiny. Envy of my work has won the day, and my market with the king has been ruined. If the sovereign's chamberlain reads these delicate words of mine he will with his fine perception understand that some of his treasure would make me happy here. (May any harm from an ill-wisher be remote from him!) Then he would mention it to his Majesty, so that perchance the seed of my labours might come to fruit.

(ii) *The story*

[When Khosrow Parviz was a youth, his father being still alive and the boy a champion warrior, Shirin was his one love in the world, as dear to him as his own bright eyes. None else in the world found his approval among the beauties or among the daughters of the great. Then, when he became king, he was parted for a time from Shirin and wandered restlessly about the world, all his concern being to give battle to Bahrām.]

(iii) *Khosrow while hunting sees Shirin*

One day Parviz the Shah conceived a longing for the chase and made all ready in the fashion of the ancient kings who had lived before him in the world. Thus, for this Khosrow of goodly name there were brought along three hundred led horses with golden trappings. On foot there were eleven hundred and sixty loyal slaves with javelins in their hands, in addition to whom he had a thousand and forty wearing cloaks of brocade with armour beneath and carrying staves and swords. Running behind them came seven hundred falconers with sparrow-hawks, lanners and royal falcons. After the falconers came three hundred men on horseback all bearing panthers. There were also there seventy lions and leopards attached to chains firmly fastened and wearing coats of Chinese brocade, and there were other leopards and lions trained and muzzled with gold chains. Also there were seven hundred hounds collared in gold which seize gazelle at the gallop. Accompanying all were two thousand minstrels ready to play airs on hunting days. Each was mounted on a camel and wore on his head a golden coronet.

There were chairs and tents and large pavilions, as well as small canvas shelters for men and stables for the animals. Before all went five hundred camels especially picked for their beauty. Now also came two hundred captains of war to kindle braziers in which were burned aloeswood and ambergris, two hundred young attendants carrying roses, narcissi and saffron before the Shah, so that the breeze might waft their perfume to him. The whole of the road was sprinkled with water, which you might have thought was rose-water mingled with amber, to insure that if a breeze suddenly sprang up it might not settle dust on that felicitously-born king. Immediately escorting the great king himself rode three hundred princes, all clad in coats of yellow or red or violet, while alongside the monarch went the Kāviāni Banner. He rode along arrayed in his crown and earrings, royal coat of gold thread, bracelets, collar and golden girdle, every button in it being set with a jewel.

When Shirin was told of the cavalcade that approached with the world-conquering king at its head, she donned a dress redolent of musk and gave to her face a rosy tint. Over her breast was red Grecian brocade; her whole frame was a mass of jewels on a background of gold. On her head she placed a royal diadem, so that she now presented a figure that appeared wholly composed of Pahlavi jewels. From out of her resplendent chamber she emerged on to the roof, but in spite of her youth she was not happy; while she was waiting there until the king should arrive, tears dropped from her eyelashes on to her cheeks. When she beheld his countenance she rose to her feet and displayed herself to Parviz in her full stature. In honeyed words she spoke to him of the days that had passed, asking what had become of that old love and what of those tears of blood for which the sight of Shirin had ever been the healer. And where had departed all that turning of night into day when hearts and eyes had wept although lips had smiled? Whither had those links and affinities of theirs gone and all those vows and oaths?

He sent a palfrey with trappings of gold and forty Greek eunuchs of good repute who should take her to his gilded inner quarters and the jewel-studded chamber. He himself continued his way on to the plain where the game abounded, being accompanied thereto by his wine, his minstrels and the cup-bearers. When he had taken his fill of the mountains and the plains he returned gaily to the city, and as he entered his lofty palace Shirin came from the women's quarters to greet him, and kissed his foot and the ground and his breast. The monarch then said to his chief priest,

'Imagine nought of me but what is honourable. Betroth this beautiful woman to me and let the glad tidings of it be given to the world.'

So he married her, with the ancient ceremonial, as custom and law at that time held right.

(iv) *The princes advise Khosrow*

While the princes were on the march, news reached them and the troops that Shirin had entered Khosrow's seraglio and the ancient attachment between them had been renewed. The whole of the capital was disturbed at the affair, and was full of doubts, pain and resentment. For three days none of the notables were present at Khosrow's court. On the fourth, when the world luminary became bright, Khosrow sent to summon them and asked them to be seated in the places of the nobles. He said to them,

'For these several days I have not seen you and I have become anxious.'

He waited, but no one made any reply, and all kept their tongues tied. Those of them who harboured a grievance or some cause of resentment turned their eyes towards the Chief Priest, who, noticing this, rose to his feet and addressed Khosrow, saying to him,

'True hero, you became king while you were still young and have since then experienced much of fortune both good and ill and heard much of good and evil fame in the world concerning the deeds of the great and powerful. Now the seed of the greatest is being defiled and the greatness of that seed has been besmirched. If the father is pure but the mother of evil character, then you must realize that the son can never achieve purity. No one ever sought rectitude from crookedness unless he was one whose sleeve was plucked away from the straight path. Our hearts have becomed grieved through the vile demon who has become the consort of our great monarch. If there had been in Iran no other woman but this one to whom the king has given his blessing [none would comment]; had Shirin not entered the royal harem, every face would brighten at the Shah's advent. Your ancestors, wise and true men, could never have imagined a story such as this.'

It was a lengthy speech that the priest delivered but the king of kings uttered nothing in reply except to say,

'We shall come to this hall of audience tomorrow at dawn.'

Whereupon the priest said,

'It may be that we shall receive an answer from the king then. Our speech today has been over-long.'

On the morrow, once the night had passed, all the princes rose and paid their homage. And then one of them said,

'The priest did not know how to speak.' Another one remarked,

'All he said was allied with good sense,' while a third said,

'Today the king will give us an answer, and it would only be fitting that he should speak in decisive fashion.'

In the Shah's presence the princes sat down in their appointed places and then there entered a man with a bowl in his hand, a bowl polished and shining like the sun. As he passed by the great nobles sitting there, they saw that into the bowl warm blood had been poured. The man came close to the king and set the bowl down before him, but those men in the assembly had turned their faces away from it, so that the place was filled with rumour. The Shah gazed so fiercely at each man that the company was abashed and in awe of him. To the Iranians there present he said,

'Whose blood is this? Why is it thus set before me?'

The Chief Priest answered,

'It is polluted blood, through which all who behold it become tainted in character.'

As soon as these words of the priest had been heard, the bowl was withdrawn, one man passing it into the hands of another. The handsome bowl was then cleansed of the blood and its gold was lustrated. Once the polluted bowl was bright and pure again the man who had cleansed it filled it full of wine, over which he sprinkled musk and rose-water. The bowl itself had become immaculate as the sun. Khosrow now inquired of the priest,

'Is the bowl still the same, or has it been changed?'

The priest replied,

'May you ever be happy! Out of the evil, goodness has appeared. You have by your command created Paradise out of Hell: goodness has come out of a base action.'

Khosrow answered,

'In the city Shirin was held to be as worthless as that bowl of poison. Now she has become the bowl of wine in my harem and thus she is redolent of my perfume. It was through me that she acquired ill repute so that she sought no friendship amongst men of substance.

The nobles there applauded and said,

'May the earth never be without your crown and throne! Goodness is magnified by the good you do. That becomes great in the world which you cause to be so, for you are king, priest and warrior. Of a truth you are God's shadow on earth.'

(v) *Shirin kills Maryam*

Thereafter the Shah increased in power and, having once been moonlike, he came to resemble the sun. He spent each day with the Caesar's daughter and she was his favourite in the seraglio. Greatly was Shirin aggrieved over Maryam and her cheeks were ever yellow with her bloodstained tears. At last she gave her rival a poison and so the Caesar's beautiful daughter departed from the world. No one was aware of the cause, for Shirin kept that secret to herself and, a year afterwards, Khosrow assigned the Golden Chamber to her.

When [Qobād] Shiruy's years reached sixteen his height exceeded that of men of thirty. Now his father brought tutors in order that his noble son might be instructed in the arts and, by the Shah's command, a priest had supervision over him night and day. On one occasion the priest had left the throne-room and come to visit the fortunate youth. Always before when he had visited

Shiruy he found that his sole need was for play. But now he saw that he had a book in front of him in which was written the story of Kalila [and Demna]. In the left hand of the sturdy youth was the dried paw of a wolf and in his right a buffalo's horn, and he kept striking the one against the other as the fancy took him. At behaviour such as this the priest's heart was grieved and he mourned at his frivolity and his idle conduct. He took as no good augury the wolf's paw and the buffalo's horn and the conduct of this sturdy youth.

Grievously he was perturbed concerning the working of fate and the unruly character of this boy of inauspicious fate, for he had observed the star in the ascendant at his nativity and moreover had made inquiries of the king's minister and treasurer. Thereupon he approached the Chief Priest and informed him that the prince's one delight was play. He reported this to the Shah, who closely considered the circumstance, his face paling for his son and his heart troubled concerning the working of destiny. He asked how the Lord of the heavens would reveal his countenance in these circumstances.

When twenty-three years of Khosrow's reign had passed, Shiruy was fully grown and his shoulders had expanded. The great king remained distressed by him, and now the child was a young man growing sturdy. His once smiling spirit was saddened and he caused the home of the youth to be his prison, into which he placed his foster-brother with him, for he too had outraged his honour. With them the Shah incarcerated those who had been their associates and had ever gone to the prince for counsel.

[Much later in the narrative Ferdowsi recounts the circumstances in which Shiruy came to be released from his prison. Meanwhile, however, the poet interrupts himself to describe some of the achievements and triumphs of the reign of Khosrow, and the events which led to its termination.]

(vi) How Khosrow repaired the throne called Tāq-e Vis

Now tell a tale within a tale, one which came from those single-hearted and single-tongued men of truth. It concerns the throne which you call Tāq-e Vis, which Parviz [Khosrow] set up in the hippodrome. Its first materials came from Zahhāk, the impious and unclean. When he had passed away and Faridun the Warrior had borne off the championship for valour from the Arabs, there appeared then on Mount Damāvand a man whom the king kept apart from his fellows. His name was Jahn, son of Barzin, and the report of his achievements had penetrated into every clime. For that renowned Shah he built a throne which was studded on each side with jewels, and Faridun rejoiced in it. When it was entirely completed he gave the man thirty thousand dirhams, a throne and two earrings, furthermore allotting to him the revenue of Sāri and Āmol. The lands thus granted him were as beautiful as Paradise.

When Faridun allotted Iran to Iraj, who was the youngest of his famous sons, he gave him three things in addition to the realm. First, the throne; second, the bull-headed mace which still exists in the world as a memento of him; and third, the jewel which the law-giving ruler called 'The Seven Fountains'. These three things were left behind when Iraj died and then Manuchehr rejoiced in them. Every successor who wore the royal crown added something to the throne. When it came to Key Khosrow the Felicitous he greatly added to the height of the throne.

So it increased until the time of Lohrāsp, and onwards again till the reign of Goshtāsp. When he beheld it he exclaimed that the work of the mighty can never remain hidden and he inquired of Jāmāsp, that man of substance, what addition he should make to the throne in order that men might lavish praises on him after his death. Jāmāsp regarded it and in his treasury of wisdom he beheld the key to the problem, for his calculation of the lofty heavens revealed its quiddity, quality and quantity. At the king's command he engraved on it all the figures of the constellations, between Saturn and the moon.

Matters continued thus until the time of Sekander, before whom every monarch who had held the throne had added something, whether of gold or silver or ivory or ebony. When it came to Sekandar, however, he broke it into fragments, in his folly accomplishing the work of destruction at a single blow. But many of the nobles secretly retained fragments of it and passed them on from hand to hand. Then came the period of Ardashir, by which time the throne had acquired the fame of antiquity. He sought out the remains of the throne and eagerly hastened from one to another. Then he died and the throne remained as it was, after he had achieved all his greatness.

So it was left, until the precious and treasured throne came to Parviz, who summoned the mighty from every clime and related to them something of its history. From them he received a great many of the fragments and with eagerness went in search of more. He then brought the throne of Ardashir and assembled every skilled craftsman in Iran, who, in the time of that monarch of triumphant fortune, restored the valued throne to the state in which it once had been. Carpenters came to him from Rum and China, from Makrān and Baghdad, as well as from the land of Iran; a thousand one hundred and twenty craftsmen were there, their minds devoted to the task of working on this throne, and with each of them went thirty assistants from Rum, Baghdad and Fars. Not for a moment was respite allowed them until, after two years, the work was completed.

When the lofty throne was set upon its feet the face of the king's high fortune shone. Its height, measured in royal cubits, was a hundred to which another seventy were added. Its width was one hundred and twenty cubits, for in breadth it was less than in height. On each morning of the thirty days of the month a different covering was laid on it, and on the front of it, all of gold, one hundred and forty turquoises were set in ornamental patterns. The nails and studs were all raw silver, each being of the weight of sixty-six dirhams.

When the sun set his lamp in the Sign of the Ram it was as though there were a field behind the throne and a garden in front of it, and when the sun waxed fierce in the Sign of the Lion the throne's back was still towards it. When the month of June arrived, the season of fruit and the festive time, then its face turned towards the orchard and gardens so that he could receive the fragrance from each kind of fruit. In winter, the season of wind and dampness, no one seated on that throne was discomforted, for it was all roofed over with canopies made of silk and sables from the royal house. Moreover a thousand balls of silver and gold were all kept heated on the fire by the guardians of the royal robes; each ball weighed five hundred misqals and the fire gave them the hue of coral. One half were kept on the fire, while the other half were placed [in braziers] before the proud champions in attendance.

The observer beheld [patterned] on the throne the twelve stars and the seven planets and the moon shining as it passed through each Sign, together with those stars which remained in their positions and those which moved on. He could also discover how much of the night had passed and to what point the sky had reached over the earth. Of the Signs some were in gold, while some few were encrusted with jewels, the number of which no man could reckon.

On the steps of the throne three other thrones were set, all richly studded with jewels. From one to the other four steps led, and each step was of jewel-studded gold. The lowest of these thrones was called Ram's Head because the head of a ram was figured on it; the most important was called The Azure Dome, because neither wind nor dust could ever touch it. The third, which was all of turquoise, warmed the hearts of all who beheld it.

To the Dehqān, or the vassal, Ram's Head was given for his seat; knights fearless on the day of battle ascended to Azure Dome. The turquoise throne was the seat of the counsellor who was concerned with the economy of the realm. Any one whose seat was the turquoise throne needed to be astute and a courtier.

(vii) *The history of the minstrel Bārbad*

The Shah's powers continuously advanced and by the twenty-eighth year of his reign there stood at his gate no person who could complain of wrong. The fame of his court reached a certain Bārbad, to whom people said that the Shah of the world chose minstrels as his companions in preference to any nobles and that if he [Bārbad] were to compete with [the court minstrel] Sarkash, he would excel him. At these words the minstrel boiled with eagerness even though he stood in need of nothing; therefore leaving his own country he came to the Shah's court and there observed the musicians. On hearing Bārbad's playing Sarkash became uneasy and going to the court chamberlain made him a gift of gold and silver and said that there was at the gate a minstrel older and more talented than himself who must not be allowed access to the Shah, because, as he said,

'We shall be turned into cast off [garments], and he will be the new.'

When the guardian of the king's gate heard what Sarkash had to say he barred the way to the new minstrel, and when Bārbad pressed him all he received in return was rough treatment and evil consequences. Despondently he turned away from the court and went with his lute towards the king's gardens, where a certain Marduy was the gardener. At sight of him Bārbad became more confident of success. The garden was one which the Shah visited at the coming of the new year [in Spring], at which festal season he resided there for two weeks. Quickly Bārbad approached Marduy, whose confidant he became that very day. He said to the gardener,

'One might say that you were the form and I the spirit. I have a request to make of you, which will be a small thing for you. It is, that when the Shah of the world visits this garden you will permit me to enter and observe him secretly, so that I may see what a Shah's feast consists of, also that I may look in concealment on the face of the Shah.'

Marduy answered,

'I will do it. Out of friendship for you I will banish all my scruples.'

When Khosrow expressed his desire to visit the garden, the gardener's heart glowed like a lamp. Going to Bārbad he told him that the Shah was coming to that festal spot. Bārbad thereupon clothed himself entirely in green, took his lute and, with songs of glory and combat, he made his way to the place where the Shah was to be, for his abode was in a fresh situation each Spring. Now there was a cypress-tree all green with an abundance of foliage and with branches intertwined like the men at the battle of Pashan. Up into it with his lute at his breast went the minstrel, there remaining concealed while the Shah emerged from his portico on to the feasting-place, where the gardener had got ready a royal seat.

A page with a peri face approached and handed a cup to the Shah, who accepted wine from the boy, the crystal of the cup disappearing before the red of the wine. Until the sun paled and the night turned azure the king sat there and then the musician in the cypress struck up his note and sang 'Salute to the Warrior'. It was a ravishing tune that he sang in the tree and the alert-minded king was overcome with wonder. In a sweet voice Bārbad continued next with the ballad which we now call 'Dādāfarid' at which the company was lost in admiration, each giving tongue to a different merit he found in it.

At such minstrelsy Sarkash was left like a man without sense, and knowing whose it was he held his peace, realizing that no one could play like Bārbad and that no one else could know the tune of 'The Warrior'. To the nobles there the Shah gave the order that the festal place was to be searched from end to end, but though they cast about everywhere they returned to the king with no success. The cunning Sarkash then spoke and said,

'Through the blessedness of your Majesty it is not to be wondered at that flowers and cypresses should become your minstrels. May your head and diadem continue to eternity!'

Again the cup-bearer brought a goblet and as the monarch took it from his hand, the singer tuned his note to a different melody and without prompting gave utterance to another ballad, which is called 'The Battle of the Brave', which title is taken from the tune.

Thus the minstrel continued to sing and Khosrow to listen, drinking his wine while the singer trolled. Again he commanded,

'Bring this fellow here; tread over the whole garden.'

They went into every corner of the garden and shone their lamps under every tree. But apart from sallow and cypress and pheasants strutting among the flowers they saw nothing. Again the monarch called for a cup and raised his head to listen to the voice. Once again the sound of melody came as the minstrel tuned his note to a different lay. It was what you today call 'Green upon Green', to which tune spells and incantations are chanted. Hearing it now, Parviz rose to his feet and called for a garden-adorning cup of wine, one which holds a maund of liquor, and which he drained at a single draught. Then he said,

'Even if this be an angel, compounded of musk and amber, or a demon—but if he were one he would not know how to play the lute—you must search the whole garden to find where he is, both orchard and flowerbed. I will fill his mouth and bosom with jewels and make him a nobleman for his singing.'

The minstrel, hearing the king's voice and his warm and gratifying words, descended from the cypress-bough and continued with his music and its gaiety. When he approached the king he bowed his face down into the dust.

'Speak,' said the king, 'what man are you?'

'I am a slave,' he said, 'alive in the world only by your word.'

The monarch was pleased at the sight of him as a garden is on beholding the moon in Spring. But to Sarkash he addressed himself in the following terms,

'You feeble performer, you are as bitter as colocynth, whereas Bārbad is as sweet as sugar. Why have you held him at a distance from me and grudged this audience his music?'

He continued happily to drink wine while Bārbad went on with his singing and drained the crystal cup to the bottom. Thus he did until he laid down his head to sleep, having first filled the minstrel's mouth with pearls of finest water. From then onwards Bārbad was king of the minstrels and became renowned amongst the great.

(My story of Bārbad is ended; may misfortune never befall you! Many a one great and small has gone before me and I do not wish to awaken you from any dream. A man who has reached sixty-six years of age cannot be happy in suffering old age. Yet when this remarkable poem of mine has come to its close, the land will resound with reports of me. Then I shall not die but shall live, having sown the seeds of my words. Any man who has sense, reason and faith will call down blessings on me after I am dead.)

(viii) *Khosrow builds the palace of Ctesiphon*

A certain clear-witted man of Fārs whose years had exceeded in happiness four times thirty told me how Khosrow sent messengers to Rum, India and every cultured land, and how three thousand craftsmen, every one of them a man of note, came from their several countries. Amongst them were masters, fully acquainted with bricks and mortar and in number about a hundred, who came from their own regions such as Ahvāz and Iran as well as Rum. From amongst them thirty stout men were chosen. And from the thirty, three were chosen, two of them being Rumis and one Persian. The most distinguished of the Rumis was an architect who surpassed the Persian in his ideas and he, coming with all his experience to Khosrow, explained the work and the constructive art required for building. The king said to him,

'Accept this undertaking on my behalf but bear in mind all the instructions which I give you. I require a place in which my offspring shall dwell for as much as two hundred years, and one which will not suffer dilapidation from rain, lightning or sunshine.'

The architect accepted the commission and said he had the ability to do what was needed. He sank the foundations ten royal cubits down, the royal cubit being five other cubits, and the materials used in the foundations were stone and mortar of the kind which those men demand who desire to do justice to their work. While the walls were being raised the Rumi presented himself before the lord of the world and said,

'If your Majesty knows of a man over whom the years have

passed and is wise in these matters, send that man with others of whom he may approve to the site of the palace.'

He conceded to him certain men of the kind he required and they went and with great exactness examined the walls. Now the architect had imported silk from which a group of men had spun a cord of the finest weave. With it they took a measurement of the palace wall, from its top down to the ground at its foot. When the length of this finely-spun rope had been measured in the presence of the men assembled, the Rumi bore it to the king's treasury, where, after having sealed it, he entrusted it to the treasurer. He then came to the Shah's palace and said,

'This new wall of the palace reaches to the moon. If your Majesty, who is swift in achievement, will give the command I will not hasten over this task. Let your Majesty rest at ease, granting me forty days' respite while the work which is done sets, selecting for me men who are skilled in such work. By the time that the business of the audience-chamber must begin the height of the wall will be that of Saturn. But display no impatience over the building nor increase my difficulties while it is in hand.'

To him Khosrow said,

'Why, you ill-disposed wretch, do you demand so much time of me? You must not stop working, and you shall not need for silver and gold.' The Shah then commanded that thirty thousand dirhams be paid to the architect that he might not feel aggrieved. Yet this honest master-craftsman knew that the experts would find fault with him if he were too hasty in erecting the arch, and that if it collapsed it would reduce both his livelihood and his lustre. When night fell that craftsman disappeared and no one saw him thereafter. When the news came to Khosrow that Farghān [the architect] had fled, he poured out before the messenger the wrath he felt for the man. He said,

'That fellow had no knowledge. Why then did he display such presumption before me?'

He commanded that the work should be inspected and that all the Rumis left should be carried off to prison. He furthermore commanded that other architects were to be imported and mortar, bricks and heavy stones be brought in. But all who saw the walls fled away and disappeared from the Shah's land and country. Being now without resource he was compelled to desist from continuing the work. But he kept his ears and mind strained towards Ahvāz, because from that city some architect might come, and work of the kind in hand could not be allowed to remain long without completion.

For three years he sought for that Rumi architect but no one saw the peerless craftsman although men constantly spoke of him. Then in the fourth year he appeared again, and an alert-minded spy, eager for honour, brought news of him to Khosrow. Simultaneously the Rumi himself arrived in haste and the Shah said to him,

'You defaulter, tell me what excuse you have for this. What would you say if you were taught a lesson?'

The Rumi answered,

'If your Majesty will send me someone in whom he has confidence I will reveal to that understanding person what my excuse is and by that excuse shall attain to my forgiveness.'

The Shah sent for someone he knew, and the valued master with the king's friend left the palace. With him the Rumi sage carried the cord and with the other man accompanying him he measured the height of the work, which in cubits now fell seven short of the length of the cord. This report they carried to the king, and the man who had accompanied the Rumi told of what he had seen.

'Had I continued the upward thrust of the work to its completion,' said the Rumi, 'nothing would have been left either of the wall or the arch or any of the work, nor could I have remained at your Majesty's gate.'

Khosrow perceived that the man spoke truly; and no one dares to conceal the truth. He released all that were in the prison whether malefactors or innocent; to the man himself he gave a purseful of gold coin and to all prisoners a large quantity of goods.

For a great length of time the labour continued, while the Shah eagerly watched the construction. When seven years had passed the palace stood completed, admired of all men of good understanding. He provided it with much water and land, expending money in large amounts on it and giving it his blessing. Men came from everywhere to look upon the palace and at the New Year the king proceeded there [to take up his residence].

Now a ring was smelted of gold from which there was suspended a wheel and from it again there was let down a red gold chain, of which every link was set with a jewel. When the monarch ascended the ivory throne the crown was hung from the chain and

when at the New Year he seated himself on the throne the Chief
Priest sat in felicity near him. Places lower than that of the Chief
Priest were kept for the nobles, the great ones and those possessed
of authority. Beneath the great ones was the place of the merchants and those who had skill in trades. Lower still was the place
of the poor who earned their bread by heavy toil, and beneath
them again came those whose hands or feet had been cut off.
Many corpses of men who had been killed were also flung down
in front of the palace gate.

> [He urged everyone to look downward, not up, in order to be
> chastened and be content with their lot. A proclamation was then
> made from the palace, encouraging all men to cast out fear and
> exhorting princes to deal justly with all people subject to them.
> A further proclamation warned the great to relinquish any am-
> bitions for power which they might have and to beware of
> stretching out their hands towards what was possessed by others.]

(ix) *Khosrow acts with tyranny*

With that renowned throne and that position of grandeur, with
his power and royal diadem, the emperor did not long remain in
harmony, and he brought Iran and Turān to ruin. The king who
had at one time been himself the giver of justice turned to injustice and rejoiced in the wrongs committed by his subordinates.
There now came on the scene a certain Farrokhzād of Āzarmagān,
a man of severe countenance ever turned to his subjects. Always
imposing new burdens, his one demand was for fresh treasure.
He extorted money from all, ever adding that to this and this to
that. The blessings of yore now turned to curses on the king, who,
after having been a mild ewe, had turned into a ravening wolf.
When the people were left sans bread, sans water and sans body,
they fled from Iran towards the realm of the enemy. Anyone who
was so overwhelmed by misery would inevitably depart from his
country.

Also there was a certain man of evil character whose name was
Gorāz, through whom the king accomplished his ambitions and
received satisfaction and comfort. He was the holder of the
frontier against Rum; and he was a man with the head of a demon,
so extortionate and vile was he. This man, when the Shah who
had once been endowed with justice turned towards iniquity,
was the first to betray Iran. Another man of the kind was Zād

Farrokh, a man well known and a favourite of Khosrow, whom none could approach unless Zād Farrokh summoned him to audience. The time came when the Shah's measure was full and the heart of Zād Farrokh too was utterly corrupted. He allied himself with the older man named Gorāz, and the secret was divulged in one province after another. This warlike Gorāz sent a letter to the Caesar in whom too he inspired evil ambitions, inciting him to arise and seize Iran, with the assurance that he would be the first to come to his aid. On reading this letter the Caesar got an army together in preparation for war and he led his troops from Rum to the border of the prosperous land of Iran.

(x) The Iranian army revolts

Warning came to the Shah of what was occurring, but although it was a grave matter he regarded it lightly. He knew that it was the doing of Gorāz to incite the warlike Caesar, because this Gorāz, being summoned to the court, on one pretext or another disregarded the royal behest. That evilly disposed man now conceived a fear of Parviz and his court and the proud men there. The king of kings himself sat with his nobles, the chieftains of Iran, having washed his heart clean of all sincere thinking and seeking on every hand for devious schemes. Then a lucid notion occurred to him. He wrote a letter to Gorāz saying,

'I approve of your action and praise you to men of valour. What you have done was very cunning and it has brought the Caesar's head low. When this letter is brought to you, put your subtle mind to work but remain where you are until I move from my place here. Then march out with your troops. Since there will be armed forces in this direction and that, between them the Caesar's plans will come to nought. We will bring him captive to Iran and imprison all the Rumis.'

From amongst his courtiers he chose out a certain ingenious fellow glib of tongue and endowed with understanding in the cunning required. To this man he said,

'Take this letter in secret, in the way that spies do; yet go in such fashion that some Rumi will take note of you on the road and question you freely. Let him bring you to the Caesar or else to the commander of his army. When he asks you whence you come, tell him that you are a poor man looking for a means of livelihood, that you have travelled this long road painfully and carry a letter from Gorāz. Have this letter fastened under your right arm and if they take it from you all is well.'

The messenger left Khosrow's presence and, with the letter fastened under his arm, went on his way. As he approached the Caesar's palace a patrician saw him and led him, his head covered with dust, his cheeks pallid and his lips blue, before the Caesar. The monarch pressed him to disclose where Khosrow was, warning him to tell the truth. The poor fellow, coming in search of a livelihood, was overcome with awe by him, and in his terror made a mournful face, at seeing which the Caesar said to his attendants,

'Search this mischief-seeking fellow; he is of evil intent, evil motive and evil speech.'

On searching him they found that letter under his arm and someone there who understood these matters opened it in his pursuit of guidance for the Caesar. A chief scribe was then found, one who could read that Pahlavi writing with accuracy. When the scribe had read the letter, the face of the Caesar turned the colour of pitch. 'This,' he thought to himself, 'is the vengeance of Gorāz and I would rashly have walked into the trap. The Shah has three hundred thousand men and no one can tell the number of his war elephants. He wished to catch me in his net, may his fate be dark!'

He immediately withdrew his army, his purposes against Iran having vanished. When Gorāz heard the news that the renowned Caesar had turned back to Rum, his heart was filled with annoyance and his cheeks paled. He picked out a certain valiant cavalier and sent him with a letter full of wind and wrath demanding to know why the Caesar had become suspicious of him, and why he had turned back from Iran, thus making him, Gorāz, once more a man in search of a living. The reason for that was, he said, that the Shah was well aware of what he, Gorāz, was doing and his heart would be filled with pain and rancour against him. When the Caesar read this letter he picked out a man of substance from among his retinue and by him sent in return a message which read,

'Did God free you from need in order that you might destroy my crown and throne and consume my army in the fire? Had I come, nothing would have accrued to my treasure but dispersal to the winds, which would have come about through your agency. Your desire was to betray me to Khosrow; may you never attain to greatness or happiness! You must know that the Iranians, as long as they have in their view a Shah of the Keyānid line, will never have a stranger in Iran, whether he be of the stock of the Caesars or a philosopher.'

Although Gorāz begged the Caesar humbly for forgiveness he could not for all his efforts free himself from the net into which he had fallen. Meanwhile Khosrow wrote a letter to him to this effect,

'You worthless villainous agent of the Div, how often am I to summon you to this court, while you remain aloof from all courtesy and good manners? To add to this now, the troops who are with you have in thought and heart become the familiars of the Caesar and secretly changed their loyalty. Send to me any who have become renegades or who are ready for contumacy.'

[These arguments passing back and forth ended in the revolt of the army against Khosrow. They released his eldest son Shiruya from the prison in which he had been held and set him up on the throne. For long the Shah was kept in ignorance of what was afoot. At this point the poet resumes the story of Shirin, which he had for long intermitted.]

(xi) *The history of Shirin resumed*

In the darkness one night the Shah was sleeping, while Shirin in disquietude remained at his pillow. Suddenly she heard the cry of the watchman, and she became alarmed and her spirit, happy till now, was perturbed. She said to him,

'Your Majesty, what is to happen? We must speak of this thing.'

At her voice the king awoke, his heart being filled with fear. He said to her,

'My lovely one, what conversation is this which you have been holding in my sleep?'

She replied to him,

'Open your ears and listen to the shouting of the watchman.'

When he heard their loud voices his cheeks grew white as fenugreek flowers. He said,

'Three watches of the night have passed. Discover what the astrologers have to say. When this villain was born I secretly gave him the name of Qobād, although aloud I uttered the name Shiruy, concealing the other name. We must depart for China while the night is still dark, or else for Māchin or the land of Makrān. By some cunning we shall be able to accomplish the journey and then I will demand an army from the ruler of China.'

His star in the heavens, however, was dark and his words fell fruitlessly to the ground. In the darkness of the night his incantations failed of their effect and his unhappy position crumbled into dust. Thereupon Shirin said to him,

'Our time has come. Our enemy prevails against our incantations. In your wisdom contrive a way of escape for yourself now. We must not cast ourselves on the mercy of the enemy. As soon as it is light, the enemy will seek their opportunity and will without doubt set their faces towards this palace.'

At once the Shah called for a coat of mail from his armoury, for two Indian scimitars and a Rumi helmet. Furthermore he demanded a quiver, some arrows and a golden shield, as well as a slave who was a man of war ready to do battle. When the night turned a dusky hue he entered his garden just as the raven was waking from his sleep. He hung his golden shield from a tree in a place remote from any path, then seated himself down on the narcissi and saffron flowers and placed one of the swords firmly under his knee.

When the sun thrust up his clear head from below, the demon-inspired enemies of Khosrow entered the palace, but when they had gone all about it they found that the splendid abode was empty of the Shah. They plundered all his treasured wealth, giving not a thought to the toil that had amassed it.

(xii) *Khosrow is taken prisoner*

Meanwhile Khosrow remained in the garden, with the tall tree above him providing him with shade. When half the long day had passed he began to feel the need for food. Now there lived in the garden a workman who did not know the king's face and to this humble servitor the resplendent king addressed himself and told him to cut off one end of the valuable girdle he was wearing. On it were five gold buttons, in each of which with great labour a jewel had been set. To this gardener Khosrow said,

'These buttons will be of service today. Go to the bazaar and buy me a piece of meat as well as some bread. But go by an untrodden way.'

Now the value of these jewels was thirty thousand dirhams to anyone who could make use of them. The gardener swiftly made his way to the bakers and asked for bread to the value of the golden girdle-end. But the baker said he did not know its value and yet dared not let it go. So they bore it to the jeweller's and asked him to endeavour to put a price on it. When the expert saw the buttons, he said,

'Who dare buy these? This girdle-end was in Khosrow's treasury. Only a hundred new ones of this kind are made each year. From whom did you steal these gems? Or did you rob some sleeping servant?'

The three men then went to Zād Farrokh, and when he beheld the jewels he ran to the newly created king, who said to the gardener,

'If you will not tell me where to find the owner of these jewels I will immediately cut off your head and those of all your vile race.'

The man said,

'Oh king, he is in the garden; he is a man wearing armour and carrying a bow in his hand. In figure he is like a cypress and in feature like the Spring. He resembles a king in every respect; the garden from end to end is lit up by him. Clad in his breast-plate he is like the flaming sun. From a branch hangs a golden shield and a slave with a girdle stands in service before him. He cut off this jewelled girdle-end from it and gave it to me, telling me to hasten here and bring him bread from the bazaar as well as something to eat with the bread. And I have just come running from there.'

Shiruy perceived that this must be Khosrow, for his appearance at the time was something novel. There and then he despatched three hundred horsemen to go swiftly as a storm-wind to the brink of the garden stream. Khosrow beheld this troop from a distance, grew pale and drew the sword of wrath; whereupon the men, seeing his face, turned back in their traces and went to Zād Farrokh, each one bearing a different excuse, such as 'We are but slaves, and he is Khosrow', 'Ill fortune to that king is something new', 'None should direct even a breath of cold wind at him, whether he be in a garden or on the field of battle'.

[Zād Farrokh now approached Khosrow alone and persuaded him to surrender. This he did and was imprisoned in a house at Ctesiphon, his reign having lasted for thirty-eight years. Qobād (Shiruy) now seated himself on the throne. To his father he sent a message upbraiding him for his past misdemeanours and at the same time requesting his forgiveness for the part which he

(Qobād) had played in reducing him to his present unhappy condition. In return he received a harshly reproachful letter; yet he
gave instructions that his father should be well treated. Khosrow
remained suspicious and refused all delicacies brought to him,
taking nothing but what was prepared by the hand of Shirin. His
minstrel Bārbad, after lamenting his patron's downfall in a touching elegy, vowed to burn all his instruments and never play again.
To ensure this he cut off four of his fingers and consigned his
musical instruments to the flames.]

(xiii) The nobles demand Khosrow's death

Those who stood in attendance upon the new Shah remained
night and day in terror of destiny. Shiruy was timid and raw, so
that to him the throne was a trap, and men of understanding knew
that his greatness would not endure. To his court flocked men
who had committed crimes or had behaved deviously in the course
of their careers, and to him they recounted their misdemeanours,
saying,

'We have said it before and now repeat it: in your head you
have something which is averse from rulership. When two kings
are seated on the golden throne, one of them occupying the
place of power and the other a lower position, then, if the relationship of father with son becomes closer, they will conspire together to cut off the heads of all their servants. This is the case now
and we are not in agreement with it. Therefore speak to us no
more of it.'

Shiruy fell into fear and trembling at their words, knowing that
he was a bondsman in their clutches. He answered.

'None but the man of evil repute would stretch out his hand
against an ensnared lion. Go to your houses and take counsel
together over this. Discover someone who will put an end to this
trouble for us.'

Those who were at enmity with Shah Khosrow thereupon
sought foreign assassins who would kill him secretly for them.
But there was no one in the world who had the temerity and the
measure of courage necessary to shed the blood of so great a royal
personage and so take a mountain of sin on his back. In every
direction they sought men who were evilly disposed against the
Shah, until at last they came on a certain man walking on the road.
His two eyes were dark blue and his cheeks yellow, his body
withered and covered with hair, his lips azure, his feet covered

with dirt, his belly hungry; and the villain's head was uncovered. No one in the world knew his name, whether among the great or the small. This hideous fellow went to Zād Farrokh [May he never behold the joys of Paradise!], and when he learned the story from him he agreed to the conditions that he made, saying,

'This toilsome affair is the task for me. If you will feed me well, this is the game I would pursue.'

Zād Farrokh replied,

'Go, and, if you can, do it; but never open your lips to speak of it. I have a bag of golden dinars for you and I am your friend, as close to you as your own son.'

The slayer took up a sharp dagger, bright as water, and departed full of haste. As he approached the Shah he beheld him in the company of a slave in the antechamber, and at sight of the man Khosrow trembled and his tears poured down on to his cheeks.

'You hideous fellow,' he said, 'what is your name? Your mother must needs weep over you.'

He answered,

'They call me Mehr-e Hormazd ['Love of Hormazd']. I am a stranger in this city and have neither friend nor wife.'

Khosrow remarked,

'My fate has come and by the hand of a base, malevolent fellow. His face resembles nothing human and no one in the world requires his love.'

To a young page who stood in attendance on him he said,

'My guide, go and bring me a bowl of musk and amber, and a very clean and handsome robe.'

The servitor heard his voice but being young did not comprehend what lay in the king's words. He appeared before him with a golden bowl which he presented to him, and then brought a robe, a towel and water. Khosrow hastened to put on the robe. He looked on the sacred *barsam* and entered on the ritual silence; it was no time for words or frivolous speech. Being clad in his robe he murmured a prayer of penitence for his sins. Then over his head he placed a fresh kerchief so that he might not behold the face of his executioner. Mehr-e Hormazd, dagger in hand, went over and locked the king's door, swiftly returned and, tearing off the robe, thrust the king through to the heart. Thus does this unstable world behave, keeping its secrets hidden from you to the last.

When news came to the market place that Khosrow had been destroyed in that way, his enemies went to the prison chambers in the palace, where the Shah's unfortunate children to the number of fifteen were held captive, and there slew them despite their innocence, in the very place where the royal throne had been overturned. Shiruy wept bitterly on hearing the news and sent twenty guards to protect the dead Shah's wife and other children. But he dared tell nothing of this and kept his sorrow hidden.

XXXIX

Shiruy and Shirin, wife of Khosrow Parviz

I have brought the record of Khosrow to its close, and now introduce the story of Shiruy and Shirin. When fifty-three days had gone by after the killing of that belauded Shah, Shiruy sent a message to Shirin, saying,

'You treacherous woman, you practitioner of witchcraft, you are well acquainted with wizardry and are the most sinful person in Iran. By your magic arts you were able to captivate the Shah, for by your wizardry you could bring the moon down out of the sky. Tremble, you sinner; come to me hither in the palace but walk with no pleasure or confidence.'

Shirin was roused by the king's message and his false and wicked vituperation. She said,

'May this man who has shed his father's blood never more keep his stature and *Farr*! I will never look on this malefactor even from a distance, neither when he mourns nor when he is festive!'

She fetched a scribe, a man who had some compassion for her, and could put together a document in Pahlavi, and to that skilled man she dictated her testament, declaring to him the worth of all her possessions. In a casket she had a portion of venom, kept there so that she need not seek for venom in the town. This she now concealed about her person and for her cypress-body she stitched a shroud. Back she sent a reply to Shiruy saying,

'Proud king, worthy of your crown, the words you have addressed to me are leaves in the wind. May your maleficent heart and soul be humbled! Who has ever heard of witchcraft in the world but its name, or rejoiced in it? If the Shah had been of the kind and quality to have his counsel refreshed by magic, there would surely have been a witch in his harem and someone would have seen her face. Me he kept for the sake of his happiness. At night, when anxieties would not let him rest, he would desire me to come from the Golden Chamber in the harem, and he would solace his spirit with the sight of me. Be ashamed therefore of such words as yours; lying speeches ill become a king.'

They bore the answer to the king, who was stirred to rage

against the guiltless woman. He declared that there was no course
open to her but to come [and do homage to Shiruy] and that she
was unequalled for her impudent words. On hearing this, Shirin
was afflicted with anguish; she writhed in torment and the colour
of her cheeks turned yellow. She replied,

'I will not come to you except in the company of people whom
you appreciate as men of wisdom, who have been about in the
world and have read much.'

Shiruy thereupon brought fifty men of wisdom and mature age
and then sent to Shirin saying,

'Arise and present yourself. Enough of speech.'

She clad herself in the blue and black of mourning and came to
the king, going directly to the garden chamber of Shādgān, which
was the place where the nobles delivered their orations. She seated
herself behind the curtain veiling her from the king, as was the
custom with chaste women, but he sent her a message to this
effect,

'Two months have passed in mourning for Khosrow. Now be
my wife, that you may be happy again and never see humiliation.
I will maintain you as my father did; nay, even more perfectly and
in more kindly fashion.'

She replied,

'Grant me first what is my right, and then my life is yours. Once
you have granted it I shall never fail to respond to your desires or
to obey your commands, your counsel and the longings of your
felicitous heart.'

At that Shiruy consented to let this handsome woman present
her petition. From behind the curtain therefore she lifted her voice
and said,

'Oh, king, may you be ever triumphant and happy! You called
me an evil woman and an enchantress, bereft of all honour and
truth.'

Shiruy replied,

'That is so. But generous people do not harbour rancour for a
sharp word.'

Shirin then turned in the direction of the nobles assembled in
this hall of Shādgān and asked,

'What evil have you beheld in me? What darkness, crookedness
or folly? For thirty years I was queen of Iran and was the stay of
valiant men. I sought nothing but honour; all crookedness and
default remained far from me. Many a man owed a province to

my words and received worldly advantage. Let him speak who experienced my protection in its firmness and saw the protection given by my crown and regalia. Let him speak who saw and heard. All my life will become patent from his reply.'

Those great ones there in the Shah's presence gave him the advice that kindliness should be vouchsafed to her, proclaiming that she had not her equal in the world, known or unknown. Shirin then spoke again and said,

'You noble men, who have seen the world and known princes of mighty prowess, there are three good things whereby a woman who is endowed with them becomes an adornment to the throne of greatness. The first is modesty combined with wealth, wherewith her husband adorns his house. The second is the bringing of fine sons into the world, through whom her husband's happiness increases. The third consists of her figure and face and also of her hair, with which she can cover herself. At the time when I became Khosrow's wife and found new life in that union, he had returned from Rum unsuccessful and disheartened and having no abiding-place in this land. But thereafter he achieved such triumphs as no one in the world had ever seen or heard of. By him I begot four sons, in whom the monarch rejoiced; they were Nastur, Shahryār, Forud and lastly, Mardānshah, the crown of the blue arch of the sky. None like them was ever born to Jamshid or Faridun. May my tongue cease to exist if I depart from the truth!'

So saying, she unloosed the veil from her face. And her face was the moon at its full and her hair was all musk. She continued,

'This is the third thing: my beauty as it is now. If it is false, let someone put up a hand. My tresses were an adornment I held secret; no one in the world ever beheld them. All my enchantment is what I show you; it never lay in witchcraft or trickery or evil inclination.'

None of the nobles had ever beheld her tresses, nor even heard report of them. At the sight the elders were astounded and moistened their lips, and when Shiruy beheld Shirin's beauty, his secret soul fled away from his body. He said to her,

'I need no one but you. You are the wife out of all Iran that will content me.'

The lovely woman answered him,

'I am not yet without some petition to make to the Shah of Iran. I have two wishes, fulfilment of which pray command. May the kingship ever continue with you!'

Shiruy replied,
'My life is yours. Anything you request is granted.'
Shirin thereupon said,
'Grant that in the future everything which in this realm has been
mine shall be assigned to me entirely. Before all this notable
company set your script to this document, affirming that I am free
to do as I will with all my possessions, small or great.'

Shiruy swiftly did as she demanded and she, as soon as she
heard his compliance with her request, departed from the hall of
Shādgān and left the presence of the great ones and the nobles.
Entering her house she freed all her slaves, gladdening them with
wealth. What was left she gave either to the poor or in larger
measure to those who were akin to her. Some she granted to the
fire-temple of Āzar, for the celebration of the New Year and the
Feast of Sada, and some for a refuge which had fallen into disrepair
and become the haunt of lions. All these gifts she made in memory
of the Emperor Khosrow, as a benefaction to rejoice his soul.
Then she entered her garden and uncovered her face and seated
herself unadorned upon the ground. Summoning all her slaves
to her she graciously bade them be seated and then in a loud voice
she said,

'Worthy people, give ear to what I say but let no one look upon
my face. Let none of you speak anything but the truth; let no
falsehood come from any of you that have knowledge. When I
came to Khosrow and newly entered his golden seraglio, becoming then queen of queens and the Shah's glory, what sin did I ever
commit thereafter? Let no one speak a word to save my face!
What specious word can help a woman in desperation?'

They rose to their feet as one and adorned their tongues with
their reply, saying,

'Renowned queen of queens, eloquent, wise and of a clear mind,
we swear by God that no man ever looked on you or even heard
your voice from behind a veil. Surely from the time of Hushang
onwards no one like you ever sat on the throne of delicacy.'

All the eunuchs and attendants, all the eager and wideawake
slaves, with one voice declared that no one could accuse her of
wickedness. How, they asked, could wickedness accord with her
beauty? Shirin then said,

'That evildoer, whom the high vault of heaven rebukes, slew
his father for the sake of the crown and the throne (may his eyes
never behold good fortune!). Can it be that he put death outside

the wall, holding his father's death as so small a matter? That man sent me a message at which my innocent spirit grew dark. I replied that for as long as I lived I proposed to devote myself to the Creator of the world and I made patent to him all my history. But I still remain in anxiety about him, my enemy. Doubtless after my death he will utter slanders against me.'

When those who reported these matters came to the king they told him what they had heard that blameless woman say. He for his part inquired whether she had any further requests to make. She sent someone to inform him that she had but one request, which was that she might open the door of the king's tomb, for the urge had come upon her to behold his face.

'That too,' said Shiruy, 'is granted; for such desires are appropriate to her.'

The guardian opened the gate of the tomb and the pious woman intoned a lament. On entering she placed her face upon that of Khosrow and, recalling certain words that had passed between them, she swallowed a deadly poison which destroyed her sweet life. Lying by the king's side with her face veiled and her body clad in a garment exuding camphor, and with her back against the wall, she died. She died and from the world carried off praises. Shiruy on hearing the news was stricken with illness, being overcome with awe by what he had seen. He commanded that another tomb be erected and that it should be crowned with musk and camphor and that the gate of Khosrow's tomb should be permanently closed.

No long time passed before Shiruy himself was given poison, for the measure of the Shahs in the world had been filled. Born under an evil star, he died in misery, leaving the throne of the Shahs to his son. Here is a man who reigned for seven months and in the eighth was crowned with camphor.

XL

The Reign of Ardashir Son of Shiruy

When the news came to Goráz, with whom Khosrow was associated in trouble, he sent from Rum [to which he had been exiled] someone who should speak on his behalf. He said, 'The crown of the ill-starred Shiruy has fallen in the dust. May his spirit be held captive in Hell and his tomb be overturned from top to bottom! Surely the eye and mind of time will never more see a monarch like him. My office as prince was granted me by Khosrow and it was through him that I returned to authority. Who could ever know that in the garden the cypress might receive hurt from the grass, that sun and moon would rob him of his greatness and take the crown and throne away from so great a monarch as he was, giving the sovereignty to such a one as Shiruy and thus casting the realm of Iran into ignominy? I did not know that Shah Parviz was destroyed at the word of that evildoer Shiruy. Now he is gone and Ardashir wears the crown, but none whether young or old can be content with him. I should not desire a ruler like him for however long our era remains without a king; he has it in his mind to become a great lord although his plans are all directed by foreign troops. I myself am arriving with a mighty army, whose commanders shall be selected from Rum and Iran. We shall see who this emperor is who favours these fine plans; I will dig out his roots from the ground and thereafter he will speak no more of sovereignty.'

He placed a swift messenger on the road with directions to the seniors of the army of Iran, and at the same time concocted another evil scheme about which he sent a letter to Piruz, son of Khosrow.

[This letter incited Piruz to overthrow Ardashir and realize his own ambitions. He was to work in secret under the threat that if he revealed anything he would be attacked by Goráz and his Rumi troops.]

Now Ardashir used frequently to delight in the company of Piruz, who was a man of eloquence and understanding and acted the part of minister to him, being also his treasurer. One dark night he arrived and was immediately given audience. He found the wine bright and the conversation easy. Ardashir was seated in his hall with a company of men young and old and when Piruz came close to him it was as though his head touched the sky for pleasure. He ordered that music be played, and the hall was filled with the strains of song. But even when half of the dark night passed, still Piruz had taken only a single cupful; but the Shah's companions lay drunk and there was no longer a minstrel there who might have taken note of what occurred. With evil in his heart Piruz sent away the king's friends and none but they two were left there. He then came forward and, seizing the king's mouth, kept his hand over it until the monarch was dead. The hall now filled with swords and arrows. All was in the hands of friends of Piruz son of Khosrow, parvenus as well as knights. To Goräz he sent a racing camel, brightening that gloomy spirit when the letter was received. Out of Rum he marched with an army so great that it barred the way even to the ants and the gnats. Swift as the wind he marched on Ctesiphon, with an army ready to wash their hands in blood. None dare utter complaint against that army; but it did not stay there long.

XLI

The Reign of Gorāz known as Farāyin

(i) Farāyin's evil character

When Farāyin assumed the crown of the Keyānis he gave utterance to such things as came into his mind. He said,

'To practise kingship for a while and sit rejoicing on this throne is better than drudging as a slave for sixty years, suffering toil and with arms humbly hanging down. After me my son will sit on the throne and place this royal diadem on his head.'

Covertly his elder son whispered to him,

'You are now sole wearer of the crown in the world but be not over-confident. Lay your plans for amassing treasure. You have become ruler of the world; once and for all arrange matters agreeably for yourself. If any of the true royal seed should arrive you would not remain here long.'

And then his younger son said to him,

'You are now wearer of the crown in the land. You have an army and treasure worthy of a king and as long as you possess treasure you will never fall into difficulties. Faridun had Ābtin for his father. Which of that family wore a crown before him? He divided the world between his three felicitous sons and found his pleasure in rendering justice in the land. Hold this land by your manliness and your wealth. No one is a king when he is born.'

The younger son's words were more to his liking than those of the elder, whom he admonished to commit no indiscretion. He installed the army's muster-master in the royal treasury and summoned all his troops to the court. Whether in the dark night or in bright daylight he lavished money on them and presented many a robe of honour, so that within two weeks there remained of Shah Ardashir's treasure not as much as the price of a feather for an arrow. When he used to go to drink wine in his garden no light was carried save that provided by candles of amber, eighty going before him and eighty behind, and he was followed by friends upon whom he could rely. All the drinking-vessels were of gold or silver and the golden ones were encrusted with jewels. It was his custom to drink all night, until at last the hearts of the nobles were filled with wrath against him. Constantly also when the night was dark he would roam about the gardens and the open squares of the city.

Soon not a friend remained to him in Iran, so that ruin fell on his reign. He ceased all generous practices, became extortionate, and was illiberal and mean. On gold alone were his eyes fixed, and he sold the world for money. He shed the blood of the innocent, until at last the army rose against him. They decked their tongues with objurgation; the whole world desired his death. Under cover of secrecy they assembled in a particular place in order to discuss his doom. One dark night Hormazd Shahrān Gorāz addressed an audience in secret. This man was a cavalier born of an illustrious family in the city of Estakhr, where all the nobles made their boast of him. He said to the Iranians,

'Noble men, this reign of Farāyin has become burdensome to us, and he looks upon us nobles as of small account. Why should your minds and hearts be placed in such distress? Because of him all eyes shed bitter tears. Will no one's heart's blood boil with rage at him? He is neither a Sāsānian nor of the seed of kings. Why should we stand prepared to serve him? Have your hearts flowed out of your breasts, or has the gall in your bellies disappeared?'

The troops there answered him,

'No one who is a man is left at the court, and no one is sufficiently conscious of grievance to tear the heart out of this base-born fellow. We are in accord with your views; now tell us what you have learned from trustworthy men—for from this mad king with his inflamed mind there comes no good word or any agreeable action. How shall we deliver this land of Iran? May there never be a blessing on him!'

Shahrān Gorāz replied,

'These difficulties of us Iranians have endured overlong. If you will not betray me or do anything not befitting men of nobility I will at once by the aid of God the pure cast him down from the throne into the dust.'

'May harm never come upon you!' they replied. 'We the whole army are your allies today; if any danger threatens you we shall be your stronghold.'

On hearing these words the loyal warrior sought the means of overthrowing that worthless king.

(ii) *Farāyin is killed by Shahrān Gorāz*

One day the Shah, having made his preparations, departed from the city in pursuit of game, with him being a retinue of Iranians, all of them of the nobility. Farāyin spurred on his horse and rode like Āzar Goshasp, now in one direction now in another, while the cavaliers encircling him galloped after their own prey on hunting bent. When the time came for the return to the city, Shahrān Gorāz fearlessly gazed at the despicable king, having first sought out from his quiver a steel-pointed arrow. He then put spurs to his black horse, causing the retinue to gaze at him in wonder, and brought out his bow, which he drew now across his chest now over his head. As though in sport he fixed the arrow in the bowstring and, when the point was fully back, he loosed the arrow from the thumbstall so that it lodged in the king's back. His whip fell from his grasp, the arrow being embedded as far as the feathers in his blood, the point emerging from his navel. At once the cavalcade drew their swords and while night came over the dusty plain the men struggled, continuing all night long, no man knowing who his neighbour was, some receiving and others dealing blows, some cursing some blessing. When the sun like brocade of yellow appeared, the mountain seemed like a leopard's back. Of the escort many lay dead or wounded; troopers and commanders all were in confusion.

The great army scattered like sheep suddenly coming on the wolf, and for long the realm remained without a sovereign, for no one emerged who was desirous of the crown. Men sought about for the offspring of the kings, but of those noble men they found not one.

The Reign of Purān Dokht

Now there was a young woman, Purān by name—when a woman rules affairs go crudely—who was the last survivor of the line of Sāsān, and she had read much of the annals of the kings. Her they seated on the throne of sovereignty and the great nobles scattered jewels over her. Afterwards she addressed them and said,

'I do not desire the people to be dispersed. Anyone who is poor I will make rich from my treasury. Let no one ever be needy in the land, for harm will come upon it from his distress. I will drive all enemies from this country and will maintain the ceremonial of kings at my court.'

She sought for traces of Piruz son of Khosrow, and exact information was brought to her. On receiving it she chose from amongst her retinue a certain man of note and by him had Piruz brought before her. She said to him,

'You evil and vengeful person, you are now to get requital for the deeds you have committed and it will be well fitted to that wickedness. The retaliation that you are to have inflicted on you now for your actions is this, that I shall cause a stream of blood to flow from you.'

From the stables she called for a colt, one that was fresh and had never known a saddle, and on to it she bound Piruz firmly as a rock and with a halter about his neck. That colt, never trained to the saddle, carried the tyrannous man out on to the open square, to which she also sent a number of mounted men with lassos at their saddle straps. As the colt galloped along it threw Piruz off from time to time, so that he was dashed to the ground and his skin was torn to pieces. Gradually the blood trickled out of his body and at last he gave up the ghost in ignominy. How shall you receive justice in return for injustice?

The queen ruled the land with gentleness so great that even the wind of heaven did not leap upon the dust. When six months of her reign had elapsed she fell ill and died, bearing away a goodly name.

[This queen was followed by another, Āzarm, who reigned for only four months before death overtook her.]

The Reign of Farrokh-Zād

From Jahrom [in Fars] they then summoned Farrokh-Zād whom they seated on that royal throne. When he ascended it he gave praise to the Creator for the glory of his position, saying,

'I am the descendant of kings and in this world I desire nought but security. If there is anyone who seeks to work harmfully in the land now that I am king he will reach no height; but anyone who pursues justice in his heart and uses no deceitfulness in his doings I will maintain in honour as my own soul. I will seek no harm to any innocent man.'

The troops all applauded him, but when he had spent a month on the throne, his head and fortunes came down into the dust. He had a slave, like a slender cypress in stature, endowed with beauty, fineness of feature and brilliance of appearance. This dissolute fellow's name was Siyah Cheshm ['Blackeye']; may the skies never produce another like him! He conceived a passion for a certain youth attendant upon the king. Of a sudden one day he came upon the youth and sent him a message, saying,

'If you will ally yourself with me you will acquire wealth beyond measure through me, and I will adorn your crown with jewels.'

The attendant listened to the message but returned no reply to it. Instead he spoke to Farrokh-Zād, who was inflamed to rage by it to such an extent that for anger he could neither eat nor sleep. He chained Siyah Cheshm in fetters and made a dungeon his dwelling-place. But only a little while had passed when the king in his justice removed the vicious fellow's heavy bonds, because so many had interceded for him. Once more he returned to the king's service; then, when he was in his confidence once more, Siyah Cheshm mingled poison with his wine, which he drank, thereafter living but for a week.

The realm was coming to its end; from every side foemen made their appearance.

XLIV

The Reign of Yazdegerd

(i) Rostam's forebodings

When Farrokh-Zād had passed away, Yazdegerd became king, in the month of Sepandārmoz on the day of Ard. The nobles called down blessings on him and named him sovereign of the land. And so he ruled until twice eight years had gone by. Then [the Caliph] Omar sent Saʿd son of Vaqqās with an army to make war on the Shah.

The standards of the kings of the world came to an end. Gold vanished and farthings took its place. The unseemly became good and the good unseemly; the road to Hell issued forth from Paradise. The countenance of the revolving firmament was changed, and it withheld its love from free men altogether.

When Yazdegerd was apprised of this he assembled troops from every region and ordered the son of Hormazd to take the road and march out with the army. His name was Rostam and he was a man of alert mind, sagacious, warlike and one who had been a conqueror. He was a calculator of the stars, of great perception; and he listened deeply to what his counsellors advised.

When the month passed its thirtieth day the Arabs sought to give battle at Qādesiya. Rostam knew the reckoning of the stars and said,

'There is no propitiousness for this combat; the path for the water of the Shahs lies not in this channel.'

Bringing an astrolabe he took the stars again and now seized his head in his hands in lament for the day of misfortune.

[To his brother he wrote a long letter foretelling calamity for Iran and an end to the Sāsānian dynasty, which for four hundred years had reigned over the country. 'New men,' he said, 'would rule in the land' and he warned him to send all his wordly goods in haste to a safe province such as Āzarbāijān, 'a land of great and free men'. He ended by lamenting his own science, which informed him of such impending misfortune.]

When the pulpit becomes equal to the throne, you will hear of no names but Abu Bakr and Omar. All our long labours will be

in vain, for the stars only befriend the Arabs. But as times pass
they shall be sated with wealth. One man shall toil and another
shall eat; no one shall esteem justice and generosity. They shall
turn away from honour and truth; lies and baseness shall be
honoured. True knights shall be dismounted, and boastful and
vain shall mount in their places. The valiant fighter shall become
useless. Lineage and greatness shall cease to bring forth fruit. This
one shall rob the other, the other this; and they shall not distinguish between praise and malediction. And what is within shall
be even worse than what is in the open—men's hearts shall turn
to rocks of granite. Fathers shall wish evil upon their sons, sons
shall conspire against fathers. A worthless slave shall become the
king, and true greatness and lineage shall count for nought.

From Iranians, Turks and Arabs there shall appear a race
neither high born [Dehqān] nor Turk nor Arab—ideals to them
shall be as playthings. They shall hide their treasures under their
skirts—only to die and leave them for enemies. No festivities, no
leisure, no felicity, for ever scheming to snare one another. They
shall seek the loss of others for their own gain, but shall mas-
querade in the name of religion. And when these events come to
pass, none shall respect the free man.

(ii) *Rostam's letter to Sa'd son of Vaqqās*

Another letter, composed of lightning and thunder, he sent at a
gallop to Sa'd. It was written on white silk and the scribe wrote
it in words that shone like the sun. On the direction was inscribed,

'From the son of Shah Hormazd, the world Pahlavān Rostam,
who desires nought but good, to Sa'd son of Vaqqās who seeks
conflict and so has rendered the world a dark and narrow place
for himself.'

At the beginning of the missive he said,

'In the presence of the pure Lord of the world we may not stand
without fear and reverence, for it is through Him that the revolving heavens endure and all His governance is justice and charity.
May there be blessings from Him on the monarch who is the
adornment of his crown, throne and seal, who by his *Farr* holds
Ahriman [the spirit of evil] enthralled, the lord of the sword and
the sublime crown.

'This deplorable event has occurred and to no purpose has this
grievous thing, this struggle, come to pass. Tell me this, who is

your king? What man are you and what is your religion and way
of life? Over whom do you seek to triumph, you, naked commander of a naked army? With a loaf of bread you are satisfied yet
remain hungry. You have neither elephants nor platforms nor baggage nor gear. Mere existence in Iran would be enough for you, since
crown and ring belong to another, one who possesses elephants and
treasures, *Farr* and sublime rank. His forebears from ancestor to
ancestor have all been renowned kings. When he is visible, there
is no moon in the sky. There is no monarch of his stature on earth.
When he laughs at a feast with his lips open and teeth shining like
silver, he gives away what is the ransom of an Arab chief without
any loss to his treasury. His hounds, panthers and falcons number
twelve thousand, all dight with golden bells and earrings. From
a diet of camel's milk and lizards the Arabs have come so far as
to aspire to the Keyāni throne. Is there no shame in your eyes? Do
feeling and honour not lie on the path of your wisdom? With a
countenance such as yours, such birth, such sentiments and spirit,
do you aspire to such a crown and such a throne? If you seek to
possess some portion of the world you will not make over-boastful
claims. Send us some man to speak for you, someone of experience,
a warrior of understanding, of the kind who may tell us what your
religion is and who your guide is upon the royal throne. I shall
send a cavalier to the Shah requesting him to grant you what you
desire. And now do not attempt to make war on so great a
monarch, for it is in his hands that the outcome of it will lie.
Observe well the contents of this letter filled with good counsel;
do not bind up the eyes and ears of wisdom.'

A Pahlavān bore the letter to Saʿd son of Vaqqās while the
great ones of Iran, illumined of spirit, remained enveloped in
their armour, their silver and gold, their golden shields and
golden girdles.

(iii) *The reply sent by Saʿd to Rostam*

When Saʿd learned of the messenger's coming he went forward
swiftly to receive him, prayed him dismount and questioned him
concerning the [Iranian] army and the Pahlavān in command of
it. He further enquired about the Shah and his ministers, his
retinue and keen-minded chamberlain and about his realm. For
the envoy, Piruz, he laid down a cloak, saying,

'We regard lances and swords as our companions. Brave men

hold no converse about brocade, gold and silver, sleeping and eating.'

He listened to what the envoy had to say and read his letter, and in his reply lavished praises on the writer. Then in Arabic he wrote his own letter, revealing in it much of what was beautiful and what was ill-favoured. He discoursed of what concerned the Jinns and what concerned human kind, of the words of the Hāshemi prophet, about the declaration of the one-ness of God, about [divine] promise and threat, about things everlasting and the new dispensation. He spoke of the pitch and the fires of Hell as well as of the intensely cold part of it, about Paradise and the streams of wine and milk that ran there, about the camphor sprinkled and the waters ever flowing, about the trees of Paradise, its wine and oxymel. If, he said, the Shah would accept this true faith, then both worlds would be his in royal splendour and felicity. He would even receive a crown and earrings, and the whole year round he would have perfume, colour and beauty. Muḥammad would be intercessor for his sins, his body would become like purified rose-water. When his actions could receive Paradise as their reward, why sow vengeance in the garden of destruction?

The eyes of the Shah, he said, were fixed on this fleeting world, being dazzled by the thought of crown and treasure. He had become assured of this ivory throne, these panthers and hawks, this good fortune and crown. Why did he keep his mind ever in anxiety over a world which had not the value of a drink of cold water? Anyone who came against him [Sa'd] in war would experience nothing but Hell and a narrow grave, but anyone who believed would have Paradise as his abode. Let the Shah consider well what his plan should be.

To the paper he affixed an Arab seal and gave adulation to Muḥammad.

When Sho'ba son of Mughira, from amongst the Arab warriors, set out to go to the Pahlavān Rostam, a certain notable from amongst the Iranians came to the commander of his army to report that an old and feeble messenger was arriving, without a horse or weapons and with no sound body. Hung from his neck he had a slender sword and his shirt appeared in tatters. Rostam considered these words and caused to be erected a pavilion of brocade, wherein they spread magnificent carpets of Chinese gold thread. The troops came forward in numbers like those of ants and locusts and a golden throne was placed ready on which the commander of the army seated himself. He paraded sixty men of the Iranians, all knights, veritable lions on the day of battle. Their purple cloaks were interlaced with gold and on their feet were golden shoes. All were wearers of bejewelled collars and had earrings and the pavilion was decked in regal display.

When Sho'ba reached the portico of the pavilion he would not place his foot on the carpet lying there, but very humbly trod on the ground making a walking-stick of his sword. He seated himself on the earth looking at no one and without regarding the commander of the army. Rostam said to him,

'Let your spirit be at ease; keep your soul equipped with wisdom and so permit your body to prosper.'

His reply to Rostam was,

'Man of goodly repute, if you accept the faith, then peace upon you!'

Rostam fell into uneasiness at these words; he frowned at the man's garb and his face paled. He took his letter from him and gave it to the reader, who repeated the contents to him. In reply he said,

'Say to Sa'd, seek neither kingship nor crown. You have not seen my fortune brought low by your lance and yet your heart has formed a desire for my throne. Words are not held in contempt by the wise; you have no vision of this way of life. If Sa'd wore the crown of kings, to fight or to feast with him were an easy matter. But now, since evil is destined for me by my perfidious star, what am I to say, seeing that this is the day of ruin? If Muhammad will be my guide, I will accept this new faith in place of my old one. The working of this curved sky has become crooked; it designs to treat me with cruelty. Return to Sa'd with this felicitous news. There is no room for words on the day of battle. Tell him that to die with honour in war is better than to live with the enemy triumphing over you.'

(iv) Rostam's battle with Sa'd

[The Arab leader's answer was to give battle immediately, and after three days' struggle Rostam was killed. Shah Yazdegerd, after consultation with his intimates and his army advisers at 'Baghdad' (i.e. Ctesiphon), made the feeble decision to retreat to Khorāsān. There he had numerous friends and troops and, in addition, hoped to enlist the aid of the Faghfur of China by a marriage with his daughter, an alliance that would bring the Turānian chiefs in on his side. He was not unopposed on his way, for he was met by a chieftain called Māhuy who entertained ambitions of himself occupying the throne of Iran, and had stirred up some of the Turānian chieftains against the Shah. In the subsequent battle the Iranians were routed and Yazdegerd took refuge in a mill, where he hid himself.]

The miller, with a bundle of grass as a load on his back, opened the door of the mill. He was a man of humble birth and his name was Khosrow. He was possessed neither of goods nor wit nor name nor prosperity. He got his food from the mill and did no work besides. On entering, he beheld a warrior like a tall cypress, seated despondently in the dust, a royal diadem on his head and his breast gleaming with Chinese brocade. His eyes were those of an antelope, his chest and shoulders lion-like and the miller's eyes could not have enough of the sight of him. On Khosrow he gazed and was astounded and in his wonderment called on the name of God. He said to the king,

'Shah of the sunlike countenance, tell me how you came to this mill. What kind of resting-place for you is a mill, where there is nothing but wheat and dirt and a little grass? What man are you, with those arms and this splendour of countenance? Surely the heavens cannot gaze on another like you.'

'I am one of the Iranians,' said the Shah to him. 'I have fled away from the army of Turān.'

In distress the miller said,

'My only accompaniment is my poverty. If some bread made of barley is of service to you, and some trivial herbs from the stream, I will bring them. There is nothing else. Men who are poor must weep over what they have.'

For three days after the battle the king of the world had had no provision either for sleeping or for eating, and he said to the man,

'Bring what you have; and bring me also the sacred *barsam* rod.'

Quickly that ill-provided man put some sour milk on the ground and laid before the king the herbs and the barley bread. He hastened away for the *barsam* and came to the house to which the taxes were brought. To the chief of the mills there, he came and requested a *barsam*. Now Māhuy [the Turkoman chieftain who had opposed Yazdegerd] had sent in all directions in search of the Shah and this official enquired why the miller required the *barsam*. He told him that a mighty warrior was in the mill, resting on some grass, that he was a slender cypress in figure, brilliant as the sun in appearance and covered with splendour. He had put some stale sour milk down in front of the man and some barley bread fit only for himself. The man had desired to hold the *barsam* and observe the ritual silence. To the miller the official then said,

'Speed away from here and tell all to Māhuy.'

Swiftly the official handed this pliant fellow to someone who brought him into the presence of Māhuy.

[The Turkoman questioned the miller about his uninvited guest and was given a glowing description of him.]

(v) *Māhuy commissions the miller to slay Yazdegerd*

When Māhuy gathered his thoughts together, he knew that this could be none other than Yazdegerd. He said to the man,

'Speed away from this company and at once sever his head from his body. If you will not do so I will cut off your head and leave no one alive of your kin.'

The nobles there heard the words he spoke; great men of alert mind and doughty accomplishments. They were stirred to wrath against Māhuy; their tongues were filled with speech and their eyes with tears. Now there was a priest there, Zāruy by name, who guided his spirit with the bridle of wisdom. He said to Māhuy,

'You man of evil designs, why has the Div thus dazzled your eyes? Be aware that kingship and prophethood are two gems set in the same ring. Your desire is to break one of the two and to trample both spirit and wisdom underfoot. Look well into what you would do and beware of this deed. Do not become an opponent of the Creator.'

[Others of the distinguished assembly joined their voices to that of the priest and endeavoured to dissuade him from his plan to assassinate this last of the Sāsānian Shahs. They warned him that the consequences of his evil deed would be visited not only on himself but on his descendants. But their speech 'availed not a hair'. Mahuy ordered the miller to kill Yazdegerd, who was stabbed to death while he was eating the barley bread. His body was cast into the mill-pool.]

XLV

Māhuy ascends the Throne

There came to Māhuy someone who told him that the Shah of the
world had found a resting-place in a tower of silence, that bishop
and priest and monks of Rum and all in the land who mourned
him, young and old, had gone with lamentations and taken the
Shah's body out of the pool. They had made a tower of silence for
him in a garden. It was so large and so high that the vultures
could not fly across it. To that, the evil-fated and malicious Māhuy
replied that never before had Iran been of the kin of Rum. He sent
orders that all who had built the tower and all who had shared in
the mourning ceremonies should be slain and the whole land
given over to be plundered. Such were his triumphs and his
values. Thereafter when he gazed about him in the world he
could see no survivor of the family of the great.

In Māhuy's possession were a crown and a royal seal, which in
that shepherd's son inspired an ambition for the throne. Summoning his confidants he spoke to them at length of what was in his
mind. And to his counsellor he said,

'The day of glory and combat has arrived. No treasure have I,
nor name, nor birth, and it may hap that I shall be throwing my
head to the winds. The name inscribed on the seal-ring is that of
Yazdegerd, and the people will not be tamed by me with the
sword, whereas to him all the land of Iran was in thrall, even
though everyone of his kin had been scattered. Those among the
people who have understanding will not acknowledge me as Shah
nor will the army be content with me, in spite of my seal. I should
have employed other means; why did I shed the blood of the Shah
of the great? All night long in my thoughts I was filled with blood.
The Lord is aware what my condition was.'

To him his counsellor replied,

'All that is past. The world is full of rumours of it. Look to
what you must do now, for you have broken the thread of your
warp. He has now become dust in his tower, dust which has
become the theriac for his spirit. Gather together all your men of
experience and turn your sharp tongue to smooth words. Tell

them that the crown and ring were given to you by Yazdegerd as token of your sovereignty; that when he understood that the army of the Turks was approaching, the Shah summoned you at dead of night and said "When the wind of battle rises, who knows upon whom the dust will settle? Take this crown and ring; there will come a day of vengeance when they will be of service to you. I have nothing but a daughter in the world, who lies concealed from the Arabs. Do not surrender my throne to the enemy but guard these treasures as tokens of my rule." Say that you hold the crown and the heritage from the Shah and that it is by his command you ascend the throne. Thus you can lend glamour to your evil deed. Who shall know whether what you say is true or false?'

When Māhuy heard this he exclaimed,

'Well said. You are indeed a counsellor and no one is greater than you.'

He then summoned all the heads of the army and discoursed to them at length of the matter. They understood that it was not the truth that he spoke and that it would be a lawful matter boldly to cut off his head. But one Pahlavān said,

'That is what you must do, whether it be right or wrong.'

Thereupon he placed himself on the seat of kingship and by his cunning got the army into his hands. To the nobles he made grants of land, declaring that he was king of the world in kindliness. He promoted men of evil desires, as was in keeping with his nature, and he made evil men governors in every province, overturning any man who might be possessed of wisdom. Thus, the head of truth being brought low, falsehood displayed itself everywhere in the world. When his troops multiplied and his wealth increased the heart of that dishonourable man gained satisfaction. He gave his army money and made it prosperous with a view to battling against [his ancient rival] Bizhan. His pretence was that by the command of Shah Yazdegerd, who was the master of the seven spheres, he was compelled to exact vengeance of Bizhan by the sword, since it was through him that the fortunes of the king of the world had been made gloomy.

[Bizhan however attacked first, and Māhuy was defeated and slain, on the ground that he had caused the death of Yazdegerd. This is the last incident related in the narrative part of the epic.]

XLVI

The Conclusion of the Shāh-nāma

Sixty-five years passed over me, during which time I had abundantly to think of pain and toil. I inquired ardently after the history of the kings, but I was confronted by a star dilatory in its action. Great men endowed with knowledge and noble birth wrote down without payment what I composed. I sat as a spectator at a distance; you would have said that I was their hired man. All the reward I received from them was 'Bravo!' My gall was like to have burst at their 'Bravo!' The mouths of their old purses remained close and my bright spirit became weary by the tightness of their strings. However, of the noteworthy men bearing great names in the realm some share is due to 'Ali Deylami Bu Dulāf who constantly solaced my spirit over my toil; he was a man of illumined soul. Another of the nobly born who never demanded to receive my verses for nothing was Huyyay son of Qotaiba; at his hand I enjoyed food and clothing, silver and gold, and to him I owe the power to move my foot and arm. So it was that I was never acquainted with land-taxation in root or branch and I have been able to luxuriate in the midst of my quilt.

When my years reached seventy-one the sky felt the worth of my verse. For thirty-five years in this fleeting abode of the world I had toiled painfully in the hope of wealth; but all my toil was thrown to the winds and my gains amounted to no more than thirty-five dirhams. Now that my age is nearly eighty my hopes are altogether thrown to the winds.

The story of Yazdegerd has now come to an end. In the month [the twelfth] of Sefandārmoz and the day [the twenty-fifth] Ard, five times eighty years having passed of the Hijra [the year four hundred of the Hijra is equivalent to 1010 of the Christian era], I completed this royal record. May the throne of Maḥmud remain ever prosperous! May his head be green and his heart content! I have praised him in such terms that my words will endure in the world, both publicly and in private. I have received much praise from the great, but even greater is my praise of him. May that wise man endure for ever, perpetually attaining to his desires and with his mind ever effective! This book of mine will remain a monument to him, the count of its verses having reached six myriads.

Now that this fame-worthy work has reached its end, the whole surface of the world will re-echo with reports of me. Henceforth I cannot die; for I live, having broadcast the seeds of my verses. Anyone possessed of sense, good counsel and religion will after my death offer up praise for me.

FINIṢ